FAMIL

Gabriel started pag... ...nal.

If anyone could call ...

Elspeth had always been an orderly, conscientious person. They had often studied together, so Gabriel remembered what her notebooks had looked like: precise, neat, files listed properly and well ordered.

But *this*! This jumble of random sentences, strange little drawings, quotations, illegible scrawls . . .

Gabriel was about to lay the notebook aside when a drawing at the edge of the screen caught his eye. He highlit and enlarged it, and the squiggle resolved itself into two words:

"*far cry*"

Gabriel stared at them in awe at his own stupidity.

Far Cry. *They sent a ship there once, long ago. . . .*

CUTTING EDGE SCI-FI NOVELS

Anvil

Nicolas van Pallandt

A ROC BOOK

to
Bregje
my wilderness queen
and to
Erland and David
who matched enthusiasm with actions and helped it happen

ROC
Published by the Penguin Group
Penguin Putnam Inc., 375 Hudson Street,
New York, New York 10014, U.S.A.
Penguin Books Ltd, 27 Wrights Lane,
London W8 5TZ, England
Penguin Books Australia Ltd, Ringwood,
Victoria, Australia
Penguin Books Canada Ltd, 10 Alcorn Avenue,
Toronto, Ontario, Canada M4V 3B2
Penguin Books (N.Z.) Ltd, 182–190 Wairau Road,
Auckland 10, New Zealand

Penguin Books Ltd, Registered Offices:
Harmondsworth, Middlesex, England

First published by Roc, an imprint of Dutton Signet,
a member of Penguin Putnam Inc.

First Printing, February, 1998
10 9 8 7 6 5 4 3 2 1

Copyright © Nicolas van Pallandt, 1998
All rights reserved

lines that swept over their heads, lacing the sky from horizon to horizon. A low growl left the lion's throat and he pulled away from the lioness. Then, as one, they turned and padded back into the dappled shadows of the nearby trees.

Elspeth Kylie was falling through a blue, moonless night. She fell, twisting, her hands flailing out right and left and closing on empty air. Her ears rang with a slow thunder.

Elspeth Kylie fell, and thirty-nine years fell with her. Not flashing before her; there was no final rerun, no fetal recollection, no gasp of glad remembrance. There was just surprise. Elspeth was surprised. She could see her life sliding from her, like a drop of mercury sliding away down an ebony slope into darkness, and she was amazed. Perhaps, if she had had time, she would have tried to follow back the thread that had led her here. But there was no time.

Her heart beat five times before she struck. One moment she was falling, then the mossy ground smote the life from Nerita Elspeth Kylie. Her hand twitched once and her pained, dark eyes lost their look of surprise in a fleeting instant of wonder before they saw no more.

For a long time there was silence. Then a lion, who had been startled into the bushes by the dry thud of her body striking the ground, emerged and padded cautiously over to investigate. He sniffed curiously, his breath berry-sweet against the lifeless face, his nose questing over the burnt almond skin and sable hair. Presently he was joined by a lioness. More nervous than he, she circled the little mound on the grass at a discreet distance before coming to stand beside her mate. She nipped at his shaggy neck in a hopeful sort of way whilst he ignored her and gazed up at the stars winking out behind the fine network of straight silver

a certain light

In the Dreamtime the Ancestors dreamed Creation. They dreamed the earth and the rivers and the seas and the beasts that lived in them. They dreamed the stars and the heavens; they dreamed into being all that ever was and all that will ever be.

Humanity had since found substitutes for most of these things, including the steam engine, the abacus, true love and the wheel. But no one had yet found a substitute for the gleam of suspicion in a good Customs official's eye.

Or a cool beer in the heat of a breathless summer, thought Gabriel Kylie as the Orbit 1 Customs official examined his passcard readout and let his gaze rove over Gabriel's bag in a ruminative and slightly hopeful manner.

"From Earth," the official mused. "We don't get many of you through here." His attention turned to Gabriel himself, taking in the dark skin, the shaggy mane of blue-black hair, threaded here and there with gray and tied back in a ponytail, loose strands spilling over a heavy brow and onyx eyes, the two silver earrings in his left earlobe and the long, mountain-stained overcoat.

Gabriel nodded and waited patiently. He knew that Earth's peculiar status within the Seventeen Planets would protect him from the worst infringements of over-zealous immigration authorities. But the curiosity engendered by a traveler from Sol System tended to offset the benefits of that protection. Fortunately, the official's ruminations were interrupted by the sound of raised voices a little further down the line.

A woman in her late twenties or early thirties was engaged in an altercation with another of the Customs officials. She was clutching a small cage to her, and protesting shrilly, "Look, he was delivered today and all my forms are in order. You are not going to take him out and scan him! I'll sue you for Privacy breach!"

Tearing his eyes away from Gabriel's leather shoulder bag, the Customs official sighed and slipped Gabriel's passcard back across the counter.

"Welcome to Thor," he said perfunctorily.

"Thanks," replied Gabriel, relieved.

He shouldered his bag and headed for the gate to the shuttle that would take him down to Thor's surface. The trip from Octavia had been a long one. Seven weeks was a long time to spend on a ship, even a luxurious vessel like the Hyperion liner, and Gabriel could hardly wait to stand under open skies once more. Except that open skies were a short commodity on Thor.

He entered the Orbit 1-to-Kyara shuttle and made his way to the main lounge, where he ordered himself a cup of herb tea. As the shuttle disengaged from the Orbit station and began its long fall down to the miracle that was Kyara City, Gabriel settled himself down next to the viewport, which rose from the center of the lounge floor like the basin of a medieval fountain. It was a six-hour, twenty-thousand-kilometer drop down to the surface of Thor, and Gabriel did not want to miss a minute of it.

The muted conversations of other passengers swirled about him. On a long settee built into the cabin wall, five members of a family who had occupied the cabin next to his aboard the liner stared in listless fascination at five individual Walk-Vs. Across from them a pride of minor executives from New Canada on Octavia rattled drinks at one another and bared porcelain smiles. And over by the bar—a group of freighter hands, back from a run to Denube.

Gabriel ignored them all. His thoughts were occupied with death. Not that that was anything new. For nineteen years Gabriel Kylie had lived with a little death upon his shoulder. And nineteen years was a long time to be running.

He was awakened from his reverie by a babble of voices. He had no idea how long he had been staring into the viewscreen. The rim of the planet had long ago extended beyond its edge and Kyara City was now visible, a bright scarab adrift in a pool of honey-dark waters.

Gabriel glanced up at the sound of a shriek. The family with the Walk-Vs had leapt up, gesticulating like gale-blown scarecrows. A woman, whom he recognized as the one who had been arguing with the Orbit 1 Customs official, was apparently trying to pacify them, whilst at the same time searching for something under their seats. The commotion had brought over the steward.

Gabriel felt something moving around his ankles. He glanced down to see what resembled an olive green ferret skittering off across the floor to disappear behind a couch in a deserted area of the lounge. With a start Gabriel recognized it as a Helios weasel.

The level of hue and babble around the woman had risen and he could make out her voice, pleading, "It's not GenTec, but it's not poisonous either. I've got it registered. It's a Helios weasel . . . yes, a weasel! It's completely safe."

Safe? Gabriel mused, reflecting on what an angry Helios weasel was capable of. And a Helios weasel was rarely anything but angry.

Apparently someone else shared this viewpoint as the woman's reassurances had served only to raise the noise level and introduce new vocabulary into the exchange, notably "civil action," "safety violations," and "lawsuit."

He raised his hand to catch the woman's eye and pointed at the couch. Thankfully she extricated herself from the group and came toward him.

"He's gone to ground behind there."

"Thanks. I just opened the cage door a fraction. They just delivered him and I wanted to make sure he was alright." They approached the couch from opposite ends.

Aware of a professionally servile presence, Gabriel glanced back to find the steward hovering over them.

"I'm sorry, madam," the steward addressed the woman, "I'm going to have to ask you to get your animal under control immediately or I'll have to inform the captain. Releasing a potentially dangerous animal aboard a commercial shuttle is a felony."

"Look, we're doing our best here," said the woman

agitatedly. "If you'd just keep those flappers out of our hair."

"I'm sorry, but if you can't secure him *now*" . . .

Gabriel broke out his "easy face," used to deflect the kind of half-witted challenges that came out of the thin end of a gin bottle in backwoods saloons.

"Listen, sport, it's not a dangerous animal, it's a Helios weasel. People keep them as pets and they're old friends of mine; I've even eaten them. If you just keep everybody's ankles out of the way, we can get this sorted out in about ten seconds."

The steward looked unconvinced, but before he could object further he was interrupted by a tap on the shoulder. It was one of the freighter hands, a wiry little gargoyle of a man.

"Dilly, dilly, dilly," he exclaimed in a voice like split wood, "we've got more serious problems west-side than loose rodents. Me and my mates are seriously dehydrated and the bar isn't serving."

The steward hesitated. Dry-mouthed deckhands presented their own perils.

"We'll be fine," affirmed Gabriel. "If you can keep everybody clear of this part of the lounge, we can catch him a lot quicker."

"This is a question of health, stike, we're hurtin' over there," insisted the freighter hand, plucking at the steward's arm.

Reluctantly, the steward was hustled toward the bar. "Good one, stike." The freighter hand leered over his shoulder, nodding at the woman. "Make a hero of yourself and I reckon you're well in there."

The woman sagged with relief. "One down. Listen, thanks for your help. My name's Isadora. Isadora Katarina Manuela Gatzalumendi, actually. It's a Basque name. Means 'castle on the mountain.' But call me Iz. Everybody else does," she chattered nervously.

"Gabriel Kylie." Gabriel stripped off his coat and wrapped it around his hands for protection.

For the next ten minutes the Helios weasel had them hornpiping about the deserted end of the lounge.

Finally, seeming to tire of the game, the weasel made a break for grounds anew. Seeing it make a direct beeline for the most crowded section of the lounge, Gabriel had no choice but to take a dive at it. He brought his overcoat down over the weasel and scooped it up.

As he climbed to his feet, Isadora came hurrying over with the box. His coat squealed and thrashed about as if possessed.

"Oh, you're great. I'm so grateful. I don't know what they'd have done if I'd lost it."

"Who's 'they'?" Gabriel did not take his eyes off the bundle in his hands.

"The Real Life Menagerie."

"There's a zoo on Kyara?" Gabriel was surprised. He couldn't remember the last time he had seen a zoo with real animals in it.

"Two rooms plus an aquarium in the hall. Teachers send their pupils. It's just a hobby, I work there as a volunteer. Here, shall I take that?"

"It's alright, I've handled these before." Gabriel looked up and gave her a reassuring smile.

That moment's inattention was all the Helios weasel needed.

Isadora cried a warning, "Care . . . !"

The next instant its wicked little head had shot out and buried its fangs firmly in Gabriel's thumb. Trying not to yell, Gabriel grabbed the weasel behind the head, hoping to pry its jaws open, but the weasel just growled and drove its teeth further into his knuckle.

Isadora was hovering fretfully. "Are you okay? Shall I . . . can I do anything . . . ?"

"I'm fine, I'm fine," Gabriel said through gritted teeth, feeling like a complete idiot. "Just let him calm down for a second."

"Are you sure? He doesn't look like he wants to let go."

"I really have handled these beasties before," he mumbled. "Here, hold the cage up ready. He'll get bored and let go in a second." Gabriel inhaled deeply and tried to breathe out the pain, wondering if he could strangle the creature without Isadora's noticing.

Isadora obeyed. "Where are you from anyway? The only liners in the last day were from Octavia, Helios, and Ho Chi, and you don't look like a spacer."

"Oh, no? What does a spacer look like?"

"Them." Isadora jerked a thumb at the freighter

hands. Gabriel's gaze followed the direction of her gesture and found the ugly little freighter hand looking right
at him. As their eyes met the other indicated Isadora
with his chin and raised his eyebrows meaningfully, nico-
tine-root smirk cracking his face open from ear to ear.
He gave an evil wink.

Gabriel returned his wink with a nod that was outwardly friendly but pointedly nonconspiratorial and
turned his attention back to the weasel. *Twit,* he thought
irritably as the Helios weasel tightened its agonizing grip
on his thumb.

"Here, what if I . . ." Isadora reached over and tried
to jam her thumb and forefinger into the beast's jaws,
which only resulted in its shaking its head from side
to side.

Gabriel could not restrain a yelp of pain. He caught
the steward looking in their direction and managed a
watery smile. "Your drink!" he hissed. "Pour it into his
nose, quickly."

Isadora leapt to obey. The alcohol dribbling into the
open wound felt like someone driving an ice pick
through his hand, but had its desired effect on the weasel; releasing it's grip on Gabriel's thumb for an instant
to draw breath. Gabriel whipped his hand away and
jammed the protesting animal headfirst into the cage.

Isadora slid the lid shut and Gabriel leaned back,
sucking at his wound in relief and swearing at his own
stupidity.

"Are you alright?" she asked worriedly. "I'll try and
find you a disinfectant peg."

"It's fine, it's fine, no worries." He fumbled in his coat
pocket for something to bandage his thumb. "Maybe you
could get me a glass of water."

By the time Isadora returned with his water and something stronger for herself, Gabriel had managed to
staunch the flow of blood with an old tissue and, for the
first time, had a chance to study her properly.

She was plump, comfortingly so, nothing sharp or
spiky about her anywhere. Her hair was coppery and cut
short to the nape of her neck. Her skin was the color of
varnished walnut and her eyes dark as a desert shadow,
cut through by a glint of open mischief. She had a Medi-
terranean look about her, although that did not say

much, with 247 nations on the Seventeen Planets, plus assorted independent moons, asteroids and colonies, to choose from.

Isadora was leaning with both her elbows on the edge of the view-window and had her fingers curled around the stem of a wineglass. The liquid in it was pale green and viscous.

"You never answered my question."

"Question?" Gabriel remembered. "Right, where am I from? Native Australian. A small town called Landing, it's about a ninety miles southwest of Alice Springs . . ." He paused. "How's your geography? Earth geography."

"High school."

"Uh-oh."

"I know where Australia is!" she said indignantly.

"Do you know where Alice Springs is?"

"Vaguely."

Brave words, but she hadn't a clue. Gabriel did not conceal his amusement. He was about to offer her a condensed lesson in Australian geography when she continued, "Biggest city in Central Australia, borders the Glass Desert, also known as the Green Desert."

Gabriel busied himself tightening the bandage around his thumb to conceal his embarrassment whilst thinking, *too many nights alone in the mountains with no one around to disagree with you and remind you what a smug twit you're becoming.* He tried to come up with an intelligent comment and heard himself saying, "Er . . . right . . ."

Brilliant.

Thankfully Isadora did not appear to notice; she was staring into the view-window. She said, "Quick, take a look."

He looked back into the view-window and started. Kyara City now filled the entire screen. Indeed, they were so close that the landing pad was clearly visible in the middle of the screen and swelling. His stomach tightened with a spasm of latent vertigo. Somehow the words "WELCOME TO KYARA," absurdly stenciled across the pad in what had to be ten-meter-high letters, only added to the feeling. But, even as he let out a careful breath, the image contracted and the viewport went dark.

"For queasy stomachs," said Isadora wryly. "Nothing like a half-mile drop to get your lunch a little lively. Don't bother," she said quickly, seeing Gabriel about to rise. "It'll be ten minutes yet. Are you staying in Kyara for long?"

Gabriel studied her carefully for about half a minute before answering.

"No, only about three local days. I just have to sort out a little personal business." He hesitated. "My sister died here a couple of months ago."

Gabriel saw her flinch.

"It's all right," he said, forestalling the flood. "Really."

"Shit, I always ask . . ." She fumbled.

"Really. No worries. No open wounds on me." He waved his thumb cheerfully. " 'Cept one." She looked sheepish.

Passengers were beginning to mill around the exit, Gabriel noted, with that studied aimlessness of people all wanting to be first through the door once it opened without seeming as if they did and without alerting anyone else as to their intentions.

"Maybe I can show you around someday if you're here long enough, maybe make up for . . ." Isadora indicated his bandaged thumb as she rose.

And another friend left behind when I leave, Gabriel thought sadly. Reluctantly he replied, "Well, that'd be fine, but, to be honest, I'm only here for those three days. But maybe we'll collide," he amended, seeing the disappointment in her face.

She shrugged ruefully. "If you change your mind, I'm in the phone files." She started to back away.

"Isadora Katarina Manuela Gatzalumendi." He grinned at her.

With one hand clutching a carryall and the other wrapped in bloodstained tissue, Gabriel stepped out for the first time into Kyara City. His nostrils flared as he took in his first breath of Kyaran air. He caught a brief impression of many layers of perfumed air freshener, forming a skin over the more acrid odor of cleansing mist and the heaving wellspring of humanity. A holographic ground stewardess smilingly waved him toward the main Arrivals Hall.

The main Hall was nonagonal and rose about him in gleaming, white planes of imitation marble that curved into a dome far above his head.

Strewth! Gabriel thought in awe, letting his eyes climb to the dome's apex. *Bloody bathroom-tile Gothic!* He would have expected far more economy of space in an enclosed environment such as Kyara. It took a few seconds before it occurred to him that the ceiling might be as illusory as the ground personnel. For a moment he was tempted to throw something up to see if the space ended a few feet above his head. One glance around made him change his mind. He had already scored enough as the backwoods greenie today. Besides, he should get on.

A glance at his blank watch face told him that the central timepiece here must be transmitting on a different frequency from that of his watch. He thumbed "SET" and a few seconds later "11:32" appeared. Morning. Plenty of time.

He looked about until he saw a phone booth at the far end of the Hall and made his way over to it, executing a neat slalom between two holographic salespeople and a robot, all wearing blissful expressions and offering promises of nirvana and a free pocket auriscope if only he attend one Psychic Divination Meeting at their nearby Id and Soul Center.

Gabriel thumbed the plate on the booth and accessed his credit account. There was a "pip" and a cardphone slipped into his waiting hand. He glanced at the number printed on it, whispering it under his breath so as to commit it to memory, then slipped the card into the thin pocket on his lapel.

Gabriel was about to turn when he felt that uncertain tingling in the back of his neck. Someone was watching him. He hesitated, then turned and casually let his eye circle his immediate surroundings.

Some distance to his left a tall, blond stick-insect of a man was bending over, fiddling with something on his shoe. He was clad in ragged work trousers and sleeveless vest. His wrists jangled with bracelets, and necklaces of colored beads and imitation bone hung around his neck. The stream of people seemed to part and flow around him as if repelled magnetically. Gabriel saw one woman step near the man, then flinch and step back before giving him a wide berth.

Since the man stood in his path and Gabriel could see no reason to make a detour, he started to walk past him, following the crowd.

Gabriel was just drawing level with him when the strange creature looked up, his wild gaze fixing on Gabriel. He straightened, limb by limb, unfolding like some stiff-jointed marionette, his eyes never leaving Gabriel's. Shocked, Gabriel halted in his tracks and stared into the other's eyes, causing the woman behind him to jostle him. Once before he had seen a look like that, back in Landing, in the eyes of a water buffalo, shot three times by offworld poachers and still alive. A horrible conflict of rage and hopelessness.

"Just a reeker," said a man's voice. "Take no notice, there's spooks keeping an eye on him."

Gabriel ignored the speaker. He had already noticed the two—police officers by the drink stand, wearing their uniforms like a warning, and he wondered that such an ungainly figure as this could excite so much interest. Seeing the uniforms, Gabriel automatically made to fade into the crowd once more.

The man spoke. "You," he said, still looking at Gabriel, his voice ragged, like someone who had been screaming for an hour without stopping. "Yes, you, I'm talking to *you!*"

Gabriel stood, riveted on the man's gaze. He started to move toward him, but hardly had taken a pace before the most unholy stench made him gasp and step backwards in surprise. It was like inhaling a witch's brew of carrion, dried fish and raw sewage.

"Hah! You got it, hey!" The man gave a yelp of laughter, a yelp of laughter that sounded more like a stifled shriek of pain. He waved his hands at Gabriel, nervous, grabbing hands. "It's okay, it's okay, you don't have to come in. You've been traveling a long way already, hey? Far enough, hey? Keep your lungs clean, clean, clean. Me? I don't notice anything. Me? Nothing!"

Gabriel eyed the other narrowly. Every big city had its tribe of sidewalk crawlers, mad-eyed and strung out on any one of a thousand alternate chemical realities. What made this man different?

"What! Still here, man?" The man laughed again. "Close maybe? I see where you come from, I can see where you're going. You're going to be staying here a while, a change of plans, man. What you like, stike. Thor holds you down, man, and she don't let go easily. She'll keep you for good if you don't watch out. Kept others just like you. Just like you, stike!" The man stopped, peering at Gabriel for a couple of seconds. Then his voice dropped. "You'll remember my face, boyo," he hissed. "You'll remember it in the uplands. Time to go, time to move on now, man. Company, no?"

It was true. The two police agents had left their perch near the drink stand and were moving in his direction. Not with any great haste; it seemed as if they were wanting to be seen by the stick-man. They did not seem to expect ever to reach him and so they didn't.

Raising his arms in front of him, the insect-man called, "Coming through, fine citizens, coming through. Would you let me marry your daughters? Would you let me marry your sons!"

The crowd parted like a bow wave before him and closed in his wake. The reeker swam through their midst like a porcupine fish.

He left Gabriel staring at the patch of floor where he had been standing, all traces quickly hammered away by passing feet.

What was it that they had called him? *A reeker?*

Gabriel soon found an information booth which scanned the name and address that he held in front of its Eye and listed the modes of transportation available.

"You could take the Worm or pick yourself up a hang-cab. It's more expensive, especially with a real driver, but it's quicker. You might find it easier, since you don't know your way around. 'Course you could walk, but I wouldn't recommend it; it would take you about two hours, more with baggage." The booth paused expectantly.

"Where can I get a hangcab?"

With a sliver of light the booth indicated an exit on the near side of the Hall. As he approached it he saw a large, portly man coming to meet him.

"Hangcab, sir?" inquired the man, already holding out

his hand for Gabriel's carryall. "Derek van Doorn, your driver."

Gabriel gave him the carryall and followed him out to a long corridor where a sleek vehicle hung, suspended by a magnetic rail running along the ceiling.

The cabbie tossed the carryall into the trunk and opened the side door for Gabriel. Then he levered himself into his own seat and peered into the rearview flatscreen at his passenger.

"Where to?"

Gabriel considered for a moment. "First I'd like a not-very-expensive hotel. Then I'd like to go to Turner Way 1773, Green Sector, Police Headquarters."

"You got it."

Gabriel leaned forward and rested an arm on the back of the driver's seat. The look he fixed upon the driver through the rearview screen was not unfriendly.

"In some places spaceport cabs have arrangements with certain hotels, which are often not the best or the most reasonable."

The cabbie's gaze was steady.

"Not me, sir. I know exactly what you're looking for."

He squeezed his vehicle into gear, and the hangcab shot forward. For a few seconds there was nothing to see but the tunnel walls, then abruptly the walls ended, the floor fell away a thousand feet and Gabriel found himself gazing out for the first time on Kyara City itself.

He gasped with delight.

Through the spun-diamond domes that lidded the city-scape, Thor's sun illuminated a tableau of braided towers and leaping columns, molded of glass and agate. As if in scorn at the tremendous gravitational forces outside, Kyara rose in spires of crystal sugar, intertwined with a web of hangcar rails and arching bridges. There were both open streets and enclosed Halls, joined by a web-work of alleys and walk-ramps and escalators, and dotted with plazas and climbing terraces.

"Knocks your eyes back a little the first time you see it, eh?" the driver said with some satisfaction, observing Gabriel in the rearview flatscreen.

Gabriel had to agree. He nodded. "It has a certain light," he said, his gaze darting from pinnacle to cleft in wonder. The streets opened up like dark, jeweled canyons below them.

The driver snorted. "I've heard it said bigger."

He eyed Gabriel in the rearview flatscreen again, his eyes like knots in heavy pine, hard and curious. "You from Helios?"

"Been there," replied Gabriel cheerfully, then added, "Didn't stay long."

The hangcab slid to a halt outside Green Sector Police Headquarters, situated in a broad covered Hall. There were far fewer people about than there had been around the spaceport. The ground did not seem to hum quite as loudly under Gabriel's feet.

After he had paid off the cabbie, he entered through the tall glass doors. As he did he felt that faint chill of uneasiness that he always felt upon entering any center of law enforcement.

The reception module inquired politely if it could help him and Gabriel shrugged off his unease. He groped in his pocket and pulled out his wallet. Opening it, he read, "I'm looking for . . . uh . . . Officer Hitedoro Izeki . . . please."

"Name and Patrial Registry number," said the module.

"Gabriel Kylie. No P.R. number. Earth resident."

Somewhat to his surprise the module did not comment upon his lack of Patrial Registry number. It simply said, "Room 261. Just follow the green line."

Hitedoro Izeki was a large, corpulent man; his clothing was an afterthought, rumpled and draped over the expanse of his body like a sartorial postscript. His expression, as Gabriel entered his office, was harried.

"Yeah?"

"I'm looking for Officer Izeki."

"Officer Izeki is off duty, come back tomorrow." Gabriel did not move and after a moment the other turned and gave him the once-over. "Well?" He sighed. "Okay, five minutes, I've been on bat shift and I want to get home."

"Bat shift?"

Officer Izeki eyed Gabriel bleakly, "You're not from

here, are you? I've been up all night, and I'm tired and pissed off. Where are you from anyway? Helios?"

"Earth."

The big man's eyes flickered imperceptibly. "Earth. Welcome to Kyara; you've got four minutes and thirty seconds left."

"Any reason why we should spend it standing up?"

Izeki's right hand swept out and gestured expansively. "Be my guest."

As Gabriel sat down, Izeki lowered his broad frame into his own chair and reached for a box of nicotine root. After offering it to Gabriel, who declined, he took one himself and popped one end of it into his own mouth.

"What can I do for you?" he inquired with a long-suffering air. "Mr. . . . ?"

"Kylie, Gabriel Kylie."

"Kylie . . ." Izeki frowned.

"My sister was killed here a couple of months ago. I understand you were the officer in charge. Her name was Nerita Elspeth Kylie.

For an instant Izeki hesitated, then his teeth clamped down on the nicotine root. "The Rainer Park woman. Right. I'm sorry. That was some time back. What can I do for you? If it's about the body, I'm afraid we follow standard Orbit Colony procedure here. Can't afford not to. Everything goes into recycle at the quickfarms immediately after last rites. We give the family a little more time to claim personal effects if there's no will. I don't know about that . . ."

"Actually," Gabriel interrupted him, "I was just looking for some information."

"Information, right." Izeki hesitated again.

"How'm I doing for time?"

Izeki shrugged and waved his hand. "That depends. What can I tell you?"

"What *can* you tell me?"

"What do you know?"

"Nothing. Just that it was an accident."

"Well . . ." Izeki chewed on his nicotine root in a ruminative manner. "She fell off a high scaffolding in the park, coroner estimated between thirty, thirty-five meters. Broken neck and a fractured skull, died instantly. You're not thinking about some kind of civil court action?"

Gabriel shook his head. "Not my style."

"Just as well. There isn't a case for negligence against the park authorities. She shouldn't have been where she was."

"Where was she?"

"Like I said, Rainer Park. She was climbing on some scaffolding which was supposed to be off-limits to the public."

"Did anybody see it happen? I mean, how do you know it was an accident?"

"Any reason to think it wasn't?" Izeki took the root out of his mouth and leaned forward. "Listen, Mr. Kylie, how long is it since you saw your sister?"

How long indeed. When Gabriel had last seen her she had been a rangy eighteen-year-old, with sharp, agile limbs and the heady drug of zealotry flaring up hand in hand with her newfound sexuality.

"About twenty-one years."

"I thought it might be something like that." Izeki sighed with the air of someone who had had conversations like this all too often. "Look, I'll be honest with you. Like I said, your sister had no business being where she was. She died in the park—it's on the east side of Green—at night, during closing hours. I don't know what she was doing there and I sure as bugsucker don't know what she was doing up on that scaffolding, but the place would have been dark . . . who knows? That's the way accidents happen. People are a little strange in the ways they pick to get killed. They fall off mountains, they drown, they jump off small moons and never come back. I think most people spend their lives choosing how they're going to die." Izeki glanced down at the nicotine root turning in his fingers.

"There were no marks of a struggle, as there might have been if someone had pushed her off. The body hadn't been moved.

"Murder is not as common in Kyara as it is in many other places. We've got our problems; there's the roof-runners and the downlanders and the freaks down on Bugout Plaza. It looks like we might even have a consortium war on our hands. But there's only one way out of town." Izeki drew a little upward line in the air with his forefinger—Gabriel presumed he was refering to the Orbit shuttle. Izeki's lips twitched into a thin smile. "The investigation was thorough, I can promise you, Mr. Kylie."

"I'm sure it was, Officer," said Gabriel reassuringly. "Wouldn't doubt it for a moment." And he smiled.

That Izeki doubted the sincerity of Gabriel's smile was certain. He rose, dropping his nicotine root into the flashtray, his jowly face creased, as far as it could crease, into a frown.

"Look, Mr. Kylie. I wasn't just beating rags when I said I was tired. I've been up for twenty-four hours. How long are you in Kyara for?"

"I'm booked out in three days."

"Okay, well, if you leave the address of where you're staying at the desk, I'll get in touch with you about re-claiming any personal effects. I'm sorry I can't do more for you."

Gabriel accepted the dismissal and rose, allowing himself to be escorted to the door.

"By the way," Izeki said, as Gabriel was turning away. "Where did you get my name?"

"The death notification was sent to next of kin back on Earth."

Izeki grunted. "You took your time getting here."

Gabriel shrugged and grinned sheepishly. "Well, it got to me via a kind of roundaboutish sort of route. And Thor's quite a ways. See you around." He turned and walked with apparent unconcern down the corridor, leaving Izeki watching him from the doorway of the office with tired, sagging eyes.

As soon as Gabriel had disappeared from view Izeki reached up and touched his collar phone.

"Extension tee-six-slash-one-one."

There was a "pip" and after a moment a voice answered, "Here."

"This is Izeki," Izeki said. "I've just had a visitor . . . and I'd say you've got a problem."

Outside the police station Gabriel paused, surveying the enclosed street before him. A steady stream of busy, purposeful people strode past, all on their way to that all-important, generic Somewhere.

"You silly cow," Gabriel muttered. "Another fine mess you've gotten me into."

He reached up and keyed his phone card. "Long-hop Travel, reservations," he said.

After a moment a female voice answered, "Long-hop Travel, reservations, Inno Noiret speaking, how may I help you? . . . Hello? Long-hop Travel . . ."

"Yes," Gabriel said slowly. "My name is Gabriel Kylie, K-Y-L-I-E, I have a reservation on Helios Starlines, traveling to Merryweather on the twenty-second, Standard. I'd like to cancel it . . ."

Several things had become clear to Gabriel in the past half hour, not least of which was that Officer Hitedoro Izeki was a liar.

in parenthesis: thor

One hundred and four years before, when the Seventeen Planets inhabited by Humanity were but Ten and the Congress of Stellar Systems not half a century old, the exploration JUMP-ship Fenris, with her crew of thirty, had come across a vast, black planet in thrall to a small, yellow sun.

The new planet circled that sun in an eccentric 732-year orbit that brought it as close as 139 million kilometers at perihelion and as far as 927 million kilometers at aphelion. Its orbital plane was almost perpendicular to that of the three other, more diminutive planets sharing its sun, leading to speculation that it might have been a wanderer, captured at a much later stage in the star system's evolution.

Further investigations revealed its surface to be composed of 70 percent iron and it was postulated that this planet was the core of a much larger gas giant which had had its atmosphere ripped away in the same cataclysm that had thrown it out to wander through deep space until it was captured by the yellow dwarf around which it now circled.

The good ship Fenris had just undergone a "constitutional mutiny" whereby a meeting had been convened and the captain, Jorn Sømmarstrom, been relieved of his duties by a unanimous vote—including that of his then wife, Astronomer Agnetha Sedelquist. He was replaced by his second-in-command, Ricardo Avriel. The grounds for impeachment, as entered in the ship's log, were "excessive passivity in the discharge of his executive duties," a pleasant euphemism for "indecisive nitwit who spends half his time in a blue funk, and the rest of the time moping about making a general nuisance of his unshaved and ineffectual self."

(The overall tone of this voyage of exploration can be gleaned by the fact that Avriel was, within some weeks, replaced by HIS second, Rae Wynot. By the time Fenris pulled into its home port of Octavia some months later, Captain Sømmarstrom was once again in command.)

As a consolation prize to ex-Captain (and Captains-to-be) Sømmarstrom (who was otherwise well liked) and in honor of the Scandinavian origins of their ship, it was decided to name the new planet Thor, after the Norse God of Thunder.

When discovered, Thor was 242 million kilometers from its sun. Its surface, though black, radiated enough invisible radiation to ignite a match. The gravitational pull on its surface was in the region of forty gravs. Under that force a watermelon would collapse under its own weight. It would have been difficult to find an environment more hostile to human life.

And so it was that Humanity, with characteristic recalcitrance and hubris, had placed upon its surface . . . a city.

From an experimental scientific station set up to test the limits of the newly developed Icarus Antigravity Field, under the administration of Akash Chandra Levinson, Kyara grew into an unlikely and—owing to the costs involved—exclusive tourist attraction. Then, with the discovery and settlement of Zuleika, Ho Chi, Ikaat and Son et Lumiere beyond Thor System, Kyara suddenly found itself the hub of several of the now-Fourteen Planets' newest commercial trade routes. Within a decade Kyara's stringent Privacy Laws had made it a haven for intersystem companies seeking the blind eye of a pragmatic government whose other eye rested firmly on the profit margin.

Protected by the bubble of its Icarus Fields, Kyara stood defiant on Thor's Anvil, its inhabitants treading their daily lives a spun-diamond windowpane away from the most deadly environment ever inhabited by Humanity.

the hollow field

The voice at the other end of the phone was brimming with early-morning cheer, the kind that Isadora thought of as the dentist-laser-on-a-live-nerve variety.

"Hallo, Iz, did I wake you?"

"Who is this? D'you know what time it is?" Isadora grumbled, thinking that perhaps she would rather have her tooth lasered.

"Sorry, look, the bakeries are open, I've brought some croissants."

"If I want croissants, I'll dial for them . . . Who *is* this?"

"Gabriel Kylie, we met on the shuttle, remember? Can I come in?"

Isadora jerked upright in bed. "Come in? Where are you?"

"Outside your front door. D'you want me to come back?"

"Yes . . . NO! Wait . . . can you wait a minute?" Isadora leapt out of bed, knocking Raymond and Skunk to the floor in a flurry of indignant feline yowls.

"Sorry, sorry . . ." she murmured, bounding naked into the bathroom.

Five minutes later she was showered and dressed and moderately presentable, although her eyes were still thick with sleep and her voice sounded like a two-stroke engine. The bed had been retracted into the wall, her dirty clothes, several books and a plate hurled pell-mell into a closet and Mack the Knife shut up in the shower cubicle with the light out for refusing to stop screeching.

"Hi," she said casually as she opened the door.

"Croissants." Gabriel flashed his white grin as he handed her the bag. "Were you asleep?"

"I was in the shower," Isadora lied. "I've dialed some coffee. If you sit down, I'll go get it."

She returned minutes later, bearing a tray laden with butter, marmalade and fresh coffee, to find Gabriel inspecting her shelves with apparent approval.

"Books," he remarked. "Not what I expected to find in Kyara."

"I'm a hard-copy lady. There's nothing like feeling the pages between your fingers."

"And all about beasties." He glanced down at Raymond, who was purring against his leg, "There can't be too many pets on Thor."

"Oh, there's plenty. You'd be surprised," she said, carefully elbowing Raymond's catnip cushion off the coffee table and sliding the tray into its place. "People tend to think of Kyara as a colony because we're enclosed, but we've got four and a half million people here. Lots of cats mainly. Mice, no dogs, Helios weasels like your friend over there."

"Adders?"

"Wang Fu's a rarity," Isadora said proudly. "No Gen-Tec, the real thing. Active poison ducts, the works. He used to belong to an ex-lover of mine when I used to work in the D.N.Amics labs." She gazed affectionately at the corner, where Wang Fu was curled up in his glass pen. "I reckon I won on the deal."

She glanced back to find Gabriel pouring coffee, a croissant gripped between his teeth.

"Sorry, I should be doing that." Isadora accepted her cup contritely. They raised cups at one another and took the first sip at the same time. The liquid was tart and bitter and hot and just what Isadora needed. She closed her eyes and let its warmth seep down her throat. Then she opened them wide and sighed.

Gabriel eyed her with faint amusement. "Long night?"

Iz pulled a face and reached for a croissant. "Long day. What brings you here?"

Gabriel gazed at her steadily for so long that she began to become a little uncomfortable. Then the left corner of his mouth lifted a little sheepishly.

"Well, to be honest, my plans have changed a bit. I was hoping maybe you could help me. I need to get to a place called Rainer Park."

"Rainer Park?" Isadora was surprised. "That's easy enough, just hop on the Worm, there's a stop right outside it. Don't you have a map? Never mind, I've got one," she said before he could answer. She hopped up and went over to her desk. The map was not where she had thought it was and it took an embarrassing amount of rummaging through drawers until she found it under a broken Window, the one that used to give views of Querin. She unfolded the map and spread it out on the table.

Seen topographically, Kyara was shaped like an irregular group of soap bubbles, seven of the nine sectors—Blue, Brown, Red, Yellow, Purple, Orange—grouped around the central axis, White, and the newest sector, Green, creating a bulge on the western edge.

"There you are, we're here." She pointed to where a blue point of light was flashing in Orange Sector. Her finger traced a line to where a large lollipop-shaped protuberance extruded from the outer wall of Green Sector. "And here's Rainer Park."

Gabriel leaned forward and rested his fingers next to hers. "Rainer Park," he murmured.

"Why the interest?" Isadora asked curiously. "Is this anything to do with your change of plan?"

Gabriel nodded. "That's where my sister was killed. The policeman I spoke to said she fell off a scaffolding there."

Isadora was momentarily taken aback, then she chastened herself. *Of course! Gabriel KYLIE!* Why hadn't she made the connection? "The woman in Rainer Park!" she exclaimed. "I didn't realize."

"You heard about it?"

"I work for Duas Voces, that's Byron Media's news section. Byron Systems built the park. You think I didn't hear? Major stink. MAJOR!" she said with some satisfaction. "The place had only been open for a couple of months."

"So it was true, what the police told me."

"What? About how she died? Yeah. There was still a bit of construction going on."

Gabriel was silent for a moment, as if weighing in his mind what he was going to say next. Then he said, "I think they're lying."

Isadora's eyes widened slightly. "Lying? Who's lying?"

"The police."

"The spooks?" Isadora scoffed. "Now why are the spooks going to lie about something like this?"

Gabriel shook his head. "I don't know. Oh, I think she was *killed* there. And she fell off the scaffolding, just like the police say. But there was something the bloke wasn't telling me. I'm not so sure it was an accident."

Isadora stared at him with growing disappointment. In her three years of working for Duas Voces she had learned to be leery of conspiracy theories and their purveyors. She had hoped better of him.

Gabriel's grin was back, rueful this time. "I suppose it sounds a little paranoid."

"A little."

"Well, maybe it is. I'm not used to cities." Gabriel shrugged. "Tell me, what is Rainer Park? I get the impression it's something special."

"It is. It's only been open six months or so. It was built by a man named Saxon Rainer. You ever heard of Byron Systems—I mentioned them just now? No? Big conglomerate. The biggest actually. Byron Systems *is* Kyara. The first here . . . and, well half of what you see wouldn't be here if it weren't for Byron Systems.

"Anyway, Saxon Rainer's the chairman of it. He's known as something of a philanthropist. He built this thing. It was his big project, a park full of trees and nature that would be open to the public here. It's huge, almost three kilometers across, it's . . ." She hesitated. "I suppose it's worth seeing."

"You don't sound overly enthusiastic."

"Well, I'm not really. There's aspects of it I find a bit depressing."

"Oh? Such as?"

Isadora gestured. "Personal tick. I wouldn't want to spoil it for you. Look, I've got to go to work soon. If you like, I'll walk you down to the Worm and point you in the right direction."

"Yeah, I'd appreciate that. Uh . . . before we go can I use your bathroom?"

"Through there." Isadora indicated with her thumb.

In the time it took Gabriel to complete his ablutions, Isadora dumped the plates and cups in the disposal slot and pulled on a pair of shoes.

They were a hundred meters from her front door before Isadora remembered Mack the Knife. She stopped and swore.

"Can you wait here a second, I've forgotten something," she said, starting back.

"It's alright, no worries." Gabriel caught her by the elbow. "I let the parrot out of the shower."

The Worm was basically a long, moving corridor. Between stations it stretched and its speed increased tenfold and you would find the distance between yourself and the next person along from you increasing. At stations it would compress and slow to walking speed. Gabriel had not spent more than half a day in a major metropolis for several years, and was unused to the crowding and the tightness of space and the push and shuffle of humans flesh. He suddenly found himself breathing quickly and shallowly.

"Steady on, old bugger, ease her up," he muttered to himself, then had to pretend not to notice the startled expression on the face of his neighbor.

He stepped out onto the platform with a long sigh of relief, only to find that he had gotten off one stop too soon. Rather than face the claustrophobia of the Worm again he walked the rest of the way with the aid of Isadora's map.

He found himself at the entrance to a molded tunnel, almost thirty yards in diameter. Its design did not match any of the surrounding architecture and it was obviously of far more recent construction. Gabriel was aware of a translucent veil of light across the entrance. As he drew nearer it congealed into the words "WELCOME TO RAINER PARK"; words which appeared to shatter and dissolve as he stepped through them.

The corridor was dim, expressly so, for Gabriel found himself drawn inexorably to the bright circle of light at the other end. He stepped out blinking and when his

eyes had adjusted, found himself standing at the edge of
a field of ankle-deep grass. It swept out on either side
of him, curving and disappearing behind a copse of juni-
per and pine that blocked the way ahead. He could smell
the sweet muskiness of the trees from where he stood.
In growing wonder he made his way around the thicket
and stood, gazing across a flat expanse of meadow, yel-
low-green and speckled with a rainbow shower of blos-
som and wildflowers.

Gabriel had a momentary impression of great space
but, almost immediately, realized that it was an illusion
created by the light and the layout of the landscape.
Gabriel inhaled deeply and smelled that mismatched
cocktail of scents that told him "park." The sense of
living things, plants, flowers, trees, being placed in close
proximity to other plants next to which they had no business being.

Gabriel walked forward, the long grass whispering
past his ankles, making his way toward a hummock in
the distance that seemed to form the base for a monument of some kind. Thumb-sized silver bees, beautifully
crafted replicas of the real thing, hummed from wildflower to wildflower, alighting and burrowing into each
one momentarily and then moving on. Ensured
pollination.

As he neared it the meadowland smoothed into manicured lawn and a few park benches appeared, situated
at aesthetically strategic points. There were a half a
dozen people in the vicinity, mostly parents with children. The children gamboled about with joyful abandon,
but the adults, Gabriel noticed, stepped with careful,
flinching steps, placing their feet as if in anticipation of
the jarring hardness of metal or concrete.

As Gabriel climbed the hummock to the monument,
he saw that it was a domed, glass cylinder, like a stubby,
upended test tube, about five meters high and three in
diameter, standing on a base of black, semitransparent
stone. The stone was polished to a high sheen. From the
apex of the cylinder hung a pendulum, consisting of a
large sphere of the same black crystal swinging from an
almost invisible thread. On a flattened rectangle on the
base of the monument glowed a series of rapidly changing red numbers. After an instant, Gabriel realized that

the numbers were a digital clock, showing the date in Standard, and the time in hours, minutes, seconds, tenths and hundredths of a second. It seemed to be synchronized with the swinging of the pendulum. Set into the grass next to the whole affair was a bronze plaque proclaiming:

"AKASH CHANDRA LEVINSON, FOUNDER OF KYARA"

A woman in mauve overalls with a Rainer Park Maintenance badge on the breast pocket was working next to the monument. She herself was huge, a centimeter or so taller than Gabriel and as broad as a two-man life raft. She had a small box clamped to the side of the glass cylinder which her chubby fingers operated with almost indecent delicacy. She was chewing gum and her jaws moved from side to side in a slow, ruminative manner.

As he looked at her she gave him a glancing once-over and he could hear the thump of the rubber stamp in her mind as she branded him "ignorant tourist." Logic and self-honesty dictated Gabriel's next step.

"I'm an ignorant tourist," he said, presenting her with his most disarming smile. "I was wondering if you could help me."

The big woman's jaws stopped working as she eyed this thin, dark stranger suspiciously.

"Could you tell me about this monument?"

The jaws resumed their side-to-side motion and the woman nodded at the plaque. "It's written there."

Gabriel regarded the plaque as if he had only just noticed it, "You're right! You know, I've always been a sucker for women who chew gravel while they work."

The big woman nodded slowly, but the look she gave him was no longer unfriendly. "You talk to everyone like this? I'm amazed you're still walking around."

Gabriel lifted his shoulders and spread his hands. "Here I am."

"Chandra Levinson founded the original scientific base which grew into Kyara. We installed this as a memorial to her about two months after the park was opened. It's *supposed* to keep time to within three-hundredths of a second a year . . ." She let her voice trail off as she made a slight adjustment to her apparatus. "Of course, somebody checked it last week and found it was already three point six seven four dot seconds off after four months. That's why I'm here."

Gabriel looked up at it, impressed. "What keeps it going?"

"Solid-state magnet in the middle. And it's in a vacuum; that helps. That fella"—she indicated the pendulum ball—"weighs 160 kilos, which is what makes resetting it like this such a fiddly job. You have to speed it up and then start slowing it down before it actually comes into sync so that when it does the swing is juuust right."

Gabriel decided the time was right to switch the conversation onto another tack. "Have you worked here long?"

"From day one," replied the woman with obvious pride. "I was one of the first people on the team when they were still working out the design. The name's Jael Nyquist."

"Gabriel Kylie." Gabriel took the outstretched hand. Her grip was surprisingly gentle. He said, "I was actually hoping you could tell me something."

"Like what?"

"There was a woman who was killed here about three months back. You got any idea where exactly it happened?"

"No." Jael's voice was all of a sudden chilly. "What are you? Tick?"

"Sorry?"

"Media man, journalist."

"No."

"Then what's your interest?"

"She was family." Gabriel matched her stare and the big woman softened.

"Kylie was her name," she murmured, comprehension dawning, "Sorry about that. No offense, but we had the ticks crawling about the place for days afterward with their noses in the turnip roots, all 'human sodding interest,' the lonely girl who killed herself!"

"Killed herself?" Gabriel was startled.

"That was one angle." Jael snorted. "It's always somebody's angle. No, I reckon it was an accident. She was messing about here after closing hours in the dark . . ."

She caught herself in mid-sentence, "Uh . . . I didn't mean it quite like that."

"No worries." Gabriel shrugged. "Could you tell me where it happened?"

"Over in the veldt." She indicated the tawny landscape to Gabriel's left. "If you wait a minute, I'll take you over there; it's my lunch break." She inspected her apparatus, then touched a switch. "Come on."

She lumbered down the side of the hummock with Gabriel in tow. The children were gone, and their place had been taken by an elderly, white-haired woman of elegant frailty and quite lovely, sitting on the end of one of the park benches. Beside her on the bench was an enormous, antique wickerwork picnic hamper and beneath the bench itself was parked a small cleaning robot, the size and shape of a chamber pot.

"That's the Litterbug," Jael told Gabriel with a wink. "Pretend to look the other way, but . . . watch her."

Gabriel did as he was told. The old lady finished the yogurt she had been eating, glanced surreptitiously about and tossed the yogurt carton onto the grass two meters away. She hunched her shoulders guiltily for an instant and then a self-satisfied smirk stole over her face and she reached into the picnic hamper to pull out a paper napkin. The moment her attention was elsewhere the little cleaning robot came to life and shot out from under the park bench. A faint grinding of ceramic teeth and the yogurt carton was no more.

"She comes here every day," Jael explained, "seven days a week. Never misses and, as far as anyone can tell, she comes for the sole purpose of littering the place up. It wasn't worth calling the spooks on her and we didn't want to start throwing people out within two months of opening if we didn't have to, so we assigned her a cleaning robot every time she comes. It follows her around the place whenever she's here. I programmed a twelve-second delay in it. No sense in spoiling her fun. Look, there's the place, over there."

They were walking through long, dry plains grass now. It was perceptibly hotter and the air was less humid. *Neatly done,* Gabriel thought appreciatively. They were heading toward some kind of movable scaffold; three platforms, one above the other, all attached to a rail that ran around the perimeter of the park.

Suddenly a whiff of animal scent passed under Gabriel's nostrils. He glanced about quickly and spotted the patch of yellow fur almost invisible in the grass twenty meters to his left.

"What's that?" he asked, stopping, all his tracker's senses alerted.

Jael looked around. "Where?"

Gabriel pointed and Jael followed his finger.

"Probably a lion . . . where? . . . yes, it is. You've got good eyes, stike." She whacked him between the shoulder blades, hard enough to knock the air out of his lungs. "Come on, the place is right over here."

Gabriel remained, watching the lion, a big, sorrel-maned male, his instincts telling him that there was something wrong here. Wrong in the bovine way this beast moved, in the faint, tarry odor of it. A smell of the earth. It was only when the lion bent and nibbled at a grass stem that Gabriel understood.

He did not need to see the square front teeth, the flat molars, made for steady grinding instead of tearing, the carefully clawless paws, to know what it was that a romantic wildlife lover like Isadora found so depressing about Rainer Park.

GenTec.

Gabriel had seen worse, but he did not allow his mind to follow that route. Some of the things he had seen still hurt.

Jael was waiting for him at the foot of the scaffolding.

"This is the place; the cleaning robots found her the next morning right next to that red stone there."

Gabriel knelt by the spot indicated by Jael, examining the stony ground, the tufts of yellow grass clawing their way up through the rocks. Finally he laid his hands flat on the ground, pushing his fingers as far into it as they would go. It was good, dry soil, but silent. It hummed, certainly, that faint hum that filled every corner, every stone of Kyara, but that wasn't it. This soil ended, half a meter down, in metal grating and humidity and fertility control apparatuses, monitoring mineral content, pH balance, correcting every aberration. Life here had no roots. When the Ancestors walked their

paths of Song and sang the Earth and the trees into
being, who had sung this ground, these trees?

"You won't find anything there, stike, it's been
months." Jael was observing him critically.

Gabriel ignored her and let his eyes roam the immediate area. They were standing on a rocky outcropping in
a stretch of woodland set against the wall of the dome,
which was opaqued to a height of three meters so that
it was impossible to look out on the surface. It was bor-
dered on either side by trees and overlooked a lake. The
edge of the trees on one side was only a few paces from
the spot where Elspeth had fallen. *Somebody could have
hidden there,* he mused, *but, shag it! Jael is right.* The
grass growing here now was not even the same grass
that had been growing here the night Elspeth died.

He turned his attention to the scaffolding. It consisted
of three platforms set one above the other at intervals
of some fifteen meters. The curve of the dome meant
that each platform overhung the one below by a meter
or so. There was a fragile-looking ladder climbing up as
far as the topmost platform.

"The platforms slide up and down. The top one goes
up to the apex. You can get to any point on the dome
with these. Mainly for maintenance, bit of window cleaning. Anything major we'd put up something more solid."

Gabriel chewed his bottom lip thoughtfully. "Have
they been used since it happened?"

Jael shook her head. "Nah, and you've got to have
clearance to use it. Thumblocked. I'd love to know what
she thought she was doing up there."

"Curious maybe," Gabriel mused. "I'd be curious to
climb up and have a look myself."

Jael gave him an amused look. "Give it a try." There
was a challenge in her tone.

Tentatively Gabriel reached out for a shoulder-height
rung. The effect was a little nastier than touching a metal
railing after walking on a synthetic carpet. Jael chortled
annoyingly at his expression as he flexed his fingers.

"Starts uncomfortable at kid height and gets progressively stronger as you go higher," she explained. "Never
strong enough to kill, but it keeps them off."

Gabriel scaled the ladder with his eyes. She could
have been wearing gloves. Lieutenant Izeki had not

mentioned whether she had been found with gloves on or not.

"And this is on day and night."

"Unless you've got the thumbprint that matches."

"Was it on the night it happened?"

Somewhat to his surprise Jael replied, "As a matter a fact it wasn't. We were overhauling the whole security system that week. There—some bugs had come up between Park Control and City. The main nerve center is in the city itself. The doors were locked, but all the infrared scanners were down. We'd been working on it for days. Otherwise, we would have known the moment they got in."

Gabriel stared at her, bewildered. They? "They; you said 'they.' Who's 'they'?"

"Yeah. Oh, you didn't know? There was some old eth-head in one of the service tunnels under the park. We found him unconscious down there. Bugout Plaza type. One of our people had seen him before. 'Course the spooks were swarming all over the place by then, so we gave him to them."

Gabriel listened to this with increasing agitation.

"You mean there was some other bugger running around here on the same night?"

Jael Nyquist managed to look sheepish, all three hundred pounds of her. "It was not our finest hour."

"Well, what happened to him . . . the man that was here on the night?"

"I told you, we gave him to the spooks and glad to see the back of him. The guy was in ethanol free fall and stank!"

Gabriel glanced back at the ground. "That's the exact place she was lying?"

"Saw it myself. Head right there, next to that sharp rock, feet there." Jael pointed.

Puzzled, Gabriel stood where she had indicated and looked up. The area that Jael had marked out was almost directly below the edge of the first platform, almost a meter inside that of the second and some distance to the side of the ladder.

"Then there's no way she could have fallen off the second ladder; she would have fallen the other way. She must have been on the platform itself," Gabriel mused.

"Reckon so." Jael was showing signs of restlessness. "Listen, if there's anything else . . ."

Gabriel took the hint, "Yeah . . . yeah, thanks for your help." He barely noticed as the big woman walked away.

Izeki was no fool. What had he hoped to achieve when he sent Gabriel home with a condescending pat on the fanny? It was not the old drunkard in the park or even the oh-so-convenient park shutdown the same week Elspeth was killed. Opportunity knocks, and if Elspeth had wanted to circumvent the alarm in order to get into the park for some reason, what better time to have done it than when the system was out on the jinglies. What smelled was the haste with which Izeki had brushed Gabriel off and the sheer clumsiness with which he had done so.

They were waiting for him at his hotel. Two slim-necked types in plain clothes. Leaning against a wall, a discreet distance from the hotel entrance. They were clearly professionals, experienced at blending into their surroundings; and Gabriel could have spotted them in a blizzard a mile off.

They approached, identified themselves as TARC officers and invited him in quiet, steel-rimmed voices to accompany them to the bureau. Gabriel acquiesced with an amiable shrug. One could never win an argument with drones and, besides, he was curious now to meet anybody who was interested in him.

He was led into a pastel blue office where he was greeted by a small, gray man with a fox-terrier smile, who introduced himself as Pelham Leel. He nodded to the two drones and they soft-soled out efficiently, the door sliding shut behind them.

"I apologize for having you brought in like this, Mr. Kylie, but I'm sure you understand I can't afford to wait in hotel lobbies. As it is my men were there all morning."

"I have a phone." Gabriel indicated his collar.

"True, but since you are only here for . . . ah . . . three days, I believe, I thought this might be quicker. Clearly no one is infallible." He smiled thinly and Gabriel smiled back. He understood. The Bogy had been flexing its muscle. From Grayscape to Luna Dome it was the same. No matter how big, or how small, even a moonlighting law officer in a one-weasel hamlet on Helios, the Bogy could never resist.

"I believe you're seeking information on the death of your sister in Rainer Park some months back. You spoke with a Municipal Police officer yesterday. A Lieutenant Izeki?"

"Yes." Gabriel leaned back and waited. He had had encounters with police on eight of the Seventeen Planets and had found that, when in doubt, dealing with the law was best handled like fishing. Let it come to you.

"And he perhaps mentioned that the investigation reverted to TARC jurisdiction," Leel continued.

"No."

"I see. Well, it did. Saxon Rainer is one of our most prominent citizens and this could have become a major scandal for him. Our commission was called in at his personal request. Many were, of course, worried that your sister's death was *not* an accident. I was fairly convinced myself for a time, despite the fact that murder is not a common crime here." Pelham Leel squinted at the wall behind Gabriel's left shoulder, pursing his lips as if trying to find the right words to express what he was trying to say.

"You see," he said slowly, "we do have our problems, like any city, but Kyara is unique in that, unlike an artificial colony such as the Terran Lagrange cities, there is only *one* exit from Kyara. It concentrates the civic-spirit enormously if a person knows that there's only one door and that can be covered with a dozen agents. It sometimes sounds a little sinister to offworlders, so it may surprise you to know that we have the strictest Privacy Laws on the Seventeen Planets. That's what prevented us from simply putting a tracer on your phone.

"At any rate, for those reasons, when there is reason to suspect that a violent crime has been committed, the matter is examined *thoroughly*."

He leaned his elbows on the table and fixed Gabriel with a gaze that was almost overwhelming in its sheer frankness and sincerity.

"Mr. Kylie, the investigation was meticulous. There is no reason to believe that your sister's death was anything other than a tragic accident. However . . . do you have a wallet computer?"

"Of course." Gabriel took it out and handed it to the TARC man.

Leel slotted it into a loading drive and murmured, "Load file 2661/36b/b." Then he removed the wallet from the slot and slid it across the table toward Gabriel. His hand, however, did not release it. "This is a copy of all files relating to the investigation. Please examine them and if you have any questions, phone me. I've included my phone number in the file." He lifted his hand from the wallet and Gabriel recognized it as a dismissal. But he still had one question, something that had been picking away at a corner of his mind since his arrival. And since everything seemed so cozy between himself and Captain Leel:

"Uh . . . I do have one question, if you don't mind," he said.

"Of course."

"Yesterday, in the airport, I saw a man. He smelled rather .. strongly. Somebody called him a reeker."

Leel nodded. "Yes, that would have been an O.T.E., an Olfactoric Transaetheric Enhancer. It's a surgical implant in the skull." He touched a point between his eyebrows. "Doesn't affect the person implanted. It works directly on the olfactory nerve, giving the illusion that the implantee smells disagreeable."

Gabriel's eyebrows lifted. "The person I saw stank like a latrine full of last year's jockey shorts."

Leel blinked. "I . . . yes, well, the effect is adjustable. We use it on chronic nonviolent anthropathic offenders . . ."

"Troublemakers."

"People who adversely influence the smooth running of the social fabric." Leel looked at him pointedly. "Was there anything else?"

Gabriel shook his head and, for the second time since his arrival in Kyara, allowed himself to be courteously, but expeditiously escorted out of the offices of the Kyaran law-enforcement agencies.

Unwilling to face the Worm again, Gabriel caught a hangcab, reflecting as he did so on the universal truth that police agencies' eagerness to pluck you off the street

and drive you downtown was rarely equaled by any
matching enthusiasm to drive you back uptown when
they were done with you.

He found a little sake house called the Edelrice, across
the street from the hotel, run by a leathery, old, oriental
crone, esconced himself behind a corner table with a pot
of green tea and a viewscreen and commenced to read
the report Pelham Leel had given him.

There were no surprises. Autopsy revealed that the
subject had fallen from a height of some thirty meters
onto a rocky surface and died instantly as a result of a
broken neck. There were no marks on her that indicated
a struggle. The subject had evidently remained hidden
in the park when it closed and remained undetected because of the inactive alarm system. One anomaly; the
presence of an elderly tramp, who identified himself as
Old Mac and was found unconscious in a service tunnel
under the park, having staggered down there in a
drunken stupor. He had sustained a mild concussion as
a result of collapsing onto a floor grating. He was unsur-
prisingly vague about what he was doing there, denied
having seen or heard anything and was subsequently
released.

The inquest's decision: accidental death.

Gabriel sipped his tea as he ran through it a second
time more slowly. Since his arrival two ranking police
officers had vehemently denied any suggestion of murder. Denied unasked.

There was a burst of laughter from one of the adjoining tables and Gabriel glanced up to find Hitedoro Izeki
observing him from the entrance.

a word from the wings

Izeki wove his way through the other patrons to Gabriel's table and drew up the chair opposite, draping his elbow over the back of it and leaning his back against the wall. His eyes were pink and his face was hanging heavy round the edges.

"I've been waiting for you," he grunted.

"I'm a popular bloke," Gabriel replied mildly. "How did you know where I was?"

Izeki jerked a meaty thumb at the door. "There's a TARC on the other side watching this place. He wouldn't do that without a reason." Izeki brightened, then scowled at Gabriel's teapot. "What are you drinking there? Tea? You've got to be kidding." He turned to the robot waiter who had slid noiselessly up to his elbow. "Atovar single malt, double. Sure you won't join me?"

"Cheers, no." Gabriel poured himself another cup of tea. "I knew a bloke in Arowan state, on Octavia, used to make his own. He used to trigger the fermentation process by drowning a few dozen of a particular local insect in it. Little scorpion-type bugger. There's an enzyme in the poison ducts that gives the process a kick start."

Izeki's jaw dropped. "No kidding." He examined with a certain dubiousness the glass that the robot waiter had set in front of him. "Bugs, huh?" He took a careful sip, pursed his large lips and shrugged. From inside his coat he produced a padded envelope, which he placed on the table.

"Look"—he hesitated—"I don't know what you want. But there's a little more to the story than what I told you yesterday . . ." He broke off, reached into his pocket for a box of nicotine root, opened it and selected one. "This is . . . off the record. The TARC outside—he didn't see me come in, he won't see me leave, alright?"

"Alright," Gabriel replied. "I've just read the official report."

Izeki made an unsuccessful attempt to hide his contempt. "Yeah, there's not a whole lot I can add to that. I was pulled off the investigation the same day. Does it mention that her phone was on?"

Gabriel touched his collar inquiringly.

"Yeah, she was talking to someone, or listening to someone, or they were listening to her when it happened. They'd hung up, of course."

"Which means somewhere out there there's someone who might have heard . . ."

Izeki shrugged. "Maybe. And then there was the old man. Old Mac, he called himself, some old curb roller who lives in Bugout Plaza. Wouldn't say what he was doing in that service tunnel—he didn't remember—just said that he'd been bullywhacked, said that someone had jumped on him. Did have a nice, fat bruise on his head, so he could have been telling the truth." Izeki paused.

"So what happened to him?" Gabriel prompted.

"TARCs took him over when they bumped me off the case." Izeki scowled into his glass as if searching it for insect residue. "A captain from Central turned up the same evening, just as I was getting ready to go home, flashed authorization and told me I was off the case. They were taking over. Took the files, photographs, material evidence and the one possible witness, who they later turned loose. And that's it." He swallowed the last of his drink, but made no move to leave.

"Except . . ." Gabriel said at last.

Izeki stared at him coolly. "Except there was a nasty little voice that wouldn't leave me alone the whole time those people were cleaning out my files." The nicotine root rolled slowly back and forth in his fingers.

"I did something I've never done before. I stashed evidence. Here." He tapped the padded envelope. "That was what she had on her when she was found. They never came back asking for it. It isn't much, just junk, but it might mean something to you."

Gabriel made no move to take it. There was some kind of battle going on inside Izeki and he felt it best to wait until it had resolved itself.

Izeki flicked his root into the flashtray and leaned across the table.

"Nobody's clean. But I'm cleaner than most. Just that much"—he made a tiny circle on the table with his forefinger—"I don't know what you're planning on doing with this." He gestured toward the envelope. "I don't know if you're a part of any of this, if 'it' is anything, so I'm taking a risk here. But after this I don't want to see you or hear from you."

"Alright," said Gabriel quietly, "that's fair enough. But I do have one question."

"You've heard what I have to say!"

"This captain," Gabriel continued, ignoring the interruption. "What was his name?"

Izeki said nothing, his expression stony.

"Was his name Leel, yes? Pelham Leel?"

Izeki rose to his feet. "Drinks are on you," he said coldly. He made his way to the bar entrance. After peering out of the doorway, he stepped out and, with a funny twist of his heel, matched his walk to those of the other pedestrians, becoming suddenly just another anonymous form moving up the street.

Gabriel sat for a while with his empty teapot, his fingers turning the tiny cup over and around. He made no move to open the envelope.

Twelve miles north of Landing, where the road forked right for Alice Springs, you could turn off into the bush and, if you walked for about fifteen minutes toward the double-humped hill in the distance, you would find a clearing in the scrub. The ground was covered with flat stones and in the center of the clearing stood a dead tree which looked like the hand of one of those figures whom Gabriel had seen pictures of, excavated from the bottom of peat marshes. There was no water there. It was quite dry. There were no stray strands of wildgrass twisting up through the stones. It was quite bare. There was no shade. Gabriel had not seen it for nineteen years. And yet, at this moment, he found himself missing it very much.

"Shag it!" he muttered in a sudden surge of anger.

He tapped for the bill, thumbed it and rose. At the door he halted, then went back over to the bar. The old woman squinted at him inquiringly.

"You want another drink?"

Gabriel shook his head and said quietly, "Is there a back way out of here?"

"No."

"No?"

"No."

Gabriel stared at her and she returned his stare, her beady eyes almost lost in their epicanthic folds and her mouth like the grin of a lizard.

"Do you know, you're a nasty old woman," Gabriel whispered.

"You pay for your drinks, Mama 'Guchi keeps serving," she replied unmoved.

"Sss," Gabriel hissed softly at her, and walked out of the sake house. He felt much better. Mama 'Guchi was his kind of people. The good feeling enabled him to ignore the TARC goon watching him.

In his hotel room, however, he sobered as he removed his coat and flung it over the back of a chair. His hunting knife went onto the bedside table.

Gabriel keyed open the envelope and emptied the contents onto the bed. With a sweep of his hands he spread them out. He caught his breath.

Within the parameters of his own knowledge, Hitedoro Izeki had been right. This was junk.

But not to Gabriel. To him this was Elspeth.

A cardphone. A pair of coral-tipped earings. A small pocketknife. An antique coin—a penny from the days when money was measured by the weight in your palm. A thin gold chain bearing an evil eye, a fish carved in jacinth, and a silver salamander. A couple of scraps of plaspyrus. A pen. A smashed wallet computer. An almond. A half-empty pack of lysergic gum. A red pebble like those they used to throw at birds when they were young. In a small, transparent plastine envelope, a parakeelya seed from the desert around Landing.

"Oh, Christ," muttered Gabriel, swallowing hard. All of a sudden his throat was constricted.

There she was, all there was to show for her life. Gabriel picked up the chain and fingered the jacinth fish, identical to the one on his own wrist. He remembered the summer they had gotten them.

Elspeth had been a fine swimmer. She had lived her tenth summer like an eel in the lake near Grandmother Lalumanji's lean-to, gurgling with glee as she left her elder brother raging in the shallows.

They had caught their first fish of that year together, she and he, a silver trout, a queen of trout, and watched as Grandmother Lalumanji roasted it over a tight little fire until it was brown and crisp on the outside and soft and pink on the inside and fell apart on their tongues like a ripe fruit.

At the end of the summer Grandmother had given them each a little jacinth fish. If you unscrewed the end of one you would find that it was hollow inside, just a tiny space, large enough to hide a pea. Gabriel had been very excited by this, but in all the years that followed he had never found anything worth hiding in his. Elspeth on the other hand . . .

"Tell me you haven't," Gabriel whispered. He gave the fish a sudden twist and it came in two in his hands. Something tiny and glittering fell onto the bedspread. It was a perfectly square sliver of crystal a half a centimeter across.

"Aw, shit," Gabriel breathed. Then he jumped as his phone pipped at him. He touched the contact.

"Yes."

"Hi, it's me," said a familiar voice.

Gabriel pulled himself together. "Yeah, hi, Iz, how're you doing?"

"I'd be doing better if you opened the door."

Gabriel went chilly, "Where are you?"

"Outside your door."

Gabriel closed his eyes, "Strewth . . ."

"What?"

"Wait a moment." Taking one of the plasper slips, he carefully scooped the crystal off the bed, placed it on the bedside table and covered it with the packet of lysergic gum. Then he wiped his eyes, composed himself as best he could and went to answer the door.

Isadora was grinning and holding up a short, green

feather, when Gabriel opened the door. "Present from Mack."

"Thanks." Gabriel returned a halfhearted grin and took the feather from her fingers, "Come on in." He stood back to allow her inside, peering up and down the corridor as he did so. There was no one there, not that he'd expected actually to see anyone.

When he turned back inside he found Isadora watching him closely. "Are you alright? I didn't really pick my time, did I?"

"Nah, it's fine, I could use a spell with a mate." Even as he said it he could feel a wave of relief washing over him. He indicated the knickknacks on the bed. "I've been having an interesting day."

"D'you mind if I . . ." Isadora was standing questioningly by the drink slot.

"No, no, sorry, have something. Maybe you can dial me up a cup of tea."

Isadora did so and took a coffee herself. Then she slid out the wall-bench and curled up on it, watching whilst Gabriel placed Elspeth's things back into the envelope. She sipped at her coffee. "So, tell me about your interesting day. What were you looking for in the corridor?"

Gabriel nodded at the door. "There's a TARC officer outside taking a serious interest in me. Now that he's seen you come in here he's going to be taking an interest in you. It would have been better if you hadn't come . . . for *your* sake."

Isadora's eyes narrowed and lowered her cup. "What's going on? What have you done?"

Gabriel sighed and threw his hands out. "What have I done? I came here for three days for a little information. I came to say good-bye to my sister; I thought maybe I could get an idea about what she's been doing for the last couple of decades. In the last two hours I've been hauled downtown for an interview with a charming little ferret posing as a TARC captain, who presented me with an inquest report and assured me that there was no question of foul play, I've had another spook sliding up to me in a sake bar to tell me that the first spook was a liar and the report in my hand is an old-fashioned whitewash and since then I've had yet one more lead-brained spook outside my door watching every move I make in or out of here! Christ, forget her bloody death. I still haven't even found out what she was doing for a living!"

"Exterminator."

Gabriel stared at her in surprise. "Exterminator?"

"Yeah, that's why I came by." Isadora reached into her breast pocket and pulled out a compcard. "I called up all the media reports on her when I was at work. I thought you might want to see it."

Gabriel took the card. "I forgot. A tick."

Isadora replied drily. "Not quite. I'm a researcher. The ticks call us honeybees. We look for the sweetness in the fields of weeds."

"Honeybee," murmured Gabriel, and held up the card, "Thanks, I appreciate it. An exterminator. Of what? Bugs?"

"Yeah, the normal kind, a few of the rare GenTec varieties, there *are* one or two around. And electronic— chiproaches, twigleggies and the like. They're the biggest problem on Kyara. We had a chiproach in one of the data-storage backups in my department a couple of months ago."

Gabriel nodded. He had never seen one, but was familiar with the phenomenon. Tiny, self-contained, self-reproducing computers on insectlike legs, smaller than a pinpoint and programmed to creep into single-crystal circuitry and introduce a virus—invariably destructive.

"Maybe you can tell me what a TARC is."

"Targeting, Apprehension and Remand Central. Official law-enforcement agency."

"The Bogy by any other name . . ." muttered Gabriel.

"What did you say?"

"Nothing. Please, just tell me what that means."

Isadora took a sip of her drink. "Would you mind sitting down then?"

Only now did Gabriel realize that he had been pacing back and forth across the carpet like a caged bear. "Sorry."

"I'll try and keep this simple but . . . well, what do you know about the political settup here?"

"I hate it," Gabriel said feelingly.

"That much? Okay, look, in a nutshell, you've got the elected Assembly, you've got the Conclave, which is a group of so-called distinguished citizens, nominated for life or until they choose to resign, whichever comes first. And then there's the president, who's elected by the Conclave and the Assembly. He's the tie-breaker. There's also the High Court, but they operate separately from the others. Still hate it?"

"Loathe it."

"Good. Now the Municipal Police answer to the Assembly. The TARCs are under the direct authority of the Conclave. *Both* answer to the High Court."

Isadora took a sip from her cup, then, when Gabriel made no response, she leaned forward, and said, "Gabriel . . . what's going on? Do you . . . do you really think somebody might have killed her? Why would they do that?"

Gabriel gazed at her, seeing the barely suppressed excitement in her face, her upper teeth biting on her lower lip. Despite the soft curve of her face there was something lynxlike about her now.

"I don't know," he said slowly, "that I care."

"You don't care?" Her disappointment in him was palpable. "How can you not care? Gabriel, there may be a murderer walking around free out there! I mean we're talking about the law here!"

"The law won't bring her back."

Isadora deliberately placed her cup on a side table. "The law may stop it from happening to someone else. Gabriel, this person . . . these people are breaking that law! Those guys outside your door, if they're still there tomorrow *they'll* be breaking the law!"

"Privacy Laws?"

"Right! On Thor that kind of surveillance can be continued for three days maximum without a serious court order. You can file a civil suit if you catch them listening at the door! Against anyone, for that matter."

"And threats?"

"Can you prove it?"

"I didn't record the conversation."

"And a good thing, too. If you had, without a High Court order, they could have you incarcerated."

"By way of the same Privacy Laws."

"By way of the same Privacy Laws, right."

"It's been my experience that if something needs protecting by law, then people have forgotten the true nature of that which they're protecting."

"And what's that bit of polemic supposed to mean?" Isadora demanded, now clearly nettled.

Gabriel gazed at her in despair. Too much had happened in the last twenty-four hours; he was tired and confused. Too tired really to care whether or not he could make her understand.

He spoke with care. "It means I don't believe in Law and I don't believe in Order; I only believe in a big, ugly Bogy that feeds on itself."

Isadora was staring at him in complete incomprehension.

"Well, for a disinterested cynic who couldn't give a damn, you've smoked quite a lot of people out of the woodwork so far!"

"I haven't done anything of the sort!" Gabriel retorted. "They came to me!"

"Then either someone's afraid of you or someone thinks you know something . . . or maybe you do."

"Well, they're wrong on all counts. Listen, Iz, maybe you'll understand this . . . I may not know what I believe in, but I know what I don't like. I don't like lies."

Isadora watched him in silence and by degrees the indignation left her face.

Gabriel turned and walked into the relative shadow of the corner near the front door. For a long moment he stood with his back to her.

"Are you alright?" Isadora asked at last. "I'm sorry; I shouldn't have pushed. I know you're upset about your sister . . ."

"Isadora . . ." Gabriel said gently, keeping his face to the darkness. "I'm in a place I don't like. In a place I don't understand. You know, to someone born in a cage the bars are the horizon. They don't even see them. I wasn't born here, and I can see the bars. I've been here less than two days and I've got the Bogy outside my door, watching me. They've threatened me, they follow every move I make, they've lied to me."

"They've got you scared," whispered Isadora.

Gabriel pursed his lips and fingered the periapt hanging from his wrist. Slowly he shook his head. "No." He turned to look at her, saw her eyes widen and body stiffen. *From lynx to rabbit,* he thought absently, and then realized that it was he from whom she was recoiling. Deliberately he relaxed his features and his death receded from his eyes.

"No," he repeated, "they've got me angry."

The smile that slowly spread across her face was triumphant. She believed in him again. "You're a complicated man, Mr. Kylie."

Gabriel shook his head. "No. I'm real plain. Elspeth, she was . . ." The shrug returned. "Here, you want to do something for me?" He strode forward and removed the packet of lysergic gum from the plaspyrus scrap and showed her the crystal.

"A chip."

"You reckon you can find out what's on it for me?"

"Is it important?" Gabriel did not bother to answer. "I'll ask a friend of mine down at the BME office. She's a good software retrieval woman. How 'bout . . ." She hesitated. ". . . maybe a bite to eat? There's a couple of personal service places I know. Real cooks . . ." She broke off, disappointed, as Gabriel shook his head.

"I'd love to, Iz. But I think I'd like to take another stroll back to Rainer Park, sniff around a bit."

Isadora glanced at her watch. "What, now?"

"It's open until late, I think, no?"

"Eleven or twelve, something like that. But I don't know what you're hoping to find. Besides, it's going to be in dark-down by now."

Dark-down. Gabriel pulled a face; he had forgotten. There might be no days or nights in Kyara, but every artificial colony had some form of night-and-day cycle. Nevertheless, Gabriel felt the pull to look once more at the place where Elspeth had spent the last moments of her life.

"I just need to get a feel of the ground. There's a trail there, somewhere . . ."

"After three months?"

"I've seen animal tracks, petrified ones, over a hundred million years old."

"You're not in the wilderness now," said Isadora, amused.

"Oh, yes I am," replied Gabriel.

conversation

—It's me. I finally got some word back about Kylie.
—What took so long?
—Long Hop Travel. They're to-the-letter sticklers about Privacy Law Statutes. All we could find out was that he arrived from Octavia and *was* booked out for Merryweather the day after tomorrow. He canceled his reservation about three hours after he arrived. We reckon it was just after he spoke to Izeki.
—Do you think Izeki told him anything?
—What could he have told him?
—That idiot Leel had to go pushing his weight around, making threats. Can't you keep your people in order?
—He did perform a useful function. If this Kylie had simply been who he had said he was, he would have taken the hint and left, or *not* gotten the hint, accepted the explanation and left. Anyway, he'd already canceled his reservation . . .
—Not a very clever thing to do if he'd really wanted to retain his cover. Can't you find out anything about him?
—He's from Earth! They don't give out information of *any* kind on their citizens, not even phone numbers, you know that. They don't even allow information on citizens to be computerized. Hard copy only. Makes it harder to get access.
—*Damn* it! Find out something! I'm going to put a curtain down. This man gets access to nothing!
—By this evening we're going to have to take the official surveillance off him unless we get a court order.
—Then make it unofficial. What about his phone?
—What about his phone? You want me to pip it? We're

talking about a major Privacy Law felony, and the way the Statutes are being tightened up at the moment . . .

—You're worrying about *Privacy Law* felony *now?* Don't you think it's gone a little beyond that?

—There is nothing beyond the Privacy Laws.

—Stop! I don't want any more excuses, I want answers. You want to do it your own way, then go ahead, but find something!

—We did check on the woman he contacted. Her name is Isadora Gatzalumendi. She's a tick. A researcher at Duas Voces. She's also an activist against opening Querin to human development. Actively campaigning for a Nay vote from Thor in the summit. Three arrests, public-disorder misdemeanors. They happened during antidevelopment protests.

—She works for Duas Voces? . . . Alright, I'll see what I can do at my end. You take care of yours.

—I always do.

the twist

Isadora did not notice the holo-artist on the street outside her building, nor the two figures who peeled themselves off the street tableau and followed her inside.

"Ms. Gatzalumendi?" the voice was quiet and couched in practiced civility.

Isadora's hand withdrew from her doorplate and she turned to find herself facing a man in the nondescript plain clothes that sang of officialdom. He was accompanied by a robot in the green-and-silver uniform of the T.A.R.C.'s Artificial Intelligence wing.

"Yes, that's me," she said nervously.

"I was wondering if I might have a few words with you," the plainclothesman said, adding pointedly, "in private."

Isadora hesitated. She knew that, without a warrant, it would be an unforgivable breach of Privacy etiquette for him to ask to be invited inside her dwelling. It was also clear to her that he expected the invitation and she resented that presumption.

"There's no one here," she said, glancing down the corridor.

The man waited. Isadora realized that she was treading the line between incivility and deliberate antagonism.

"Have you got I.D.?" she said coldly.

Without changing expression he reached inside his coverall pocket and slid out a small card. At the slight pressure of his fingers it lit up. He did not hand it to her, and Isadora was forced to tilt her head in order to read it. Touché.

"Leel, Pelham. Captain, Targeting, Apprehension and

Remand Central, Green Sector," she read. As she'd expected, TARC.

"Come in," she said with bad grace, touching the doorplate and leading the way inside. It was only as she heard the door slide shut behind Leel that she remembered the chip in her pocket. She turned and saw with a chill that the robot had followed them both inside and was standing near the door, its burnished, featureless face reflecting the entire room in distorted miniature.

Composing herself, she gestured for Leel to sit down, which he did with cool grace. She sat on the edge of the wall-couch and tried not to think of what she was carrying in her pocket.

"I didn't want to inconvenience you by asking you to come down to the station," he said with a slight smile. "It's come to our notice that you've had contact with a man calling himself Gabriel Kylie."

"Yes," Isadora said shortly. "We . . . met on the Orbit shuttle." Leel's fingertips were rhythmically pressing against the arm of his chair, the fingernails biting like incisors into the smooth plastine.

"On the Orbit shuttle. I see. What did you and Mr. Kylie speak about the three times you met? Did he tell you about himself? About his reasons for coming here?"

"Why are you asking? Is this official?" responded Isadora coldly. "What Mr. Kylie and I said was strictly private. If you've got anything else to say, I suggest you produce some kind of warrant."

Leel glanced at the robot, silent by the doorway, then let his gaze rove about the apartment in an absent-minded sort of way until it alit on Wang Fu's corner. He rose and went to crouch next to the adder's pen.

"Careful, he's poisonous," Isadora said warningly, adding, "And yes, he is registered. A warrant?"

Leel continued to gaze at the snake. "Not a GenTec then. Earth species?"

Isadora hesitated. *Earth. Earth snake. Earth man.* Was there an implication? Before she could reply Leel spoke again. "Ms. Gatzalumendi, I came here hoping for your voluntary cooperation. I see no reason why we should be speaking of warrants at this time. Do you?"

The robot glistened darkly from the doorway. The chip seemed to grow hot against her thigh. If this was official, she had no reason not to cooperate. If it was not official and they searched her . . .

Isadora realized that she had been fingering her pocket and withdrew her hand as casually as she could.

"We talked about where he was from. He's from Australia, near somewhere called Landing. His sister was the woman killed in Rainer Park three months ago. We talked about that." She paused, but Leel did not respond. "And I told him about Kyara, you know, tourist stuff. Lent him a map to get to Rainer Park. That kind of stuff."

"Just that?"

"Yeah. Just that." Isadora stared at him defiantly.

Leel's over-the-shoulder gaze was long and piercing.

"And what was his purpose in coming to Kyara, did he tell you that?"

"His sister was killed, I told you. He said he wanted to find out what she had been doing the last twenty-one years. That was how long it had been since he had seen her."

"I see. Doesn't that strike you as strange?"

"Strange?"

Leel rose and walked back to his chair. "Unlikely then? That after having not seen her for twenty-one years he should suddenly appear. Why the sudden interest? And three months after her death, no less."

Isadora was taken aback. Nothing up until now had given her reason to doubt the veracity of anything that Gabriel had told her about himself. But Leel was right. The constituent parts of Gabriel's story did not quite seem to add up.

And she remembered that look he had given her from the shadow of the doorway. That terrifying gaze, like death was staring out of his eyes. She realized suddenly that Leel had spoken again.

"What? What did you say?"

Leel leaned forward. "So he gave you no inkling at all about why he was now suddenly interested in his alleged sister's life?"

"No . . . *alleged* sister? What do you mean?"

"And he never mentioned the blue box?"

"The what? No, he never mentioned the . . . anything like that." To Isadora the conversation was taking on a surreal edge. "Look, what the flock are you talking about?" she asked angrily.

Leel regarded her for a moment, then rose to his feet. Isadora felt a sudden surge of fear.

"Thank you for your help, Ms. Gatzalumendi," he said politely, and walked toward the door. The robot swiveled to open it. For an instant Isadora was too surprised to react, then she burst out, "Hey. Hey!"

Leel stopped and turned slowly. The robot's hand hovered over the doorplate. "Yes?"

"What is this all about? What d'you mean 'alleged' sister?"

Leel sighed, and said in a patient tone, "Has it never occurred to you to wonder if your Mr. Kylie is really who he says he is? Hm?"

Isadora's eyes narrowed suspiciously.

Leel went on, "You've met him three times, but what do you really know about him? What could you know about a man that you claim is a casual acquaintance? Who is this Gabriel Kylie? Is he an aggrieved brother? Or is he something else? Did he mention that he was a cyborg?"

Isadora was taken aback. "A cyborg?"

"Loosely speaking. He has a prosthetic. Did he mention that?" Leel pursed his lips with satisfaction. "Clearly not."

"Why should he? What kind of prosthetic?"

"Well, now, that would be in breach of the Privacy Laws, wouldn't it? My point is simply this—what do you really know about Gabriel Kylie, Ms. Gatzalumendi?"

Pelham Leel turned, waited for the robot to slide the door open and stepped outside, the robot following him like a gargoyle shade.

"Well, who do you think he is then?" Isadora called out. "Hey!" The door closed on Leel's ironic leer. Isadora took two steps toward it and then stopped, knowing it was useless. She drifted back onto the couch, breathing hard. "Shit," she whispered. "Shit."

Gingerly she reached into her pocket and pulled out the fold of plasper containing the chip. She stared as it. *I don't belong here and I don't belong in this,* she thought. *Who are you, Gabriel Kylie? And if you're who you say you are, then who is Pelham Leel?*

Isadora's hand darted to the wall-phone. What had it said on the identification card?

"T-A-R-C, Green Sector. Voice only," she added quickly.

An instant later a female voice said, "Targeting, Apprehension and Remand Central, Green Sector. May I help you?"

"Do you have a Captain Pelham Leel there?"

"Yes we do, I'll connect you," chirruped the voice. Isadora's finger poised over the "DISCONNECT" button.

Then, "Pelham Leel's office, may I help you?"

"Yes, I'd like to speak to Pelham Leel, please."

"Captain Leel is not available at this moment. May I help you?"

Isadora hesitated, then decided to press ahead. "I must speak with Captain Leel, it's really very urgent."

"I'm afraid that Captain Leel is in a meeting with the commissioner. Who may I . . ." Isadora broke the connection.

"Oh, boy," she breathed. "Dumb. Dumbdumbdumb. Why don't you mind your own business, Iz? This was not your business and you minded it."

So there was a Captain Leel, but Captain Leel was in a meeting with the TARC commissioner. Then who had she just been talking to? Involuntarily her eyes darted to the front door. Her fingers tightened on the fold of plasper in her hand, then flicked out another code. The woman's voice that answered was petulant. "What is it?"

Isadora said, "Chuen, I need a favor."

Gabriel's feet swished through the dry veldt. Rainer Park by night seemed more full than by day, though Gabriel knew that that was just an illusion. The black trees crowded close and clawed starkly out of the gloom the light of the floating glowglobes that dotted the park.

Gabriel's examination of the scaffolding had only confirmed what he already knew. For Elspeth to have lain where she was found someone must have moved her body. In hindsight he was no longer sure why he had come or what he had hoped to find. Perhaps he had just needed to soak up the presence of the place by night, see it as she had seen it.

During his footloose days on Octavia, tracking animals through the rich forests for food, he had often arrived at a point where a trail came to an apparent end, perhaps near a stony place where the padded feet of small mammals left no imprint. Usually it was just a matter of soaking up the place, trying to see where the beast he was trailing would want to go, what would attract it, what its purpose was.

But here? *And after three months!* He marveled at his own folly.

Gabriel was just reaching the line where the veldt greened into meadowland when he caught a whiff of scent, a familiar tang that stopped him in his tracks. His mind raced to catch up with his body, which had already identified the smell and frozen. It was a scent that he had not smelled for sixteen years. Eucalyptus.

His eyes scanned the dark landscape. Somewhere out there must be a slice of eucalyptus forest, a piece of . . . home! Gabriel pulled himself back from the brink of going in search of it. Now was not the moment.

It'll be there when you want it, chum, he told himself, and turned away.

Before long he saw the transparent cylinder of Chandra's Clock rising before him, an island in a pool of globe-lit lawn. Away to one side someone was juggling fire-sticks. There was a surprise. Who would have expected to find a primitive street art like that here in Kyara? The juggler himself was in shadow and the flames arced up and down, curving back and forth, one-two-three, one-two-three, seemingly of their own volition.

Gabriel grinned and cast about until he spotted a frail figure sitting on a park bench just outside the circle of globe light, near where a tiny, artificial stream looped out of a copse of Nordic pine. The Litterbug. So she came here in the evenings as well.

Even as Gabriel watched she drew her arm back and threw something invisible onto the grass before her. A few seconds later a metallic flash told that her cleaning robot had gobbled up whatever it was.

Gabriel made his way over to her. At the sound of his approach the old woman looked up and he saw that her eyes were the palest of green, and paler yet in way of the eyes of the elderly.

"Hello," she said, without surprise, and nibbled at her chocolate. She watched Gabriel brightly as he sank down beside her on the bench.

Her face adopted a look of mischief. Her hand curled round the chocolate wrapper and she drew her arm back and threw it, watching as it landed soundlessly on the dewy grass.

She stared at it intently until, with a whir, her tiny nemesis shot out from under her bench. She sighed as her brief triumph was consumed in a frisson of tooth-some efficiency and gazed at the empty spot on the grass while the cleaning robot resumed its station.

"Gone," she said sadly, in slightly accented Standard. "Every time."

They sat in silence for a moment, then she brightened a little and turned to study Gabriel's face.

"So," she said softly, "you've come back as a man."

Her gaze was curiously absent, looking at some distant place that only she could see.

"You know me?"

"I will always know you." She turned away to look at the grass where she had thrown the wrapper. She sighed. "They spoil it. Every time they spoil it. Even this they take away, like they took away everything else."

Gabriel began, "I was wondering if perhaps you'd seen a girl here, a . . ."

"A girl?" the old woman interrupted. "What girl? There's only you. And me. Just us."

"I didn't mean now, I meant . . ." Gabriel broke off, realizing he had made a mistake in approaching her. Unwilling to give up immediately, he tried again. "What is your name?"

She looked at him in disappointment. "Ah, you've for-gotten. Well, they often do when they return. It's a long journey." Then she brightened. "But I remember. I would have known you reborn as a blade of grass. Or one of the silver bees. Or . . . Tant pis. I'm Louise. I came back Louise Daud," she said gaily. "And nobody knew me either. Except Ellis. He used to meet me every night in the park. Did you come for a story? It's been

a long time since we told each other stories. Which one
would you like to hear?"

"I don't remember the stories," Gabriel said
regretfully.

"Ah, no, you wouldn't. It's a long journey." She
searched about and finally stared up at the dark sky.
"The Twist is out tonight."

Gabriel followed her gaze to the long, corkscrew-
shaped nebula that trailed across the night sky.

"Tell me about the Twist," he suggested, settling back.

"You remembered!" she said happily. "You always
liked that one. Let me think." She pondered for a time
and Gabriel watched her sadly, wondering what it had
taken to drive her back to childhood. Grandmother Lalumanji had always spoken of such people as walking
both worlds at once.

"They called it the Twist, and no one is quite sure
how it came to be there, or why it's shaped the way it
is," she said slowly and pointed. "Look, you see that
bright star on the end, the white one."

"Yes."

"That's the Beacon. It's a pulsar. It rotates very
quickly and sends out a beam of light. Like a lighthouse
bringing the ships home," she whispered, "and she has
a secret sister, la Hermanita Rojita. That means 'the little red sister' in Old Spanish. She is hidden in the
nebula."

"How do you know all this?"

"You know how! Or don't you read anymore?" Louise chastised, then seemed to reflect. "Ah, but books
are not knowledge. You can't preserve knowledge, only
fossilize it. They sent a ship there once, long ago. It was
called the *Far Cry*. They went and . . ." She paused.
"And they came back and no one went there again. Just
like that. Nobody asks anymore, for the sake of asking.
Nobody seeks for the sake of seeking. It all needs a
reason, it all needs something coming out of the factory
door." Her voice was bitter. "They ask because they
want, not because they need. *You* ask though. You always ask about the stars."

"I do?" Gabriel said and then, when she did not reply,
went on, "I know the stars as a traveler."

"Ah, as a traveler," she said, sad again. "Beware of the snake in the desert."

She gazed back up at the sky and suddenly she began to weep. "They took it away," she whispered. "*He* took it away. It was just a dream, just a . . . small dream . . ."

Discomfited, Gabriel reached out and touched her shoulder, but she flinched away from him and she pulled herself in tight, weeping silently.

Sadly Gabriel rose and moved quietly away. The person he really needed to talk to was Hitedoro Izeki. As he walked toward the exit he spotted two familiar figures waiting, still and patient, just outside the circle of light cast by a glowglobe.

"Bugger this," he muttered. He stopped as a gleeful glimmer of an idea came to him.

You're in MY terrain now, he thought with satisfaction. He headed purposefully into the nearest patch of woodland, choosing a path through the wettest patches of earth and moss. His feet left clear footprints behind him.

With his peripheral vision he saw them start after him; he could soon hear the thump and crackle of their feet as they stumbled through the woods after him. His own passage was silent. When he was sure that he was out of their line of vision he halted at the edge of a muddy area and began to walk backwards, literally retracing his own steps.

His feet automatically found his own footprints, fitting neatly into them. He stopped beneath a broad oak, reaching up and seizing an overhanging branch that he had spotted when he passed here a few seconds before, and swung himself up. Without a sound he swarmed up the trunk of the oak. By the time the two TARCs passed under the tree, following Gabriel's footprints, their quarry was already six meters above their heads.

He waited until they were a safe distance away, then leaned out to drop down. As he did so the branch he was holding on to suddenly gave a sharp "*crack!*" Instantly Gabriel let go and crouched, hugging the trunk of the tree to steady himself. He held his breath, but the two TARCs were apparently too far away to have heard him.

He examined the branch above him curiously. Where the branch joined the main trunk a split ran down the trunk for almost half a meter. *If I'd put my full weight on that,* he thought.

As he reached out for a different branch, he saw that that, too, was on the verge of breaking off. This was one unhealthy tree. Something in the soil here was not right.

Gabriel silently cursed his own stupidity. He could have broken his neck through this absurd stunt.

Awkwardly he leaned out again and dropped down to the ground, being careful to leave no trace. The TARCs' mistake had been to follow him rather than simply cover the entrance, and he had to get out of the park before they smartened up.

It was with a feeling of release that he made his way to the nearest Worm station. Not that he had accomplished much, he had to admit to himself. *The buggers'll be up bright and early, in time for breakfast,* he thought grumpily. But, at least, for perhaps the first time since he left Hitedoro Izeki's office, he did not have some token of government responsibility dogging his footsteps.

It was just as he was thinking this that he felt hands seize both his arms in a firm grip and something flat and cold touch his neck. For a fraction of a second Gabriel's body tensed.

"Twenty thousand volts, you won't enjoy it," said a woman's voice behind him.

Furious with himself for his own sloppiness, Gabriel allowed himself to be maneuvered into a waiting hangcar. *There's nothing like a good mood,* he reflected, *for making a slob out of a man.*

Pelham Leel thought a curse. He *knew* he should have assigned a robot, even if it meant having to explain the assignment away in a report.

Out loud he said into the phone, "They just called me."

The voice at the other end of the connection was harsh. "How the hell could an offworld stranger have given two trained agents the slip in a park with only one exit?"

"I don't know, unless my hunch was right and he's a professional himself."

"Damn it. How long since they lost track of him?"

"About ten minutes."

There was a pause. Then the voice on the other end of the line said decisively, "Alright, pip his phone."

Leel hesitated. "His phone? Look, we're already pushing the edge of the Privacy Laws as it is, following him about without due cause. You want to pip his phone and we're stepping into serious felony."

"You're worrying about the damned Privacy Laws?"

"The point here is that getting a position trace on his phone means using agency descramblers. There's too many forms and too many outside witnesses involved."

"Leel, just do it! We're losing time. I'll arrange authorization later if we need it."

Leel's face twisted as if he were chewing on bitter bread. He nodded to himself. "On your guarantee. I should have people on the street with a lock on him within ten minutes."

"If that's the best you can do . . ."

Leel flicked off his phone, and muttered, "Bitch."

dark-down

Lee Chuen's face glowed marble gray in the light of Isadora's old flatscreen monitor. She smiled a smile of self-satisfaction as Isadora set the cup of steaming coffee at her elbow.

"Like spitting through a hoop," she murmured. Chuen was the most senior researcher at Duas Voces.

"You've done it? That was quick." Isadora slipped eagerly into her own chair and sipped at her coffee. Lee nodded at the screen.

The two women were sitting in the offices of Duas Voces. During the day this floor of the Byron Media Entertainment buildings was swept by a constant passage of media personnel; ticks, honeybees and the resident lolligaggers pursuing the age-old art of appearing to be busy whilst setting one's cortex on idle. Now the office was still, a stillness broken only by the whispered passage of the occasional security robot.

Lee Chuen had turned out all the lights, as was her wont whenever she was absorbed in her work. She said that it helped her focus. Leaning back in her seat, she ran her fingers over her shaved pate and fingered the Sisters of Tanit tattoo on her forehead. The Sisters of Tanit were the leading female-separatist movement in the C.S.S.

"What have you got?" Isadora asked her.

"It's quite an odd assortment really." Chuen picked up her light pencil and expertly manipulated the thumb-wheel at the aft end of it. The monitor screen flickered. "There was some minor damage to the chip, so there's the odd chain lost here and there. My guess is it came from a Notebook of some sort . . . am I right?" Chuen shot Isadora a shrewd look.

When Isadora did not answer Chuen arched a sardonic eyebrow and went on. "There's some official-looking accounts and suchlike . . ." The screen froze and Isadora found herself faced with a series of columns.

"Kylie Exterminations. Dates, names, credits." She pointed to the right-hand column. "That would be the client's name. This"—her finger shifted—"would be the date, and this the amount."

"Busy little beaver, wasn't she?" Chuen remarked. "Looks like the extermination business was booming."

"Is there a lot of this?"

"Oh, pages and pages of it." Chuen thumbed her pencil and let the columns scroll up. "What are you looking for?"

Isadora shrugged. "I'm not sure . . . maybe nothing."

She slowed the scrolling and they went through the last few pages carefully. And then a second time.

As they neared the end, Chuen suddenly said, "Go back a second. Back . . . back . . . yes. That's funny."

"Calaban Transport," Isadora read out loud. "What about it?"

"Well, it's the only one that's repeated. See? Three visits. Bum, bum, bum. Within two weeks. If I remember rightly, they're quite a big firm."

"So?"

"Look, I know I may be making something out of nothing" Chuen admitted. "And let's face it, love, you're not giving me anything to work with—but still . . . I mean, how many insects could there be in one building? Unless they had a bad chiproach problem in their information system. There are quite a few mischief makers coming up with some real nasty little twigleggies. You can't find them without wiping half your files and can't get at them without tearing out half your circuitry. But even so. *No* exterminator comes back three times, unless they've botched the job."

"Alriiight," Isadora said slowly. "So she was a lousy exterminator. Or . . ."

"Exactly, love." Chuen's face shone with grim satisfaction. "An exterminator has *access*. She peeks through the computer's keyhole. She might get to see sensitive material. That's why they're so highly paid. You need a guarantee of confidentiality. Remember how much head office paid out to that clown who was here last month?"

"And she could not have been a lousy exterminator, or she wouldn't have been freelancing to a firm like Calaban Transport . . . No"—Isadora was seized with a sudden doubt—"no, we're reaching."

Chuen shrugged. "If you say so, love, it's your kiddie. Odd coincidence though," she observed thoughtfully. "And Calaban . . . Calaban . . . what do I know about Calaban?"

"The monster in Shakespeare's *Tempest?*" Isadora suggested.

Chuen frowned and shook her head. "No, that's Caliban, sweetie. No, there's just something . . . Calaban, shit, I can't think."

Chuen made as if to rise, but Isadora waved her down. She was eager to find out what else was in the files and the less Chuen was involved the better.

"Leave it for now, I can look them up. What else is there on the chip?"

"Well, like I said, um, quite a hodgepodge, really." Chuen retrieved her light pencil and the orderly columns were suddenly transformed into a tangle of handwritten words, doodlings, illegible scribblings.

"Sterike!" Isadora stared at the mess in fascination.

"I guess this was some kind of journal." Chuen shook her head pityingly. "I'd love to have had a peek into this lady's id. Here, let me show you the interesting bit. There's only three basic files in here: her accounts, all the scribbles here—there's a *lot* of these, endless pages—and then . . . this."

Isadora found herself staring at some kind of technical ground plan. Chuen was eyeing her, a self-satisfied smirk on her face. Bewildered, Isadora studied the screen. "I'd guess it's some kind of . . . factory? I don't know."

Chuen sat forward. "The detail density is pretty high, you can zoom into an area about the size of this desk. Of course"—it was obvious that she was enjoying keeping Isadora in suspense—"the giveaway is if we pull right back and look at the whole thing."

Isadora was now looking at a partially melted dish, covered with hieroglyphics, on a stick.

"Come on, Chuen!" she groaned. Chuen's smugness was beginning to grate.

Chuen raised her eyebrows. "Still don't see it? Then let's remove the interior detail." The hieroglyphics disappeared leaving only the wobbly outline. Isadora caught her breath.

"Shiiii . . ." she murmured in astonishment. Now she understood why Chuen had been so smug, "It's *Rainer Park!*"

"Mmmm." Chuen restored the interior detail. "I'd be curious to know where she get ahold of this. The file is about twice as big as one would have expected for just a ground plan—which is what it is. Detail goes down to about one square meter."

"Could there be a detail-enhancement key you've missed?"

"Probably." Chuen placed her light pencil decisively on the desk. "However, love, if you want any more out of Chuen, you'd better come across with some answers of your own."

Isadora met Chuen's hard gaze and realized her friend was serious. "Please don't ask. Right now it's just curiosity."

"Has this got anything to do with this 'Gabriel' man you met on the shuttle?" The quotation marks were audible and bitter.

Isadora looked at her friend sharply. "What if it does?"

"You're the only person I know who can make a garden out of an appleseed," Chuen said. "It's gotten you in trouble before."

Now it was Isadora's turn to go cold. "I'll go with whom I want, when I want! And I'm too old for a mother!"

"Iz, love . . ." Chuen placed her hand on Isadora's thigh.

"Please don't!"

Chuen's hand shifted to Isadora's knee and gave it a sisterly squeeze. "I know, it's just not you." She almost managed to keep the hurt out of her voice.

Isadora calmed at once. "No it isn't me," she replied gently. "And I can't even wish that it was. I'm sorry."

"You'll never learn," Chuen said cheerfully. "You

know that when two lines of evolution diverge they can never come together again."

"You might like him."

"Who? Your Gabriel? I doubt it. And I *don't* want to meet him! Here, Isadora, I'll make you a spare copy of this." She reached into a drawer and pulled out an old Notebook.

"I'd like hard copy," Isadora put in. "If you don't mind."

"Shit," Chuen grumbled. "You and your hard copy. I don't know how you persuaded the front office to invest in that old printer. You're the only one who uses it."

"I'm an old-fashioned girl, with old-fashioned charm."

"You're an old-fashioned pain in the ass. Next time I'll hang up on you."

"Here, I'll do it." Isadora took the Notebook out of Chuen's hands. "But, do me a favor, Chuen. Keep this quiet?"

"The soul of discretion, love, but . . ." Chuen's face became suddenly grave. "Please be careful." She tapped the screen. This has a bad smell about it."

Gabriel was sardined in the backseat of the hangcar between the two men. The woman climbed in after them, touched the automatic button on the hangcar's dashboard, and whispered something inaudible. Then she opaqued the windows and turned, flint-eyed, back to Gabriel. "Did you scan him?" she asked.

"He's clean," replied the man on Gabriel's left, a sallow-faced individual with an obvious prosthetic hand. As if to emphasize the point he reached up and plucked Gabriel's phone out of its collar pocket and snapped it in two.

The woman, fine-boned and fragile-looking in the way of a praying mantis, got down to business.

"Now look, Mr. Kylie, we can do this easily or it can be difficult. You've got about—" glance at the car's dashboard—"five minutes to keep it easy. Now, where is it?"

Gabriel shook his head uncomprehendingly. "Where's what?" An elbow from the goon next to him drove his breath out with a gasp.

"That was the wrong answer, Mr. Kylie. Where is it?"

"Where's *what* . . .?" The elbow slammed into Gabriel's ribs again. Angrily he said, "Stop bloody hitting me and tell me what it is you're looking for! Maybe I can help you."

"You can. Just tell us where it is." An edge of boredom was creeping into her voice. A hint that this was business as usual and Gabriel was fulfilling her expectations by his recalcitrance.

He could use that expectation. *Familiar territory fosters inattention,* he told himself.

"Tell you where *what* is?"

"Time is passing, Mr. Kylie."

"Where is it, Mr. Kylie?" said the man to his right, speaking for the first time.

"Where is it?" One Hand picked up the refrain.

Gabriel slowed his breathing and loosened his shoulders. Sweat beaded the palms of his hands.

The man on his right was the larger of the two. The other man, the one with the prosthetic arm, had the prod. Gabriel didn't know precisely what the laws governing prosthetics here were; on most planets the law forbade cyb' power from exceeding the average strength-to-body/weight ratio of the wearer. Excessive cyb' strength was considered a form of lethal weaponry. That made One Hand the weak link. If there was just a right moment . . .

"Where is it?" the woman repeated.

"Alright, look, just let me speak a second," Gabriel began. "I don't know who you people think I am, but, really, I think you've made a mistake." The elbow jabbed into his rib cage again, not hard, but as a warning. "Look," Gabriel said, "I don't know what you're looking for—you won't *tell* me what you're looking for! How am I supposed to answer you? What d'you want to hear?"

"Where is it?"

Gabriel let out a long breath and studied the faces, watching him intently. He felt the hangcar descending and slowing.

The woman raised her eyebrows a little. "Where is it, Mr. Kylie? Last call."

Gabriel lifted his shoulders, pleading.

"Your choice." The woman shrugged.

The hangcar stopped and the woman climbed out, followed by the big man. As Gabriel had hoped, One Hand lifted his hand up behind Gabriel's head and Gabriel felt the same tingle of cold metal on his neck.

"Out," said the woman.

No sudden moves, Gabriel thought. *Feed their expectations* . . .

As his foot touched the sidewalk Gabriel leaned forward ever so slightly, as if shifting his weight. For a split second the metal left his neck. Instantly Gabriel spun away to his left, bringing up his arm and knocking aside his captor's arm. With his right hand he grabbed the nape of the man's neck and pulled him forward out of the car, sending him sprawling onto the ground. The prod skittered away out of sight.

Fully confident of the deterrent effect of their little prod, the second man and the woman were taken completely by surprise as Gabriel reached down, lifted his trouser leg and drew his hunting knife out of its sheath. In one lithe movement he had hauled the prone man's head back by his hair and was holding the dull blue ceramic blade to his neck.

"Not a bloody move," he said.

The other man had frozen in the act of drawing something out of his pocket. Both he and the woman seemed shocked. Obviously neither of them had expected an attack of this sort.

Gabriel nodded at the man. "That a squirt? Let it fall."

The man hesitated until the woman nodded. "Do it."

The weapon slipped out of the man's fingers and clattered on the ground. Gabriel judged the short, slim-barreled weapon to be some sort of slumbergun, firing stun-pellets.

"Scanning isn't much use on knives, is it? Now, you two, lie down on the ground, slowly, arms above your heads." The woman and the man obeyed, watching him all the time. One Hand was clearly in some discomfort.

"Let go of my hair!" he pleaded. "I'm not going to try anything."

"Quiet." Gabriel cast about frantically for something to tie the man's hands behind him with. He saw nothing.

"Shit," he muttered under his breath. He was out of

his depth here. Defending himself in a barroom brawl,
skinning rodents, trapping birds, these were all the arts
of an honest backwoodsman. Taking prisoners? Here
Gabriel was a little short on practical experience. He
was, in fact, starting to feel rather foolish.

He caught the glance passing between the other two
and tightened his grip on the man under his hands.

The slumbergun. He could not get to it without releasing his grip on his captive.

"You," he addressed the other man. "Kick that
squirt . . . kick that slumbergun over here."

"Don't do it!" snapped the woman.

"You be quiet!" Gabriel snapped back. "Kick it over
here! Carefully."

"Don't do it," repeated the woman. Then, addressing
Gabriel, "You want to take us out, do it! We're three
and all you've got is a knife." Slowly she began to rise
to her feet. The other man followed suit.

"Stop!" Gabriel said hoarsely.

"What are you going to do? Kill him?" Her voice was
quiet as an adder's. "Be my guest, then we'll have you."

"Don't bloody try it!" Gabriel's voice rose and he
increased the pressure on his knife, feeling it bite into
flesh.

The man under his hands was trembling and Gabriel
could feel his fear and pain, feel the man's clammy sweat
against his wrist as he brushed against the man's neck.

The fingers grasping the man's hair were beginning to
cramp up.

Gabriel realized that the woman was staring intently
at his knife. A thin line of black blood had slipped back
along the blade. Even as he glanced down a single drop
fell to the sidewalk and shattered into brilliant crimson.

For an instant that ragged red nipple held them all
mesmerized. Then fury welled up in Gabriel Kylie, fury
that they, and the woman in particular, would have allowed things to go this far. And for what?

Without warning he whipped his knife away from his
captive's neck, his hand releasing its grip on his hair.
The man let his face sink onto the sidewalk with a sob.
The knife hand slashed out toward the woman and the
other man, both of whom leapt back instinctively.

One step forward and Gabriel was reaching for the

slumbergun. Just as his fingers closed around it, he felt his foot seized from behind and he found himself stumbling to his knees.

Then the other man was on him, arm around Gabriel's neck. Gabriel threw his weight sideways and together they rolled over the ground in a tangle of thrashing limbs. A shape, the woman, flickered across his vision. He waved the slumbergun, trying to turn it so he could fire it, and the shadow ducked away. He could feel his heart in his ears, slamming like a door in a strong wind. His lungs spasmed, seeking to drag air through his blocked windpipe. Desperately Gabriel reversed his knife and jabbed down twice.

There was a shriek in his ear and the arm abruptly loosened. Gasping for air, Gabriel tore himself free and slewed to one side. He was barely able to focus and did not realize that the second man was leaping at him until the last instant. He was just able to bring up his knife hand to block the blow from the man's cyb' arm.

It was like trying to stop a swinging H-beam.

Gabriel heard himself yell with pain as his arm was smacked away, the knife arcing out of sight. Gabriel tried to scrabble away backwards but his right arm would not respond and his left was still holding the stunner. He could hardly see. With fingers that would not respond groping for the trigger, Gabriel brought up the weapon. He did not ask himself why the man suddenly flinched away.

There was an unpleasant spitting sound and a red spark leapt out of Gabriel's fist. Then Gabriel's field of vision was clear and he heard something soft strike the ground. Feverishly Gabriel waved the slumbergun around to ward off another attack. But none came. The other man's cries had formed themselves into words.

"Shit! He's down! He shot him!"

Only then did the truth penetrate. He was not holding a slumbergun, but some kind of kinetic-energy weapon that fired self-propelled bullets. Primitive, but very deadly. Abruptly, Gabriel came to. A prone form was lying on the ground, limbs feebly moving in little circles.

"Oh, God," Gabriel whispered in horror. "Oh, my God." The gun was suddenly white-hot in his hand and he twitched it away in revulsion. He had killed animals before, many times, for food, in the way of a hunter. But he had never shot a man before. Carefully he approached his erstwhile opponent, the one, detached corner of his mind leading him around to the right side. Away from the prosthetic arm.

"Oh God," he heard his voice whispering. He willed it to be quiet.

Numbly, he knelt. The bullet hole was a couple of centimeters below the right collarbone and about a centimeter and a half across. Some kind of expanding bullet. Blood welled up from it, spreading around the man's neck and ear. Quickly Gabriel stripped off his coat, folded up a corner of it and pressed it against the wound to staunch the bleeding. With his other hand he searched through the man's pockets. This same individual had snapped Gabriel's phone in half. Gabriel hoped against fading hope that he had one himself.

Some scraps of plaspyrus, a hangcar license. Gabriel glanced at the name. Dana Sotack, Security Officer, Kyaran Ventures 99, P.R. No. 3462238 . . . Gabriel dropped it. Nothing.

Gabriel grabbed the man's real hand and pressed it against the makeshift bandage. "Hold this," he said distinctly. "Hug yourself." When he was sure that the man had understood and obeyed he let go and moved to stand behind the man's head. He hooked his arms under his armpits, and said, "Hold still, I'll try not to hurt you."

With some difficulty Gabriel managed to maneuver the man into the back of the car. When he had settled the bandage back into place he climbed into the front, keyed the starter panel, and said, "Nearest hospital."

Nothing happened. Thumblocked.

Gabriel ground his teeth in frustration. *You would be, you bastard,* he thought bitterly as he climbed out of the hangcar. The man seemed to be barely conscious. He was bleeding to death in front of Gabriel's eyes and Gabriel stood helpless as a clown in an empty circus ring.

He glanced vainly about his surroundings. Where the flock was he and why the flock was there no one around?

He was standing in a cavernous, partially enclosed Hall, lined with struts, like skeletal Doric pillars. Random spills of light broke up the dimness and defined the forest of struts.

A little further down an alley led away at right angles. Gabriel started toward it at a run. He had to find a wall-phone, or *steal* some bugger's personal phone.

Gabriel had almost reached the alley when he heard a faint hiss, followed by a hum, coming from behind him. He spun around, braced to defend himself again.

"What the bugger . . . ?" To Gabriel's amazement he saw through the forest of struts that the hangcar's doors had closed. Even as he watched the hangcar was lifting up and gliding away down the Hall. "Jes . . . Wait!"

By the time Gabriel arrived back at the battle site the hangcar was gone. His blood-soaked coat was lying in a heap on a quiltwork of pale gray and wet crimson. Drained and confused, Gabriel brought a hand up to his face. It was sticky. Blood had crept into the crevices of his palm, creating a scarlet web.

Gabriel's guts gave a heave. He bent over and was violently sick.

When he could move again, he picked up his coat, rolling it up so as to hide the bloodstains. Then he searched around until he had located his knife. His right arm ached and every time he moved his fingers slivers of pain shot through it.

Wearily Gabriel started to weave his way down the Hall.

And unseen, hundreds of meters above him on the rooftops of Kyara, two tiny figures leapt from perch to giddy perch, black insects moving through a landscape of glass-Gothic spires.

The roofrunners were abroad tonight.

lalumanji's grandchild

By the time Gabriel reached Isadora's front door it was almost two in the morning. It had taken him four and a half hours to get there, flitting from one deserted Hall to the next, trying to hold himself erect and hide his blood-encrusted hands and clothing whenever he was forced to pass other pedestrians.

The moment a peevish Isadora keyed the door open, Gabriel stepped inside, swaying with exhaustion. Her apartment was dark, except for one glowglobe and the dim dark-down light coming in through the window.

Isadora took his arm and guided him to the wall-couch.

"Sterike! Gabriel, what happened? I tried calling you and your phone was off-lined . . . Oh, my God!" She had seen the blood covering his rolled-up coat. She pulled away from him in shock.

"It's alright, it's not mine," he croaked. "Not my blood . . ." *Sure, that'll make her feel better.* He almost laughed.

"But what happened?" She was afraid. Of him, he realized.

"It's not me, I got jumped . . . here, ouch!" Gabriel tried pulling his sleeve up and realized it would be easier to take off his shirt. "Could you help me?" His arm was a solid ache from shoulder to fingertips.

She hesitated, then reached for him. "Come to the bathroom." She guided him to the sink and eased off his shirt. His arm was swollen and badly bruised—not that bruises ever showed up on *his* skin. "Damn it, tell me, what happened?"

"Got smacked by a guy with a prosthetic arm. Bugger had it boosted."

"Boosted? That's illegal!"

"No kidding. Must have been double . . . triple strength." He leaned his elbows on the edge of the sink and held his hands under the water outlet. Water began to pour, flooding the crevices in his hands and draining through his fingers. It made a pink spiral as it swirled away down the plughole. "I'm amazed he hasn't dislocated his own shoulder having it boosted up that high . . . No!" Isadora had been about to throw his rolled-up coat into the incinerater slot. "No. Please . . . just wash it."

Reluctantly she shoved the sticky bundle into the washer slot, setting the washer on its maximum three-minute cycle.

Gabriel examined his arm. For all the pain there appeared to be nothing broken.

"Here, strip off the rest of that stuff and get in the shower," Isadora instructed. She showed him how to adjust both the water and drying temperatures, dialed him up a bathrobe and left him to his own devices.

When Gabriel emerged some fifteen minutes later, he found Isadora waiting with a tube of anesthetic spray. She made him sit on the couch whilst she tended his arm.

As the anesthetic spray reduced the ache to a tingle Gabriel ran through what had happened.

"Kyaran Ventures 99?" Isadora frowned when he had finished.

"Heard of them?"

"Well . . . yes . . . They're the second biggest conglomerate on Thor next to Byron Systems. I don't understand why they would send people to attack you . . . it just doesn't make sense." Isadora hesitated. She seemed drawn into herself.

"Here, lie back," she said at last, pushing him back and lifting his feet onto the couch.

"What is it?"

"Nothing," she replied, going to the drink slot. A moment later she placed a cup of herb tea next to his elbow. As she straightened up Gabriel reached out and caught her wrist. "Iz . . ."

She shook him off. "I'm fine. I'm tired, I was sleeping." She walked back to the drink slot and retrieved a second cup, then went over to the desk.

"Iz," he asked, "did something happen to you?"

"No. No." He watched her closely. The blanket of fatigue that had enveloped him earlier had dissolved into a comfortable tiredness that imposed no demands on him.

"Here, look." Suddenly decisive, she picked a flat-screen Notebook up off her desk and brought it over to him. "I got that chip of yours hooked up."

She handed him the Notebook, then reached over, scrolling through Elspeth's account files.

"I looked through these . . . there was only one thing that seemed unusual. It may be nothing." She told him about her suspicions concerning Calaban Transport. She spoke fast, keeping him at a distance with her flow of words.

"I looked them up when I got home. Not much of a transport company. Mainly storage warehouses these days. The point is, they're owned by Byron Systems. In itself that's not much of a surprise—they own bits of everything—but I was looking for connections with Rainer Park and Byron Systems also built Rainer Park and look . . ." Isadora touched a key and the map of Rainer Park appeared on the Notebook screen.

Gabriel examined the screen briefly, then returned his attention to Isadora.

She sat on the edge of her bed, cradling her drink. It smelled like hot cocoa. Her shoulders were narrowed, her whole body wrapped around her cup. Her eyes steadfastly avoided his gaze. He waited.

"Gabriel," she said at last, "you haven't lied to me, have you? About . . . something . . . anything. About what you are, or where you come from maybe? It doesn't matter, I'd just . . . like to know if you have." Her eyes met his.

Gabriel had been about to laugh it off, but the look in her face stopped him, as if for a moment she were completely defenseless, completely vulnerable.

He said gently, his voice stolen by an unexpected ache that had nothing to do with his arm, "I've told you the truth." His mouth curled up in a new-moon smile. "Lies are heavy baggage to carry around when you've traveled as far as I have."

She stared at him intently, picking his face apart with her eyes, as if she were examining the individual tiles on a mosaic. The streetlight from the window made wells of her eyes, blue shadows of her cheeks, and he suddenly saw in her the same tenuous beauty that he had seen in the face of the old woman, Louise Daud. His breath caught—it had been so long since he had been with a woman. He saw that she had seen the change in his face and she had not moved. He wanted to stand, to walk over to her . . .

Gabriel remained where he was and the moment faded. A moment later she, too, began to dissolve in a wash of shifting gray.

He heard her voice, but the words were blurred around the edges and he had difficulty making sense of them. He dragged his eyes open.

"What? Blue . . . box?" He wished she would wait for now and let him sleep. "Blue box. Somebody asked me about it today. Asked if you'd mentioned it." She hesitated. "He said you were a cyborg. He said you had a prosthetic."

"He? who said?"

"Some . . . body. A TARC officer."

A TARC officer? He was too tired to ask. "A prosthetic? Does that make some difference?"

"No . . . no . . . I just . . ."

"You figured I was lying to you." *So many lies. And now truth disguised as lies.* Gabriel sighed in disgust. He tapped his chest. "Iz, behind this rough exterior beats a ticker of purest MemPlas."

"Your heart," she said in wonder.

"My heart. Yeah. The old one rolled over and died when I was nineteen. Wanted to take me with it, but I reckoned, piss on that. And here I am."

She was contrite. "I'm sorry, I didn't mean to pry . . ."

"Yes, you did."

Isadora regarded him uncertainly. To show her he wasn't angry with her he forced his mouth into a weary smile and she smiled back, relieved. Then her face faded away again, leaving only her smile, like the Cheshire cat in some forest he'd once heard of. Except the forest had

been larger . . . or had he been smaller? Then it was
gone and he heard her voice speaking softly.

"Lights dim."

Perhaps they did. Gabriel was beyond noticing.

*The pain tore up his arm and squeezed his chest into
a knot. He felt as if his ribs were caving in. The hospital
stank of disinfectant and cations from the ionized walls.*

*"Oh, God." He wept. "Oh God." He remembered he'd
refused the antipain tabs. Through the pain he became
aware of someone sitting beside his bed. "Who is it?"
he gasped.*

*He felt breath against his face, the familiar aroma of
burnt wood and baobab tree, and suddenly Grandmother
Lalumanji's face filled his vision. She smiled. "Does it
hurt, Gabe?"*

"It hurts."

*"It'll fade. They've taken it away," she said. "They just
left the pain. And that'll fade. You've got a whole new
inside, tickin' away there. Like the croc that swallowed
the clock. Remember?"*

*"Oh, Jesus . . ." He shut his eyes, tried to squeeze the
pain away with his eyelids. "It was Old Man," he whispered. "He was holding the killing bone. I saw it."*

*"Shh," Lalumanji whispered. "You don't really believe
that, do you? The myall just bin tellin' you stories again."*

*"I saw . . . he pointed it at me . . ." He thought he
had seen . . .*

*Shh. You think Old Man would have wasted his time
with old magic an' killing bones if he'd wanted you damaged? Not him. He's too busy bludgin' an' drinkin' an'
hidin' from Daisy wife. He'd've waited 'till the next time
you got home from getting pissed with your mates and
put a spear in your back."*

*Gabriel let his eyes flicker open. He gazed at Grand-
mother Lalumanji's kindly face and knew then without a
doubt. The pain that knowledge gave him was worse than
the pain in his chest.*

*For the first time in his life, his grandmother had lied
to him.*

Isadora seemed less subdued the next day. She had to
take the Helios weasel to the menagerie first thing, so

Gabriel spent the early-morning hours going through Elspeth's Notebook. He skimmed through the accounts, ignoring the file with the Rainer Park map. Then he started paging through Elspeth's journal.

If anyone could call it that.

Elspeth had always been an orderly, conscientious person. He remembered her bedroom, each toy in its place, from a very young age. They had often studied together, so Gabriel remembered what her Notebooks had looked like: precise, neat, files listed properly and well ordered.

But *this!* This jumble of random sentences, strange little drawings, quotations, illegible scrawls.

He scanned each page, picking out fragments of coherence.

"Home is a well. Every world has a gravity well, Thor's is the deepest well of all. They even spell it with a capital 'W.' 'Life in the Well' they call it here."

"There's not much difference between a circle and a square. It's a question of faces."

"Kyara. Gabriel would love this. No, Gabriel would hate it. No mud to play in. And Mighty Mickey has a finger in every pie."

"There's something in my eye.

"Sometimes I go out to the viewing terrace near Rainer Park and look out on the Anvil. It looks like a greasy hot plate. No mountain peaks, no valleys. It's strange to think that nobody has ever touched the real surface of Thor. Anyone who did would be squashed flatter than a beetle on a hangcar's windshield, no time for spit. And yet here, just a few meters above the surface, there are children playing."

"Someone stole it. I stole it. Someone stole it. I stole it . . ."

"Wimburro Brook was where my totem sprang into Mum's belly. Old Man told her that Crow had claimed me. Grandmother wasn't so sure. How could she say that

*Old Man was wrong? He's the know-all. But Grand-
mother Lalumanji could always see. If Crow-woman was
my totem, she'd have seen the wings. She'd have seen
the claws."*

*"They've shut the only door tighter than a tiger's smile.
Laz has promised me a way out. I'm too big to fit through
a keyhole."*

"The ground is warm in Rainer Park."

*"Fabiana has a kiss like honey, like honey, like honey.
And she'll kiss you anytime, for money, for money,
for money . . ."*

*"The Ancestors walked the Paths of Song and sang life
into being. There are no Singers on Thor but someone
must have been playing a harmonica."*

*"I tried to press needles into my skin to make the hurt.
The hurt keeps me alive. Without it I couldn't be sure I
was still living. But the fear keeps me back. I need the
hurt to drown the fear, but I fear the hurt."*

"Dying children always draw butterflies."

Page after page Gabriel sought Elspeth and found
only shards of her. *What happened to you, Elspeth?* he
thought in bewilderment.

He stretched his right arm. The soreness had abated
somewhat, but his arm felt stiff and weak. Leaning back
for a moment to rest, Gabriel thought back to what Isadora had said to him the night before. The memories
were vague, like a smeared painting. What had the
TARC officer said? Blue box?

On a sudden hunch Gabriel tapped the "SEARCH"
key and typed in "blue box." After about six seconds
scrolling, the Notebook came to a stop on a page filled
with doodles and nightmarish little drawings. On the bottom left side of the screen a flashing rectangle highlighted two short lines of writing.

*"found the blue box in the hollow by the Hall,
hanging by my slaphappies, starfished to the wall"*

The two lines made little sense to Gabriel. He tapped the "SEARCH" command again, but after three seconds it pipped "DESIGNATION NOT FOUND" back at him.

Blue box.

The rest of the screen was densely filled with gargoyle faces, undecipherable scrawls, small rocket shapes.

Gabriel was about to lay the Notebook aside when a drawing at the top edge of the screen caught his eye, a face with a huge, wide-open mouth and a speech-bubble, containing an almost illegible squiggle, ballooning out of it. He highlighted and enlarged it and the squiggle resolved itself into two words:

"far cry"

Gabriel stared at them in awe of his own stupidity.

Far Cry. *They sent a ship there once, long ago.* Long ago.

At that moment the door slid open and Isadora entered, carrying a bag of shopping. She halted as soon as she saw Gabriel's face.

"What is it? Have you found something?" she asked, putting down her shopping.

Gabriel flipped the Notebook around so that she could see the screen. "Yeah, the prodigal brain returns."

"Far cry," Isadora read.

"Ring a bell?"

"No, should it?"

"That old woman in Rainer Park last night. I can't believe I didn't see it. She was talking about this. It was an . . . expedition of some sort."

"An expedition? What kind of expedition?"

"I dunno, some . . . exploratory thing to . . . there's a nebula, like a corkscrew. You can see it at darkdown . . ."

"The Twist."

"That's the one. . . . but there was something else. She said . . ." Gabriel strove to remember her exact words. "She said to me 'You've come back as a man.' She recognized me. She talked to me as if she knew me. I had my head screwed on backwards, I thought she was nuts. I should have known better. She must have talked to Elspeth!" He threw down the Notebook and stood

up. "What was her name . . . er . . . Louise . . . Louise . . .
shit . . . Daud! Louise Daud! I'm almost sure."

"Well, there's one way of finding out," said Isadora,
striding over to her desk-terminal. "Phone listings.
Search Daud, spelling check D-A . . . U-D . . .?" Isadora
looked at Gabriel questioningly. He shrugged helplessly.
She continued, "First name, Louise."

Almost immediately the terminal flashed back:

"NUMBER/ADDRESS NON-LISTED. Refer Privacy Statute; Article 12, Chapter 11, Code 6142/a"

"Yeah, that would have been too easy," muttered Gabriel wryly. "You're going to tell me there's no way
around this, right? No way to get her number."

"Not unless you have a police warrant."

"Bugger. I'll have to go back there. Apparently she
goes there nearly every day," he said. "Something else.
Have you any idea where we can find out who runs
Rainer Park on a day-to-day basis?"

"I know who does—the same man who built it," Isadora said immediately. "Edom Japaljarayi."

Gabriel started. "Come again?"

"Edom Japaljarayi," Isadora repeated. "I did a little
research while Chuen was installing the chip. What's up?"

"Japaljarayi, that's a Native Australian name," Gabriel muttered, thinking hard.

"Well?" Isadora looked blank.

"Well. It's unusual." Gabriel mused. "How often do
you find Earth citizens anywhere but Earth? Have you
any idea how unusual it is to find a Native Australian?
I'll tell you how unusual. Very bloody unusual. We have
to see this bloke. Christ, if the park was built by a Native Australian . . ."

"D'you think it has some significance?"

Gabriel shrugged helplessly. "It explains something I
smelled when I was there . . . eucalyptus. I bet if I go
there, somewhere in that park I'll find a piece of the
old country."

"And you think she might have known Japaljarayi."

"No. I reckon it might have been simpler than that."
Gabriel's face fell, his voice grew quieter. "She'd been
away a long time. Maybe she was just trying to get
home."

*   *   *

Down on the carpet by the front door something moved. Isadora's door left a two-millimeter gap between the end of the door and the edge of the frame, so the twigleggy had survived being shut in.

The twigleggy resembled a pinhead-sized mercury drop, its long legs thinner than a human hair and almost invisible. Unlike a chiproach, which might contain any one of a myriad of computer viruses, the larger twigleggy's mission was simple: to destroy information.

The twigleggy scanned the room, seeking that specific magnetic field generated by a computer. It touched Isadora's tabletop installation and a pulse of recognition went through it. Scanner locked on, the twigleggy began making its way across the carpet.

bitter lips

Edom Japaljarayi had bitter lips. That was Isadora's first impression of him. He was a little man, hair close-cropped, with a sheen of gold, skin almost black, with a heavy brow and those bitter lips. Only the eyes offset the hardness of him, they were large and warm. It was almost as if someone had joined the upper and lower halves of different faces, with the seam running across the ridge of a once-broken nose. The lips parted and bared white teeth, and the eyes wrinkled and turned it into a warm smile.

His body was thin to the point of emaciation and he seemed to move with difficulty as he crossed the room to greet them. When he held out his hand Gabriel realized that he was wearing some kind of mechanized, movement-assisting harness under his clothes.

"Mr. Kylie, Ms. Gatzalumendi?" His smile was a bell—his voice, surprisingly deep and very soft.

It had taken considerable determination on Gabriel's part to arrange this meeting. The automatic receptionist had been all courtesy until Gabriel identified himself. The "one moment, please" that followed, though all burnished robotic perfection, had been followed by a pause so long that Gabriel knew something must be up. Soon he found himself up one rung of the ladder, talking to a human secretary, who in turn shunted him laterally to a woman identifying herself as being from legal affairs.

Mr. Japaljarayi—she pronounced it Japjarai—had been advised by his legal counsel not to speak directly to any members of the deceased woman's family.

Gabriel's assertions that the visit was of a purely informal nature was met with frank disbelief and his denial of any wish to press a civil suit against the Rainer Park authorities provoked faint hostility, disguised beneath a blanket of prolixity in which the word "regret" featured prominently.

Eventually he gave up and called Jael Nyquist, who snorted loudly when he explained the problem and promised him to speak to Edom personally. She phoned him back twelve minutes later and told him to be at the control center at two o'clock and she would arrange a pass for both him and Isadora.

They met him supervising a repair crew who had removed several floor panels in one of the corridors. Edom Japaljarayi pointedly greeted Isadora first before turning to Gabriel.

The similarity between the two men was remarkable. In a human race that had grown progressively more uniform over the past three centuries since the wars following the GenTec Plagues and Humanity's spread out to the stars, it was nigh impossible anymore to trace any one person's racial heritage. The skin of most members of the human race ranged from light to dark brown, the hair from dark to darker brown to black. Blond hair and blue eyes were a comparative rarity and there were places where a head of red tresses was known to stop traffic.

Except Earth, reflected Isadora. It was funny how the word Earth, with a capital "E," was almost invariably prefaced with the word "except." Unique among all the Seventeen Planets.

Gabriel was from Earth, and Edom Japaljarayi's parents had been immigrants from there. Isadora had looked up his biography that morning when she was at the office.

The two men took each other's measure silently before Edom smiled and released Gabriel's hand.

"Had to be, with a last name like Kylie. Native Australian?"

Gabriel nodded. "Aranda ancestry. I was born in Landing."

"Ah, yes. Yes. Lovely place. Never been there, but . . . one hears. Pardon my inquisitiveness. My parents were from Tasmania."

Edom led them into an adjoining room, which obviously served as his office, and indicated they should sit. He, himself, carefully lowered himself into a chair opposite. He caught Isadora staring at the skeletal harness running up the back of his hands into his sleeves.

"Not to worry," he said, seeing her embarrassment. "It's a congenital condition. Without this"—he indicated the harness—"I'd be in a wheelchair."

"A what?"

"A wheel . . . ah . . . no, you might not ever have seen one. Primitive transportation device for people unable to walk," he explained.

Wheel . . . chair? Iz wondered why he hadn't had the condition GenTec-corrected like any normal person. Nevertheless she found herself warming to the little man.

Gabriel remained standing and slowly surveyed the room. Its walls were hung with ancient 2-D photographs. On one wall two long, thin spears, with shorter, hooked pieces of wood beneath them. On another were several flat blades of wood, crudely made, with a right-angle bend in the middle.

"I hear you had a few difficulties at the front office," Edom said. "I do apologize for that. I had one of the usual anal retentives from the legal division in here yesterday telling me not to have anything to do with you. Something about a possible civil action. Apparently they told my assistants the same thing." He paused. "I take it you *aren't* planning anything of the sort?" he inquired cautiously.

Gabriel shook his head. "No time, no funds, no inclination."

"I thought not." The little man was obviously pleased to have his faith in human nature confirmed. "As far as I can tell they divide the entire human species into two genera: plaintiffs and defendants," he asided to Isadora. "Anyway," he went on, "tell me what I can do for you."

Gabriel pursed his lips and studied Edom for a moment. He appeared to be trying to formulate the words.

"It's about the night my sister was killed," he said, finally.

Edom's eyes dropped. "Of course, of course . . . I'm sorry. You must understand, though, that there was nothing anyone could have done. Nothing anyone could have done."

"Oh, I realize that." Gabriel raised a hand reassuringly. "Not to worry. It's just . . . umm . . ." He reached into his pocket, started, tried another, and then looked imploringly at Isadora, who was already brandishing her Notebook. "Thanks," he muttered as he took it. "I wonder if you'd look at something for me . . ."

They fed the file into Edom's big tabletop screen. The engineer's eyes widened as the Rainer Park plan appeared. "I . . . where did you get this?" He seemed quite stunned.

"From my sister's Notebook files."

Edom bent and examined the plans for a second or two. "Yes, I thought so; these aren't anywhere near the complete plans. For a start the detail is only to the nearest square meter or so, so there's no actual functional design information with regard to the machinery. And there's a lot of stuff which simply isn't shown."

Gabriel said, "I'm just curious . . . what isn't shown on this plan?"

"Like I said, nothing smaller than a meter square. And vital stuff, the security systems, alarms, all that kind of thing. And the Icarus Field grid, of course," he added. "That's the biggest guarded secret on Kyara. There probably aren't a half a dozen people who know the location of the three City-generators, or a fraction of the grid layout. And as far as the park is concerned nobody knows AT ALL! And that includes backups, alarms, the lot."

Gabriel frowned. "What about the people who built it?"

"For the few humans, well, a lot of misdirection: you know what you're working on, but you don't know how you got there, and it's sealed off once you leave. For the rest it was automated—programmed automatons which were deprogrammed at the end of each day by me personally."

Edom regarded Gabriel, whose expression was sceptical.

"Believe me," Edom averred, "if there's one thing *nobody* gets sloppy with on Thor, it's the Icarus Field. A fluctuation of point zero zero zero one of a grav in either direction and every alarm in the damn place'll go off like you've never heard!

"Come," he said, rising from his desk. "Comecome-come. Come and have a look at the control room."

Edom limped across to the door. He led them down the corridor to an unmarked, cream-colored double door. Edom's left eye flashed briefly laser red as it was scanned.

"Three to enter." The door slid open and they entered the nerve center of Rainer Park.

The control room was one of those nondescript beiges that look like the result of mixing all the leftover paint tins standing in the garage. The walls were lined with monitors and controls whose purpose defied deduction. There was a large screen on one wall which was showing a section of the park near Chandra's Clock. The most spectacular feature, however, was the ceiling, which consisted of a holographic projection of the entire park. It was covered with a myriad of tiny red lights, some of them moving, which Isadora took to represent people and animals. Five technicians were slowly circling the room, checking dials. One of them was Jael Nyquist. She grinned at Gabriel as the three entered.

"Welcome to the real Rainer Park," Edom said, smiling as he lowered himself into a chair which hovered half a centimeter above the ground on some kind of repulsion field.

Gabriel was staring in delight at the ceiling.

"Bloody hell," he muttered, his eyes darting hither and thither. "The little red lights are people, I suppose?"

"That's right." Edom was watching his guests' reactions with evident enjoyment. "This is where we control everything." He slid his chair over to a central desk-console. "Monitored pollination of the flowers, heat, humidity, soil-checks, even how many kilos of refuse are gathered by the cleaning robots on a particular day. The lot."

"And the animals, their movements and so on," said Gabriel.

Edom's face fell, his voice grew chilly. "All the animals are GenTec, licensed and safety-certified," he said stiffly.

"You don't sound like much of a GenTec lover," Gabriel observed.

"It wasn't my decision," Edom said, his voice lowering. "The choice of GenTec was made by Mr. Rainer."

"Mm-hm." Gabriel glanced up again at the ceiling display. "And that's how you check to see if everyone has left the park at night?"

Edom shook his head. "No, no, we have automatic counters at the gate that count the number of people going in and out and alert us to any discrepancy at closing time. Of course, we've got infrared and motion trackers throughout the park as well, but with all the trees and other foliage *and* the wildlife, however tightly controlled, they can be deceptive."

"Then I take it the counters weren't on that particular night," Gabriel said.

Edom nodded grimly. His frail hand clenched itself into a fist and beat a soft tattoo on his desk-console. "No. They weren't. We'd been having trouble with a couple of the security systems and we'd shut down a whole section of the net to deal with them. There was still a manual watch, through the cameras, but . . . it's a big park. Stupid," he whispered, seemingly to himself. It appeared to Isadora that he was trying to contain his anger. "Stupid," he repeated.

"Who was on watch that night?"

Edom's hand stopped its tapping and the little man looked levelly at Gabriel.

"I was," he said, and his tone was bleak. "I was . . . the responsible party. I was working with Jael Nyquist over there and Abdul Halal. We were trying to sort out the glitches we'd been having. You must understand that with any newly built system such as this there are bound to be things one has overlooked. Little . . . problems that need to be ironed out. There's always things. It's in the nature of engineering. And the place where she was killed was on the other side of the park, almost three kilometers. Even if we'd seen her we couldn't have gotten to her in time to do anything." It seemed to Isadora that Edom's tone was almost pleading.

"And this place was manned the whole time?"

"Of course! Apart from twenty minutes or so when Jael and Abdul were checking some circuitry behind a

corridor panel, we were all three here the whole time.
But, without the counters . . . she was just a dot."

Edom raised himself and went over to a control console. Shakily his fingers caressed its smooth surface, then
he placed his palms down flat and leaned upon them.
"How could I have known that that was her?" he
muttered.

Isadora felt Jael standing behind her.

"You alright, Edom?" the big woman asked.

"Fine, fine, yes . . ." Edom turned and his hands
twitched at her. "It's alright, Jael. I do apologize."

"I reckon it's time we were off anyway," said Gabriel.
"You've been a help." He paused. "There is one thing.
Jael, do you know if the Litterbug is here today?"

Edom's brow furrowed into a quizzical frown aimed
at Jael.

"*The* Litterbug, Edom, there's only the one," Jael reminded him. "Hey, Abdul. Everybody's favorite Litterbug here today?"

One of the other technicians leaned back and squinted
at a distant panel. "Uh-uh, her robot's still in place."

"Why the interest in the Litterbug?" Jael asked as she
led Gabriel and Isadora back to the main entrance.

"Oh, I dunno." Gabriel seemed more cheerful than
she had seen him in a while. "Just like to ask her opinion
on a couple of things."

They came to a large transparent door. But Jael made
no move to open it.

"You know," she said, her face turned away from
them, "Edom went ape when it happened. We thought
he was going to lose it. He didn't sleep for three days.
He finished the work on the alarm himself. It's . . . grunt
work, any of us could have done it. I don't know how
he managed in that harness of his. He loves this park.
It's not just some flockin' ego trip. Something you slap
your name on 'cos your company paid for 10 percent
of it."

"Would they have closed it down?" Isadora asked.

"Nah, are you kidding?" Jael snorted. "Saxon Rainer's got too much invested in it. You think he'd let anyone shut *Rainer* Park? Not a chance. No. But they might
have pulled Edom off as manager and chief engineer,

though I doubt that as well, no matter how much him and Rainer've been fighting."

"Fighting?"

"Yeah. Chemistry, I guess. The whole thing came to a head over the GenTec thing. Edom wanted the real thing, real wildlife fitted out with restraint collars. Rainer made him take GenTecs." Jael finally keyed the door open. "I think what really got to Edom was the fact that those repair platforms and the dome itself are the only thing in this entire park he hasn't checked every weld of personally."

Isadora and Gabriel raised their eyebrows questioningly.

"Acrophobia," said Jael. "Get's dizzy standing on a chair. See the irony? The one thing he never checked out personally and that's where she got killed. Look, I got to get back."

Gabriel and Isadora thanked her and stepped out of the main doors.

They were waiting for them on the other side. Two TARC agents and three police robots, featureless faces gleaming menacingly.

"Gabriel Kylie," one said, "you're under arrest."

walled

Isadora had been smacking her head against the brick wall of courteous TARC intransigence for almost two hours. They had taken Gabriel into custody, loaded him into a hangcar, refused to allow her to accompany him, refused to tell her where they were taking him and it had taken a dozen phone calls to find out that he was being held in the TARC station on Malian Hall in Purple Sector. She had followed these calls with a thirteenth, to Kynan Christmas, a lawyer friend, who had promised to come and meet her.

Arriving harried and angry at Purple Sector TARC Headquarters and finding no Kynan, Isadora had been stonewalled by two spooks in succession. Despite her threats, entreaties and a fair-sized tantrum they had remained calm, polite and utterly unbending. And *that* was what stank. With the way she was behaving they should have arrested her long ago.

The walls of the cell were a closed fist. The cell was empty, save for two chairs and a table rooted in the center of the floor. Gabriel had no idea how long he had been sitting there. They had taken his watch from him, along with his shoes, his overcoat and his knife.

Closing his eyes he hugged himself and tried to tell himself that they would let him out, that this was only temporary. But there was no window to tell the passage of time and every second the fist closed tighter, pressing against his back, bending his neck forward, pushing his arms into his shoulders, his knees against his chest . . .

The door slid open and someone stepped inside. Gabriel kept his eyes closed for a moment, carefully releasing every contracted muscle in his arms and neck and chest, listening.

There was a faint sourness of nervous sweat in the air. Whoever it was breathed shallowly, tensely. He or she was physically light but walked with the weight of personal assurance. Before he opened his eyes Gabriel knew who it was.

"I'm sorry to have kept you waiting, Mr. Kylie," said Pelham Leel. He took one of the chairs and rested his wrists on the edge of the desk. As he did so a police robot took up a position inside the doorway and slid the door shut with a touch on the doorplate.

Leel placed a square of silver on the table and touched it with his forefinger. A holo of an elderly woman's head appeared in the air above the table. Gabriel recognized her immediately.

"Do you know this woman?" Leel inquired.

"Ask your goons. They've been following me around for the last three days."

"I'm asking you, Mr. Kylie."

"Do I know her? No. I've spoken to her once. Look, why am I here?"

"You've only spoken to her once?"

"I spoke to her in the park, yesterday evening."

"And what did you talk about?"

"That was private, between me and her." Gabriel put a hard edge into the word "private."

"You are not being coerced here, Mr. Kylie," said Leel, "but a straight answer would certainly prejudice your case in your favor."

"You've got no bloody right to hold me here!" Too late Gabriel tried to bite back the word "rights." "Rights" were the Bogy's territory. The Bogy loved to slice "rights."

Leel's tone was bored, "Yes, I do, Mr. Kylie, under Article 15, Chapter 6, Code 3611 which allows a citizen to be held for twelve hours for questioning in Class 1 felonies, provided that no form of physical coercion is utilized."

"What's a Class 1 felony?"

"In this case, suspected murder."

After all that had happened Gabriel should not have been surprised, but he was.

"Murder? But . . . who?"

Leel's expression was stony. "Who did it? I'm afraid that's what we're looking for . . ."

"No! Who was killed?"

Leel let the silence grow. "A woman named Louise Daud. This woman." He indicated the holo.

"What . . . ?" Shock choked Gabriel's voice to a whisper.

"In fact, according to witnesses, you may have been the last person to have seen her alive. Now, perhaps you'll answer my question. It's really a very simple one." Leel reached up and picked something from the corner of his eye. He glanced down at his finger, then returned his gaze to Gabriel. This little interaction of theirs was formulaic to him. He could do it by rote.

Gabriel felt his chest constrict. Murder? That gentle, bewildered old woman. "Streamin' hell," he whispered, appalled.

"What was that?"

Gabriel gathered himself together. "We didn't talk about anything . . . I mean, it's not as though I didn't try. I don't know, she wasn't all there . . ." He broke off. *Jesus, why would anyone want to kill her?* "I don't . . . nothing she said made much sense and I don't remember any of it."

"You don't seem like the kind of person who suffers memory lapses, Mr. Kylie . . . if that's who you are."

"What d'you mean, if that's who I am?" retorted Gabriel.

"Why did you cancel your reservation to Merryweather?"

"What the hell business is that of yours?"

Leel leaned back in his chair. "Nerita Elspeth Kylie," he said slowly. "Your sister."

"Yes, my sister!"

Here it came, the pushing, the flexing of petty power by minions, smiling gap-toothed smiles with the fangs of the government Bogy grinning in the space behind them.

"There were certain things," Leel began, "that we omitted to tell you about your sister when I gave you that report. At the time you were still the aggrieved brother, so we didn't want to distress you needlessly.

Your sister was mixed up with people that . . . well, wrong people."

"And what's a wrong person?" demanded Gabriel.

"I think we both know what we're talking about, don't we, Mr. . . . uh . . ." Leel's lips curled into a sneer. "Well, you tell me."

"Kylie," Gabriel stated. "My name is Gabriel Kylie."

"Uncheckable. You'll have to do better than that, Mr. *Kylie.*"

"Smile when you say that."

"Is that a threat?"

"I just want to know what you want."

"I want the truth."

"I've told you the truth!"

"Have you?" Leel was obviously disappointed, as if he had been expecting something else from his prisoner. He shrugged. "I've always had a certain respect for liars—and I've known many. You find out that there's only one lie, and it comes in a myriad of disguises. But it's always the same lie. Being a law-enforcement agent you quickly learn what a ticklish thing the truth can be. The lie becomes the only constant and you learn to recognize him when you see him. You become friends. Because he's a far truer guide than the so-called truth. You just have to learn to hear him and then follow the line of him back to where the real lie sleeps." Leel smiled a little self-consciously. "You understand what I'm saying here."

Gabriel shook his head, but said nothing.

Leel leaned his elbows on the table. "He's all over you, Mr. Kylie. And you don't honor him. Because you're not very good." He sighed, a little regretfully. "You came here for something, and it had nothing to do with family feelings . . ."

All at once Leel's phone gave a squeak. "Leel here."

He appeared to be listening, but Gabriel heard nothing. Leel's phone was obviously directional. Slowly Leel's eyes rose and fastened on Gabriel and the corners of his mouth pulled into a smile. The maleficent satisfaction in that smile was chilling.

"All right, I think it's just moved onto the endangered list."

Gabriel knew instantly that Leel's "it" was himself.

"It looks like you've had a busy evening, Mr. Kylie," Leel said comfortably. "That was our lab, which was just running a routine analysis on your coat and knife, and guess what we found?"

Gabriel knew and his anger turned inward upon himself. What perversion had made him keep that coat instead of incinerating it like Isadora had wanted to?

"And your shoes tell us that you were probably down in the plastines industrial area in Brown Sector," Leel went on. "Since she didn't die by a knife wound, I doubt that the blood is going to match Louise Daud's. In fact the chances are it's natural causes and I'd still be happy, now that I've found this. I wonder what we're going to find down in the plastine sector."

"I was attacked," Gabriel muttered.

"I beg your pardon?"

"I was *attacked!*" Gabriel burst out. "I was picked up off the street by a bunch of wide boys, who threatened my *life!*"

"Can you prove it?"

"No, I can't bloody prove it . . ." Suddenly Gabriel broke off. A name returned to him: Dana Sotack, Kyaran Ventures 99. The man he had shot. If they could find him . . . The thought died as Gabriel realized that the only thing standing between him and a cerebral Probe might well be the fact that they could not connect the blood on his jacket with any individual, alive or dead.

Pelham Leel was scrutinizing him. "Inspiration, Mr. Kylie?"

Gabriel gave his head a sharp shake. His mind clawed for purchase. There had to be some way!

"You know, beyond physical violence and cerebral Probing coercion is not codified."

Gabriel snapped to. Something had subtly altered in Leel's tone, like a cat weary of the game and deciding to strike the death blow.

Not codified. Meaning that they could use any of a variety of less-than-recipient-friendly methods to get what they wanted out of him. But what if he did not *have* what they wanted? Or was Pelham Leel's statement simply another lie?

"Where is it, Mr. Kylie?" There was a barbed intent hidden in Leel's voice. He repeated, "Where is it?"

Only hours ago someone had asked Gabriel the same question.

"Where is what?"

"That which was stolen."

Without really knowing why, Gabriel said, "The blue box?"

"Ah." The tips of Pelham Leel's fingers came to rest on the desktop. "The blue box."

Gabriel hesitated. Should he string Leel along, hoping for a moment to escape? But there would be no escape, Gabriel realized, not from this place. Moreover, his lie was a triumph that he refused to give the Bogy.

"I don't know what the blue box is," he said slowly. "To me it's just two words. And that's all it's going to remain, for as long as I'm sitting here with you."

There was a long silence as Pelham Leel studied Gabriel. He peeled Gabriel and found his prisoner's own death staring back out at him.

Slowly he rose to his feet. His thin lips pursed briefly. Then he gave an odd little tilt of his head and walked out of the cell.

A sense of calm pervaded Gabriel. It was the moment when the rat stares into the eyes of the dingo and knows that his life is beyond his own recall and becomes a gift bestowed.

Gabriel let the last of his anger settle into the pit of his stomach and wash him clean. The police robot still stood impassively against the wall, the only movement visible from it that of Gabriel's own reflection in its burnished face.

"You the eyes and the ears?" Gabriel whispered to it. The robot did not reply.

By the time Kynan Christmas came rushing up to the TARC reception desk, Isadora was nearly at the point of despair. It was all that she could do to restrain herself from screaming at him. "Where the hell have you been; I called you two hours ago!"

Kynan blinked, a little taken aback, "I . . . had something else going on." From his Gladland-induced eyes it was clear what that "something" had been.

Isadora had known Kynan for two years, ever since they had found themselves in the same Municipal holding tank after a "Hands Off Querin" protest march that had gone awry. Traditionally, public protest on Kyara was done via electronic petitions on the Web, but, Privacy Laws restricting accessibility and mobility within the Web the way they did, the Querin protesters had decided to adopt the more ancient method of a public gathering, complete with signs and chanted slogans.

Kynan had not been on the march; he had been jailed for disorderly conduct in court after suffering a lysergic acid flashback during a small-claims hearing where he was representing the plaintiff. As it was his first case as a full-fledged lawyer, he had been excused on the grounds of youthful exuberance at having just graduated and suffered no permanent blemish on his record.

Kynan had subsequently laid off prehistoric hallucinogens, but had never lost his taste for altered mental states. Isadora wondered just how far down the path to Neverland he had been this time and just what he had taken to bring him down so fast.

"Look, Kynan," she said more gently, "could you just take on this clown. If I keep on, you're going to be defending me on a homicide charge pretty soon."

"No problem, Iz, no problem, I'll take care of it." He turned an unsteady gaze to TARC Officer Mugambe and took a deep breath.

"Good afternoon, my name is Kynan Christmas, accredited lawyer. I'm representing . . ." Kynan stopped. He turned to Isadora and muttered, "Who am I representing? What's his name?"

Isadora rolled her eyes in exasperation. "Kylie, Gabriel Kylie."

"Right." Kynan turned back to the TARC and continued, "I'm the legal representative handling Mr. Kylie's case. I would like"—he ticked off his fingers—"a) an immediate meeting with my client, b) pending a formal charge against my client being forthcoming, the immediate release of my client and, c) should a charge have already been brought against my client, an official copy of said charge delivered to me within, say"—Kynan glanced at his watch—"three minutes."

"I'm afraid I can't oblige you, sir," said the TARC

officer. "As I was telling the lady here, I am not in a position to confirm or deny the presence of this Gabriel Kylie in our custody, I refer you to Privacy Statute, Article 12, Chapter 11, Code 3146 . . ."

"Two minutes and fifty seconds," Kynan interrupted, laying his compuwallet on the counter and touching the "AURAL-RECORD" switch. "You people try and use that Statute every time and you know as well as I do that it cannot be used to deny counsel access to its client. Now, I hereby notify you, Officer, that I am openly recording this conversation. What is your name?"

For the first time the TARC officer seemed a little taken aback. "Mugambe. Desmond Mugambe."

"A little louder please." Kynan smilingly tapped his compuwallet.

"Desmond Mugambe."

"Right," Kynan said. "Now, I, Kynan Christmas, counsel to Gabriel Ky . . . er . . . Kylie, am hereby lodging a formal complaint under Article 2, Chapter 7, Code 1001 of the Statutes covering right of Private access to counsel. I can be back here in about two hours with a Lower Court order demanding an encrypted denial of my client's presence here, which I can then have delivered for inspection to a Lower Court judge within about twenty minutes. Refusal to submit such a denial will be taken as a confirmation. Moreover"—Kynan paused for breath but continued before Officer Mugambe could interrupt—"moreover, the court's decision will be, ipso facto, retroactive, meaning that if Mr. Kylie was in TARC custody at any time between the time this complaint was lodged—like *now*—and the time of the court's ruling, you—and I mean *you,* Officer Mugambe—will be waving good-bye to a promising career in Kyaran law enforcement. Do I make myself clear?"

Officer Mugambe stared at Kynan for a long moment, his jaw twitching. Then he said stiffly, "If you'd wait one moment, please, sir. I'll have to talk to my superior." He started to turn, but Kynan's upraised finger halted him.

"Officer Mugambe," he said gently, "I will be shunted up the ladder of command precisely once. If the next person to whom I speak is not of sufficient rank to allow me access to my client, the next time you see me will

be in the presence of a Lower Court official, facing a
charge of violation of Privacy rights. Follow?"

Mugambe nodded sourly and disappeared through a
doorway leading to the main office complex.

"I'm impressed, Kynan," Isadora said admiringly,
squeezing his shoulder. "You're better than I thought."
When earthbound.

"Yeah, I thought I was pretty good," he said, bright-
ening. "I'll tell you something though," he went on in a
lowered voice. "This"—he pointed at the doorway
through which Mugambe had disappeared—"is just a
stall."

Before Isadora had time to agree, Mugambe was back
in the company of a pale woman who introduced herself
as TARC Sergeant Jasmin Keterelli.

"I understand there is some kind of a problem."

Kynan straightened up and gave her the nearest thing
he could manage to a basilisk glare. "It's very simple. I
wish access to my client. Your subordinate refuses even
to confirm his presence in TARC custody. I'm going to
give you the same ultimatum that I gave him to grant
me that access, starting now. Three minutes."

"Please"—Keterelli held up her hands placatingly—"I
don't think there's any need to be issuing ultimatums.
Look, you must understand that for us to confirm this
Mr. Kylie's presence to any but his immediate family or
to his lawyer would be a violation of his Privacy rights."

Isadora muttered, "Ste*rike!* Do you people check in
your brains with the enrollment form or was your parents' gene pool getting a little small . . . ?"

"Iz," Kynan cut her off sharply. He turned back to
Keterelli, who was glaring poisonously at Isadora. "Sergeant Keterelli, apparently we're still experiencing a
communication problem here. I . . ." he enunciated each
word clearly, "Am . . . Mr. . . . Kylie's . . . legal . . .
counsel. And . . . I . . . wish . . . to . . . see . . . him.
Are you following me?"

Keterelli responded coolly, "According to Officer Mugambe here, you were not even acquainted with your
supposed client's name. We have no way of knowing
that you are in fact Mr. Kylie's accredited counsel."

Kynan replied, "That is not for me to prove. Therefore"—and his voice rose—"unless you can prove that

Mr. Kylie has already obtained other representation, you will give me access *right now,* or face personal legal consequences under Privacy Law Statute who-the-flock-knows and don't think I'm kidding! Now! Do you still deny that Mr. Kylie is in Targeting, Apprehension and Remand Central custody? You have five seconds before I lose patience!" Kynan held his compuwallet in front of her face.

Keterelli regarded the compuwallet distastefully. She hesitated. Kynan raised his finger.

"I'll check for you," she muttered.

"Thank you."

Keterelli turned to her terminal and said something inaudible. Her face flickered with hol-display light and she said, with bad grace, "Mr. Kylie is in TARC custody."

Isadora heaved a sigh of relief and Kynan relaxed visibly.

"Good," he said. "In that case, under the right of an accused or a witness to private, legal counsel, I request to see him."

"I'm afraid that's impossible," said Keterelli.

"Impossible?" Isadora exclaimed. Kynan shot her a warning glance.

"I think," he began patiently, "we're encountering that little communication problem again."

Keterelli interrupted him, "Under Article 15, Chapter 6, Code 3611, in the case of Class 1 felonies a witness or suspect can be held for twelve hours *without* right to counsel."

Class 1 felonies! Isadora went cold.

"Class 1 felonies?" Kynan repeated in surprise and gave Isadora a worried glance. He pursed his lips, and said, "Well, in that case I'd like a copy of the charge. As his counsel I *do* have a right to that."

"I'm afraid I am unable to help you there," said Keterelli. "You'll have to go to the station where he's being held."

Isadora's eyes widened in shock and Kynan's jaw stayed open just a little longer than was strictly dignified. He was clearly flummoxed.

"What do you mean, 'the station where he's being

held"?" Isadora demanded when she had recovered. "I thought he was being held here!"

"I'm afraid not. You'll have to go to the TARC Headquarters, Green Sector," replied Keterelli with in-your-face courtesy.

Isadora wanted to throttle her. "You people lied to me! The arresting officer told me he was being held here!"

"Do you have a recording of that conversation?" Keterelli asked mildly.

"No, she doesn't," Kynan interrupted hastily. "An unauthorized recording is a felony under Privacy Law, as my client well knows."

"This woman is also your client?"

"Business is booming, Officer. Isadora, let's go!" Kynan hissed.

She allowed herself to be hustled out of the building by him.

"They lied to me!" she exclaimed.

"Maybe, but you can't prove it," Kynan replied bluntly. "Now, we'd better get ourselves over to Green Sector and find out what's going on, don't you think?"

It could have been an hour later, it could have been a day later, when the robot finally came to life and spoke. Gabriel, who had been dozing, started up.

"You are required elsewhere, please step through the door," it said. On cue the cell door slid open.

Gabriel rose to his feet. Were they letting him go? No. "Required elsewhere" had been the phrase. And that could mean any number of things, none of them pleasant. Had they decided to charge him formally perhaps?

Tentatively he stepped through the door. He was in a room identical to his cell, but without furniture and with a second door directly opposite his own. His cell door slid closed behind him and he was aware of a sensation of movement.

He spread his bare feet out against the warm plastine floor, gripping with his toe, and bent his knees slightly. He set himself so that he had a door on either side of him. Whatever happened he would be ready for it.

He felt the elevator slow and stop. Ready.

The door on his left slid open. The light beyond outlined two uniformed TARC agents. Rather to Gabriel's surprise there was no robot present. Since he had been arrested he had not seen a TARC officer go anywhere unaccompanied by one of the ubiquitous, spoon-faced TARC robots. One of the agents was a small, ratlike man, the other man was taller, taller than Gabriel himself. Both had strangely expressionless faces. Gabriel felt as if he were looking into the countenances of two corpses.

The smaller man beckoned to him, and said, "This way, dilly. Just follow me."

Gabriel obeyed and sensed the taller TARC fall into step behind him. As they led him down the corridor he noticed that both men were thin and moved with a kind of spidery grace. It was not until they reached the first door that he felt that something was amiss.

The little man palmed the palmlock, but instead of placing his eye in front of the ret-scan he held a small card in front of it.

"Three for passage," he said. There was a red flash and the door slid open.

Gabriel hesitated and immediately felt the second man's finger in the small of his back, prodding him onward. There was nothing to be gained by trying to make a break for freedom there, so Gabriel reluctantly obeyed.

With mounting unease, Gabriel allowed himself to be shepherded down several more corridors and through several more doors. Each time the little man in front of him went through the same procedure, palming the lock and holding the card in front of the ret-scan. Gabriel could detect an air of increasing tension in the two men. It was visible in the neck of the agent leading him, his head darting left and right like a bird's. It showed in the way his weight was shifting increasingly onto his toes, as if in readiness for some form of violent action.

They arrived at another door, this one broader than all the others. The little man glanced over his shoulder and winked at Gabriel, a weird, dead wink.

"Last one, dilly," he cracked.

And then Gabriel knew what was wrong with the man's features. His face was not his own.

the face of the uplands

For a few moments it looked as if the TARC sergeant at Green Sector H.Q. was going to continue this day's tradition of stonewalling. However, after Kynan had run through his by now well-oiled speech, she simply said, "Please wait one moment," and disappeared from sight.

Only Kynan's reassuring hand on her arm stopped Isadora from exploding.

"Easy, easy, please," he pleaded. "Spare my headache and let's see where this takes us."

A moment later the TARC was back with someone Isadora instantly recognized.

Pelham Leel gave no indication of having recognized her. "Ms. . . . Gatzalumendi," he said, glancing down at the terminal screen as if for confirmation. Isadora felt a twinge of the same fear she had felt yesterday when he had visited her apartment.

Nevertheless she began stoutly, "I want to know . . ." But Kynan interrupted her.

"Captain, I'm sure you were notified that we were coming and what we want, so I won't waste either your time or mine. Where is Gabriel Kylie?"

"Mr. Christmas," Leel acknowledged Kynan with a stare, "as you've been told, Mr. Kylie's presence here involves a Class 1 felony. It is only some five and a half hours since he was arrested."

"Aw, c'mon, Captain! You and I both know what that twelve-hour isolation time is worth! Now you've had him for five and a half hours, do you really think there is anything you can get out of him in the next six and a half hours that you haven't already got out of him without resorting to a cerebral Probe or any kind of physical coercion?"

Leel pursed his lips for a moment, eyeing Kynan and Isadora in turn. "Alright," he said quietly, "but your consultation will be observed and recorded." Then he gave a short, sharp nod to the TARC sergeant and walked away.

The TARC sergeant said, "I'll have him brought to the private consultation rooms," and turned to her console.

Isadora's sigh of relief was choked off halfway as she caught the expression on Kynan's face. He looked like he was sucking on a slice of lemon peel.

"What is it?"

Kynan shook his head and pinched the bridge of his nose with his finger and thumb. "Too easy," he grunted.

"Easy! After all this?"

"No, not back in Purple Sector. Here. Ten minutes and it's 'Go ahead.' If they're willing to let me see him this easily, it means they're confident. It means they've got enough on him to keep him here beyond the twelve-hour isolation limit, in which case it makes no difference if I speak to him now or later."

"Still," Isadora pointed out, "they're sticking to not letting us have a *private* consultation with him until the twelve hours are up."

Kynan shrugged.

In the empty cell behind door 155/C the guard-robot stood silently. Its featureless face registered no reaction when the order came in to escort prisoner 155/C to visiting room 11. Nor did its body so much as twitch as it sent back the message: "Prisoner 155/C not present."

The door in front of Gabriel slid open to reveal a narrow deserted alley.

The smaller TARC jerked his head. "Come on, dilly, let's get along."

Gabriel hung back. Something here was not definitely right. "Who are you two?" he asked suspiciously.

"Move it." The TARC behind him gave him a prod, but Gabriel had been expecting it. He twisted to one side and a gentle shove was enough to send the bigger man stumbling.

Instantly the small man's hand swept up, gripping a slumbergun, which he pointed at Gabriel's chest.

"Let's not be muckin' about, dill," he said. "Come along, out the door!"

The big man started circling around behind Gabriel, who backed away.

"I'm getting tired of people pointing weapons at me," Gabriel said tightly, his indignation rising again. *Doesn't anybody in this bloody city know how to say 'please'?*

The small TARC's finger tightened. "Listen, laddibuck, we can carry your tired backside out or you can walk out. You choose."

The big man feinted at him, but Gabriel skipped a step back.

"Fine! Bloody go ahead," he said hotly. "If you're going to shoot me, then bloody shoot me. I don't give a piss anymore."

The little man licked his dead lips nervously, "We don't have time for this . . ."

"No you don't. Because you're not TARCs and I'm not going another step until I know who you are."

Pelham Leel walked away from the reception desk with a feeling of satisfaction. Legally he would have been within his rights to disallow the meeting between Kylie and his so-called solicitor. Under surveillance there would not be much that they could accomplish and indeed, if this lawyer was the kind of narked-out ambulance chaser experience told him he was, they might spill a lot more than they intended. At any rate, he had enough to keep this "Kylie" well wrapped for the next few days until they found out what his real game was. Even if the agents scouring the plastines industrial sector came up empty-handed, which Leel strongly suspected they would—street-cleaning robots would have wiped away any traces by now.

"Captain?" Sergeant Bork's voice stopped him just as he reached the door to his own office. He turned.

"Sir, Kylie is not in his cell; he seems to have been moved."

Moved? Leel frowned, puzzled, a sudden doubt gnawing at him. "Moved? Where to? Who's moved him?"

"Pelwil and Chance, sir . . ." Bork broke off, mirroring Leel's frown.

"What is it?"

"I thought Pelwil and Chance were off-duty today."

Leel froze. His eyes twitched over to look at Isadora and Kynan.

Off duty? Sudden realization swept through him. "Alarm! Code 34!" he shouted. His hand snapped up and pointed at Isadora and Kynan. "Hold them!"

The small TARC (so-called) was growing increasingly agitated. "This ain't the place to talk biolifes, stike. *Stop!*" This last was directed at the big man, who was about to lunge at Gabriel again. "We need him walking! Alright, you're right, we're not TARCs . . ."

At that instant a piercing whistle tore through the air and the outside door began to slide shut. The little man's reaction was instantaneous. He threw himself into the doorway. The door stopped closing and an automated voice said, "Free the doorway. Code 34 in progress. Free the door . . ."

"Shag it! We're made!" the little man snapped. "Toh! Out!" The big man leapt through the doorway. The little man cocked a look at Gabriel and pointed at the chamber's inner door. "They know where we are now and there'll be toymen here in five seconds. Your choice, stike, you coming?"

The words "your choice" decided for Gabriel. For the first time since he had arrived, somebody had given him a shagging choice! He darted through the doorway as the inner door began to open and the little man followed. Gabriel caught an impression of bright, blank, robotic faces before the outer door, freed of its obstruction, slammed shut.

Then he was running, up the narrow alleyway and out into an open, crowded street. The big man, Toh, led the way. As they rounded the corner into the street Gabriel chanced a glance back and saw TARC robots piling out of the now-open doorway.

"Move, move!" shouted the little man.

They charged down the street, weaving through the

passersby. Behind them an amplified robot voice said,
"Fugitives are ordered to halt now!" Its dispassionate
tone was at odds with its volume. Shocked faces swept
through Gabriel's vision, people twisting their bodies
into clumsy angular shapes to avoid him. His shoulder
collided with a green-haired woman, eyes like marbles,
who clawed at him and yelled as she went down.

They rounded another corner. The man ahead seemed
to know exactly where they were going, as if their escape
route had been perfectly planned beforehand. Toh drove
straight into the crowd, sending bodies tumbling right
and left amidst a chorus of indignant cries and swearing.
Then Toh went down, but before Gabriel could stumble
over him, he had scrambled to his feet again, hardly
losing any speed and trampling two people as he did so.
Gabriel tried to jump over the prone forms. He glimpsed
an arm thrown up to protect a face. He landed. Fingers
squirmed beneath his bare foot and there was a yelp of
pain. Gabriel flinched, stumbled, then he was in the
clear. Behind him he heard a smack of flesh on flesh as
the man following him struck a part of somebody's
anatomy.

Gabriel glanced back again and saw a half dozen
TARC robots rounding the corner. The robots had not,
to his surprise, gained on them, but it was immediately
obvious why. Programmed against willingly injuring
human beings, the robots were having to be much more
careful about potentially injurious collisions with pedestrians. The on-the-surface-lunatic decision to flee down
a crowded street was starting to make sense.

Toh dropped back and thrust something at him. "Put
these on!" he panted. Gabriel found himself clutching a
pair of thick, black, elbow-length gloves with broad
straps to secure them to the forearms. The palms were
shiny and made of some other material.

As he ran Gabriel obediently pulled on the gloves and
tightened the straps around his wrists and elbows. His
lungs were burning.

"All pedestrians please lie flat!" the TARC voice
boomed.

"Shiiiiiiit!" the man behind Gabriel hissed.

All around them pedestrians melted to the ground like
candles on a hot plate.

"Kipper! Where?" Toh shouted.

"Left, you blag! Wake up!" the little man shouted back.

They rounded another corner into a narrow alley just as a hail of slumber-bullets spattered across the far wall.

"Kipper . . ."

"Fine!"

They hurtled down the alley. If the TARC robots reached the alley before they had reached the far end, they would be caught like ducks in a shooting gallery. Gabriel could feel that the seven weeks inactivity on the interstellar liner had already taken their toll on his stamina. His lungs were raw, his bare heels striking the ground harder and more heavily with every step. Three minutes had passed since the alarm had gone off and they had been going at a flat-out sprint the entire time.

Suddenly Gabriel found the little man, Kipper, abreast of him, his short legs a blur. "You slap them down . . . you peel them up . . . okay?" he said between breaths. "Slap down, peel up . . ."

"What . . . ?" Gabriel did not understand.

"Make sure . . . you're secure on three points . . . two's enough . . . three for sure . . ."

"Kippeeeeer!"

Toh's wild eyes were staring out of his inert face, back over Gabriel's shoulder, and Gabriel knew that the TARC robots had reached the end of the alleyway. He dragged up strength that he did not even know was there and managed to increase his speed. Just a half dozen paces more to the end. There was a splutter behind him. Gabriel dived flat. Slumber-bullets tugged at his hair. His bruised right elbow struck the ground first, blinding him for an instant with a flash of pain. Before the rest of his body had landed he was already rolling to the right. A hand grabbed his shoulder and there was a voice in his ear.

"Put these on and follow us."

Gabriel fumblingly pulled on the soft, ankle-length slippers that Kipper had handed him. The trample of robot feet echoed out of the alley. As he was tightening the second strap he realized that the other two were no longer with him. He cast about in surprise before a flicker of movement above him made him look up.

Toh and Kipper were slithering lizardlike straight up the wall, slapping their hands and toes against the tusk yellow marbeline and pulling them up like gum from a tabletop. They were heading for an open window some ten meters above the ground.

Slap them down, peel them up.

Finally Gabriel understood. He sprang upward. Slap! Slap! His gloved palms struck the marbeline and stuck fast. With a grunt he pulled himself up. Agony lanced up his right arm from fingertips to shoulder. It *hurt!*

He tried favoring his left arm and kicked with his feet. His toes stuck fast. He peeled his right hand up from heel to fingertips and it came away easily. But even as he reached upward with his hand for a new purchase Gabriel knew that he could not make the window in time before the TARC robots arrived. They would pick him off the wall like a fly.

Yet Gabriel realized that he did not care. The only thing that mattered was that when they caught him they would catch him *running.*

Slap! Slap! *Pull up, peel off.* Icicles of pain shot through his arm every time it took his weight. Slap! Slap!

The drum of feet grew louder and suddenly glittering toymen were spilling out of the mouth of the alley. Gabriel froze, absurdly hoping that they might pass him by. But even that faint hope flickered out as he heard the feet stop and a second later an amplified voice rasped:

"Gabriel Kylie! Halt and return to ground level! You have now received the statutory mandatory warning. Obey immediately or bio-intrusive methods will be adopted."

In other words, "Stop or we'll shoot."

"Come and get me, you bunch of slugs," Gabriel muttered. Defiantly he peeled his left hand away, reached up and slapped it down again. He pulled himself upward.

"You are ordered to return to ground level!" the voice repeated.

Gabriel's right hand peeled away, reached out, slapped down. His toes kicked out and gummed to the wall. With a hiss of pain he heaved himself up another half meter, his back tingling in anticipation of the volley of slumber-bullets.

The TARC voice remained silent.

Puzzled, Gabriel twisted his head to look down. The TARC robots were arrayed in a ragged, silver semicircle at the foot of the wall, their mirrored heads tilted toward him, their right hands raised and pointing at him. He could see the holes in the ends of their index fingers out of which they fired their little mosquito bullets.

And suddenly he understood. He was too high! The six-meter drop could seriously injure or even kill an unconscious person falling and the robots were unable to hurt him intentionally.

Gabriel almost laughed. As he watched, several of the robots broke away and started running for the building's main entrance. Hope fueled panic in him and Gabriel scrambled up the last couple of meters to the open window. There hands seized him under his arms and jerked him over the sill and inside.

"You're a quick study with those slaphappies," said Kipper as he led Gabriel and Toh pounding down the corridor toward the elevator. Curious heads ducked back into doorways.

"You're just lucky the spooks are too lazy to do their own running and sent robots or they'd have shot you off that wall, no pause for a spit," grumbled Toh.

"Ah, stop whinging," said Kipper.

"Let's see who's whinging if Sharry hasn't diddled the override on that front door lock!" retorted Toh.

"Sharry's a genius girl; she's never let us down yet."

The elevator door dropped open and they tumbled inside.

"Roof!" snapped Kipper and leaned back against a wall, a grin cracking open his mannikin face. "Holy joy, here come the uplands!" The floor pressed against their feet.

"Unless they get to the elevator override first!" mumbled Toh glumly. Kipper was fiddling inside the collar of his uniform.

Gabriel, who had still not quite gotten his mental bearings, interjected, "Excuse me, I don't want to be too much trouble here, but maybe you'd care to tell me what's going on."

Kipper's fingers ceased their fiddling and began to tug upward. "This is the rescue committee, laddibuck. Lazarus Wight would like a word in your shell-like ear." His hand tightened into a fist and pulled. His cheeks wrinkled, the grin withered to a prunelike grimace, his nose collapsed and twisted and with one movement he peeled the flesh like taffy from his face. A new and familiar face blinked up at Gabriel, stretching and wriggling like a newborn snail, a face Gabriel had last seen leering at him over Isadora's shoulder in the Orbit-Kyara shuttle. It was the little freighter-hand who had winked at him in the shuttle lounge.

"Shag-a-lackey, it gets hot in there, stike!" Kipper exclaimed happily, holding up the mask. "Self-heating to body temperature. Fools the infrared in any toyman's eyes."

"Provided they don't look too close," muttered Toh. There was a rubbery "snap!" and a second mask was hanging from Toh's fingers, revealing a basset-hound visage.

"Nice to meet you face-to-face," said Gabriel, wincing as he massaged his right shoulder.

"Pleasure's all yours," replied Toh rudely.

"Ignore my sidekick," cackled Kipper. "His mother was a tadpole. Kipper Gibbons at your foreign service . . . with a smile!"

Before Gabriel could answer, the floor gave a shudder and Gabriel felt that the elevator had stopped.

"Oh, man, they're inside already. We're shagged!" moaned Toh.

"Clever boys," remarked Kipper. "But just too late. *Door open.*" Nothing happened. "Shag it, Sharry, you useless bitch!" he turned to say something to Toh, but Toh was already busy slicing open a section of panel with a pocket buzz-knife.

"Ready for another run?" asked Kipper, scooping Toh's mask off the floor and flinging it into the flashcan hatch along with his own.

"Maybe," said Gabriel carefully. "But maybe not in the same direction as you."

Kipper looked troubled. "That's up to you, stike, but we just laid our wee backsides on the line for you. I reckon you owe us few minutes of your time."

"So far you've got me stuck in an elevator with half the TARCs in the world trying to shoot bits off me," retorted Gabriel." How much of a favor is that?"

Kipper smirked. "I see your point."

"So tell me who this Lazarus Wight is."

"That's too long a story, stike! Lazarus Wight is the One. *The* One, you know?"

Gabriel flinched inwardly. Anyone referred to as "*the* One" by his adherents could only be trouble.

"I'm done," called Toh. On cue the door dropped open to reveal a broad balcony enclosed by a marbeline railing and overlooking a forest of glassy spires and bright, slanting roofs.

"Welcome to the uplands," Kipper said as they bolted out of the door onto the balcony. Gabriel skidded to a halt and gasped.

The roofs of Kyara swept up around him in ornamented spires of glass and marbeline, all brittle and glistening like the combers on some frozen sea. The peaks were split by chasms and window-studded walls that plunged hundreds of meters to the floor of the city. Each edifice was bridged by closed Halls and ribboned by hangcar rails. Above his head, closer than he had yet seen them hung the spun-diamond domes of the city, supported by a webwork of impossibly thin struts that extended up from some of the buildings.

A wave of vertigo swept over Gabriel. "Bugger me," he whispered in awe. But there was no time to gather his wits properly. Above a second elevator at the other end of the balcony a light was flashing.

"Here they come," groaned Toh.

"And here we go, dillies!" exclaimed Kipper. He turned to Gabriel. "You want to stay free you do as we do, compris?" Then he leapt up onto the ten-centimeter-wide balcony railing and began to run along it. Toh followed suit, dancing along the narrow rail as if this were some deranged game of follow-my-leader. Gabriel hesitated. The other side of the rail dropped two meters down onto a slanting roof, which in turn dropped into a void as deep as forever. Far below grains of colored sand scurried back and forth and shiny beetles slid along silver twine.

None of this made sense, but by now Gabriel had given up looking for the sense. With a deep breath he hopped up onto the railing. He ran giddily along the rail behind Toh, swaying like a spinning top on a shoelace,

suddenly caught up in the fun house lunacy of it all. He
saw Kipper drop off the end of the balcony, heard him
land a second later. Toh followed like a ripe apple.

The hiss of the elevator door dropping open behind
him sent Gabriel's arms windmilling for a purchase that
wasn't there. He drew into a ball, caught his balance and
kept running, every nerve screaming for him to get down
off the rail before the spit and sting of a TARC slumber-
bullet sent him plunging unconscious over the precipice.

Yet, for the second time within minutes the expected
did not materialize.

At once it all came into focus. That was why Kipper
and Toh deliberately threw themselves into perilous situ-
ations. As long as the TARC robots ran the risk that
their shots would kill the person they were after they
were unable to shoot.

Gabriel ran the last few steps along the balcony rail
and dropped off the end. He landed on a broad ledge
rimmed with gargoyle heads and found that Kipper and
Toh were already hightailing it around the far corner of
the building, deliberately keeping to the outside edge of
the shelf rather than hugging the wall. Kipper shot a
glance back, saw Gabriel on their tail and hooted with
glee. "Welcome home, dilly, you're a roofrunner now!"

The next few moments took on the visage of a dream
for Gabriel. Gleaming TARC toymen bounded out of
entrances on different roofs, fanning out and pacing the
fugitives, attempting to encircle them. An occasional
shot revealed the presence of a couple of flesh-and-blood
TARC agents coordinating the pursuit. They were in no
way bound by the constraints of the robots.

Gabriel followed Kipper and Toh in a deepening
trance, feeling like a captive on a dark and glorious
carousel ride. It became a game where the boundary
between capture and death was a dance along the brink
of a half-kilometer drop. And there came a point when
Kipper glanced back at him and cracked his squirrel grin
and Gabriel found himself grinning back and the next
moment he found that even somber Toh was giggling to
himself as he wobbled, threw out his arms for balance
and reclaimed life by a nail's breadth yet again.

But all the while the TARCs drew their net tighter.
Gabriel and his two companions reached the point of a

pyramidal roof to find themselves at a dead end. The building was octagonal, with eight ornamented ribs, each as high as a low wall, that ran from the apex to each of the eight corners. Gabriel found himself sheltering in the triangle formed by two of the ribs at the apex. On the other side of the point the TARCs were closing in on them. Behind him the roof sloped down steeply for some fifty meters, then dropped into nothing. Running past the roof, about two meters above the outside edge and six meters out, was a hangcar rail. Far too far to reach, even at a running jump.

Gabriel was leaning back against the wall, panting, holding himself secure with his slaphappies. The elation that he had felt whilst running had died. His body felt clammy with sweat, his left arm was throbbing and he found that he was shivering. He could feel the walls of the TARC prison cell around him already and had to fight to choke down the rising panic within him. Beside him Toh was white with fear, mumbling almost unintelligibly.

"I goin' to *skin* Sharry, man, I'm going to *skin* her . . . !"

Kipper was staring into the air in front of him, "Cork it, Toh," he said quietly. "It isn't Sharry's fault. She couldn't suss they'd override that front door lock so fast."

There was no sound from the other side of the roof. At last, unable to stand it any longer, Gabriel raised himself up to the edge of the ornamented wall. He held his breath and quickly poked his head up and glanced about. Standing on the peak of a neighboring roof, three TARC agents were observing the action through fargazers. Two dozen TARC robots were carefully making their way along the bottom edge of the roof, slowly encircling it completely. Five of the eight faces of the pyramid were already covered and toymen were even now clambering over the dividing ribs to encompass the faces on either side of the one on which Gabriel and his companions were crouching.

Despairingly Gabriel cast about for some avenue of escape that he might have missed. His companions seemed already to have resigned themselves to certain capture. A red sheen was covering the rooftops. Gabriel

looked up and saw that the sun was turning a deep car-
mine, signaling the onset of dark-drown. Even as Thor's
sun dimmed the Twist seemed to leap out of the suddenly star-drenched sky, the Beacon gleaming like a
beckoning eye. Farther along the underside of the hangcar rail a hangcab cruised slowly.

Gabriel caught a glimpse of movement to his left and
jerked his head back as a spray of slumber-bullets raked
the top of the rib.

"Bloody sod this!" he swore. He turned on Kipper.
"This is it? This is your bloody escape committee?"

Kipper cocked an eye at him. "What'd you prefer,
stike, staying in the bastillia?"

"In about half a minute I'm going to be back in the
bastillia and they won't have to think up any bright excuses to keep me there!" retorted Gabriel.

"Oh, you reckon spookland were goin' t'let you out
of there, do you?" Kipper snorted. "We've called a lot
of favors and flashed a lot of hands to get you out!"

"And a fat lot of good it's done us! In about one
minute they're going to have us freeze-wrapped tighter
than a spaceman's dinner!"

"There's always a way out, stike," said Kipper slowly.
"There's always one way out." He glanced at his watch
and snickered. "Let's go, dillies. It's flying time." He
started to rise.

Toh's lips pulled back, baring his teeth in a rictus
smile. The cords in his neck were tight as stays. "Call
it," he said hoarsely.

"Now!"

As one they stood and, to Gabriel's amazement, began
running straight down the side of the roof, whooping
like boys freed for summer recess.

For a surreal instant Gabriel was suddenly transported
in his mind back to Landing, to Mackay's Rock, a pie-
shaped hill of red stone, scoured smooth and sloping
down to where it dropped sheer for ten meters into a
deep, turquoise-rimmed lake.

That was where his nine-year-old self and his best
friends, Billy Halfpint and Dig-Dig, used to run, hooting
and crying with glee, arms waving for balance as they
tried to catch up with their own legs. As the edge approached the lake would come into view, staring up at

them like a giant reptile's eye, until the drop-off, where a final kick-off would send them soaring out in wavery swan dives, and plunging down into icy waters.

Suddenly, near the bottom edge of the roof, four robot heads appeared over the corner ribs, gleaming redly in the dark-down light. And Gabriel was back in the present. His breath caught and before he knew what he was doing he had leapt to his feet and was running after Kipper and Toh. On either side of him silver fingers pointed, tracking him as he ran past, unable to fire because of the risk of killing him, despite the clear inevitability of his death.

So this was what Kipper had meant when he'd said there's always one way out.

And Gabriel discovered that he did not mind.

Sorry, Iz, Gabriel spoke silently to himself. *Guess I'll be a little late.*

Faster and faster he ran down the slope, arms windmilling. And suddenly Toh and Kipper were Billy and Dig-Dig and the lake was smiling up at them. Already they were only meters from the edge, unable to stop themselves if they wanted to, as he was unable to stop himself. Gabriel spread out his arms like a bird released and whooped with them and the eucalyptus trees were gray with dust.

Just at that moment the hangcab that Gabriel had seen earlier appeared round the corner of the building. It swerved toward them and came to a dead stop directly in their line of motion, at the point on the rail nearest to the roof. Gabriel, drunk with flight, hardly registered it. Nor did he comprehend as Kipper sprang outward and struck the side of the hangcab with his slaphappy palms, *slap! slap!* and hung fast. Then Toh was soaring into space, *slap! slap!* and he, too, was swinging by his hands from the cab's rear door.

The cab began to move, but Gabriel barely noticed. His mouth opened and a roar freed itself and echoed across the rooftops. He inhaled death and was filled to the brim with life. His foot struck the edge of the world and, with a final spring, Gabriel Kylie launched himself into the void.

the mask of the foole

Isadora had been arrested thrice before, but that had been by Municipal Police, who had simply held her overnight with her fellow protesters and then released her. This was different.

Twice Pelham Leel came in and methodically ran down the same list of questions:

Where had she first met Gabriel Kylie.

What did she know about tonight's escape.

Why was it that she just happened to be there when the breakout was taking place.

Where had she first met Gabriel Kylie.

What did she know about . . ."

By the time Leel entered the cell for the third time and seated himself on his side of the plain, white wall-table, Isadora's nerves were as tightly strung as high-C piano wire.

Leel regarded her stonily. "Three previous arrests, causing a disturbance, impeding pedestrian traffic," he recited, reading off the flatscreen. "Querin riots, weren't they?"

Isadora raised her chin and tried to match his gaze. "No, not riots. In about a month the Congress of Stellar Systems is going to vote on the status of Querin. They're going to vote on whether the sentient species there possesses a—quote—valid—unquote—culture, capable of developing out of its present Stone Age state . . . kind of a moot point considering the Neanderthals we've got posing as law-enforcement officers . . ."

Leel interrupted, "I thank you for the lecture . . ."

"I'm not finished. If the Querin culture is ruled invalid the C.S.S. will open Querin to exploitation . . ."

"Ms. Gatzalumendi, I follow the news . . ."

"Then you'll know it's a debate. A debate! Maybe you've never heard of one of those. It's when two parties have a difference of opinion and try to resolve it without the use of thugs posing as law-enforcement officers. The protest marches were a means for our side of the debate to draw attention to itself. A legal means."

"Legal means don't result in arrests," Leel pointed out drily.

"Look, you've got no grounds for keeping me here."

"Considering you've been consorting with a suspected murderer . . ."

"If it hadn't been for me, you wouldn't have known he'd escaped for hours!"

"So you concede we have a case against him."

"That's not what I said!"

"Ms. Gatzalumendi." Leel reached into a pocket and produced an I.D.-sized holograph. "Do you know what this is?"

Isadora reached out for it, but Leel twitched the card out of reach. "It's a holograph of a certain TARC officer's retina. One of two officers who happen to be missing at this moment, Jason Pelwil and Del Chance. The quality and resolution are extraordinary; it wouldn't have fooled any high-grade security system, but it was quite adequate for the holding tank here." The holograph disappeared into Leel's pocket again.

"The point is that Kylie would seem to have broken out with the assistance of roofrunners, but no roofrunner or downlander has ever had the means to produce a holograph of fine enough resolution to fool even the most basic TARC security system. That opens up a myriad of questions. And we need answers."

Isadora spoke slowly. "Officer Leel, I don't know how he escaped. I don't know what he was doing. In fact, as was pointed out to me last night, I don't even know who Gabriel Kylie really is. But I am certain of one thing. Whatever it is you're trying to pin on him, he didn't do it."

"Pin on him?" Leel's eyebrows kissed his hairline. "I'm a law-enforcement officer; I don't pin things on people. Have you see the charge file? Suspected murder, accessory to the kidnapping of two TARC officers—

that's assuming they're still alive and unhurt—breaking out of a TARC detention center whilst under arrest, resisting rearrest. Even if I were what you seem so anxious to paint me, I don't *need* to pin anything on Gabriel Kylie."

"Then what do you want from me?"

"I want answers."

"I don't have them."

"Obviously."

"Oh, so you . . . what?" Isadora broke off in shock.

Leel stood. "You're free to go. The security robot will escort you out presently." He spun on his heel.

Isadora had no idea what made her blurt out the next thing she said. Perhaps it was just the resentment at the way Leel seemed to feel that he could manipulate her, confusing her, throwing her own belief in herself into question and then casually dismissing her.

She said, "Well if I'm free, why don't you answer some questions for once. What about the blue box?"

Pelham Leel froze. Slowly he turned and looked at her quizzically. "The what?"

"You heard me. You asked me about it when you came to my apartment last night. That's what all this is about, isn't it? What is this blue box?"

Leel frowned. "I'm not following you. Who was at your apartment last night?"

Isadora blinked, taken aback. "You. You came to my apartment with one of your robots. You were admiring my adder. Birds of a feather . . ."

Leel interrupted. "I wasn't at your apartment last night. What's all this about, Ms. Gatzalumendi?"

Isadora gaped. "But, you were. At about eight o'clock. You asked me about Gabriel Kylie, you seemed to know where I'd met him and when, and you asked me about the blue box."

Leel sank back into his chair. He sat straight, not touching the table.

"Tell me about this . . . blue box," he said slowly.

"Now, wait a second . . ." Isadora tried to clear her head. "I can't . . . you were the one . . . You're not trying to tell me you weren't at my apartment last night. I *saw* you! I recognized you today down at the reception desk! You knew my name."

Leel studied her narrowly, "Ms. Gatzalumendi, the duty officer told me your name. You're quite right. I did know that you had met with Gabriel Kylie and when and where, I've made that quite clear this evening. But last night at eight I was in a meeting with TARC Commissioner Tamara Lennox and two other police officers. Now. Suppose we stop fencing here for a second and you tell me what you think is going on."

The silence was long. At length Leel leaned back and spoke to the robot. "Last order rescinded. She stays." He studied her for a few more seconds, then rose. The door whispered shut behind him.

They released her the next morning, twelve hours to the minute from the time she was arrested. She emerged, tense with exhaustion, to find Kynan waiting for her, asleep in one of the reception-room chairs. He looked like a piece of chewed gum stuck to a park bench. Isadora only hoped he looked worse than she did.

They caught a hangcab. As it was twenty to ten, Isadora had Kynan drop her off at the BME building. Kynan was too hungover to hold a coherent conversation, but as she climbed out of the hangcab he caught at her shoulder, nearly tumbling out of the cab as he did so.

"Iz, do me a favor," he pleaded. "The next time you need a favor, you know, breaking people out of TARC detention centers, stuff like that. Call someone else, not me."

The concern in his eyes belied his words.

"Thanks, Kynan," Isadora said gratefully. "You're a good friend."

"Oh, god." He groaned miserably as she shut the hangcab door. "I hate being good friends with people."

She made her way to the Duas Voces offices, barely aware of her surroundings. The news office was in full swing. Outline faces glanced in her direction when she entered. They fanned around her with all the individuality of a deck of cards. As she passed through them they rattled and brayed at her.

"Hey, Iz!" a Jack of Diamonds chirruped at her. "You hear about the stike who escaped from Green Sector TARC holding tank? We got it on the air eleven point four seconds earlier than any other news station on the air. Eleven point five! Yessah!"

"Nice going, Jörn," she murmured automatically.

Lee Chuen was not at her desk, but two men were. They both had Maintenance patches on their overalls and were busy administering to Chuen's terminal. Isadora recognized them as the exterminators who had taken care of BME's last virus alert.

"Where's Lee Chuen?" she asked in astonishment. Chuen never let others mess with her terminal.

"Who?" one of the men inquired. Then his face grew sullen. "Oh, you mean the charmer that uses this terminal? She's talking to her boss and she's welcome to her. If that's her bedside manner, I doubt she'll be her boss much longer."

The other man snickered.

Isadora hurried over to the office of Marushka Vladeck, the senior Duas Voces editor. Through the wall she could see Chuen hammering on Marushka's desk and Marushka leaning back as if she were in the presence of a reeker.

"Marush, you've got to get those clowns off my terminal!" Chuen was bellowing, her voice turning heads throughout the newsroom.

"What's going on?" Isadora wanted to know.

Chuen rounded on her. "Those flocking morons are replacing my terminal!"

"What? Since when?"

"Iz, would you wait outside?" Marush attempted to intervene.

"They're screwing with my files, my programming." Chuen turned her fury back on Marush. "Marush, you've got no flocking right to do this, that's my *terminal*!"

Marush weathered the blast with barely a blanch. "Chuen," she said, attempting to remain calm, "that terminal is Byron Media Entertainment property and we've got every right to replace it. The thing's an antique. The only reason we've left it there this long is because you've badgered me and badgered me, but a terminal is no use if no other staff member can even USE IT!" Marush's self-control broke on the last two words. "Shag it, I don't know what it is with you researchers, you with your terminal, her with her damned hard copy." Marush indicated Isadora.

Isadora attempted to speak but Chuen was already in full throttle. "I've got stuff on there that's private! So help me, I'll get the legals on you for Privacy breach!"

"That terminal is BME property," Marush repeated stubbornly. "That means that everything on it is BME property. Check your contract."

"Bullyshag! There isn't a person in this office who doesn't have private files in their cyberspace."

"And the office tolerates it, the same as it tolerates the political activism of some of its employees."

Chuen went pale. "Are you threatening me?"

Isadora reached out and grasped Chuen's forearm. She had to get Chuen out of here before this went too far.

Marush railed on, "I've put up with your 'Hands Off Querin' agitating, and bailing you out of jail every time you get arrested for hassling people in the street and I've done it because you're the two best researchers we've ever had in this office . . . yes, I'm talking to you, too." Isadora suddenly found herself on the receiving end of Marush's ireful glare. "But I've had enough. The powers that be have ordained that this start looking and operating less like a synth-tank warehouse and more like a newsroom!"

"But they've got no right to interfere in the running of this office!" Isadora objected. "We're an independent news organization!"

"Independent from who?" Marush shouted. She reined herself in. "I mean," she said in a quieter voice, "independent from *whom.* I'm an editor and my grammar is going to pot."

"Screw your grammar, this *stinks*! This STINKS!" Chuen raged. Then to Isadora's horror she added, "You've never pulled us off a story before, *ever*!"

Marushka was too astute not to pick up the implications. "What story? I'm not pulling you off a story. What story am I supposed to be pulling you off?"

Now Chuen hesitated, apparently realizing that she had said too much. Isadora seized the opportunity to tighten her grip on her friend's arm and drag her toward the door.

"Chuen, let's go, *now*!" Isadora said, trying to keep

her voice as gentle as possible. Marush seemed only too relieved to see the back of them.

"Take the rest of the day off, Chuen," she called after them. "Come back when you're ready to stick to the job description!"

"What the hell did you think you were doing in there?" Isadora demanded when she had maneuvered Chuen into a secluded corner near the canteen slot.

"Don't you get it?" Chuen hissed. "She said it herself. This is the lean! Someone upstairs has been monitoring our terminals and hasn't liked what they saw!"

"But what? What have you been sniffing around?"

Isadora flinched under Chuen's scornful stare. "What have *I* been sniffing around? Wake up, Iz! Marush said it herself. We're active members of the 'Hands off Querin' lobby. That's 180 degrees opposed to BME's editorial stance. Of course they've been monitoring us!"

"But why now?"

"You tell me, Iz! I've worked here six years and nobody, *nobody* has ever tried restrict my access or censor me in any way. That was your chip we were looking at last night and now, all of a sudden . . . Where the hell did it come from? Where did you get a chip belonging to the Rainer Park woman?"

Isadora recoiled, dazed.

Chuen shook her head in disgust. "How stupid do you think I am, Iz? You think you can shove something like that under *my* nose and not have me know what it is? I'll tell you something else, Iz," she continued. "I'll tell you what I think. Calaban Transport. Remember last night, we were wondering about them? Well, after you left I looked them up. Guess who owns them?" Chuen did not wait for an answer. "Byron Systems!"

Isadora looked away and Chuen pounced on her triumphantly.

"Ah, you knew! Big Mother herself! No? Then let me spell it out for you. Eight months ago Kyara gets within a tinker's fart of having the first Consortium War in forty years anywhere on the Seventeen Planets. Of course no one can prove anything, but *we* know, the spooks know, everybody who 'knows' knows. And who are the protagonists? Why, our old friends, Kyara Ventures 99 and *Byron Systems*. Who do we work for? Duas Voces, slash,

Byron Media Entertainment, owned by, yes, Byron Systems. And did you happen to notice the dates on those visits to Calaban by 'Kylie Exterminations'? Almost eight months ago to the day! Shit!" Chuen smote her hand against the wall. "My search request last night must have registered on their watchdog program and bingo! the boys with the hats turn up the very next day."

Isadora remembered what she had learned in school about the Consortium Wars of the early thirties. Corporate sabotage escalating into terrorism, trade blockades, the closing down of power grids, the cutting off of essential resources. A consortium war was insidious in that it was nonterritorial in nature, its battlefields, supply lines, communications intertwined and braided like the threads on some mad tapestry, its protagonists two opposing cancers, rampant and fighting for supremacy in the same host body. She dared not believe it.

"It's too thin, Chuen," she said feebly. "There can't be anything that's such a hot potato that one request for information brings a crew down . . ." Even as she spoke she thought of Gabriel's attempted kidnap by KV 99 agents and then his arrest and his escape and her arrest. She pulled her fingers back through her hair, trying to clear her head. "And anyway, why didn't they just send in a cleaning virus if they wanted to get at your files?"

Chuen hissed. "Use your shagging brains! How would they get at my off-Web files? If you don't believe me, you wait until those exterminators have finished with my terminal and we'll see if I've lost anything. One gets you ten they'll come here with long faces to tell me, 'Oops, sorry, sister, file damage, nothing we could do.' And if your file is one of those missing we'll know."

Isadora could no longer be surprised when one of the exterminators approached them some minutes later, his face the apologetically smiling mask of the eternal incompetent to tell the two women, "Oops . . ."

"Thanks a whole bunch," said Chuen acidly. The man backed away, satisfaction clear in his eyes.

An instant later Isadora snapped out of her trance.

"The chip. Gabriel's chip."

Chuen gave her a hard look. "What did you do with it?"

"It's at home . . . oh, god . . ." Isadora spun round and ran for the door.

"Iz, wait . . . !"

Isadora ran out onto the street, feeling Chuen on her heels, and hailed the first hangcab she saw. They made the journey in tense silence.

Isadora leapt out of the cab the moment it stopped, leaving Chuen to pay. Her hands were shaking as she thumbed her door open and stepped inside.

She paused at the doorway, scanning her apartment. Skunk came bounding up to her, rubbing the length of his body against her ankles and chittering. Mack the Knife was stretching his wings and twitching his head from side to side, apparently awakened by her entrance. The sheer normality of it all made her hair prickle against her scalp. Something had to be wrong.

She heard Chuen come panting up the corridor and the next instant her friend had pushed past her and was looking around.

"Well?"

Isadora shrugged helplessly. "I don't know, it seems to be okay."

"Where's the chip?"

"Over here." Isadora marched over to her desk and reached out for the plasper envelope containing the chip. Before her fingers could reach it, however, her wrist was seized in Chuen's cold grip.

"Wait! Look." Chuen was pointing to a tiny, scorched mark on the mikette desktop. Isadora did not need to hear Chuen's next words to know what that meant.

"Twigleggy. There go your files . . . your Notebook . . ." Chuen indicated the Notebook also lying on the desk.

Dazed, Isadora sank down onto her desk chair.

"CompSystem on," Chuen said. Nothing happened. The computer's hol-screen remained blank. "You voice-keyed or codelocked?"

Isadora shook her head.

"Then it's dead." She picked up the Notebook. "And this. Probably everything in a one-meter radius from the look of the burn mark, including your chip. You don't have anything else . . . ?" Chuen trailed off as Isadora shook her head again. "Flocking twigleggies! You better get your animals checked, they might have taken some radiation burns if they were close enough when it went off."

It was gone. Everything. And yet . . .

On the verge of tears Isadora felt her mouth twitch, heard Chuen's sharp intake of breath.

"You're happy," whispered Chuen in incomprehension. "You're glad all this has happened."

To Isadora's own shock she realized Chuen was right. A perverse corner of her being was truly enjoying this. The enemy had solidified into something tangible and in doing so had just displayed its first weakness.

She smiled as she remembered something that Gabriel had said this morning:

"Far Cry."

Then her eyes lit upon on a stack of plasper on her desk and she began to giggle.

Chuen regarded her apprehensively. "What the flock is wrong with you?"

Iz pointed, still giggling. "Nobody reads books anymore."

This particular Hall in the plastines industrial sector never got any lighter than it was now and that made it a logical place for a bullywhack.

TARC Officer Zbegniew Romanov knelt beside the blackened stains on the Hall floor. "What a mess," he muttered to himself. The dried bloodstains were smeared over a broad area.

He rose as TARC A.I.unit $\alpha \delta$ 554 approached, shimmering as it walked through the Hall's scattered lightfall.

"Officer Romanov, Municipal Officer Sukarno says she has found something of interest," said the robot.

"Show me."

As they walked over to where the Municipal officer was waiting, the robot continued, "In accordance with your orders I have been monitoring communications traffic concerning your missing colleagues. Officers Pelwil and Chance have just been located in an alley off Carroway Hall in Gray Sector."

"Bugout Plaza?"

"Well within its environs. They were unconscious as a result of excessive ethanol use."

Romanov winced. *Drunk? Oohboy!*

Three Municipal Police officers were standing around the dead cleaning module, the pudgy Sanitation Department man kneeling by the module's intake slot.

"See . . . here. That's where the shooter's jammed." The san-man's words were slurred by the king-size nicotine root in his mouth. "You can see it. The teeth should have been able to grind it up, but the bugsucker went off. Lucky shot. The bullet blew its way right through a circuit crystal." The san-man climbed to his feet. "Lucky for you dillies or it would have had this place cleaned up clean and you would have found bullyshag."

Romanov had already heard this over the comm. He said, "Officer Sukarno, what have you got for me?"

The young Municipal officer held up a plas bag containing what appeared to be a blood-encrusted identity card. "We found that over yonder." She pointed to a spot near a support strut.

"Dana Sotack, KV 99," he read out loud.

"It's got prints all over it," Sukarno said helpfully.

Romanov shook his head. "That's no good, fingerprints are inadmissible, you know that. Too easy to fake, and it's too late for an infrared pattern analysis. Still"—he let the satisfaction show in his face—"we've got enough. Gunny!" The robot stepped forward. "Run this to the lab for analysis. Get a few samples of blood from different areas here, we'll want to know if it's all from the same person and if it matches the stains on the card . . . and on Kylie's coat. Then get someone to run a check on one Dana Sotack, P.R. No. 3462238. Find out if he's been reported missing. Then report to the captain. I'm going down to the KV 99 offices. I think we may have enough to nail this Sol-side dilly."

"Provided you catch him," one of the other Municipal officers observed. There was a trace of scorn in his voice and Romanov flushed. Kylie had escaped from TARC custody and by now every Municipal officer in Kyara must be privately gloating.

Romanov replied icily, "Oh, he's already ours, Officer."

in parenthesis: seventeen

First there was Terra Nova, the first habitable planet discovered in or outside Sol System—

Terra Nova was a kindly world, with a greater total dry-land area than Earth. Over its pristine continents chlorophyll-rich vegetation spread a verdant carpet, home to a plethora of animal life, diverse and abundant.

During the initial twenty years of colonization human beings managed to cover a large percentage of these continents with roads and buildings and amusement parks and other goodly stuff. Until StarrTx came into being and brought things to a screeching halt, instituting strict guidelines for the exploitation and development of this and any habitable planets discovered in the future.

The miracle had happened, Humanity had learned from its own history.

In the decades that followed, human exploration was guided by StarrTx, the agency for stellar travel and the exploration and exploitation of planets set up by what eventually came to be the Congress of Stellar Systems (C.S.S.). The three "R's" of the StarrTX code were: Respect for Life; Room for Diversity; Restraint in Growth. In the long run it was the third of these R's that was to be the greatest wellspring of dispute.

Less than three centuries after the GenTec Plagues ravaged Mother Earth and thermonuclear fires created the Glass Deserts in North America, Australia and Greater Europe, the children of Earth had spread their seed through Seventeen Planets and multitudinous independent colonies, scattered across twenty-six star systems, and created a Congress of Stellar Systems that embraced every one of these planets and colonies. The two marginal mem-

bers of the C.S.S. consisted of the penal colony on the great gas planet Leviathan's moon, Retreat, which was governed directly by the C.S.S. and Earth.

Though a member of the C.S.S. and officially one of the Seventeen Planets, Earth's membership was half-hearted at best. In the free flow of people and information between the C.S.S.'s member systems, Earth was the pro-verbial snag. Its population of 900,000,000 was the least homogeneous, either racially or culturally, of any plane-tary population in the Seventeen Planets. The strictness of its Privacy Laws was legendary. As well as having the largest proportional number of bureaucrats, civil servants and assorted pencil pickers of any of the Seventeen, its government was also the slowest and, oddly, one of the most conscientious. There was not a bureaucrat on Earth who was not proud of the leaden pace at which its rela-tively honest wheels of parliamentary power turned.

In the century following the discovery of Terra Nova, a decade rarely passed without the settlement of yet another planet suitable for human habitation, twelve more in all (Mars, Grayscape and Thor, though settled, were hostile to human life). Thereafter, however, no more were discov-ered. It would be forty-seven years before another habit-able planet was discovered.

That planet was Querin. A beautiful world of jungle-carpeted continents and deep oceans, Querin was the an-swer to the developer's dream. There was just one catch.

Someone was there already.

They had come a long way; their culture was well into the late-Neolithic: stone tools, fire, primitive ceremonies. The anthropologists who watched them through remote spy-eyes were ecstatic. Here was an oxygen-breathing, tool-using, quasi-mammalian race, equipped with (four) opposable thumbs and still in the state that Humanity had been in fifty thousand years ago.

StarrTX imposed an immediate quarantine on the planet.

From the start Querin's status as a newly-discovered planet was a thorn of political contention. Arrayed on the one side were the dozens of multisystem corporations to whom the discovery of a new planet presented the usual promises of wealth beyond the dreams of CEOs. Sharing common cause with, but in no way allied to these multisystems were the thousands of special-interest groups—invariably religious—each with its own dream of creating a personal (and naturally exclusive) paradise tailored to its own individual precepts. Both of these groups lobbied for throwing Querin open to human development.

Standing against this nascent feeding frenzy were the combined governing bodies of the C.S.S., in the shape of its StarrTX wing. StarrTX had not been caught unawares; indeed, the agency had been preparing for the eventual discovery of alien intelligence for over a hundred years. Using the post-Plague Charter for the Protection of non-Tech-Utilizing Societies, set up to protect the rights of low-technology cultures by effectively removing technological status as a final criterion for a culture's validity and rights of individual self-determination under planetary law StarrTX mounted a campaign for noninterference and right to self-determination for Querin.

The dispute simmered in the corridors of power for three Standard years.

Things were ultimately brought to a head by a paper first published on the Denube Web by Pedro Jesus Mondigas and Louisa van Straten, under the title, "The Querin: a species frozen in history?" Robotic excavations in the areas around the two Querin villages under study seemed to indicate that the native Querin had been stranded at this stage of cultural development not for a couple of millennia, but for, at the very least, three hundred and fifty thousand years!

This gave the would-be developers the key that they needed. Although a culture could not be judged purely on its technological development, it could be judged on its ability to develop and respond to changing circumstances. The Querin had become stranded at the late-Neolithic stage of their evolution for three hundred and fifty millennia; ergo, they were incapable of change and had essentially arrived at an evolutionary cul-de-sac.

The battle for Querin was fought in parliaments, senates, assemblies, conclaves, cabinet rooms, and advisory boards throughout the C.S.S. By the narrowest of margins the movement for noninterference on Querin emerged triumphant. It was narrow, but it was decisive. Officially the decision hinged on the question of whether or not the

thor's anvil

Gabriel's right arm did not hurt anymore when he awoke, but everything else did. A web of shadows drifted across the ceiling above him, broken by amorphous islands of light moving in time to the swell of traffic passing outside. He tried wiggling the fingers of his right hand and found that he could barely feel them.

He closed his eyes again, letting the pieces that made up last night's events gradually merge into a coherent whole. He remembered the wild, snaking ride, swinging by his slaphappies hundreds of meters above the city streets as the hangcar careened in and out of the traffic. Then into a darkened Hall, being bundled into another hangcar, another ride, the car filled with the smell of sweat and fear and the whispers of his two companions. Then running, being hustled along black halls, red and orange doorways gaping brightly like wounds in the darkness. Unhealthy laughter and the sad faces peering out from behind cracks and corners; the bugheads of Bugout Plaza. He heard the name repeated twice.

Then another hangcar ride and, finally, hands, many hands, helping him inside, peeling off his shirt and blessed relief as an anesthetic spray was applied to his arm and shoulder. Then he was pressed onto a bed, hard and cool, and for a moment he smelled something, foul, unnatural, and then it was gone.

And then sleep.

"You're a heavy sleeper, dilly; you've slept right into tomorrow afternoon."

Gabriel opened his eyes again to find Kipper standing over him, face cracked in its usual smirk.

"I've been awake." Gabriel heaved himself stiffly up into a sitting position, feeling a tugging at his right arm. His body felt as if it were made of unseasoned wood.

"Watch the pain tabs." A woman appeared at his side, pale and reedlike, with long, stringy hair hanging over her eyes. She removed two tabs from Gabriel's arm. Gabriel's arm was covered by a fine mesh that limited its movement. As she rolled up the leads of the tabs and replaced them in their box she peered at him sidewise in the manner of a nervous sparrow. Gabriel noticed that she had the twin arches of the Church of Cornucopia tattooed on her left wrist. "It'll start hurting again in a moment. Best to let it rest for a while," she muttered.

She was right, the pain surged and snapped him into wakefulness. He gazed about at his surroundings.

He was in one corner of a large room, one wall of which was completely transparent and leaned inward; he had the impression that he was in some kind of belfry—maybe in one of the hundreds of spires that adorned Kyara's skyline.

It was obviously well lived-in. At the far end, fragments of optic wires and single-crystal circuitry covered a large worktable. There were clothes scattered about the room and used, disposable cups, standing undisposed and by now evolving their own closed ecologies. On a low table in the center of the room were several plates of food, none of them particularly appetizing.

"Come and grab some giblets, stike," said Kipper cheerfully, indicating the table. "You did earnworthy last night. Never seen a dilly take a leap like that with a pair of slaphappies first time round. Shagging upside stuff, stike! Shagging upside! Thought we'd lost you and the whole run had been for nothing, but you came up rightly upside!" Kipper clearly meant it as praise.

Gabriel stood, wobbling slightly. *Iz,* he thought, *what's happened to Iz?* Had she been arrested as well? Had they hurt her? Ignoring the food, he limped over to the window to get an idea of where he was. It took a few seconds before he understood what he was looking at.

He was, indeed, on the topmost story of a building. A little below him a hangcar rail ran past the window. Just beyond the hangcar rail, less than twenty meters from where Gabriel was standing, gleamed the spun diamond of one of Kyara's outer domes. And beyond that an eerie, black plain stretched away to a horizon that was far higher than it should have been.

Gabriel realized that for the first time he was looking out onto the true surface of Thor.

Like a greasy hot plate, was how Elspeth had described it. As his eyes grew accustomed, Gabriel saw that it was not really black, but a muddy dark gray. There were no high peaks, Thor's tremendous gravity had pulled everything flat, but there were no gentle slopes either. Everything was sharp-edged ridges and low, knapped blocks, as if anything that attempted to defy Thor's gravity was simply snapped off. On the flat surfaces dark streaks curled unmoving over and in upon themselves like an oily slick. All veiled by the pearly shimmer of the Icarus Field.

Old Man. If you had only seen this. Gabriel had the vertiginous urge to reach out and touch it.

"That's Thor's Anvil," Kipper said from just behind him. "Biggest view on the Seventeen Planets. You'd be amazed how many people in this town have never actually seen it."

"What do you mean?" Gabriel found that hard to imagine.

"Not a nice reminder, that, stike. It's easy to forget that you're living in the Well, easier not to remember. You never noticed how far from the ground the outer domes are opaqued? And a lot of the perimeter buildings got no windows on this side. Three steps beyond the dome and your dick is around your ankles." Kipper made a gleeful clicking noise with his tongue.

Gabriel said, "I've been to some of the Orbiting Cities at Terra Lagrange and in the Helios system asteroid belt. All it takes is an open airlock door and it can cost you a lot of lives."

"Not the same thing, dilly, not the same thing." Kipper shook his head.

Gabriel knew that he was right, of course. In a space colony it was the Nothing outside the pressurized environment that could kill you. Here the enemy had a face, broad and black and terrifying.

Suddenly it came home to him. Last night he had broken out of TARC custody; he was free. *As free as a fly in a gin bottle,* he thought wryly. *With the hand of the bogy holding its thumb over the mouth. As free as a bug in amber.*

"You going to eat something, stike?" the woman broke in suddenly. "Laz is going to be wanting to talk to you."

Kipper clicked at her reproachfully, "Give the man a space, Sharry, he's just awake and we were bit-shafting late."

"Yeah, and every head on V.T. is talking about it. They're pulling in every uplander they can get the grip on." Toh was standing in the doorway, his basset-hound face as sullen as ever. He was holding a bundle of cloth carefully in his arms. "We're lucky we're here at all."

"Listen, stike, I did an upside crosswire on that door! *And* the lift!" Sharry shot back indignantly. "They just caught some luck with the override. It can happen. I did my damned best!"

"Dilly, dilly, dilly, sure you did." Kipper hopped between them. Gabriel guessed that this argument had been going on all morning. Kipper planted a kiss on Sharry's forehead and then leapt over to take the bundle gingerly out of Toh's arms. "My queenie-queen," he cackled at it. The bundle gave a wriggle and a small white hand reached out clumsily and poked Kipper in the eye.

"Four and a half months and she's got the rule of silence down like a kiddie twice the brainweight!" said Kipper proudly, winking at Sharry. Gabriel caught the warm look that Sharry returned.

Kipper Gibbons, family man, he thought with some surprise. It awakened a small pain in him that he quickly supressed. Then he saw the glint in Toh's hangdog eye and realized that family, in this case, extended further than one might expect.

Kipper settled down, next to the table with the infant and a feeding bottle that had appeared from somewhere in the jumble.

Gabriel managed a few mouthfuls of the food that was on display. There was nothing particularly wrong with it, but it was bland to a fault, clearly the product of some prehistoric food-synthesizer. As he ate he could not keep his eyes off the stark view outside the window.

Rule of silence, he reflected grimly. That was something that would be needed by people who hid a lot, although with infrared Eyes on police robots that rule was probably as much symbolic as anything else.

"Elspeth was hooked on the Anvil, too," said Sharry suddenly. Gabriel snapped to in shock. "She used to spend hours staring at it."

"You knew Elspeth?"

"Oh, yeah." Kipper was gazing slyly at Gabriel, pleased at the latter's astonishment. "We knew her well as anyone."

"But how . . .?"

"Ah, there." Kipper went back to feeding the baby. Toh glowered silently from his corner. It was left to Sharry to pick up the thread.

"Did her share of roofrunning. Hung the slaphappies with us for a while up until . . . well, you know. And did some . . . stuff."

"What kind of stuff?"

"*Stuff,* stuff." Sharry shrugged and looked away. As the light caught her face Gabriel noticed that she had had her face pigment-treated, a subtle tan-line tiger-stripe that ran across her eyes and emphasized her cheekbones. "She got the Anvil-eyes first time she came up here. Had it bad as I've ever seen. She used to spend an age and an age just staring out at it. Fringe-line bug-out at times."

"She was not, she was an upside dam." Kipper looked up from his feeding chore to chastise her. "A little Anvil-eye never hurt anybody. We all got it some, someways. You don't' run the upland unless y'do."

Sharry snorted. "Even Laz figured she was half-gone to bugland by the end and you know that rightly! If she hadn't lost her three-point the way she did . . ."

"Sharry." Toh's eyes had suddenly become black glass and Sharry subsided.

"Ah, rest it. We've an upside gent here," said Kipper easily, his eyes never leaving the baby's. Toh responded with a sour purse of the lips.

"I didn't mean anything wrong by that," Sharry said to Gabriel. "We all got our reasons why we go to the upland and some people come up here just to take the long drop. I could never figure what her reasons were . . .

but . . . she was never hanging three points fast to the wall, y'know? You get the Anvil-eyes bad enough . . . some day the hammer gets you. The hammer got her rightly."

"I guess it did. The question is, what am I doing here?" Gabriel asked quietly.

"Ah, yah. Shhh, oh, you've got the appetite tonight," Kipper murmured to his daughter, then, "Oh, I one-eyed you up in Orbit 1, comin' through customs with the crowds. That's what I do, I work up there as a deck-hand and check out the incoming and you were hard to miss. One Earthman walks a head taller than the masses, know what I mean? And you sure entered center-screen on the long drop in the shuttle . . . chasing rodents, wasn't it? By the way, you ever get in the squeezies with that sweet girlie-girl?" Kipper added hopefully.

Gabriel shook his head.

"Well, there's them that does and them that sits with their balls in ice packs," Kipper remarked ruefully. "Anyway, I sent the word down and came down with you to caretake. And there you've been and here you are. And, dilly, have you stirred up a nest of cockroaches!"

"It wasn't part of my vacation plans."

Kipper cackled loudly and long and even Sharry seemed amused. Then, suddenly as it began, his laughter broke off and he looked toward the door. The same instant Toh stood up and Sharry reached for a roll of some filmy substance lying next to the bed.

A moment later the door opened to admit another ragged individual. He looked to be clad in sackcloth, bound tightly around his arms and legs. His face was bearded and his head strip-shaved, nose like an axe-head between small eyes. He had slaphappies on his hands and feet.

"Monk." Kipper waggled a hand in greeting.

"Lazarus sent me. Big company topside," said Monk, and nodded at Gabriel. "That gotta be him."

"That's him," Toh acknowledged.

"Welcome to the uplands," said Monk gravely.

Sharry had been wrapping a length of film around her upper torso. "Kipper." she tossed him the roll. With practiced movements Kipper wound the film around the child, until the child was encased in a gleaming cocoon. Then he got up and walked over to Sharry, who turned her back to him. Kipper spun the child about and pressed her back against Sharry's. She stuck fast.

Toh beckoned to Gabriel, and said, "Let's go, you're on . . . watch your arm, I didn't patch it together for you to strip it apart again."

Gabriel said urgently, "Kipper. Can you get me out of here? Can you get me out of Kyara?"

Kipper's head twitched like a gecko's and he stared at Gabriel side-on. His grin was a mask. "Who knows? I'm not the person you should be asking. Come on. Our way is your way." He motioned at the door.

Gabriel hesitated for a fraction of an instant—he was without shoes and his slaphappies had disappeared. But there was no mistaking the determination in the features of the four roofrunners. He shrugged and reached up to rearrange his ponytail. "It's your show . . . and thanks," he added warmly, hoping to irritate Toh. Toh scowled and Gabriel decided that he was liking Toh better every minute. *Never trust a man you can't piss off.*

Kipper gave a cackle as he ushered Gabriel out of the door.

Gabriel found himself in another hangcar with opaqued windows, squashed in the backseat between Toh and Monk. The ride was long. At length the hangcar slowed and sank to ground level. "I thought you people were roofrunners. You don't seem to spend much time up there," he grumbled as he climbed stiffly out of the cabin.

"Even the beasts of the field and the birds of the air go to ground on a bad day," replied Monk, unfazed. He leaned into the car and muttered something into the dashboard. "Half-hour holding pattern, be back here every thirty minutes," he told Kipper, as the car rose and slid away down its track.

The five of them were standing in a small, dark square. A cleaning pod swish-swished its way around the square's edges. On the sullen green-gray walls graffiti flashed and writhed, mad, luminescent visages and fragments of hole-in-pocket wisdom. Gabriel had forgotten; in hi-tech cities the graffiti moved. A line of lime green text near the ground caught his eye, jigging its way along the bottom edge of the wall:

> *"A great thought was thought here and immediately forgotten"*

"Remind me to ask you what it was," Gabriel muttered as the words disappeared around a corner. *These buggers could use all the ideas they can get.*

A set of slaphappies was pressed into his hands, and Kipper said, "The words of the poets are alive and well. Throw these on and let's go."

They made their way up an emergency stairway inside one of the buildings, then slipped out of a broken window and slaphappied their way up the rest of the way. Gabriel balked slightly as they maneuvered him onto the sill—his right arm was useless for any kind of climbing. But Toh and Kipper flanked him, holding him fast whilst they climbed "two-point" themselves. Sharry led the way, the infant asleep on her back and dreaming woolly dreams.

At the roof's edge Kipper gave a whistle and slaphappied hands emerged to pull Gabriel up and to safety.

He was standing on a smooth, flat roof that gently sloped up to a huge, glistening, abstract, black-glass sculpture, towering fifty meters above the roof.

Scattered along the roof on either side of him were thirty or forty roofrunners, squatting in the pools of their own shadows, like emaciated toads. They were, without exception, ragged and wild-haired, though not in a way that indicated poverty or lack of pride. More like itinerant wanderers than vagrants. Around two there was a circle of empty space, as if no one dared venture nearer. Gabriel understood: reekers.

A third circle of emptiness surrounded a dark corner under the overhanging sculpture and, squinting, Gabriel could make out a lanky silhouette reclining there. Another reeker. The two in the open were a dough-faced man with a wandering smile and a raggedy-Ann woman, swaddled in mauve bandages down to her wrists and ankles.

Another woman, raven-haired, crouching with her left leg hanging over the edge of the roof, slowly raised herself to her feet. She glared at the newcomers, turquoise eyes rippling over a wolverine snarl. Her face was beautiful, brittle, like unbaked porcelein.

"Well, well, well. Look what the cleaning pod's dragged in, Kipper. This the flatfoot the toymen are all looking for?" she drawled.

"They got better taste than to be looking for you, Snapper," replied Kipper cheerfully.

"Upside of you to turn up, now that you've got every spook in flatland up round our ears. They've already picked up Dogheart and Bannerman!"

"They *always* pick up Dogheart and Bannerman! Those two couldn't find their way anywhere above the second story if they had road maps tattooed to their foreskins. The spooks won't get widdle out of them anyway."

"We did what we were supposed to, Snapper. If something went downside and leaked out, it has here at homeroof," Sharry put in, as Toh peeled the still-sleeping baby off her back.

"And that opens the old can of Q-marks, doesn't it?" added Kipper gleefully.

Snapper scowled. "You better watch your grip, Kipper. You've been spending so much time in flatfeet country your slaphappies are getting greasy."

"The day I lose my grip, it'll be on the snail-trail you left behind, Snap, my queenie-queen."

"Oooooh!" chorused several delighted voices. The dough-faced reeker collapsed in a heap of giggles.

Snapper rose to her toes. Suddenly she cartwheeled along the edge of the roof toward Gabriel, fingertips and toes pattering along the rim. She came to a stop before him, balancing on the balls of her feet, her heels hanging out over the edge of the roof, the slip of a toe away from a thirty-story plunge. But she stood solid and Gabriel had no doubt that if he tried to dislodge her, he would be the one taking the long drop.

"Care to dance, flatfeet?" she cooed.

Oh, no, Gabriel sighed inwardly. Through the corner of his eye Gabriel saw the other roofrunners watching him expectantly. Kipper's face was unreadable. *A test? Initiation? Shit.*

After a moment's reflection Gabriel resignedly broke

out his easy smile. Fine. But if he needed to make a
point, it was as well that that point were well made. "My
pleasure," he said amiably. "Be right with you, don't
move." With his left hand he reached down and peeled
off the slaphappies on his feet. Snapper's eyes narrowed.

He had her attention.

Barefoot, he straightened up, adjusted his ponytail and
held out his good hand, palm down. "You on?" He
stared at her and let death creep up onto his shoulder.
Snapper hesitated, just a minute hesitation, but she knew
he had caught it. Defiantly she held her right hand out.
Slap! Gabriel's slaphappy palm gripped hers, his eyes
never wavering.

Keeping her at arm's length he circled until they were
standing side by side, backs to the seventy-meter chasm.
Very carefully he did not look down. He kept his features immobile, whispering silently, *Don't look down,
don't look down, only idiots look down, is this bitchkitty
worth it? No, but Elspeth is, Isadora is . . .*

Slowly he shifted his right foot backward so that his
heel was hanging over the edge. Kipper shifted uneasily.
Gabriel could feel Snapper's hand instinctively loosening
its grip. Much good it would do her. They were slap-
happy-bonded, bonded for life. *Or a long drop.*

Steadysteadysteadysteadysteadysteady . . . His right foot
took his weight, his calf muscle trembling as he brought
his left foot back and stood, balancing on his toes and
noticing, belatedly, that slaphappy slippers gave you
sweaty feet. Roofrunners stirred, glancing up-roof over
their shoulders.

*Steadysteadysteady . . . This would be easy if you were
three feet off the ground . . .*

Except that he wasn't. He could feel himself losing it.
Snapper leaned forward fractionally. Automatically Gabriel leaned back. The chasm touched the back of his
collar and ever so gently *pulled.* His left foot slid a bare
millimeter. He felt his weight go to his right foot, saw
his hand reach forward. His mouth opened to release a
shout which died stillborn, as he heard Snapper yell,
"Loose!"

Slap! Slap! Slap! Three roofrunners were a chain jerking Snapper and himself forward to safety. His feet shot
back, his right arm darted out to break his fall, then

changed its mind. A moment later he was being helped
painfully to his feet by Kipper and Sharry and somebody
else was peeling his palm loose from Snapper's.

"You've got a slight coordination problem, stike."
Kipper was cackling. "First the arm, now the knees."

Gabriel saw Snapper's turquoise glare stabbing out at
him from between two roofrunner heads, a witch's broth
of equal parts fury and reluctant respect. She had
blinked first.

. . . *By a midgie's eyelash,* Gabriel thought, *and she
knows it.*

He searched the other roofrunner faces and found
both respect and trepidation. Toh was looking sour as
lime peel, as if he had had his worst suspicions realized.
Kipper was inscrutable mischief.

He also noticed that his slaphappy slippers were gone
and that nobody was offering to give them back.

So the point had been well made. The only question
was, which point? What was he now in their eyes?

"It's been a ball, dilly." Snapper's drawl trailed back
over her shoulder as she walked casually away. "Maybe
sometime we'll make the sweet-time nose to nose on a
dark wall somewhere and I'll show you some spider
tricks."

Sharry muttered, "One day she's going to lose her
three-point and end up with her nooglies spread all over
the flatlands from here to Bugout Plaza. You won't catch
me shedding anything but skin."

The dough-faced reeker rolled toward Gabriel, sending roofrunners shuffling aside. "I reckon if Kipper says
you're upside and Lazarus says the same, then . . . we
were all flatfeet once."

Kipper threw Gabriel a shrewd but not unfriendly
glance. "I reckon he's a flatfoot who's seen places.
Hangs the slaphappies like he grew them."

"Welcome upland," the female reeker said, and she
was echoed by several "Welcomes" and one "Chuck the
flatfoot over the side."

Gabriel looked about at the tangle of kobold limbs
and slaphappy palms raised in greeting and thought
wryly, *Welcome to the tribes of Kyara, bring your own
fleas.* And Lazarus Wight, "the One" of this tribe
wanted a word in his shell-like ear? *What the hell does*

HE think I've got? The more Gabriel thought about it the less he relished the idea of meeting this Lazarus Wight. He surveyed the area behind the throng, seeking some way out of here. Without his slaphappy slippers—who was he kidding?—even *with* them the prospects were not good.

" 'Ware cleaner!" called someone suddenly.

A cleaning pod on jackstraw legs picked its way over the lip of the roof. A couple of roofrunners eased lazily out of its path, but the cleaning pod did not seem to notice the alien presence in its domain.

"Blinded," commented Kipper. "All the cleaners round here operate off one central brain. Get a finger in the single-crystal circuit pie that controls them and you can fix it so the dillies don't 'see' anything human-shaped, they don't register it. Still got to sideline yourself when they're comin' or they hit you and sound the alarm out rightly and the whole world knows you're here."

"Your sister was upside at that kind of thing. A really real specialist with the single-crystal touch." The dark figure up in the far corner spoke for the first time. "We got her into the brain and she blinded every cleaner on this whole block." He leaned forward slightly and Gabriel's eyes widened.

It was the reeker from the first day at the spaceport.

The haunted look was still there, the ashen, pain-lined face smiled a death's-head smile and his head was a ragged narcissus of short, white-blond hair. Stick-insect limbs pulled a mantid body forward as he moved into the light. "Guess you made it to the upland after all," said the reeker with a rattle of beads, the smile shriveling into a grimace and then back to a smile for just an instant.

And Gabriel understood.

The Stick-insect man inclined his head toward Kipper. "You had an honor guard coming down and a reception committee upon arrival and you never noticed either of them. That either makes you a saint or a little self-absorbed. Which is it?"

"Maybe I just need a good breakfast to get my head out of my ass," suggested Gabriel.

The reeker laughed quietly through clenched teeth. "Well, the big town doesn't seem to have gotten you down any, Gabriel Kylie. By the way, my name is Lazarus Wight."

pulse

Elspeth's journal:

I've found a place to rest my soles. I can put my toes in that sand and imagine I'm home. The ground smells right, it touches right, it eyes right, it tastes right, but it doesn't sing to me. There's no Path of Song leading through this dirty little garden. There's just the sand and the stones and the shadow of the eucalyptus tree and a big, empty, hurty space in my breast, between my heart and home. I know it will never close up. I know it won't. It's already too late.

Imagine if his brother had been intelligent. Imagine if he'd had the kind of brother you could wrestle with, the kind who would compete with you for girls, put viruses in your V.T. games, exchange black eyes and insults and peace made with shrugs and sheepish grins. Imagine if Mother had not spent half her time with her head in the V.T., hadn't seen the program on ancient Earth religions, had not adopted historical Japan's Buddhist beliefs, muddied by centuries of secondhand interpretation.

When the Down's syndrome characteristics had shown up in the unborn uterus, she might have had the pregnancy medically redirected *in utero*. It would have extended the pregnancy by a month or so, but the baby would have been normal.

She had chosen not to.

As Hitedoro Izeki watched his brother clear the breakfast table, fastidiously placing the plates, forks, spoons, glasses, into the disposal slot along with the leftovers, he was once again grateful at mother-san's choice. These breakfasts with his brother and his brother's wife, Aysha, did him good. At those times when the dirt from the streets would build up and start to suffocate his spirit, when he would wake up at night sweating Bugout Plaza, the taste of corruption on his tongue, the stench of lies on his breath. Then he would come here within these walls, with their simple dreams and transparent desires, and he would be clean again.

"Why are you sad?" Isaao had finished clearing away the dishes and was standing, watching him. Hitedoro noticed a sliver of fried egg clinging to Isaao's sleeve. He plucked a tissue from the table dispenser and gently wiped it away, holding Isaao's wrist steady with his other hand.

"It's not sad, Isaao . . . it just feels like that sometimes when things are good," he murmured. "You know what I mean?"

Isaao frowned. "I think so. I get that sometimes when I look at Aysha. It feels so good that she's there that it . . . you know, it hurts."

Aysha, pulling on her shoes in the corner, colored and shook her head happily, avoiding the men's gaze.

Hitedoro smiled. "Yeah, that's it." He reflected, what were the chances of a soul like Isaao finding another Down's syndrome victim in a city like Kyara where Down's could be remedied by a simple intrauterine treatment. And being able to marry her? And yet one day Aysha had appeared and Isaao had found that which had been denied Hitedoro. Not that Hitedoro had not been married, but the union had not been a happy one and the parting less so. In the giddy enthusiasm of new-found love he and Elena had taken a ten-year contract with no annual review-and-opt-out clauses. One year later things were ugly. From the moment that they palmed and ret-sealed the bloodstained divorce agreement they had never spoken again.

"Here, let me help you with that." Hitedoro made to assist Isaao with his work overalls but Isaao shook him off.

"I can do it, I do it every day, you know. I'm not helpless."

"He's never helpless," whispered Aysha in agreement.

"No," Hitedoro agreed wryly, "you're never helpless." Still, he'd had to bail the couple out of trouble more than once down on the quickfarms.

"A man's got to feed himself with his own hands," Mother had always said. Easy for her to say, but just as well. For a treatable birth defect like Down's the state provided no pension plan.

The job at the quickfarm was the first one that Isaao had managed to sustain for any length of time. Hitedoro had succeeded in getting him in with the live produce, knowing that the vegetables and fruit there were a lot more tangible to someone like Isaao than the yeastvats that bred the raw material for food-synthesizers.

Both Isaao and Aysha were starting to become restless. Hitedoro knew that they were worried about being late for work. He let his reverie drift away and reached for his coat.

Bidding farewell to Isaao and Aysha, Hitedoro stepped out onto the street. The morning crowd was moving like thick dough, the kind of disjointed flow that spoke of police presence somewhere nearby. A quick glance left and right and he'd spotted it. He did not even need to see the green-and-silver TARC uniform to know that it was he the robot was waiting for.

"Officer Izeki."

Hitedoro glanced at the serial number and recognized an old acquaintance. "Hullo, Lobo, who's got your leash today?" he drawled. "Or can I guess?"

Lobo indicated a hangcar hovering by the street corner. "My superior officer would like a word with you. He's waiting in the hangcar."

"He would be."

The hangcar door yawned black and he climbed inside. The robot slipped into the driver's seat and the hangcar was rising even before the door murmured shut behind him. The only other occupant of the car examined him with lead gray eyes.

"Officer Izeki," he said politely.

"What can I do for you, Officer Leel?" Hitedoro replied, disliking the courtesy, recognizing the politesse for the cupboard love that it was.

"You no doubt know about Gabriel Kylie's escape last night?" Pelham Leel said.

"Seeing as I'm not deaf, blind, or brain-dead, yeah. Word got around." Hitedoro let some satisfaction creep through.

"Then you also know that he got broken out by roofrunners."

"Yeah." Hitedoro frowned. "I heard that, too. That's the part that doesn't make much sense."

"Yes, well it's just another question to be added to the growing list on Mr. Kylie," Leel said sourly. "You met him; what was your impression of him?"

Hitedoro's chubby features molded themselves into a smirk. "Sterike, you must be up against it if you give a downland spit about what the Municipals think."

"Not the Municipals. Just you."

"Yeah, you're up against it." Hitedoro chuckled grimly.

Leel did not react. He held out his left fist. "Do you recognize this?" The fist unfurled like a deadly flower to reveal a tiny jacinth fish, lying in the center of Leel's palm.

An icy finger ran down Hitedoro's spine.

"Ah." Leel nodded with satisfaction. "Then I'm sure you can tell me where we found it."

Hitedoro hid his suddenly shaky hands by searching his coat for his bubble of nicotine root. "You tell me," he said in as even a voice as he could muster.

"We searched Kylie's hotel room, of course. We found this and several other items belonging to the late Nerita Elspeth Kylie inside a sealed envelope . . . just like the ones I use in my office, funnily enough. And yours."

"No kidding."

"No. No kidding. It just so happens that we did some cross-checking in our records. The items we found were listed amongst those that were in Ms. Nerita Elspeth Kylie's possession at the time of her death. The list was made out by yourself, Officer Izeki. Apparently I made a slight blunder when I collected the evidence from your office"—Leel managed to look a little sheepish—"and I never picked these up. Which means they stayed in your possession. Now, what I was hoping you could help me with, Officer Izeki, was how they came to be in Gabriel Kylie's possession."

Quickly Hitedoro ran through the facts in his mind,

but there was no way around this. Leel already knew and he could prove it. The only way was to brazen it out. He matched Leel's stare and slipped a nicotine root into his mouth.

"I gave them to him."

"Of course you did. Now let me ask you something else. Why did you become a policeman?"

Hitedoro was taken aback. "What?"

"Humor me, I'm interested. Why did you become a policeman?"

Hitedoro hesitated. "The same reason as most, I thought I could help. I thought . . . you get respect."

"But you didn't. Instead you'd tell people what you did for a living and suddenly the conversation would die. And in a crowded room you'd have a bigger circle of empty floor around you than a reeker. So you started lying at dinner parties, telling people that you were . . . what? An INworld program salesman?"

"No. Other things sometimes."

"Right. Other things. Anything except the truth."

"Look, is this going to take much longer?"

"Officer Izeki, I'm just trying to make a point here," Leel said soothingly.

"Well then make it!"

Leel leaned back and regarded Izeke sadly. He sighed. "Do you know why I joined the Targeting, Apprehension and Remand Central?"

Hitedoro shook his head slowly.

"Same reasons you did. Games. Children's games. Tag through the Halls, hide-and-seek, tracking each other on the Worm, one to one on the Virtuals. The goodies and the baddies," Leel's hand described a metronome. "Just like you, I decided I wanted to be with the goodies. No?"

"Maybe."

"Maybe, yes. Well, that's why we're sitting here, Officer Izeki, to make sure we both understand the distinction." Leel tossed the jacinth fish into the air and caught it." He held out the closed fist again. "Let me clarify." He leaned forward. "Reporting Kylie's visit to me: that was good. Witholding material evidence in a murder investigation and then turning it over to what is now a

wanted felon,"—the hand blossomed again, empty—
"that was bad."

Abruptly Hitedoro grew weary of Leel's baiting.
"Who d'you think you're talking to, Leel, some flockin'
infant? You think this puppetmaster TARC shit scares
me? You got something clear to say, then get it said.
Otherwise, do what you've got to do and you let me
out here!"

Leel's expression was stony. "You could go into Retreat for what you've done, Officer. Who'd look after
your family then?"

"My . . . family?" Hitedoro stopped, shocked,

Leel leaned back in his seat and called forward to the
robot, "Take us for another round, Lobo." He stared
out of the moment out of the window, his face suddenly
a twitching mask of agitation. "Do you read history, Officer?" he asked absently.

"No."

"Nor do I." The myriad parts of his face closed ranks
again. "I know I should, but it's a bore. I did hear once,
though, about pre-Plague Earth. There was a disease
called leprosy. It was rampant in underdeveloped parts
of the world. The irony, though, was that you were far
better off catching it in the parts of the world least
equipped to deal with it, medically speaking, then in the
high-tech areas with all their advanced medical facilities—I'm talking relatively, of course, all very primitive
by our standards. Because there was so much leprosy in
the poorer areas they were quicker to recognize it and
your chances of getting it treated at an early stage were
better. The point is"—and here Leel turned back to
Hitedoro very calmly—"our society is oddly ill-equipped
to deal with the kind of theoretically curable afflictions
like that of your brother. You must worry sometimes
what he would do if one day you were not around to
help him out of trouble."

Hitedoro whispered, "You piece of GenTec slime! I'll
have you six ways for Privacy breach!"

"Privacy breach?" Leel looked amused. "You'd have
to prove an awful lot, Officer, about where I got my
information, or even that I had it. Or are you expecting
Lobo here to testify on your behalf?" Leel sighed. "You
know, police work hasn't changed an awful lot in the

past couple hundred years. We keep finding new methods, the baddies find ways of getting around half of them, the law courts ban the rest.

"Fingerprints? Inadmissible, too easy to fake. Photographs? Hol or 2-D, still or moving, can't prove a thing. Voiceprints? What else? There was a brief time when all these things were conclusive proof that could send you to Retreat. Forget lie detectors or psych-Probes now. The Privacy laws took care of those. You virtually need to be able to prove guilt on available evidence to be able to administer them. So we're back to the plod. Motives, witnesses, it's basically like pre-tech times again.

"Which makes it so important that people like you and I remember which side of the line we're standing. You understand? Basically, you and I want the same thing." Leel gestured at the window. "Out there. We're the street cleaners. That's our work. We keep it all clean. And what we can't clean up"—he shrugged—"we make sure it goes somewhere where people don't trip over it. The law that we uphold is not our friend. Our friend is that thin line. We're on one side, and the garbage is on the other." Leel pursed his lips and raised an eyebrow. "It's important for you to know where you are."

Hitedoro swallowed. "I know where I am."

"Good." the jacinth fish appeared again, a glittering arc drawn through the air, from hand to hand. "We can forget about this"—Leel's eyes hardened—"but I want Kylie."

"How did . . . ?" Hitedoro hesitated, knowing that his asking would only irritate Leel. "The reports. Nothing was said about how the Daud woman died."

Leel's reaction surprised Hitedoro. He leaned in, eyes locked on Hitedoro's as if imparting a secret. "We didn't know until last night, it took all day to pin it down. Statrecks. It's a specialized poison used in GenTec labs to paralyze the heart muscles. It was injected into her wrist. Her window was broken in—probably some kind of subsonic pulse, going by the fragment distribution—and whoever did it ransacked her apartment." He paused for effect. "She lived on the tenth floor."

"Roofrunners?" Hitedoro looked disbelieving. Roofrunners tended to be misanthropes, with a bent for theft and other petty crime among the extreme cases, but not murderers.

Leel was unequivocal. "Has to be."

Hitedoro thought for a moment. "You've tried . . . the people he was with?"

"I'm not blind or brain-dead either. We've got the tick he was seeing under surveillance, that's all covered. Anything she does or says we'll know about and we made sure to muck with her head a little when we had her in the tank. She doesn't know which way is south." His face twisted into a gleeful smirk. "But you're out there on the streets and in the Halls, Officer Izeki, Lobo!" The car started descending and slowed. "Have I made myself clear?"

"I don't want any of your Central clowns shadowing me."

Leel's nostrils flared. "You choose your own course, Izeki, but I want Kylie found. You understand me?"

"Yeah"—Hitedoro's tired eyes were seeing very little—"I've got you."

through a glass brightly

Elspeth's journal:

I remember when Dig-Dig went through his initiation. Rumor was they really cut him. They say he wanted it for real, like the old times, and soon Billy Halfpint and the others were all bragging that they'd do it for real, too. Such a bunch of boys! Swinging their lowlives like that makes them men.

Except Gabriel. He just did what he always did and shrugged and said they could do what they wanted, but him? Not him! Grandmother told me that Gabriel and Dig-Dig had had a fight, with Old Man watching. Dig-Dig had said that we were the only people on Earth whose traditions stretched back unbroken to pre-Plague times. Gabriel said, unbroken? How did He know? Here he was—Dig-Dig— the first boy in his family to get circumcised in generations and now he was saying that the tradition was unbroken? Old Man had to pull them apart. Lucky for Dig-Dig, or he might have lost more than his foreskin. Gae's got a sharp smile.

Old Man wasn't smiling though. Nor was Grandmother.

Carla looked up from the diagnostic-screen and shook her curly head. "No, he's okay, he must have been far enough away." She snapped off the diagnostic and pushed her chair back. "Anyway, collateral damage to living tissue from a twigleggy burst is real overrated. You can stare right into one and you'll just see green spots for a day."

"Thanks anyway," said Isadora, relieved, lifting Skunk out of the diagnostic tank and smoothing his fur. "It's just for my peace of mind."

Carla was a slim, gray-haired woman in her mid-fifties and founder of the Real Life Menagerie. She had worked as a vet for twenty-seven years, tending to the ills of a large proportion of Kyara's pet population. At length, wearying of the holographic Adventure Zoos and their bogus representations of animal life in the wild, to say nothing of GenTec Petting Zoos ("Tiger, king of the jungle, deadliest Earth hunter—guaranteed safety-certified"), she had set up the Real Life Menagerie with the help of a group of volunteers, funding the venture out of her own savings.

She talked as she folded up her diagnostic equipment. "Well, if it's for your peace of mind, maybe you can do me an extra favor when you've finished the feeding."

"Sure, anything."

Carla pointed at the Helios weasel, who was still in the cage in which Isadora had brought him. "Your little friend? You can take him off my hands for a day or two until I've got a scent-sealed cage rigged up for him. The two Helios gullipods can smell him and I'm afraid that they're going to go into permanent shock if I have him here for another day."

"Of course." Isadora held up Carla's jacket for her.

"What's a gullipod?" inquired Chuen.

"A Helios weasel's preferred diet."

"Ah."

"And don't forget to give the lynx his powder."

"I'll look after it," Isadora promised, going to the window. "A little daylight wouldn't hurt here, either." She de-opaqued the window and flinched back as a blaze of color flared out at her.

A naked female body, sweat-sheened, squirmed and then morphed into an Atlean male torso and the word "Levinad! The choice of a city!" flashed through all seven colors of the visible spectrum in as many seconds, followed by a flurry of sexual-associative imagery and subliminals.

Isadora groaned. "Aw, Carla, did you forget the shut-out subscription again?"

Advertising on windows was legal, but the broadcasting company was also obliged to offer a service that allowed you to polarize out the broadcast. It was cheap, but occasionally people would forget, and the intensity of the visual barrage was geared to take advantage of those momentary lapses.

Carla shrugged vaguely. "I paid it yesterday, but you know, there's always a delay."

"There never seems to be any delay in messing up your view if you forget to pay," muttered Chuen acidly.

Isadora was stern. "Carla, if they still haven't done anything about it tomorrow, you call Kynan and have him force-feed them some legalese!"

After promising to lock up when she was finished, Isadora ushered Carla out of the door. She turned to find Chuen watching her, a sardonic expression on her face.

"What?" Isadora asked.

"You tell me," Chuen replied.

"Well, look, I'm going to clean up a few things here, finish the feeding, then I'm going home. You don't have to wait for me."

"That's very considerate of you, darling, but you're not getting rid of Chuen that easily."

"What do you mean, 'getting rid of you'?" Isadora feigned innocence. "I don't want to get rid of you."

"No?"

"No," it's just . . ." Isadora avoided her eye. "I just have to finish here and you don't have to wait."

"I'm not leaving until you tell me what you're up to," said Chuen.

"I'm not up to anything," Isadora said ingenuously. "I've just had a stinker of a night . . . and I want some time to myself if you must know."

Chuen regarded her coldly. "You're really not learning, are you."

"Learning what?"

"Learning you know what! The moment I'm through that door you're going to get behind that computer terminal and go digging through cyberspace."

Isadora sighed in exasperation. "Alright, maybe I am, but that's not your business, it's mine!"

"Bullyshag."

"*Yes* . . . it's my business! Look, I don't want you

involved. You don't need to be and it's better that you weren't, alright?" Isadora turned her back on her friend and made herself busy with the sheaves of plaspyrus that she had brought from her apartment. "You've done enough. Thank you. Now please go." She waited.

Chuen's angry breath hissed through her teeth. "You're something, you know, Iz. What is it with this Gabriel stike? You know, I've seen you do it again and again, with one loser after another . . . what was that, last year, you had that D.N.Amics exec? The one with the dino-sized credit account and the INworld fetish . . . ?"

"Gabriel's not a loser!"

"No, he's a shagging criminal! Shit, we *know* he busted out of the TARC tank, everybody on Thor knows about that one now. *They* think he killed some old woman, you told me that yourself!"

"He didn't kill anybody!" Isadora retorted.

"Oh? Oh? How d'you know? How do you know? He told you so? You don't know this man from a GenTec glowworm! How long has he been here and how much of that time have you spent with him? Two hours? One night? Male pheromones getting to you already?"

Isadora spun around and slammed the stack of plas down on the table. "Alright, enough! Okay? Enough! Leave me alone! I had to listen to this all night from the shagging TARCs! I trust him isn't that enough? I trust him!"

"You don't know him!"

"I *trust* him!" Isadora glared wild-eyed at Chuen, conscious as the words left her mouth that she was *not* sure, the image of Gabriel's blood-soaked coat vivid in her mind. "I trust him," she repeated, drawing a shaking hand across her eyes. A growing part of her wanted to cry, to curl up under some fetal carapace and hide from the doubts screaming in her own head.

She looked up and saw Chuen watching her, her face etched hollow, and realized how much her trust in Gabriel was hurting Chuen, almost as much as her implicit distrust in Chuen herself.

"I'm sorry, Chuen." Isadora bit her lip.

Chuen's features softened. "It's alright, Iz," she said kindly. "It's just me. It's still just Chuen, you know?" A tiny light glinted at the corners of her eyes, to disappear in a blink. "Why won't you just . . . let me help?" Without waiting for a reply, Chuen walked over to the terminal and seated herself, her hands in her lap.

Isadora could see that her back was tensed, poised as if for a blow. She swallowed hard and said hoarsely, "Thank's, Chuen, I'd appreciate it." Chuen's neck muscles relaxed and she wriggled her shoulders, loosening them up.

Still hesitant, Isadora took up the pile of plaspyrus from the table and slid a chair up next to Chuen. They exchanged a glance, and it was as if for one moment they shared the gift of their own pain, laid bare the bruises of the soul that are hidden even from a lover. And for an instant Isadora glimpsed the wound of Chuen's love for her and knew what that fleeting nakedness had cost her friend. Isadora looked away, regretting the chasm which would always lie between them, knowing the impossibility of desiring to desire that which one did not even wish to desire.

Chuen smiled sadly and laid her hands on the keypad, taking a deep breath. "Computer on," she said, and the holographic display winked to life. "Alright, Iz, so what are we looking for?"

"And don't"—Chuen held up a warning finger at Isadora—"don't try to do me a favor by putting blinkers on me this time."

Relieved but uncertain, Isadora shuffled through the pages of Elspeth's journal. "I don't really know," she said at last. "I . . . don't really know."

"This is not going to get us far," Chuen observed drily.

"No, I know," Isadora agreed unhappily. "Look, maybe you'd better let me do that." She pushed Elspeth's journal at Chuen, but Chuen waved it aside with disdain.

"I don't read hard copy."

"Nor do the scumbags who twigleggied my apartment, which is why we've still got it."

"And which shows a rare display of good taste on their part. You leave this to Chuen. Now tell me, what? Where?"

It came to her. "Far Cry," Isadora said.

"Animal, vegetable or political lobbyist"

"I don't know." Isadora leafed through the stack of paper on the desk. "It's just something Gabriel asked me to look up . . . wait"—she thought for a second—"a ship, it was an expedition."

"Fine." The keypad spattered under Chuen's fingers. "Far Cry. We'll start with those in active service. Um . . . central Ships' Registry . . . okay, accessed. Now, Far Cry. 'F' for 'fons et origo,' the source and the origin." She waited until the words "Error: subject not found" appeared above the hol-screen.

"It was an expedition to the Twist," put in Isadora.

"Uh, some little details help, darling, but not that one, not just now," muttered Chuen. "Alright, let's assume she was permanently dry-docked, we'll go back year by year." Chuen thumbed the light pencil and a flurry of symbols swarmed past. She was humming to herself, "Nothing, nothing, nothing," fitting the words into something posing as a tune. Suddenly the scrolling stopped to be replaced by the words, "Subject found."

"Well, well, well." Chuen's eyebrows described twin arches. She drew the light pencil through the words and Isadora suddenly found herself looking at a ship, floating in miniature above the computer console. It had a classic three-pointed star-shape of a kind rarely seen nowadays, streamlined for entry into the atmosphere and painted pale indigo. Judging from the size of the visible view-windows, she was not large. The words "Far Cry XC73" were stenciled in midnight blue on her sides.

Chuen said, "There she is. I mean, we can go on searching back, but she was already decommissioned twenty years ago. Pretty little thing."

Isadora did not know much about starships and murmured noncommittally. A small ship, scrapped some twenty years ago. Now, why would Gabriel have thought this was important? For that matter, was it even the same ship?

Chuen was reading off the ship's technical specifications and ownership papers, "Maximum crew of twelve. Basically a yacht as far as I can tell. A big one, but . . . yeah. Not really built for long hauls. Owned by . . . let's have a look . . . the Xaaron Corporation. Oh." Chuen pulled her chin in and pursed her lips in disappointment.

"What? What's that?"

"I haven't the foggiest, that's what's disappointing. Xaaron, Xaaron, Xaaron," Chuen hummed tunelessly. Isadora knew the signs. Chuen was in "search" mode now, at home in her Web. "So where do we go from here? Your expedition? Where did you say it was to?"

Isadora pointed a thumb at the ceiling. "The Twist."

"The Twist? There's nothing there." Chuen pouted. "What was this, some kind of Survey?"

"I don't know, I just know they went there."

"Any idea when?"

"No, Gabriel didn't tell me." Isadora shrugged helplessly.

"Hm!" Chuen snorted. "Not good for much, is he, old Gabriel Cryly . . . joking, joking," she added, forestalling Isadora's angry retort. "But this isn't getting us anywhere."

Isadora mused, "They would have had to have filed a flight plan."

"Tch. They'd dump it out of the computer as soon as the ship got back."

"Assuming they got back."

"Aah, yes, good, darling." Chuen looked pleased. "Now, Space Traffic Control does have lists of ships gone missing, if I can find them. We'll have to check both Intrasystem and Interstellar." She cleared the display, except for the image of the ship, which continued to drift above the desktop, slowly rotating. She reached her hand out to it. The sensor field above the display allowed her to "grasp" the ship, squeeze it a little smaller and place it on the topmost corner of the display.

A quarter of an hour later Isadora was staring in disappointment at the words "Error: subject not found." Chuen, however, was if anything even more pleased.

"Goody, so we know she never went missing," she said gleefully, then she noticed Isadora's despondent face and sighed. "Iz, Iz, how often have I tried to teach you that the word 'error' is a lie perpetuated by linear thinkers. In research there can be no errors. We've just narrowed our search down that much." She held her thumb and forefinger a few millimeters apart.

"I know." Isadora did know, but the romantic in her

had hoped that the ship had gone missing. Far more delicious as a mystery.

"And *I* know," Chuen agreed. "Go out, come back safely, have a drink, very dull. Never mind, look, let's backtrack here a second. Let's check all records of Surveys sent out. If it was a Survey, it'll be listed, unless it was privately owned . . . She broke off, chagrined. "Which it was, of course. Xaaron Corporation. Shag it!"

"Dull," Isadora repeated ruefully. Then she suddenly lit up. "Unless she wasn't so dull. Maybe she wasn't. Maybe she was interesting enough to make the news. Why don't we check media records?"

"What media records?" Chuen scoffed. "Whoever reports a Survey? They're a credit a dozen."

"Presupposition!" accused Isadora. "And anyway, since when do we not check media records *first?*"

"Touché, shame on me," agreed Chuen. "We don't even know for sure it was a Survey. You're learning. Media files it is. We'll cross-reference *Far Cry* with the Twist . . . and Beacon, just for good measure," she added.

Whilst they waited for the computer to complete its search Chuen ran her hands back and forth over her shaved pate. The tattoo on her forehead yawned and grinned with the movement of her scalp. She was clearly happier now and Isadora envied her that happiness and her ability as a researcher. Isadora was an above-average researcher at best, not through any lack of intelligence, but because she lacked that pit-bull determination which would seize a problem and worry it and worry it until it surrendered. That and Chuen's willingness to accept the open-endedness of an assignment, not projecting a particular goal, but allowing the trail to wend where it might.

For that matter, Isadora had never, in all her thirty-three years, shown any marked brilliance for anything that she had done, not during her years in the GenTec labs at D.N.Amics, nor in her studies before that. She wryly recognized that secret, subversive part of her which whispered the lie that one day she would be "discovered." And with sadness she also knew the lie for what it was.

Suddenly the display froze.

"Bingo! Subject found. Dead man's knickers, you were right!"

Leaving her musings, Isadora studied the display. "Two files, one year apart. Try the second one first."

"No, we'll try the first one first," said Chuen calmly. "That's why it's the first one." Success always seem to make her icy cool. She called up the first file and found a list of articles from all the major broadcasters, all from within a three-day period. She selected the Duas Voces entries. The first one read:

"SURVEY SHIP ON LONG DROP!

In the latest in a recent series of intraorbit mishaps, Space Traffic Control has reported that a Survey ship, with its crew of nine on board, is presently headed on an inward spiral which should bring it into collision with the surface of Thor in a matter of hours.

The Xaaron Corporation vessel *Far Cry,* returning from a three-month survey of the Twist nebulae and its environs, suffered a sub-light drive failure at 05.32 local/ship's time. Although the captain, Jean-Claude Barr, describes their present situation as grave, he has expressed cautious optimism that the crew will be able to restart the drive before their present course causes their ship to impact near Thor's southern pole. The crew is presently in contact with technicians on Orbit 1 and their combined attempts to trace the source of the drive failure are said to be yielding some concrete results. Barr's tone was more upbeat than that of S.T.C., which stated this morning that they have no available ship able to match course and rescue the crew within an acceptable margin of risk. Meanwhile they are diverting two satellites whose course intersects that of the *Far Cry.*"

The entry for the following day read:

"LONG DROP AVERTED!

Disaster was narrowly averted for the crew of the Xaaron Corporation vessel *Far Cry,* trapped in a collision course with Thor's surface yesterday, as a result of drive failure. Less than an hour before impact the ship's crew succeeded in restarting the drive, using procedures that Captain Jean-Claude Barr describes as "eat it or meet it." The low angle of impact meant that only a minimal course adjustment was necessary to avert a crash. As it was, the *Far Cry's* course brought the ship to within two and a half kilometers of Thor's surface, the closest ever flyby by a ship without Icarus Field shielding. The ship is said to have suffered severe structural damage and several of the crew are presently receiving onboard medical treatment for injuries sustained by exposure to gravity stresses of over seven gees.

In contradiction to yesterday's statements Space Traffic Control now claims to have had two ships on standby, which might have effected a rescue of the crew in the early stages of the incident."

The third Duas Voces article consisted of a brief entry covering the safe arrival of the *Far Cry* back at Orbit 3 Station. Isadora and Chuen patiently scanned all the other media references to the incident without finding anything new.

"Alright," said Isadora at last, "let's have a look at that second entry."

"Hm?" Chuen seemed momentarily distracted. "One thing at a time. We might get some more background on this direct from Duas Voces' research files. They were bound to have done a bit of background work on this."

Isadora was dubious. "Even after twenty years? Anything that small they'd have dumped by now."

"You'd be surprised. The copy was written by . . . Del Schultz? Never heard of him. Probably retired to fondle himself on the INworld. Still, they'd have kept whatever his references were in the background files."

She accessed Duas Voces' research files, palming the computer's palmplate to identify herself. "Well, at least I'm still on the payroll," she observed drily, as the Duas Voces' system granted her ingress.

But as it turned out Isadora was right—there was no background, or references at all to the articles. "That's not right," Chuen grunted. "Someone's been very sloppy. Or else . . . Hmm . . . However—" Chuen's mouth drew into a thin line as she considered. She seemed to be trying to make up her mind about something. Isadora waited expectantly.

"Okay," Chuen said decisively, "Chuen's going to let you in on a little secret. Oath of silence."

"Hm? Oh, of course," Isadora affirmed mildly.

Chuen's eye took on a wicked glint. "I have a back door into Eye-I-Eye Broadcasting's research library."

Astonished, Isadora exclaimed, "You're beating rags!" If there was one thing all the Kyaran news services guarded more closely than a Vestal her chastity, it was their own background files.

"Would I lie to you? I haven't used it in a while and I try not to, but this seems to be a good time." Then she added sternly, "But you spill this to Marush or anybody . . . !"

Isadora did not need the warning. She also didn't need to mention that Chuen's back door might be monitored and that if someone decided to trace precisely who it was accessing Eye-I-Eye's information library, they could find themselves cut off and facing a computer-theft suit.

Isadora waited eagerly whilst Chuen accessed a line to Eye-I-Eye and then conducted the surreal on-line conversation, made up of words, numbers and images, that made up the back door's security code.

"Still open," Chuen sighed, pleased, as the Eye-I-Eye library menu flickered up on the display. After that it was simply a matter of calling up the background files on the *Far Cry* articles again.

The technician who had come across Chuen's back door during a routine operation on Eye-I-Eye's cyber-space had been discreet. He had not closed it. Instead he had set up an alarm system that would cause a light to flash on a certain holo-display—presently unmanned—in the Eye-I-Eye newsrooms. That light began flashing now, awaiting the touch of a single button that would spring the toothsome little booby trap that he had assembled during a three-day sick leave. He had been ludicrously proud of it and had dubbed it *Dust Devil.*

The two women quickly scrolled through the dozens of pages detailing the ship's manifest for this voyage: its projected course, its mission—it was indeed an exploratory Survey mission—its estimated cost, and so forth. When they came to the crew list, however, Isadora's hand slapped down and stopped the scrolling.

Crew register/Xaaron Corp. Vessel Far Cry/XC 73/ 34.TVT/E§¶c

Jean-Claude Barr	Captain, Astrogator
Ellis Quinn Macintire	1st officer, Engineer
Maria Delaney	Astronomer
Philip Mwabea	Geologist
Sian Harewood	Biologist/as.Physician
Kam Fong	Biologist
Heloise Amiée	Physicist
Jaap Esterhuis	Chemist
Chao Gan Tai	Physician

As she scanned the list Isadora felt a mounting excitement. "Sterike!" she whispered. "I've seen this! I've seen this before! Here—" She grabbed Elspeth's journal and started riffling through the pages. After a few moments she found what she was looking for and slapped the page down on the desk. "There!" She pointed triumphantly at a list of names scrawled in the top left-hand corner.

Jean-Claude Barr
Chao Gan Tai
Maria Delaney
Heloise Amiée
Jaap Esterhuis
Kam Fong
Sian Harewood
Ellis Quinn Macintire
Philip Mwabea

Chuen examined it curiously. "Right, so she got there first. Why though? And what's this?" Her finger indicated a faint arrow from the name Kam Fong, pointing to two words scrawled almost illegibly.

"Loki file," read Isadora.

"What's a loki?" asked Chuen.

"Not a loki, *the* Loki. This I know," said Isadora, pleased to be able to demonstrate some knowledge of her own. "I remember this from an article I researched on Thor's origins. Loki was another Nordic god, a sort of prankster, a mischief maker. He used to play a lot of tricks on Thor, till he lost a bet with him and they sewed his lips up. The story goes that when he pulled out the stitches his mouth was twisted into a cruel smile forever afterward."

"They sewed his lips up," Chuen mused. "And so silenced him."

Isadora digested this for a moment. "So now we've got something else on the list. Loki file. Let's have a look at that second Far Cry entry."

The second file was dated a year later than the first and consisted of articles spread over a number of weeks. The headline of the first stopped Chuen and Isadora dead in their tracks.

"EXPLOSION ABOARD SURVEY SHIP KILLS ALL ABOARD"

"Sterike!" breathed Isadora.

Chuen read grimly, "The Survey ship *Far Cry*, three days out of Thor, apparently disintegrated two hours ago en route to the Twist Nebula. It is feared that there are no survivors."

The next hour was spent in silence, broken only by the occasional rustle of plaspyrus sheets and whine and skitter of the animals in their pens. The advertisers juggled incandescent images of fear and desire against the window.

The two women skimmed through the articles, seizing on and storing snippets as they went.

"10/2/244 ST . . . the Space Traffic Control ship *Agamemnon*, sent to the last-reported position of the Survey ship *Far Cry*, believed to have exploded three days ago, has reported slight radiation residue in keeping with shield loss on JUMP-drive engines . . ."

"14/2/244 ST . . . A review commission, chaired jointly by the S.T.C department of safety standards

and an investigating team from the T.A.R.C. has been
set up to review the safety record of all ships owned
by the Xaaron Corporation . . ."

"21/2/244 ST . . . A service was held today for the
nine scientists and crew of the Survey ship *Far Cry*.
Family, friends and Xaaron representatives were pres-
ent. The eulogy was spoken by Liam Redfern, a
Byron Cybertree executive and a close friend of Jean-
Claude Barr.

"16/4/244 ST . . . The joint S.T.C./T.A.R.C. comis-
sion reviewing Xaaron Corporation's safety standards
has submitted a decision ruling out any question of
safety standard violations or negligence on the part
of Xaaron. This may prove both a relief and a disappointment for the families of the deceased, who had
threatened legal action in the event of negligence . . .

They mused for a few moments. Then Isadora suggested that they check the crew list for the second expedition. "Elspeth was obviously interested in the crew,"
she pointed out.

"We're assuming that the lady knew something worth
knowing," muttered Chuen as she dug into the background material on the tragedy. At length a list
appeared:

Crew register/Xaaron Corp. Vessel *Far Cry*/XC 73/ 34.TVT/¶A§¶e

Jean-Claude Barr	Captain, Astrogator
Maria Delaney	Astronomer
Ruth Dobrowen	1st officer, Engineer
Chao Gan Tai	Physician
Carole Wojtas	Chemist
Benedetto Gui	Biologist
Philip Mwabea	Geologist
Sian Harewood	Biologist/as.Physician
Abelard Künneke	Physicist

"Five," Isadora breathed. "Five of the original nine."
"So what?" said Chuen, irritated.

"What do you mean 'So what?' "

"I mean, so what? This is nothing. We've got nothing. A Survey ship goes out surveying, it goes out again, has an accident. There are accidents every day! This is nothing."

"Then why would anyone be interested in it?" demanded Isadora. "'Why would Elspeth be interested in it?'"

Chuen shrugged sourly. "Shag it, I hate conspiracy crap." She grunted. "If it wasn't for what happened this morning . . ."

"Suppose," Isadora interrupted impatiently, "supposing . . ." Her eyes widened suddenly. "Sterike . . . supposing . . . they found something out there."

"In the Twist?" Chuen snorted. "What could they have found out there that no one else has ever found?"

"I don't know," Isadora said, her eyes shining. "But that would explain an awful lot."

"About *what?*" Chuen's groaned in disbelief. "We haven't got anything!"

"Okay, you doubt? You doubt? Fine!" Isadora retorted. "But"—her face slipped into a grim smile—"it might be interesting to find out exactly how many Surveys have ever been sent out there."

She studied the little ship again with renewed interest, suddenly appreciating its grace, its petaled delicacy. *Far Cry.* Had those who christened it realized how appropriate their choice of name would one day turn out to be?

Suddenly the ship gave a flicker and it seemed to turn into sand, crumbling in an instant before her eyes. It took a fraction of a second before she realized what was happening, then she cried, *"Virus!"* Even as the cry left her lips she saw Chuen's hand coming down on the mains cutoff switch. The computer went dead and Chuen was swearing, "Shit! Shit! *Shit!* The bastards booby-trapped us! Shot one right back down the line!"

Isadora reached forward and clicked the computer on again, but the display remained blank. "Brilliant," she said bitterly. "Flockin' brilliant."

Chuen's brow was furrowed as she considered. "There could be something left," she muttered. "It looked to me like a bit of an amateur job."

"That dust-blowing-away effect?"

"Yeah, a real pro wouldn't have bothered messing around with display effects; she'd concentrate on maximizing damage. And there was an appreciable delay, so I reckon the guard-dog mechanisms in this unit were putting up a solid fight. Still, there's only one way to find out and that's to yank out the chips and see what we can retrieve from them on another system."

"*Another* system?" Isadora glumly wondered how she was going to justify herself to Carla for having gutted the Menagerie computer. "We," she grumbled, "are running out of computers."

She caught Chuen's eye. Her friend's lips were pressed tight. And suddenly they both burst into laughter simultaneously.

"Ah, sterike!" sighed Chuen, wiping her eyes. "There's nothing like a little paranoia to end the day."

Electronic surveillance had never been so difficult. Yet, ironically, the technology for carrying it out had never been so refined. The section on Forbidden Technologies in the tome that was the Privacy Law Statutes ran to thousands of screen pages of design specifications for miniaturized microphone, cameras, long-distance directional pickup devices that enabled you to hear what was said by a person a kilometer away but screened out their neighbor's voice, telephone signal descramblers; scanners for interpreting the electrical activity of the brain, allowing you to analyze what a person in a room was saying without having to hear their voice; the list was endless.

The field of Privacy Law was pitted with gray areas, but in the area of surveillance they were clear-cut and they were *enforced*. Eavesdropping on a telephone conversation without a court order was a mandatory fifteen-year sentence to Retreat, with no possibility of parole or voluntary Adjustment; drilling a hole in a wall for the purpose of a quiet ogle, ten years; planting hidden cameras in a private residence, twenty-five.

But the most powerful deterrent was the ingrained notion, instilled in each individual from birth, of the sanctity of personal privacy. So deep ran this social conditioning that it would simply never occur to a person that the phone card in their pocket collar could be used as a microphone by determined ears.

But the woman monitoring Isadora's phone knew better. She also knew better than to actually listen in on what was said. The conversations recorded would be analyzed shortly by others. And that was fine by her. On this quiet afternoon, ignorance was truly bliss.

conversation

—Any word on Kylie?

—No, none

—Oh, for heaven's sake . . .

—What would you have me do? Robots are useless up there as long as there's any chance of them killing anybody and the damned roofrunners know that. And you can't expect my agents to go leaping about up there the way they do, I mean two of them nearly got themselves killed last night! We're dealing with a bunch of semipsychotic deviants . . .

—Shit! How the hell did they get him out?

—We've been through that.

—I know we've been through that! And I'm still waiting for something other than excuses!

—I don't give excuses.

—No, you don't. What about this missing KV 99 security agent . . . what's his name? Sotack?

—Dana Sotack. You didn't really expect him to turn up just like that, did you?

—If he's alive, yes, so we may be in luck.

—Don't count on it. We'd have an easier time if he were dead. Chances are that he's alive and they don't want him turning up, 'cos that leaves a question of guilt over Kylie's head. And something else. I just got word from the surveillance on the tick. She's been looking into the *Far Cry,* her and her colleague.

—What do they know?

—So far, nothing that isn't on public record. It's more a question of whether or not she can put the pieces together. Moreover she seems to have something on hard copy . . .

—Hard copy?
—Yes, our tick is something of a recessive. We don't
know what it is or where she got it; possibly she received
it from Kylie.
—So what's the significance?
—The Loki file.
—Alright, we shut this whole damned thing down now!
I want it disinfected! Right now!
Disinfected!
—Disinfected.
—From the floor up.
—I'll . . . have to talk to the Watchmaker again.
—I know that. Do it.

the people who see forever

Elspeth's journal:

*I've been out on the Glass Deserts. There's no sand
or dust there, just green, pebbled glass, as far as you
can see. Back in the Dreamtime the ancestors sang
the world into being and left behind them the Paths
of Song, the dreaming-tracks, that join the sacred
places. The sacred places are still there and the elders
still visit them—Grandmother Lalumanji, Old Man
and others—only now they carry a bullroarer in one
hand . . . and a Geiger counter in the other.*

They had gathered in an orifice near the top of the
rooftop sculpture, a black cavern with walls that glittered
like a coal seam. The rooftops of Kyara were laid out
below them like a shattered ice floe. They were close
enough to Kyara's perimeter that the Anvil was visible,
a vast, inky plain that rose and melted into the black sky.

Most of the roofrunners had disbanded, flea-hopping
into the forest of peaks and spires to vanish as locusts
from a barren land. Only fifteen remained, the inner
circle, Gabriel presumed, among them Kipper and his
family, Monk and Snapper. The raven-haired woman reclined in a corner, never moving, just watching, watching. Monk and another woman were busy, up to their
elbows in what appeared to be a bath-sized urn filled
with earth.

The rest of the throng were gathered around a small
fire to one side of the cave. It was barely more than a
flame really, just a fist-sized fuel brick. But an open fire
was the last thing that Gabriel had expected to see in

Kyara and it both comforted him and made him more aware than ever of his solitude. In the darting flames he saw a thousand campfires, scattered like stars in the wake of his life's passage, on worlds as diverse as Terra Nova, Las Palmas and Octavia. Years spent under open skies, breathing the musk of wet tree bark and the sour-sweetness of grass.

God, his missed it so much it hurt.

The cavern was filled with the murmur of conviviality, verbal scrapping and off-color jokes. But Gabriel wryly noted the two roofrunners, hovering alertly near the cavern's entrance. There would be no sudden escapes from here. He felt someone slip down next to him. It was Sharry.

"Tell me about Earth," she asked, observing him shyly through fronds of lank hair. Glancing about him Gabriel realized that he was suddenly the center of attention again. Monk had finished his excavations in the flower-pot and Gabriel saw something already moving in the soil, a thin green shoot that weaved slowly upward like a tiny entranced cobra. GenTec, he realized, his mouth setting in a hard line.

"So, what about it, Gabriel Kylie? Are you our story-teller for the evening?" Lazarus Wight was lounging a strategic distance from everyone else. The roofrunner patois had vanished from his speech, and his voice was soft and chalky.

"Don't know really what there is to tell," Gabriel said uneasily. He was less disturbed by the threat that Lazarus exuded than by his odd magnetism. For moments at a time the brittleness would vanish from Lazarus's features and a weary softness would descend upon him. Gabriel would find himself staring, waiting for that other self to emerge and hoping its attention would linger on him, for just a moment, fulfilling a promise of safety, nurturing, benevolent wisdom. "It's a . . . place," Gabriel went on. "Where d'you want to hear about?"

"Your home," urged Sharry, "tell us about your home."

Gabriel had been afraid of that. "My home's much like your home, just people trying to find their way," he said evasively.

"Aw, come on, stike, big-picture it for us, give us the

seeing eye. What's your home like?" Sharry urged. "It's got to copy a fair way different from Thor. Elspeth showed me a seed once, that she'd brought from back where she lived."

"I know. A parakeelya seed," Gabriel said. He relented in the face of Sharry's palpable disappointment. "The Anvil," he found himself saying. "It's like the Anvil. Flat and . . . but not black . . . red, as far as the eye can see. It's the patient country. Earth's oldest continent. It's so eroded and flat that water doesn't even flow anymore. People come from other places and they think it's dead, dead trees, dead grass, no rain. But, no. It's just being old and patient. It won't rain for years and then one day . . . the rains come. Parakeelya seeds, like the one Elspeth showed you, that have been lying like dead for years, swell up and bloom and in a couple of days it's not the Anvil anymore, it's not old, it's pink with parakeelyas, pink like the palm of a baby's hand. Suddenly a plain becomes a sea. There's even frogs . . . you know what a frog is? Little amphibian. The waterholding frog. It makes a little bag for itself and seals itself up inside and waits there, under the ground. The rains come, the water seeps down to where he's sleeping and before you know it the place is crawling with frogs. Food, drink, sex, babies, it's all got to happen in a few weeks . . ." Gabriel realized that he was smiling like a fond parent and broke off. "It's . . . that way," he said shortly, resentful at having been drawn out in this manner.

Lazarus Wight laughed softly. "It would seem that spinning out a good yarn is up there amongst all your other talents."

"And what other talents are those?" Gabriel inquired coldly.

"You'd know them better than I, although I've witnessed quite a few in the few days you've been on Kyara. Not often I find myself thinking along the same lines as the Thor authorities."

"I'm not sure I want to ask what lines those are."

Lazarus chuckled again, a sound like a steel file on porcelain. "In nature one of the favored ways for a hunter to seize its prey is to adopt the appearance of something innocuous."

"And one of the favored ways for an innocuous prey to escape the hunter is to resemble something deadly," Gabriel returned immediately.

"Quite. So which are you?"

Gabriel bit back his exasperation. *Flock it,* he thought, *doesn't anybody take anything at face value anymore?* He changed the subject.

"What can you tell me about the blue box?"

"The blue box." Lazarus's eyes darted toward Kipper, who smirked and winked at Gabriel. "What do you know about the blue box?"

"You know," Gabriel remarked steadily, "it seems like answering questions with questions is endemic in this town. Any particular reason why?"

"Alright, Gabriel Kylie." Lazarus rose and went over to the GenTec plant, which was now half a meter high and developing its first buds, and caressed one of its leaves. "It was something that your sister was interested in acquiring. She came to us . . . she came to Kipper there . . . asking if we would help her get it." Lazarus shook his head. "Petty larceny is not the kind of endeavor that stimulates my adrenaline."

"What was it that she wanted you to steal?"

"Did I say steal?"

"That's what I heard."

"Did you, Gabriel Kylie?" Lazarus turned on him snarling, his face distorted with rage. "You heard me say 'steal?' And what else did I say, Gabriel Kylie? What else did I say? What are we? A den of footpads? A flock of petty thieves? This is the eagle's nest, Gabriel Kylie!" he screamed. "The eagle's nest!"

Gabriel reared back in shock at this outburst. Most of the assembled roofrunners were studying the floor, except for Kipper, who's eyes were flick-flicking from Lazarus to Gabriel and back. The baby gave a squawk of protest and Toh jiggled her absently back and forth to quieten her. Lazarus turned his attention back to his beanstalk. "So," he said in a calm tone of voice, as if his previous outburst had never taken place, "what else did you hear me say?"

Gabriel was still trying to fathom what had triggered Lazarus's ire in that way, so he said carefully, "You said you didn't indulge in petty larceny."

"Nor do I."

"So what is the blue box?"

Lazarus shrugged. "I don't know. Really. Elspeth considered it important, and the people who own it consider it important as well."

"Well then, who owns it?"

Lazarus raised an eyebrow and lifted his shoulders in a strange shudder. "Do I look like I care? Do I look like the kind of person who cares about such matters? Your sister . . . your sister was a fanatic. Always railing against the powers that be. Fight the powers, fight the powers, fight the powers." Lazarus looked contemptuous.

There was a rustle amongst the throng and Gabriel caught a whiff of food, synthetic, in self-heating packaging. An instant later a steaming carton and a fork were pressed into his hands by Sharry, who gave him a fleeting smile of encouragement.

"Top of the food chain, that's us," remarked Kipper over Gabriel's shoulder. "Every dilly needs a choke and a bite to keep the three-point tight."

Only Lazarus was not eating. He reclined again, surveying his kobold tribe with icy majesty. "Are you a law-abiding man, Gabriel Kylie?"

"Not really," Gabriel said truthfully. "I've never much trusted the Bogy and its ways."

"The Bogy?"

Gabriel shrugged, unwilling to be drawn into whatever web Lazarus was in the process of weaving.

"The Bogy," Lazarus mused, eyeing him. "And what does your Bogy mean to you, Gabriel Kylie?"

Gabriel considered. "It means the oldest protection racket in history," he said at last. "I reckon the government—any government—is just the same old gang who's always wanted to run things. To keep the people loyal they'll make them promises they can't keep, build them roads they don't need and, when all else fails, they'll say, '*We* may be bad but we're protecting you from those clowns just the other side of the mountains. *That's* what you're paying us for. And you *will* pay us. Or you'll pay.' And all down history people have paid, in sweat and blood and their life's purpose."

"And the Law is just a euphemism for 'do it or else,' is that right?" Lazarus added mildly.

Gabriel agreed, somewhat sheepishly. His own arguments always sounded hollow to his own ears when he aired them out loud. Rarely could the inflexible voice of rationality convey the intuitive core of an argument based on feeling.

Lazarus pointed out, "But Earth's got the tightest Privacy Laws in the C.S.S. What's it like to live under them then?"

Gabriel hesitated, reluctant to delve into those memories. "Where I grew up we never paid them a whole lot of attention. We kind of had our own solution."

"And what was that solution?" Lazarus prompted.

Gabriel's smile was wintry. "We minded our own business."

Lazarus stared at him for a moment and then burst into a roar of laughter. The sound was like a shriek of pain. It echoed off the cabin walls like a joyless banshee wail and Gabriel flinched and closed his eyes.

As if by some signal, the rest of the roofrunners began laughing with their reeker chief. Monk came forward and gleefully slapped Gabriel on the back.

"Knew you were our breed of pickle, stike. Saw the Anvil in your eyes the moment I netted you twenty-twenty, and that's rightly right." There was a sense of relief in the air, but Gabriel could not help but ask himself just how eager he was to be adopted by what appeared to be a clan of mad goblins.

Only Kipper seemed to abstain from the general mirth. His smile was broad but thin as plaspyrus.

"I wouldn't laugh too loud." Lazarus's voice eventually cut through the general mirth without his having to raise it. "Our guest's glib little aside has highlighted the differences between revolutionaries and vandals."

"Hay, Laz, the dill's downside on Mighty Mickey," scoffed Monk. "His way is our way, no?"

Lazarus allowed a shoot from the GenTec vine to entwine his finger. "We're living outside the law," he said coolly, "not without it."

"But it's their law," ventured Sharry.

"Whose law? Whose law! It's *our* law, and it's for us to claim back! Do you have any idea—" Lazarus grasped the main stem of the plant, as if meaning to uproot it. It writhed in his grasp like a honey-drowned python. "Do you have any idea what kind of a place we would be living in without the Privacy Laws, or the GenTec laws, or the Proscribed Technology Statutes? "You really think minding our own business is going to be enough here? Look back pre-Plague to see the same things happening then as now. Look what you had then, covert surveillance systems for the government and portable entertainment systems for the folk, and a bit of both for the ticks in the middle, making sure that the flow of information goes both ways. After all, the folk have a right to know. Cameras and microphones the size of pins in the hands of every man, woman and child. The government and citizens playing a glorious game of I-saw-you-first against one another . . . and against themselves."

Lazarus made as if to move toward Sharry, then he remembered himself and for the first time his face softened into a rueful expression. "Ah, Sharry"—he released his grip on the plant stem and stroked it—"what a time. There's only one basic story in fiction and once you've told that same story over and over again, twenty-four hours a day, every day, every year, how long can you keep it up before you've exhausted the possibilities? How long before people turn away from fictional dramas and start filming, recording and watching real-life dramas for entertainment: diseases, accidents, wars, violent crime . . . hah!" He shook his head in disgust. "As if these are any more real than the fictions . . . as if there's any real way of telling the difference. But it's up there on the display, and lo! it must be true!

"But you know, there're only so many accidents that you can watch and will be entertained by, so the folk turn to the only thing left available. The neighbors!"

A few people laughed and Lazarus smiled indulgently. He started to pace the cavern, his arms gesticulating, their motion independent of the rhythm of his speech. Gabriel felt as if he were watching a great boulder rolling down a mountain slope, slowly gathering speed and, with every passing second, becoming more unstoppable and more dangerous and unpredictable.

"Tune in and discover a family more dysfunctional

and miserable than yours," Lazarus whooped, "and they're not fictional, they're real and they live *just across the road!*" His voice returned to normal and he spread his hands. "After all we've got a right to know! The public, the whole unwashed, miserable anthill has a right to flockin' know!" He rasped out a bitter chuckle. "How do you protect yourself? You can stop people from stealing your possessions, but how do you protect yourself against people stealing your *life? Your* life! Your . . . moments. When the thief is too small to see. There is no protection. No *mechanical* protection! And with no protection possible against miniature surveillance apparatus, invasion of privacy is no longer against the law. Soon it's not even considered rude. And not long thereafter privacy as a concept ceases to exist . . . almost.

Lazarus waggled a finger at Gabriel, and said, "Human beings are ingenious and they did succeed in stuffing the genie back in the bottle. But they didn't notice that they had left a couple of fingers sticking out. And those fingers are wriggling about."

Gabriel said carefully, "But . . . I always thought that Kyara had the toughest Privacy Laws next to Earth."

"Oh, but she does," Lazarus affirmed urgently, "which is why the rot sets in." He tapped his brow just above the bridge of his nose. "This little implant? Even as we speak they're busy pushing legislation through the Conclave that'll add a tracking chip to O.T.E. implants. That way Mighty Mickey can keep tabs on where all his naughty children are. And you think for one moment it'll stop at us reekers? Hm? No, stike, the bad old days are coming back and it's happening *here*! It's starting *here*!" he spat. "*Not* Octavia, *not* Zuleika, *not* Terra Nova, *not* Bell country on Joy, *not* Las Palmas, *not* the Sol System Lagrange, *not* Grayscape, *here*, right *here*! Thor System, Kyara! And you know why? You know why?" Lazarus's cackle became a hiss. "Because you cannot forbid the prime imperative, dilly! People will *have* what they *want*! They will have it, if it takes a thousand generations, they will have it! And the powers that be want *that*, they want to know everything, they want to know where everyone is and why and when, because *that's* the key, don't you see? Your sister had it ass-backwards, stike! The power's not the end, it's just the means so that the wielder can feel that his ass is covered! They want to feel safe! And what they want they will have! And no amount of rubber legislation is going to hold back the flockin' armies, stike! And it isn't going to be the 'Save Querin' breeze-heads with their banners. No, stike . . . it's going to be *us*, Kil's people! Look around you, dilly, 'cos this is it!" He was screaming now." *We* are the revolution! *We* are the rain-cloud warriors! Washing it clean! Bringing everything back to the soil! Back to the soil . . . Creation's living earth, dilly, Creation's living earth." Lazarus's voice dropped to a whisper. "The spirit of Kil has shown us the way. The way back."

A long sigh rippled through the roofrunners. "Back to the soil."

Holy strewth, Gabriel thought, appalled, *the spirit of who?* This was worse than he had imagined. There was nothing more deadly than messianic delusions. He noticed that the GenTec plant was curling in upon itself, leaves, tendrils intertwining grotesquely as if it were determined to strangle itself.

Lazarus Wight turned back to him, his face granite. "So maybe you're what they say you are. Or maybe you're not. Maybe Elspeth Kylie really was your sister and you're just another runner, like her. Maybe that's all you are, just the running type. What's your price to stay put, Kylie?"

Gabriel swallowed hard, trying not to let his anger suffuse his expression, but he could tell that Lazarus Wight knew. "My price," he said tightly, "is the truth. Who killed my sister?"

Lazarus's head moved slowly from side to side. "I don't know," he said slowly. "But get me what I want and I'll help you get what you want."

"What do you want?" Gabriel asked warily.

In answer Lazarus raised his right arm, a regal gesture. He clenched his fist and Gabriel blinked in surprise as a holo-projection of Kyara city appeared above him, almost three meters across and slowly rotating. It was as Gabriel remembered it, looking down upon it from the viewport of the Orbit shuttle. At one end of the city Rainer Park was outlined in red. Roughly a third of the

way around the perimeter of the city another protrusion
was also red-rimmed. The shuttleport, Gabriel guessed.

Lazarus reached up with both arms and seemed to
caress the projection, his fingertips dipping into the city
domes as if he were stirring up ripples in a luminous
pool. Longing shone from his face.

"I want . . ." he murmured, ". . . anonymity. I want
to brush through a crowd of people and not have them
even know that I'm there. I want the dignity of passing
unnoticed through a room. I want privacy. The sanctity
of solitude with myself." Absently he rubbed the spot
on his forehead above his nose, as if working away a
stain. He appeared confused. "I want . . . so many
things," he said vaguely. There was a long silence. Gabriel took the opportunity to search amongst the assembled faces. Hunkered in the far end of the cavern, the
little dough-faced reeker was sobbing, a bubble forming
on his chubby lips.

Lazarus dropped his arms. "I want. But Kil has chosen
me for another path." His gaze fastened on Gabriel
again. "You asked me what I want? I want Rainer
Park."

"Rainer . . ." Uncomprehending, Gabriel mouthed the
word. "You want Rainer Park? How can I get you
Rainer Park?"

"Ah, that is the difficulty, isn't it?" Lazarus's face
showed faint amusement. "Anyone connected with the
Icarus Field has a forced mental block put in by psych-
Probe, Kyara's sole and unique exception to the Privacy
Laws. That covers anyone in the engineering unit supervising Rainer Park's construction and day-to-day func-
tioning, including and especially the chief engineer. You
couldn't get a copy of the plans from them—even, dare
I say it, under something as barbaric as torture. But your
sister claimed to have found another source."

Understanding dawned on Gabriel. "Elspeth . . . was
going to get you the plans to Rainer Park?"

Lazarus nodded.

Puzzled, Gabriel said, "But, if she couldn't get it from
Japaljarayi and his people . . ."

"Somewhere else, dilly," Kipper said suddenly. "The
question is, who, apart from the park people and Saxon
Rainer himself would have access to the plans?"

"But, why not Rainer . . . no, of course not, he's not going to hand over his own pride and joy." Gabriel shook his head. "I can't get you Rainer Park."

Lazarus advanced so that Gabriel was at the very edge of his O.T.E. field. Gabriel's nose hairs were twitching, but Lazarus seemed to know to the centimeter the effect radius of his O.T.E. He leaned in, as if seeking to bridge the distance that still separated them by the intensity of his will.

"Get me Rainer Park and I'll get you your sister's murderer."

Gabriel felt the blood drain from his face. For the first time someone had said it. Someone had verbalized what he hitherto had only guessed to be the truth.

He bowed his head, trying to order his thoughts. A thousand images had appeared before his mind's eye at Lazarus's mention of Elspeth. Gabriel barely felt Kipper slip down next to him and whisper, "so what's the next move, stike?"

"Next move?" Gabriel wondered vaguely.

Uncle Bull hadn't always been dead, but he was dead now.

Old Man had died once, when the Iruntarinia spirits cut him open and took out his guts and liver. They'd killed him first, of course, with a spear through the head and another through his neck and tongue, sliced him open and put an amethyst in his belly and magic stones in the joints of his arms and legs. Then they put his guts back and woke him up, good and bright as a new pen. From then on he knew how to suck the bad spirits out of skin, cure a man or woman who'd been sung by their enemies and fly over the land as an eaglehawk.

Now Old Man stood next to this brother's body and his eyes were dry. But Gabriel could see the rage in him by the way he showed no rage. Because Uncle Bull wasn't coming alive again. No clever ways were going to stop up the laserburn in his forehead or chase away the blank page that death had made of his face. And only the ka-daitja, the path of revenge, would ease the pain of his loss.

It had been offworld poachers. There were always one or two around, but not for many a year now. Since the GenTec Plagues had decimated Australia's wildlife, the red kangaroo—the purebred, unsullied by GenTec imitations—had numbered a pitiful few hundreds. No one could explain why, in the two centuries since the GenTec Plagues ended, the numbers of what had in olden times been considered a fast-breeding pest, had never risen beyond a thousand since.

The penalties for unauthorized hunting were high all over the planet and none but the very rich, the very assured, or the very foolish would run the risk of being caught for the privilege of owning a pelt that could never be exhibited publicly. Or privately, for that matter.

But here in Gabriel's eleventh year, for the first time in years, someone had. And foolish old Uncle Bull had stumbled across them, probably whilst singing his way through the gum trees, or chasing Iguana man through the ocher dust.

And Old Man stared with his dry, dry eyes. He stared all the way into next week and never blinked.

"Gabriel? Gabriel?" Kipper was still waiting for him to respond. "What are you going to do?"

Gabriel looked for Lazarus, but the roofrunner chief appeared to have lost interest in him and was tucking into his share of the repast.

Slowly Gabriel replied, "I think I'm going to go talk with an old man. If I can find him."

In the flowerpot the GenTec plant had reduced itself to a mash of dry, brittle fiber, dead by its own hand.

"Hey, dilly," murmured Kipper suddenly. "What speak we go hang the slaphappies under four eyes, hey?" Gabriel felt something being pressed into his hands. It was his slaphappy slippers.

"Hang the slaphappies?"

"You and me, stike."

Nobody seemed to notice or care when they slipped away and Gabriel soon found himself walking along the curved top of a hangcar track, the city's hum echoing up from far below and punctuated by the hiss of the odd hangcar, passing directly beneath them on the underside of the rail. Kipper was playing his own private game of guessing each one's manufacturing brand.

"Lamont 22, Avenger, that one," observed Kipper

smugly. "Reckon three average-weight passengers or two-bulemics."

"How can you tell?"

"Feel it through my soles, stike, easy as long as the traffic's light, and it's always light in the dark," he cackled, skipping on ahead. In his own way, Gabriel realized, Kipper Gibbons was a true woodsman, too, his terrain was just a different kind of wood. "I reckon you could toe it, too, if you gave it your try," the little man observed. "Your sister had it in her."

"Was she really the way that Lazarus said?"

"You don't care much for old Laz, do you?"

Gabriel hesitated, detecting a sudden tense expectancy from the little roofrunner and aware that he was on dangerous territory. "Maybe we can leave Laz and you can tell me some more about my sister," he suggested.

"Maybe we can leave your sister and you can tell me why you're looking for the old man in the park?" Kipper shot back. "You can't reckon he broke her three-point, it'd take more than some old curb-roller to knock her off her perch. She was a pec-wired dam, Elspeth. Nearly gave Snapper back there a terminal-V one-way peekaboo at the flatlands and that takes some trying, dilly."

"Snapper? What was she fighting with Snapper about?"

"Hah! Two angry dams over one roof is one too many. The sweet double-X's have got their own agenda and it's for you and me to step aside and let them sort it out for themselves . . ." He broke off, concentrating. "Lance, Railrunner 204, and the guidance system's on the bugout. Dilly's going to cause an accident driving with that."

"Kipper, I need to find out what's happened to Isadora, if she's alright."

"Your girlie-girl from the Orbit drop? What's the interest there? Thought you didn't get the sweet-time in."

"There's more to . . . things than just the sweet-time," Gabriel said patiently, wondering how he could explain. "She . . . trusted me."

"*I* trust you," said Kipper expansively.

Gabriel eyed him sceptically. "I don't think you'd trust your mother to feed you with her own tit."

Kipper hooted delightedly. "You speak it like it lies, dilly. You don't miss a thing!"

"Good, so tell me how I can get word to Isadora."

Kipper shrugged. "I got word up from the flatlands that some woman and a man were turnkeyed bastillia-side in the same hole we pried you out of. Spookland let them out this morning."

"Isadora?"

"Media's not allowed to publish suspects' names, but tongues slipped that she was a tick herself. So I reckon she's in the prime and limelight."

"I need to know for sure."

"And I need to know why you're so interested in this old eth-head." Kipper's eyes glittered dangerously.

And Gabriel suddenly wondered if Kipper had had some other reason for bringing him out, other than just to "hang the slaphappies under four eyes." As casually as he could he scanned the area, seeking perhaps some hidden figure, ready to take him out if he gave a wrong answer. "I should think that were obvious. Because nobody else is."

Kipper did not miss Gabriel's surreptitious appraisal of their surroundings. "There's just us, stike."

"And Laz."

"Oh, yes, he's everywhere."

"Then tell me something else. Who's Kil?"

Kipper shied away slightly. "Oh, well, he's the guide. He's the one gives Lazarus his guidance." Kipper's expression was suddenly concerned. "He's trusted you, you know," he said urgently. "You could wing the word to Mighty Mickey and bring spookland upland and down around us. Laz is the one, dilly. He's going to lead us back to the soil, back to the earth." Kipper placed his hands on his own chest. "Me? I'm Thor, five generations. Came out of the cold-trays, grew up in the pens. Mother went bugout, Pater was a donor's number. I'm an Ironworld man to the marrow, never strolled further than Orbit and back. What do I know, but welding and stress-points? Shag-a-lackey, Sharry's got twice the know-what that I do . . . aaah." He smiled fondly. "We got ourselves lucky with her, me and Toh, we got ourselves lucky. And Kata. She's goin' to have the upsider's life ahead, thanks to Laz." Kipper's expression became grave again. "*He's* got twice the know-what Sharry does. He's been places, seen the thousand ways. He's not some off-the-belt reeker, dilly! No, they messed when they O.T.E.'d him and set him loose, because he's out to horn-to-horn it with Mighty Mickey. He's going to bring us back, dilly, back to the . . . earth, y'know?"

"And how's he going to do that, Kipper?"

Kipper made a conspiratorial gesture, tugging at his right eyebrow. "We're not the bugouts here, stike. The Plaza"—he snorted derisively—"that's flatland. You see anybody here on acrovak? Fabiana? You see anybody here playin' the INworld? No, dilly, we're smooth up here. This is the uplands." He spread his arms in an all-encompassing gesture. "We're *out*side. And Laz . . . he knows the way, 'cos he's *been* there. He's gone running through Mighty Mickey's guts and he knows them from the inside.

"Take a look, dilly." Kipper's arms encompassed the totality of Kyara. "You tell me what that is . . . no. No, I'll tell you. That's me. And Sharry. And small Kata. There's nothin' like it anywhere in the big Seventeen. We shouldn't be here, none of us. Flatland tries not to think about it"—he waved a scornful hand at the streets far, far below—"but *we* do. We know that Ironworld would love to squeeze us, squeeze us small as putty, make Kyara just a thumbprint on the Anvil. But Kyara's *here*. We're here, 'cos we've got *philosophy!*" He stepped in close to Gabriel. "Philosophy, stike, in two words: 'Up' and 'Yours.' " Kipper collapsed in glee. Presently he recovered and grew serious again. "Aah, we're going to spin the pointer back, stike, Laz's promised us that! Oh, yeah."

Gabriel asked, "So where do I fit in, Kipper? What makes him think I can deliver?"

Kipper spread his hands in a sign of helplessness and grinned a penknife grin. "I don't know, stike, I don't know where you fit in. You're a tricky read, but I figure you know rightly right well where you fit in. Mighty Mickey seems to know. And spookland? They're pickin' the scabs off every nook and noogly trying to lay their grip on your neck, stike. They wouldn't do that to some twenty-cred-a-day tourist."

"Oh, no?" Outwardly calm, he stepped forward and

placed a brotherly arm around the little man's shoulders. "In that case I wouldn't blink at throwing you over the side."

Kipper snickered craftily. "Try to throw me over the side and we'll be making the long drop in tandem."

"What makes you think that prospect bothers me? I've taken the dive once already, last night, thinking I was in for the long drop."

"No, you didn't," said the little man shrewdly. "You knew somebody was there to catch you. You weren't really ready to let go."

Gabriel removed his arm from the other's shoulders. You're right," he admitted, "so where does that leave us?"

"That leaves me ready to help you . . . no questions asked. Course, if you're really what you say you're *not*, you might not be needing my help."

"So who am I, Kipper?"

"There's a whole shagging hive crawling out of the walls and floor and asking themselves the same question."

And at that moment an image inserted himself in Gabriel's mind and he found himself laughing softly. "You know what I am, Kipper?" he said. "I'm the rains. I'm just the rains."

Kipper looked at him quizzically.

But Gabriel laughed with himself, for himself . . . and did not explain.

needle

Isadora peeled the bedcover off her head and peered irritably at the luminous dial of the clock. "Four fifty-eight," she groaned. She flapped her arms free of the cover and lay spread-eagled, her eyes closed, trying to convince herself that she was sleeping, that she had in fact slept at all this night and that she did not have a full bladder.

But the carousel in her head would not stop. *Gabriel, Roofrunners, blue box, Loki, Byron Systems, Chuen, TARC,* images skipped and pranced, snatching grins at her as they passed. She had spent hours poring over Elspeth's journal, tracing her way through the labyrinth of worm-tracks, scratchings and incoherence to pluck from it islands of lucidity. Bitterly she regretted not having made hard copy of Elspeth's financial records, or of the map that they had found of Rainer Park. What was it that Chuen had said about it that first night? That the file was twice as big as necessary? What had they missed? If only they had made another copy of it somewhere, anywhere where they could get at it.

Her eyes snapped open. "Sterike!" she breathed. *They had!*

She stared stupidly at the ceiling for a few seconds, then her bladder reminded her of its presence. The nightlamp came on automatically as she swung herself out of bed and stumbled to the bathroom. A file that was too big might conceal something. It would need a codeword, a number, to get access. Isadora caught herself. She was getting ahead of the facts. She still was not sure that the file was where she thought it was. After she had washed her hands and splashed some lukewarm water in her face she studied herself in the mirror, flipping it to the reverse setting so that she faced herself as others faced her; her reflection's right to her left.

A short, plump woman stared back out at her, eyes sleep-puffed small, face round and dimple-chinned, a tiny bird wing tattooed just above her left nipple—relic of a youthful run with the Halfway Houzer Freedomrights Club, when the world was fresh and full of promise. Before it shrank like the ever-decreasing spiral of a snail's shell.

She had never been able to bring herself to have the tattoo removed, to do so would be an admission of failure, a final defeat in a search for something that she had never been able to define. Isadora had been unable to overcome her scepticism enough to delve into any of the religions and cults—the Church of Cornucopia, the Hollow Sky Society, the Temple of Adam's Apple, to name but a few—whose big, shiny promises of eternal jollity and self-satisfaction slipped into her Web-mail box every day. No. Isadora was the kind of girl who, three years employment at D.N.Amics notwithstanding, ultimately became . . . a researcher. One of these nameless persons who crouched, concealed behind their function, until they and the function melded into and became indistinguishable from one another, even to themselves.

Isadora grimaced with annoyance at her own self-pity. To spite herself she set the tap water at one degree above freezing and plunged her face into it, blowing air out of her nose and mouth and sending icy threads spattering up behind her ears and neck.

As she dried herself off she forced herself to smile at the maudlin bent her thoughts had taken. What else could one expect at 5 A.M.? There was nothing wrong with her that sleep couldn't cure.

She palmed the bathroom door open and froze.

Her bedroom was unchanged, the walls fingerpainted by soft, nightlamp shadows, Raymond and Skunk two dark mounds on the foot of the bed, the Helios weasel a-chitter in his cage. But somewhere a wasp was faintly buzzing.

And there were no wasps in Kyara.

Then she spied it. A pinprick gleam drifting through the gloom above Wang Fu's corner. Involuntarily her hand twitched on the palmplate, even as a second quick-silver droplet floated into her peripheral vision. The bathroom door started to close. In the same instant the gentle buzzing rose to a mosquito whine and Isadora, unable to move, had just enough time to see the twin points of silver dart out at her like the forked tongue of a serpent, before the bathroom door slid shut. There were two sharp raps on the door, as if someone had just flung two marbles against it. Only then did Isadora jump back as if stung.

She had had a fleeting impression of a jeweled insect, thumb-sized, two vertical, jagged rows of teeth, topped by a single black teardrop eye in the center of its head, sickly delicate legs curled up against its body. Whatever it was there was no question in her mind that it was deadly. It? Them! Two of them!

Her body trembled with shock and it took a conscious effort to slow her breathing to a normal rate. Pointless to scream for help, every residence in Kyara was completely soundproofed and her bathroom had no windows. Her clothes, and therefore her phone, were all out in her bedroom. She was trapped in here. She fumbled into her bathrobe to cover her nakedness. Perhaps if she waited long enough . . . ? Her hands stopped in the action of fastening her robe as she was alerted to a faint scratching at the bathroom door. She felt her abdomen contract with fear. "Oh, sterike," she whimpered. "Oh, sterike."

It took an effort of will to go up to the door and place one hand against it, touching its surface as if it were white-hot. Vibration. The faintest hum against her fingertips. She placed her ear against the door and instantly flinched back. That was no scratching. Something—some things—were boring their way through the door. She could hear them, tiny cockchafer teeth gnawing, splintering the brittlefoam to dust.

Frantically she cast about for any kind of weapon, something she could smash them with as they came out of their self-made tunnels. Absurdly she found herself grabbing at a discarded sock from the ground that she had dropped on the way to the disposal slot and then throwing it down again in frustration.

"Shag it, Iz, think, think, think!"

Suddenly a small black spot appeared at the lower, right-hand corner of the door, visibly growing to reveal a blur of ratchet teeth and a single gleaming eye. With a shriek Isadora snatched up a mug from the sink and struck at the hole. The head instantly withdrew and then darted out again. Isadora turned the mug around and covered the orifice with it. There was a last buzz of disintegrating brittlefoam and something struck the base of the mug and began to rattle about inside. At the same moment a second spot appeared, high up on the door, out of Isadora's reach.

"Oh, no," she whispered in terror. The rattling inside the mug had stopped and been taken over by a grinding noise. Isadora felt something touch the flap of skin between her index and middle fingers. Then a long, gleaming needle snicked out from between her fingers, pinpoints of wetness striking the back of her wrist.

Isadora hurled the mug away from her with a scream. It struck the wall, dropped, but before it could strike the floor it seemed to levitate and fly straight back at her.

Sobbing with terror Isadora scrabbled across the floor toward the shower stall. She tumbled inside, slapping at the palmplate as she heard the mug hit the ground and an already-familiar gnatlike whine. She twisted her head around, saw the shower-stall doors sliding shut, defined by a narrowing rectangle of light. In the center of this rectangle something was streaking toward her and she saw a second *thing* emerging from the hole it had made in the top left-hand corner of her bathroom door.

The shower-stall doors snapped shut, leaving Isadora cowering at the bottom of the shower stall.

Tap! Tap!

They were visible through the semitransparent doors of the shower stall, two black thumbprint blurs. She could see them moving, crawling, one upward, the other down.

"Get away from me!" Isadora screamed. "Get away!"

She could hear the peck of their multiple legs as they skittered across the door's surface. Then the gnawing began again. They would be through the thin plastine within seconds.

"*Think!*" she whimpered to herself. "*Think!*"

They had come into her apartment at night, through

the ventilation system perhaps. They hadn't hurt the animals, which meant . . . what? That they knew what they
were looking for?

Their outlines were growing sharper as they came at
her through the semitransparent plastine, as if they were
emerging from a mist.

Isadora tried not to look, fought down her terror,
clutching at her scalp. There must be a way out of this,
there *must* be. How did their eyes work? Did they react
to movement? No, or they would have gone after one
of the animals. Or were they like a police robot's eyes,
also seeing into the infrared spectrum? She tried to con-
jure up everything she had ever read on the subject.

Maybe that was it. If they had come at night . . .
whoever had sent them would have expected her apartment to be in darkness. They'd be looking for the heat-
registration of her body. Maybe there was a chance.

Isadora's breath was coming in spasms as she fumbled
for the shower's controls. She set the water for "vertical
blanket" and the highest temperature on the dial, then
slapped the "ON" plate.

Nothing happened except that a calm female voice
said, "Water is set at a temperature above human
tolerance."

"Turn it on! Turn on the flockin' water, you bitch!"
Isadora hammered at the "ON" plate, "Override! Override!" she screamed. She threw herself back against the
rear wall of the shower cubicle. The scream caught in
her throat.

From two holes in the top and bottom of the shower
doors two insect heads observed her through beady cyclops eyes.

"Temperature is set at 78 degrees Celsius," intoned
the voice impassively. "Please confirm override."

"Override confirmed," whispered Isadora. Nothing
happened.

Legs wriggled out around the heads, hooked themselves around the edges of the holes and began to pull
the silver insect bodies forward. Needles snicked out
and in from between wicked little teeth, tonguing
anticipation.

"Override confirmed," Isadora cried out.

Instantly a half-meter cylinder of scalding water

dropped from the ceiling down the center of the cubicle. Within seconds the cubicle was dense with clouds of steam. Isadora pressed herself flat against the wall to avoid it but hot water splashed painfully over her feet and she raised herself up onto her toes. The moan that escaped her lips was part pain, part fear.

Through the steam and spray she could make out the two drones hovering at about shoulder height. They were less than an arm's length away from her. From the way they swiveled right and left it seemed as if the hot water and steam had confused their heat-sensitive eyes. They drifted a little to the left, then seemed to change their minds and halted again, hovering.

Her ruse had worked, for a few seconds anyway. She was certain that before long they would start working their way around the water to search for her.

One of the drones began to circle to the right. If only the other one would move in the same direction. As long as it stayed where it was it was effectively blocking her passage. Within three seconds the one that was moving would emerge from around the stream and see her.

"*Please let the second one move,*" she prayed. "*Please move.*"

Then it did. Straight through the water toward her.

Isadora edged her way around the shower stall, weeping from pain and terror, keeping the water between her and the drones. She reached the doors, fumbled for the palmplate, felt the doors open behind her. Then she turned and was running, slapping the doors shut. On her third step her wet foot slid away from under her and she tumbled to the ground, fetching up against the bathroom door.

"No!" she cried, slapping at the palmplate. As the door started to open she scrambled through the gap on all fours, lunging for her front door. Behind her she could hear *them* emerging from their holes. Their high-pitched whine bit the air.

In a frenzy she struck out at her front door, clawed at it with her nails as it slid unhurriedly open. The corridor was very bright. Even as she dived through the doorway she knew it was too late. The whine became a shriek in her ear. There was a whisper of breath against her neck, a butterfly touch.

Isadora struck the floor, skidding across the corridor to slam against the far wall. Instinctively she brought her knees up, her elbows gripping her head, curling up in a fetal shell as if this would offer her some protection. She held her breath, waited for the sting of the first needle entering her flesh. And then . . .

Nothing.

Warily she exposed her face to look back over her shoulder. They were there. Floating just inside her doorway, two evil scarabs, their legs tucked in, their single eyes focused intently on her. They made no attempt to come after her, they just hovered, waiting. Waiting for what?

Gradually, it dawned on her. They must have been programmed to remain inside the confines of her apartment to prevent accidents.

Isadora did not know whether to laugh or break down completely. A part of her wanted to thumb her nose at them, make faces, taunt their sudden impotence. She pulled herself together and climbed to her feet. Her robe was soaked, her feet bright red and scalded. Gingerly she palmed her door shut. Only then did she let go, leaning her face against the cool marbeline wall, her body wracked with shudders. She was alive. She was alright. Then a thought came to her and she gasped.

"Chuen."

Lee Chuen was bathing in Debussy. His *Sirènes* Nocturne was her favorite. The little Soundcloud at her neck created an envelope of music around her head and the aural deadening field blocked out all outside sounds.

Traveling home by hangcab at five-thirty in the morning was nothing new to Lee Chuen. She generally preferred to work after dark-down, when the city was quiet and washed with gray and the only brightness was the Twist, bleeding faerie dust across the night sky.

She had spent tonight with Angela, stolid Angela, who clung tight to the separatist ideal, never entertaining the doubts that roiled Chuen's moments of reflection. Chuen had been to the Sisters of Tanit homeland on Zuleika once, that unisex El Dorado, free of the Patriarchy and dedicated to nature's own true principle of gynocracy. It had cost her two years' savings to get there and once there she had found a grubby little country filled with the same petty jealousies, vices and politics of ego that she had left behind her. Campaigns were waged on strident promises of free-insemination rights, swords crossed in debates on the morality of *ex utero* fertilization procedures and exogenesis.

Chuen had lasted six months before disillusionment sent her packing, creaking her way home to Thor on an ancient freighter with passengers.

But Angela, who had never been to Tanita, was still a believer, addressing men in the third person and capitalizing the male pronoun with contempt. And when Chuen needed her she was always there.

After they had made love, Chuen had sat herself behind Angela's computer terminal and bathed her soul in the Web, reaching out with fiber-optic fingers to riffle through the data banks of the Central Library, Corporate Register, Small Company Register and other more familiar playgrounds. At this time of night there was no one else awake with whom she could converse, but that hardly mattered. On the Web a response from a person was often all of a piece with that of a research library bank and, where it was distinguishable, it was usually made so by the presence of dogmatism and fuzzy-minded conjecture.

She felt the hangcab descend and slow. Sighing wearily she palmed the cash register, which automatically debited the fare from her central account, checked once out of the forward and rear windows before opening the door and climbing out. Her street was deserted, but for the swish-swish of a cleaning pod working its way slowly toward her and a hangcab coming round a far corner.

Strange, Chuen mused, how, by dark-down, with the streets deserted, Kyara seemed to live more of itself. It was at moments like this that she realized how much she loved the city.

Still trailing Debussy, she entered her apartment building and made for the elevators. She stepped aside to allow a thin, robed figure to shuffle past her; Brother Sigurd, one of her upstairs neighbors, heading for morning prayer at one of the—generally unused—Anvil viewing galleries on the perimeter of the city. He beamed at her, his lips moving soundlessly, and she answered with a cursory nod. Nothing Sigurd could say rated turning off her Soundcloud and interrupting Debussy.

Sigurd was an Æsir worshiper, a "gravity bug" to non-believers. His equivalent of a goathair shirt was the harness of lead weights under his robe, worn to reflect the burden of Thor's gravity field, the actual weight worn being an indication of a worshiper's individual rank. An Æsir layman carried his own weight, whereas a bishop might labor under twice the weight of his own body plus some. Chuen often wondered if any of them ever thought about how long they would last if they were ever exposed to Thor's real gravity. Probably not; that would be a betrayal of faith.

A few seconds later she was on the fifteenth floor. The corridor outside her apartment was dimly lit—that obnoxious seven-year-old in 156B must have been shorting out the lights again. She was reaching up to open her front door when something made her hesitate, as if somebody had just cried out for her not to enter her apartment.

Chuen smiled wryly to herself. Isadora's state of mind must be contagious. With Debussy still chiming in her ears she opened her front door.

Isadora hammered on her neighbor's door, for the first time in her life cursing absolute soundproofing, cursing the habit that led people to turn off their doorbells with their lights. She needed a phone and there was no way that she could reenter her apartment to get her own. With increasing frustration she worked her way down the corridor, from one door to the next.

"You lazy bastards!" she shouted at the last door. "Don't any of you work in the mornings!?"

Isadora took the lift down to the ground floor and ran out onto the street. There was nobody about except for a couple of curb-rollers asleep in a doorway. She spotted one man a block away, entering his building.

"Hey!" she shouted. "Hey, wait! Wait! Wait!"

He glanced at her coldly and she was suddenly aware of how she must look, running around the streets at night in bare feet and a bathrobe. He turned and entered the building, closing her out. Feeling suddenly very vulnerable, she pulled her robe closer about her.

Then she spotted the robot standing impassively on the corner, bathed in the red light of a skin-dye shop window and sagged with relief. It was wearing the gray uniform of the Municipal Police.

"Help! Help me! Police!" she cried. "Police!"

The robot's featureless face turned, acknowledging her presence. It swiveled on one heel and came toward her. As it stepped out of the red light Isadora skidded to a stop. What had appeared at Municipal gray in the red light was in fact Targeting, Apprehension and Remand Central green.

Two days ago the difference would not have mattered, but now, all of a sudden, Isadora found herself wondering what a TARC robot was doing walking the beat. The TARC A.I. wing never did street patrols unless it was for a specific purpose.

"Halt," said the robot as Isadora began to back away. "I am here to assist you. You have requested assistance."

"No . . ." Isadora continued to back away, "No . . . I'm alright, I'm f . . . I'm alright."

"You have requested assistance."

"No, I'm alright, I'm fine now."

"You have requested assistance. Please clarify the nature of assistance needed," the robot continued remorselessly.

"I don't . . . I was just . . ." Isadora stammered. "Really, it was a mistake."

"Halt," the robot said calmly, and Isadora suddenly found herself facing his outstretched forefinger, its hollow point aimed directly at her chest. "You have requested assistance."

"I don't need assistance."

"It is an offense to shout for police assistance where none is required."

"I know that . . ."

"Hoaxes account for 7 percent of all calls to Justice Central, resulting in the spurious removal of police presence from areas where it may in fact be needed."

"I didn't do it on purpose, it was a mistake."

"Please identify yourself."

Isadora hesitated.

"Please identify yourself," repeated the robot in exactly the same tone of voice.

Isadora took a deep breath, "Isadora Manuela Gatzalumendi, P.R. Number 67b. 113. I live just here." She indicated her apartment block.

"Please confirm." The robot held up its left hand, palm outward.

"Hey, I live just . . ."

"Please confirm." The hollow index finger was suddenly pointing straight at Isadora's face.

Gingerly Isadora placed her right hand against that of the robot. The robot's palm glowed for an instant. "Identification confirmed," the robot acknowledged stonily. "Previous arrests, two: creating a disturbance, participating in unlicensed public demonstration. No permanent felony record . . ."

"Aw, look, please," Isadora pleaded, growing desperate, "there's a friend of mine who's in . . ." She broke off. By the time she cut through all the officialdom it might already be too late, if it wasn't too late already. "Please, look, it was a just a mistake. I was . . . I was having a nightmare and . . . suddenly I was here. Please. Please?"

For the first time the robot seemed to consider, then it said, "Offense registered. Court appearance scheduled for 6/9/264." The forefinger dropped.

Isadora backed away from the robot, turned and walked away down the street resisting the urge to run. With a surge of relief she saw an unmanned hangcab coming down the street toward her and hailed it.

By the time the hangcab descended outside Chuen's front door Isadora had no fingernails left. There was another hangcab standing outside Chuen's apartment building. The door was open and a familiar figure was stepping out of it. Isadora watched disbelieving as Chuen strode toward her building.

"Chuen!" she yelled, hammering at the door. "Chuen!"

"The doorlocks will be released after the fare has been paid," murmured the hangcab.

Isadora hurriedly palmed the register and scrambled out of the cab. Chuen was just entering the building. Isadora cried, "Chuen! Wait!" But Chuen appeared

not to hear and disappeared inside. Isadora hammered
on the door, shouting, "Chuen!" She could see Chuen
through the transparent panes stepping into the elevator,
past a skinny man who was just coming out. She waited
until the man opened the front door, then nearly
knocked him over as she pushed past him, screaming,
"Wait! Stop!"

The man grabbed at her clumsily as she went past
with a querulous, "Hey, what's this?"

Isadora was nearly weeping with rage as she slammed
her hands against the closed elevator doors. "Chuen!"
A second elevator door opened and she dashed inside.

Five seconds later the elevator was opening on the
fifteenth floor. The corridor was dark. In a splash of light
at the far end Isadora saw Chuen standing outside her
apartment, preparing to go inside.

"Chuen!" Isadora screamed. "Don't go inside!
Chueeeeen!"

Chuen hesitated in the act of touching her doorplate.
Then she seemed to come to a decision and, to Isadora's
horror, she saw Chuen's hand come down on her doorplate and the door slide open. Why didn't Chuen hear
her?

Then, just as Isadora opened her mouth for one last
despairing wail, a huge shadow swarmed out of the darkness behind Chuen and tackled her around the waist,
hurling her to the floor.

Chuen was instantly transformed into a mad wolverine, arms and legs kicking and clawing as her attacker
attempted to pin her to the floor. Before she had time
to consider the prudence of her actions, Isadora found
herself charging down the corridor and leaping onto the
back of Chuen's assailant. He was a big man with a back
like a church door. Isadora wrapped her arms around a
neck as thick as her own thigh, trying to choke him.
Chuen was screaming and swearing. "Let go of me, you
bastard, I'll kill you . . ."

The man was also shouting something that sounded
like, "Please!"

Chuen hissed, "I'll tear your stinking . . ."

"Please . . ." Their assailant's voice choked off with a
squeak as Isadora felt Chuen's knee come between her
own and she knew that the man had just taken a solid

blow to the testicles. She reached her hands around to his face and tried to gouge his eyes, then felt the man's shoulder come down, heard the smack of knuckles against flesh and saw Chuen's face jerk to one side. The next instant she was clinging to the man's neck for dear life as he roared to his feet like a rising tide.

Chuen was yowling wordlessly in pain and fury. The man was bellowing, trying to make himself heard above the din and Isadora suddenly realized that he was not pleading at all.

"Chuen, stop . . . uhh!" A smoked ham elbow slammed into her abdomen loosening her hold and sending her flying back against the wall.

She was vaguely aware of Chuen's snarl, "Let go of me, you scum-sucking . . . !" Then she saw the man's hand emerge out of his coat and point something at Chuen. He shouted something indistinctly and tore at Chuen's collar.

"Don't hurt her!" Isadora managed to gasp, mesmerized by the slumbergun in his hand. Only then did she hear clearly what the man was shouting. Not "please" but . . .

"Police! I'm with the police!" he roared.

Isadora could see Chuen staring at him in disbelief. The man reached into his pocket, pulled out a card which lit up as he pressed it.

"Municipal Police," he panted. "Lieutenant Hitedoro Izeki, and this thing is set for nerve-shock *not* stun, so do yourself a favor!"

running the flatlands

Elspeth's journal:

> Here is the heart . . . here is the way . . . fit the
> pieces to each other. Found an ancient jigsaw in a
> basement once. It was damp and the pieces had
> swelled. Nothing fit. Nothing fits. Nothing fits.
> Nothing . . .

Despite her shock, Chuen's voice was acid. "This a
new approach to law enforcement?" she panted.

Izeki pivoted and pointed his gun at the open
doorway.

"What's in here?" he snapped at Isadora over his
shoulder. "You, on the floor! Why shouldn't she go
inside?"

Isadora roused herself. "Little artificial drones,
like . . . flying insects with hollow needles. I think they're
poisoned. They just came after me in my apartment, but
they wouldn't cross the threshold of my front door. I
think they were programmed only to function within
my flat."

"Drones . . . with needles, you say?" Izeki was fumbling at his belt. He produced what appeared to be a
blue glass ball the size of a table-tennis ball, and a small
viewer that he clipped behind his right ear and over his
right eye.

"View on," he said, then with an underhand sweep of
his arm he sent the ball rolling into the apartment.
"What am I looking for?" he demanded.

"Er . . . little silver, flying robot . . . thing," explained

Isadora, aware that she was not making a very good job of it. "About the size of a large hornet, but fatter."

"A large *what?*"

"A small synthfurter."

"What the hell are you talking about, 'drones?'" Chuen hissed at Isadora. Izeki waved her into silence. He was guiding his floating camera by way of verbal commands.

"Left pivot . . . stop . . . forward," he muttered. "Z-axis ten degrees . . . minus ten degrees . . . return to level." This went on for a few minutes until the big man finally tore off the viewer with a growl of dissatisfaction. "Shag it . . ." He sighed angrily. "I think we're clear . . ." A mutton-chop forefinger was raised briefly in warning. "You two stay put. And that means you especially, bitchkitty," he said to Chuen.

The moment he disappeared into Chuen's apartment Chuen began complaining. "I don't believe this, this is shagging harassment." She groaned. "Aah, gaah, my jaw and . . . look at this! He broke my phone! Look!"

Isadora only half heard her remarks; she was too busy listening for any sound out of the apartment. At length Izeki emerged from the apartment, dropping his Eyeball into a belt pocket.

"Well, if there was anything there, there's nothing there now," he said flatly.

"Then, maybe He would like to tell us why He was lurking around my apartment at 5:30 A.M.," growled Chuen.

Izeki squinted through the gloom at the tattoo on Chuen's forehead and audibly suppressed a groan. "Sterike, I might have known, Sister of shagging Tanit. I was waiting for you. Knew I couldn't get a private word with your friend here; she's got more people trailing around after her than a stripper with a GenTec pheromone boost." Then he turned to Isadora. "Maybe you'd better tell me what this is about."

"And why are you wandering about in a bathrobe?" Chuen demanded, having just noticed her attire.

Ignoring her, Isadora patiently went through what had happened at her apartment. When she had finished Izeki's expression had become bleak. He gazed at her long and hard, his little eyes narrow. Then, suddenly, he turned and started kicking at the wall swearing, "Shag it! Shag it! Shag it!" Chuen and Isadora exchanged a puzzled glance. After a few moments Izeki seemed to tire of his wall abuse and turned his attention back to the women.

"Well," he said heavily, "you can't stay here and you can't go home. Have you got anywhere you can hole up for a time?"

"I don't really know . . ." began Isadora, but Chuen interrupted her indignantly.

"Now, wait just a second, l'homme, hole up? What's this about holing up?"

"Chuen . . ." Isadora tried to cut her off.

". . . This is something for the TARCs, for Macca's sake, somebody just tried to kill her!"

"CHUEN!" Isadora exploded in exasperation. "Ster-ike! Don't you *get* it yet?"

Chuen subsided. Too quickly. And for the first time Isadora saw fear written on her friend's face and she suddenly understood that Chuen was getting it all too well.

"You're the policeman that Gabriel went to first, aren't you?" Izeki acknowledged the fact with a grunt. Isadora continued. "He called you a liar."

"He was right . . . then. Maybe still," Izeki replied shortly.

"So what would you have us do?"

"Excuse me—'have us do?' " interrupted Chuen.

"I think you'd better come with me." From the expression on Izeki's face he was less than happy with the thought. "It would be safer for you not to go home."

"But I have to, I've got . . . animals back there," Isadora objected.

"Hello?" Hitedoro was taken aback.

"I've got animals, I can't just leave them there."

It was clear that Izeki was completely baffled by this. His mouth opened and closed twice. "Uh-huh. And . . . how are you going to get them if you've got those little friends of yours waiting for you there? You expect me to come clear your apartment, too?" He waited. "This offer's about to close; you come now or you don't come at all."

"I can't leave my animals there," Isadora said stubbornly, knowing that she was being absurd and unreasonable in his eyes, but knowing also that she had to get back there. "Please."

Izeki growled impotently, "Ste*rike!* Okay, go! Do what you have to do, fetch whatever you have to fetch. It's on your head! When you're through, you head for the nearest Worm station. I'll meet you there. And you, sister, you do the same, and stay together." Izeki turned on his heel and shuffled back into the shadows.

"Hey, just a sound bite here . . ." Chuen started after him, but Isadora grabbed her arm.

"Wait . . ."

"You *must* be kidding. You don't honestly think you can trust Sammy the Spook there?" Chuen protested.

"Who else am I supposed to trust then? Hm?"

"Well, maybe for a nice change you could maybe try someone who isn't wanted by the police or assaulting women outside their homes." Chuen clutched at her jaw again, moaning. "Ah, that bastard hit me . . ."

Nervously glancing up and down the corridor, Isadora took her friend by the arm and hustled her into the apartment. "Come on, let's spray some anesthetic on that and get your stuff together."

Chuen continued to complain whilst Isadora administered to her bruised face. "You truly pick 'em, don't you, darling . . . ow!"

"Hold still."

"You aren't seriously going back to your apartment for those shagging animals of yours, are you?"

"There's a matter of a little journal as well."

"Riiiiight, the journal. Well, maybe you'd enjoy this, too. Yours truly spent half the shagging night retrieving what we got out of the Web yesterday. Thank you . . . ouch!"

"I said, hold still!"

"I am holding still! And guess what else I dug up? Remember Xaaron Corporation? Well, guess who owns it?"

"I can't," Isadora replied shortly.

"Nobody now." Chuen was smug. "It doesn't exist anymore, *but* it used to belong to Cross Star Shipping, which is a minor subsidiary of Kyaran Ventures 99 but, until a few months ago—it gets cute, doesn't it, love—

Cross Star is a subsidiary of KV 99, but up until a few
months ago it *used* to belong to . . . wait for it . . .
Calaban Transport! Ow!"

"Sorry," Isadora swallowed, her mind racing. KV 99.
Byron Systems. *Caliban Transport, the name in Elspeth's files.*

Chuen's expression was grimly triumphant. "Sounds
familiar? Okay, okay, that's fine"—Chuen brushed Isadora's hand aside impatiently—"I'll get my stuff together." She hesitated. "Look, what stuff am I supposed
to get together here exactly?"

"Chuen . . ." Isadora suppressed her irritation. She
recognized her friend's complaints as a way of disguising
the same dread that haunted Isadora herself.

Chuen continued ranting as she cast about her apartment which, in contrast to Isadora's own, was as well-
ordered as a surgeon's operating room. "I mean what
precisely do you bring when you're going into hiding?
A toothbrush? Nobody ever seems to ask that in the
Virtuals, do they? Grab your stuff? I don't even know
how long we're going for! A day? A month? Wait! Underwear! That's something! Everyone needs underwear
and there might not be a dispenser."

"Underwear would be good," Isadora agreed absently.
Chuen's phrase, "going into hiding," had rung like a
knell in her head. *Is that really what we are doing?*

"What about a weapon?" Chuen considered, picking
up a stone sculpture, a female fertility symbol. "Yes,
that'll intimidate them, won't it," she muttered, replacing
it. "Put that gun away or be cloven in twain by my left
nipple!"

At length Chuen settled for three pairs of clean underwear and her toothbrush, downloaded her personal files
from her desk computer into her wallet, lent Isadora
a change of clothing and pronounced herself unwilling
but ready.

She was still complaining sporadically when they
reached Isadora's front door by which time Isadora's
nerves were so tightly strung that she was ready to add
another bruise to the one Chuen already had.

"It's endemic in the male species," Chuen muttered.
"Steal the other kid's toys and if He won't give over,

hit. They should ban the second trimester of pregnancy, that's when that Y chromosome kicks in . . ."

"Oh, for crying out loud, be quiet!" Isadora snapped in exasperation. "Just be quiet for a moment!"

Chuen went silent, her jaw rigid with tension.

Gingerly Isadora palmed her door open. For a long moment they stood, listening, peering into the thick darkness beyond the doorway; with the absence of human movement the nightlamp had turned itself off. Isadora's ears strained, but all that she could hear was the tremulous hiss of the Helios weasel's breathing.

She threw a quick glance at Chuen, who was watching her wide-eyed, her upper teeth nipping at her bottom lip. "This is really not very clever," Chuen muttered.

Ignoring the remark, Isadora took a deep breath and stepped forward. She paused just inside the doorway, ears alert, but heard nothing. Growing more daring she inched forward, almost jumping out of her skin and then bursting into nervous giggles as the nightlamp came on in response to her movement. For one absurd moment she wondered if any of it had really happened, then she passed the bathroom and saw the two dark holes in her shower doors.

At length, after she had circled the entire apartment twice, carefully twitching the bedclothes aside and then closing the bed up to look underneath it, she gave a sigh and nodded to Chuen, who was still watching her from the doorway.

"It's okay," she said, exhaling with a shuddering laugh. "Nothing here."

Chuen entered, giving the shower door a hard stare.

Quickly they bundled the animals up into their carrying cases, giving each a puff of tranquilizer to keep them quiet (after a moment's reflection Isadora gave the Helios weasel two). Isadora changed into some clean clothes, slung a few odds and ends into a bag, remembering at the last moment to include Elspeth's journal and her own phone, which was still in the collar of yesterday's coverall. One last, longing glance around her apartment and she was ready to go.

The light-up sun was glowing pink through the domes when they emerged. The early-morning crowds were sallying forth, on their way to work, their faces set in varying degrees of hopeful productivity and resignation. The bugheads and curb-rollers who had littered the urban landscape just a scant two hours ago had all but disappeared. But here and there the residual late-night carousers, homebound, betrayed themselves by the way they stepped over invisible bricks lying on the pavement or flinched away from nonexistent insects.

The two women reached the Worm station, following the expanding crush of people through the slip-styles and onto the platforms with no sign of Izeki. Isadora craned her neck, peering left and right. Despite the tranquilizers the Helios weasel was growing restless in his carrying case, sizzling and spitting and causing passersby who came too close to start back in surprise. One elderly woman with a Merryweather bubble-rat floating on a leash above her head, whined something about complaining to the Nonhuman Species Safety Licensing Commission, but they brusquely ignored her.

At the fork leading to the two platforms they paused. "It's your call, darling," said Chuen. "Clockwise or counterclockwise?"

"Clockwise," Isadora decided, leading the way.

"We're going to look very silly if we spend the rest of the morning riding round Kyara," muttered Chuen. "Personally I can think of much funner ways of going nowhere . . . like nailing one foot to the floor and taking that weasel for a walk."

They had no sooner stepped onto the Worm and watched the crowd elongate as their section of the Worm left the station and gathered speed, when they each felt a ham-sized hand settle softly on her shoulder.

They turned to find Hitedoro Izeki leaning over them, a mangled nicotine root sticking out of the corner of his mouth. Putting his finger to his lips he reached for Isadora's neck . . .

They left the Worm two stops further down, following close behind Izeki as he waded through the crowds. From there they hopped into a waiting Municipal Police hangcar with opaqued windows.

There was no driver and the car was set to full auto, so that after Izeki had mumbled the destination at it—incomprehensible to Isadora around the nicotine root—

he was able to turn and face them, his eyebrow cocked cynically as he eyed the carrying cases.

"Those what all the fuss was about, huh?" he grunted. Then he eased back into his seat. "Well," he rumbled complacently, "at least we shook your tail."

Chuen snorted. "Getting off the Worm and into a police hangcar within an open street is what *He* calls 'shaking off our tail'?"

Izeki smirked, the nearest thing to a smile that Isadora had yet seen from him. "The thing about T and R Central is that they always think they need an industrial laser to slice a piece of bacon. They're a bunch of overtrained prima donnas, with too many toys and too many resources. On the other hand"—his face grew serious—"they make up for that by being nasty." Izeki gestured toward Isadora's now-empty collar. "You'd better think back close on what you've been saying, 'cos Privacy or no Privacy, I'm willing to bet you haven't been alone for the last twenty-four hours."

Isadora digested this in silence for the rest of the journey.

Izeki's apartment was located at the western edge of Green Sector, overlooking the quickfarms. Izeki lived on the ninth floor. When they opened the door they were greeted by the sight of a young man, who bore a vague resemblance to Izeki, standing at a kitchen counter. The counter before him was covered with vegetables and synth-meats and assorted cooking pots and mixing bowls. He started guiltily as he saw Izeki.

"Isaao! What are you doing here? Why aren't you at work? Has something happened?" Izeki's face was suddenly naked with worry.

Isaao smiled cheerfully. "Half day today, it's Meal-day, and Aysha went to play jockeypuck and our V.T.'s still broken. Meal-day Holiday," he repeated helpfully.

"That's right," Izeki tutted. "Your boss is a Church of Cornucopian, isn't he." He looked disapprovingly at the mess of ingredients around his brother. "And this?"

"Oh, I'm . . . trying things," Isaao said vaguely. Then his gaze focused on the two women. "Hi." He waved. "I live upstairs."

"Hullo." Isadora studied him curiously. She had only

ever read about Down's syndrome and it had taken her a few moments to recognize the physical characteristics that went with it, the epicanthic folds less noticeable in Isaao's already Asian features.

"These are some friends of mine,"—Izeki gestured toward Isadora—"this is . . . er . . . Isabel and this . . ."—he indicated Chuen—". . . is Doris."

Chuen awoke out of her stupor long enough to shoot him a look of pure venom.

"Now, if you're trying things, you might try cleaning this up." Izeki made a circling motion with his finger. "And then go home; I'm sure you've been here all night." He beckoned to the two women and led them past the kitchen cubicle into the main living area, emitting a groan and then calling back over his shoulder, "And if you're going to have the V.T. running, at least watch it!"

"At least someone in your family has manners," remarked Chuen.

"You *only* cook by hand?" Isadora had noticed the absence of a functional food dispenser.

Izeki patted his waist. "Can't you tell?" Isadora was taken off guard by the unexpected touch of self-effacing humor so it took a little longer before she noticed the Windows. Every wall in the living room was covered with them. There must have been over a dozen, looking out on a variety of land- and seascapes. Several of the Seventeen Planets were represented—an emerald valley on Denube, recognizable as such by the cloud of crimson windroses drifting over the treetops; a flat, leaden gray Zuleikan plain, speckled with sprigs of lime green Creepyweed. And above the drinks dispenser, yes, a seascape, a school of spheroid finbulbs traversing the roiling azure waters of Las Palmas. There were forests, meadows, snowcapped mountains and views of billowing desert dunes.

Before she could take them all in, however, Izeki was opening a door in the far corner. "Here . . ."

He ushered the two women into what appeared to be a guest room. Its walls were sparsely decorated with off-the-shelf Windows, portraying several unremarkable views. The single real window was easily identifiable by the expanse of quickfarm complex laid out below it.

Izeki showed them where the bed was and then left them alone to settle in. Isadora had hoped that Chuen did not notice her hesitation when he asked her if she and Chuen minded sharing the same bed. Chuen's pointed placement of the Helios weasel at the center of the bed, a domestic Maginot Line, indicated that she had and spoke a silent reproach. Chuen might not like other people's choices when they conflicted with her own wishes, but respect them she did.

As the door murmured shut on Izeki, Chuen threw herself back on the bed and closed her eyes.

"Talk about a room with a flocking view! At least he's got a decent Web terminal," she muttered sleepily. Within seconds she was asleep, her mouth open, gently snoring. She looked very young.

Although she was nearly as tired as Chuen, fatigue only served to increase Isadora's wakefulness. She sank onto the edge of the bed, her eyes wide. She hugged herself, nursing an unfamiliar, emotional numbness. She would have expected herself to cry, to react with anger, perhaps, to rail against the injustice that had chosen her to confront an implacable enemy at the possible cost of her life. The dizzy elation, the excitement that she had felt only twenty-four hours before, was gone. Even the confusion that had replaced it.

After a time, true exhaustion set in and a moment came when she felt that her locked muscles had loosened, that confusion had resumed its rightful claim on her and she accepted it with a certain resignation that was, nevertheless, free of resentment.

When Isadora opened the door half an hour later she found that Izeki had dimmed the lights and polarized the outside windows and was ensconced on the wall-couch, a glass of something magenta and probably alcoholic in his hand. The room was blue-lit by the Las Palmas seacape.

Isadora extruded a chair near the terminal desk and sat facing him at an angle.

"You've been to these places?" she inquired at length.

"No. No, I haven't," he grunted. "Function, lights up." The lights brightened obediently. He drained his glass. "Time you and I had a talk," he said in a voice that would brook no contradiction. Above his head cinnabar dust blew over a range of shattered clay mountains on Helios.

Isadora mused, trying to measure to what extent she could trust him. Isadora realized that the Municipal officer was fighting some inner war of his own, but who the antagonists were she could not discern.

She began at the beginning.

The two TARC agents trailing Isadora were getting fed up. They had been sitting on the Worm now for over an hour. In that time they had circled Kyara twice, and still their tracer showed that Isadora was sitting, unmoving, fifty meters ahead of them.

"She's mucking with us," muttered one. "She knows we're here. We should go up and visually confirm."

"Hey, the orders were to keep fifty meters between her and us. The grand muftis don't pip someone's phone without a stinker of a good reason. You want to question their orders, you go ahead."

Grumbling, his partner settled back to keeping one eye on the tracer.

Fifty meters ahead of them Millie the Mover was dreaming of gray roses in a crimson meadow. What they signified she had no idea, but she wasn't much concerned with dream symbolism. Acrovak addiction tended to bring its own reality with it and that reality was notoriously fickle. Still, in that reality the Worm was the best place to catch a few snores, much safer than any of the alleys or Halls in Bugout Plaza. Provided you could sleep sitting up straight and didn't keel over on the floor no one would bother you and you could snore your way round and round and round the city.

When the phone woke her up she thought it was someone else's. She was much surprised to realize that the chirping was coming from her own pocket. Fumbling amongst the folds of her voluminous and tattered jacket, her hand closed on a phone card. As she brought it out she accidently closed the manual "ON" connection.

"Iz? It's me," said a quiet voice. "Your . . . weasel catcher. Iz? Are you there?"

Somehow Millie had ended up with a phone card in her pocket. This had possibilities! It was still on-line; whoever had lost it hadn't canceled it yet. Why, she could phone . . . Millie's brow furrowed as she tried to think of anybody that she could phone. She examined the phone speculatively. Certainly she could get a price for it from some roofrunner. On the other hand, there was an equal chance that it would be reported stolen, the spooks would pip it, and she'd end up with the Municipals around her neck for theft. And what was the point of that?

"Iz? Are you there? Answer me!" the caller's tone was growing more urgent.

With a resigned sniff she snapped the phone in half, slipped it behind her on the seat and closed her eyes. She was snoring in seconds.

Which was why Millie the Mover's ears, usually able to detect a spook's footsteps at half a klick, did not pick up the swearing of two angry and frustrated TARCs some fifty meters away staring at a suddenly empty tracer-screen.

Kipper plucked the phone out of Gabriel's hand and closed the contact. Then he broke the phone in a gesture that was growing all too familiar to Gabriel's eyes.

"Safe phone's only guaranteed for about a minute," he tutted. "Even Sharry can't do better."

"Something's wrong," Gabriel muttered. They were standing on the street opposite Isadora's apartment block. "That wasn't Isadora's breathing."

Kipper's eyebrows shot up. "You can recognize her *breath*, dilly?"

"You've got your toes, I've got my ears. It sounded like . . ." Then Gabriel had it. "It sounded like the Worm! Like it was in the Worm!"

Kipper considered. "Well, if it went as dead as rightly you say, then whoever it was probably did what I just did." Then he seemed to make up his mind about something. "You hang here." Before Gabriel could stop him Kipper was crossing the street. A moment later he had disappeared into the apartment building.

Gabriel reached up to scratch his nose and touched dead skin. He had worn masks before, but never in the literal sense, and this one took a little getting used to. Not because it was uncomfortable—it was not—but because he almost forgot that he was wearing it. Then he would try and touch his face and would be reminded.

Kipper had explained that the slight warmth he felt from it came from a mesh of filaments embedded in the latezine. The mask served the dual function of altering his features to the naked human eye, as well as his face's heat signature, as seen by police robots. The filamented body stocking he wore under his clothes served the same purpose.

Kipper's face was grim when he emerged from Isadora's apartment block. When the little man walked right past him as if he had not seen him, Gabriel followed at a discreet distance until they had rounded a corner out of sight of the building.

"What is it?"

Kipper looked disgusted. "Nothing. She's wentsome. And she's got the spooks all over her apartment."

Gabriel went cold. "Something has happened to her."

"No, not to worry yetly, stike. It's just a skim, carpett'-ceiling the place twenty-twenty. If something had happened to your dam, they'd be thicker than crabs on a curb-roller, but there's just two of them."

"Was one of them a smallish, wiry bloke? Looks like he's gray from the inside out?"

"One of them. You netted him before?"

Gabriel's voice was hard. "Yeah. Oh, yeah."

"And something tells me that he's the bugsucker turnkeyed you bastilliaside." Kipper plucked at Gabriel's arm. "C'mon, stike, let's move before the whole hive gets here."

"Wait."

"Comealong . . ."

"*Wait!*" Gabriel tore his arm loose.

"Stike, this is not the place to be," Kipper hissed urgently. "A safe phone's only so safe. You want, I'll get eyes on this place, day and night. If the spooks have got her, she'll be alright. Nobody *likes* it in the bastillia, but you get your three square. If it isn't the spooks, then the upmost favor you can do her is go digging and *this* is not the place for that!"

Gabriel hated it, but he could find no fault with Kipper's reasoning. There was no way he could get to Isadora now. Which left only one alternative: digging.

"Alright, then where?" he muttered.

Kipper winked. "You want to find worms? You go to the wormtree. You want to find an old curb-roller? You go to Bugout Plaza." He paused, fumbled in one of his pockets and drew out yet another phone. "Here"—he handed it to Gabriel—"a Sharry special. I've got its twin in pocket. You just hit 'ON' and it'll connect us, but don't expect a happy gab—she's safe for one minute, max, okay?"

Gabriel nodded and pocketed the phone. "I've got you."

Kipper's kobold grin appeared again. "Then step right along, dilly, for the grand flatland tour."

Pelham Leel surveyed Isadora's apartment critically. His gaze wandered over the bookshelves, the old, flat-screen monitor—a good example of neo-Novan Design from the hundred-nineties—the "Save Querin, Save yourself" posters, framed above the desk, their slogans rippling lazily. He had seen enough homes belonging to disruptive regressives to recognize a fairly typical example when he saw one.

And she had been ticketed for causing a disturbance at five-thirty this morning, calling for the police or some such nonsense. He swore under his breath. Why hadn't he seen that report sooner? A third offense, it would have given them an excellent excuse to pick her up. What had she been *doing?*

Leel frowned. There was something not right about this apartment, something missing.

Sergeant Hanna Bork emerged from the bathroom shaking her head. She shrugged. "Nothing, not a thing that would take us anywhere. It's hard to tell, but it just looks like she's headed out to work."

Leel growled irritably, "She's not at work. Mazzo called them already."

"There are the two holes in the bathroom door and the two in the shower-cubicle doors," observed Bork. She snickered. "Even has a washing machine. Recycles her own clothing."

"Yeeees . . ." Leel's eyes suddenly alit on the empty glass pen in the corner. "Animals," he murmured with satisfaction.

Bork registered puzzlement. "What?"

"Animals," Leel repeated. Why hadn't he seen it before? He explained impatiently, "She was an animal fanatic. She had animals here. Real ones. They're not here now."

"People take their pets out for walks, don't they?" suggested Bork.

"Nobody takes a poisonous snake out for a walk, for Macca's sake! This was a pure-gene. No legs. No." Leel bit at his underlip in frustration. "If she meant to come back today, they'd be here. What is it?" He had noticed that his companion was growing restless, sneaking glances at the door.

"Well . . . this"—Bork looked sheepish—"I mean we may have pipped her phone, but that didn't give us permission to . . ."

Leel stopped her with an impatient wave of his hand. "Don't worry. We've got grounds enough for being in here after that little disappearing act of hers. I've got people arranging a search warrant retroactively. Still"— he took one last glance around—"I reckon we're finished in here for now."

Pelham Leel settled back in his hangcar seat and stared thoughtfully out of the one-way windows. Once again he had struck the web around Gabriel Kylie.

Grimly he touched the phone at his neck and said, "Extension 8600-slash-B."

"Yes," said a quiet voice.

"She's gone," Leel said.

"I'm beginning to weary of that note of failure in your voice." the voice at the other end was icy quiet.

"I can only operate effectively to the extent of the parameters set on the information you choose to give me," Leel replied tightly.

"I think the point is more what good use are you making of the information we've given you? How long do you think it's going to take for you to find her?"

"That depends on how far you want to go."

"Meaning?"

"Meaning we know they've been digging via the Web."

There was a pause. "Unfortunately *that* is the one

thing that we're in no position to prevent. Or have you got something else in mind?"

Leel nodded grimly. "Bait."

"Bait." A note of understanding came into the voice at the other end of the line.

Leel smiled to himself. *There's life on this side of the desk as well, lady.* "I assume we know what information matters. Pinpoint something that they'll have to get to if they're putting a puzzle together and tag it. Find one particular file, somewhere. If someone—anyone—accesses it, they get tagged along with their terminal location and we've got them. We could set up a small enough tracer program that the chances of a watchdog or anyone else running across it in the next day or two are insignificant."

"Well thought out. As it happens we did just that about an hour ago." There was no hint of smugness, which made it all the more insulting. Leel managed to hold himself in check.

"Congratulations. It's about time I had a little assistance," he replied sourly. "What did you tag?"

"Need to know only." The reply was brusque. "What about Sotack?"

"The KV 99 security agent? Nothing. I've got people on it. He hasn't been seen for two days, nobody's been to his apartment.

"So he's dead."

"Looks that way."

"Well, we need more than looks if we're going to nail Kylie with this. Keep at it."

"One more thing . . ." Leel began.

"I know, the search warrant you need just got cleared. They should be lining it down to you any minute." Leel nodded with satisfaction and the voice went on, "Now, something else. The old Rainer Park curb-roller who got out of custody. We have to find him."

Leel closed his eyes in exasperation. "Brilliant!" he rasped. "And how fast do you expect us to pull that one off? He could have headed off-planet months ago!"

"Don't be absurd. How? With what? Where's an eth-head going to find the fare? He's a witness and we need to find him before anyone else does."

"I'll take care of it." Leel nodded absently and broke

the connection, his mind working furiously. He was being bypassed, he was sure of it. Shag it! They were bypassing him!

He dropped the aural dampening field between himself and Bork in the driver's seat.

"Hanna, have we got anyone who owes us a favor in the Cyberspace Crime Unit?"

"Backroom or field agent?"

"Backroom. Someone with an overview of what's going on in the whole unit."

Bork considered for a moment, then nodded, "Yeah . . . ummmmm . . . what's his name? Nosey little prune . . . Narajan! You got him out of that tramline thing last year."

"Right, right, right!" Leel looked pleased. "Good, get him on line for me. Time to call in a debt."

bugout plaza

Kipper led Gabriel down a long Hall. Eldritch figures leaned in doorways, darkly watchful, yet without any gleam of curiosity. Scuttling along the walls, palm-sized graffiti-killers fought a losing battle with the slogans of the street poets. The people he saw reminded Gabriel of caged cats he had seen, listless, fur matted and greasy, like badly cast cracked-mold copies of their brethren in the wild.

Already Gabriel had realized that Bugout Plaza was not so much a place as a state of spirit. And every big city had its Bugout Plaza.

Kipper turned into a narrow alley, at the end of which the words "Big Lila's Lizard Pit" flashed garishly above a slowly revolving door. After a beat they morphed into, "In-house INworlding: The Mountains of Lust! The Valleys of Love! The Rivers of Ersatz Violence!—safe/flat rats."

Flat rats? Gabriel puzzled. Misspelling or some exotic game involving ground vehicles and rodents?

As they neared the entrance the door suddenly stopped revolving and the words "Keep Clear!" flashed on either side of it.

"Whups!" Kipper stepped to one side, pulling Gabriel with him. "Traffic coming thr . . ."

Before he could finish, the door suddenly spun and a yelping figure was catapulted sprawling onto the ground. He paddled feebly with his limbs, like a beached seal, muttering epithets to no one in particular.

"Bouncer bait," remarked Kipper. "Lila keeps a clean house . . . ah-ah!" He put out a restraining hand as

Gabriel moved to help. "Privacy, dilly, privacy," he cautioned. There was no irony in Kipper's tone.

Big Lila's was indeed a clean establishment, but no more welcoming at that. The music was too loud, the subsonics thumping up through the soles of Gabriel's feet, but that seemed to be deliberate. Just a tad too much for comfortable conversation, it forced you to lean in close to your partner and blanketed your exchange from prying ears. Primitive, but probably more secure than only having audio dampers around individual tables.

Through a doorway on the far side of the room Gabriel glimpsed the INworld tanks. Each, he knew, contained a person living a reality that had no existence outside cyberspace. In such short-term INworld trips a numbtab in the neck paralyzed the body from the neck down. Eyepieces and audiosystems and olfactoric enhancers supplied sight, sound, and smell, and stim-tabs on the main nerve junctions supplied a rough simulation of tactile contact. Much more intense than simple virtual reality, the experience was still only a crude approximation of the permanent INworld, where the brain was surgically disconnected from the voluntary motor functions of the body and the experience was supplied directly through the nervous system of the subject. But permanent INworld retirement was only for the filthy rich. INworld junkies, such as those who frequented places like Big Lila's had to make do with third-best.

Nobody looked around as they entered, but Gabriel did not doubt their presence had been noted by every pair of eyes in the place.

Kipper led him between the tables toward the bar, where a tall woman with African features and peroxide hair sat enthroned on a barstool.

"Lila, dilly-dam!" Kipper beamed at her.

She acknowledged their arrival without enthusiasm. "Kipper. I'd have thought you'd be top-shelving it today." She directed her words at Kipper, but her shrewd eyes were fixed on Gabriel, grid-mapping his face and body and storing everything away in her private memory files.

"And why would I be going that, dilly?"

"Word is rightly the spooks have been putting the grip

on every uplander in finger reach." For an instant Lila's eyes flicked away to something or someone behind Gabriel's right shoulder and Gabriel felt himself tensing.

"Ah, so's the word," affirmed Kipper easily. "And so it is."

"They get any of yours?"

"Give you three guesses."

Big Lila smirked knowingly. "Dogheart or Bannerman."

"Both." Kipper snickered.

Lila laughed silently. "Well, it never hurts to feed the spooks a few crumbs if it keeps 'em away from your dinner." Then her expression grew chilly. "But I don't know if I like you bringing new faces into my den at a time like this."

"Ah, Lila, would I bring in the bug? This is a friend of mine, an upside stike all the way." Kipper brushed her concerns away with his fingertips.

"Your upside friend got a label? Or a voice?"

Kipper grinned broadly. "All and everything."

Gabriel understood that a response was expected of him. "I reckon you can choose your own label," he said evenly. "Seems to me you picked one the moment I walked in the door."

"Meaning?" Lila's eyes narrowed with hostility.

"Meaning nobody comes in here without you knowing what to expect."

Lila indicated the INworld booths along the walls. "My customers come back for the service I give 'em. I keep it clean here. I keep it safe. They know that nothing'll get to them while they're INSIDE and when they come OUT things'll be the same. Gives me a nose for problems, y'know?"

"And I smell like I'm trouble, is that it?"

"Like used socks on a reeker."

"Then you'll . . ." Gabriel began, then jumped as he felt something snuffing around his ankles. A blue-gray mammalian, was peacefully licking the floor around Gabriel's and Kipper's feet. Gabriel knew it for an assitek, a graceful hunter from the temperate plains that made up the heart of Denube's largest continent. Powerful rear haunches gave the beast an acceleration unparalleled even by Earth's extinct cheetahs. Yet here it was, calmly lapping away at dust clods on the formina floor, like a bison at a salt lick. As Gabriel shifted his feet it broke off its lapping and regarded him with equanimity. Having sized him up, it lowered its toothless maw to the floor again and shuffled happily off to investigate some spilled ale under one of the tables.

"Sweet new wrinkle from D.N.Amics," said Lila helpfully. "Redid the whole guts they say. Eats, drinks anything, and it keeps the floor spankier than a cleaning pod . . ." She trailed off as Gabriel refused to meet her eye.

"They always pick the predators," he muttered.

"Hey?"

"Always pick the predators," he repeated, acid coming through in his voice. "Never the grazers. The society of convenience. People always seem to like having something dangerous about the place, but without the danger. Have you noticed?"

"I don't track you," said Lila quizzically. "You prodding me the cold-spikes?"

Kipper was looking worried. "Now, Lila . . ." he began.

"It's alright, Kipper," Gabriel interrupted. He let out a long, slow breath. *For all things a time and a place.* He could feel that someone was behind him, ready to intercede at the flicker of an eyelid from Lila. "Maybe," he suggested, "you could tell me how I could put your mind at rest."

"There's a door over there. You might use it." Lila's reply was tart.

Gabriel shrugged and smiled helplessly. "That's the trouble with revolving doors, you never know if you're coming or going."

"I could show you in about three seconds."

"Ah, but that's because you're a wise and perceptive lady, whereas I can turn myself inside out just putting on my underwear."

Lila regarded him for a moment and allowed a certain amusement to seep into her expression. "And inside out is the point, isn't it?" she said softly.

Kipper eased himself back into the exchange. "Now, Lila, where's the house hospitality?" he chided. "You've got two thirsty gents here."

"Well, now, we can't have that, can we?" she mur-

mured archly. "Still want a drink if I tell you that we
had some spook in here yesterday, looking for Bimo?"

"Bimo?" Kipper tensed and something passed between him and Lila. "Uniform?"

Lila's lip curled. "You think I need to see a uniform
to twenty-twenty spookland a klick away? The stike was
sticky with Mickey from the navel out."

Kipper frowned. "This spook: TARC?"

Lila shook her head. "No: fairboy. Big bugsucker.
Raccoon knew him from Green Sector. Says he plays it
in plain view, no double-spikes, but you never know with
the opposition." She shrugged and glanced over as a
customer lurched out of the back room. "Alby," she
called over to him, "been good places?"

Alby stared about him vaguely, seemed about to head
for the bar, but then changed his mind. His fingers curled
into chicken claws and he struck out at empty air, swaying, as if fighting a headwind.

"Shit, a disconnect! Hua!" she hissed, but the bartender was already leaping over the bar and two figures
had stepped out of the tank room to seize Alby. Gabriel
had only seen this kind of thing once before. On occa-
sion an INworlder could temporarily lose his ability to
differentiate between external reality and the INworld.

Alby let out a howl of terror as they seized him and
dragged him, struggling, back through the doorway. Lila
slid off her barstool and followed, gesturing sharply for
the bartender to resume his post.

"Shag-a-lackey! What the flock is wrong with you hag-
heads! How long have you been working here that you
can't twenty-twenty a disconnect when he's losing his
rags right in front of you?" Her voice faded.

"Who's Bimo?" Gabriel inquired.

"Uplander. One of ours," replied Kipper shortly.

"Why would the spooks be looking for him in
particular?"

Kipper grunted. "We think he's a mouth. Trickles the
word spookland-ways." He smirked. Not a lot of mouths
in the upland. Doesn't pay. Too easy to lose your three-
point and find yourself heading for the flatlands at a
terminal-V. But with Bimo we always make sure we feed
him the bug. Send spookland heading off wrongways."

"At that moment Lila returned, leading Alby by the

arm. She was speaking softly to him, her manner reassuring. As they watched, the INworlder smiled weakly and broke away from her and tottered over to the bar, grasping it with both hands, as if afraid that it would dissolve. Lila tweaked a finger at the bartender, who plucked a glass from a dispenser and set it before him.

"Part of the service," she explained casually, as she resumed her perch. "I always keep a live bartender. Brings 'em back down more easily if they've got someone to spill to."

"And you never know what they'll spill, hey, Lila?" Kipper's twinkle was wicked.

"I keep my customers," she replied primly, "the ones don't get shown the door. Now what do *you* want?"

"Not what, dilly, who," replied Kipper. "We're looking for an old curb-roller, Old Mac labeled. Got pinched by the TARCs in Rainer Park after hours a few months back."

"Sooooo." Lila breathed grimly, and she stared at Gabriel straight on. "You're muckin' in big places, Kipper, dilly. Dark places."

"You know where he is then?"

"No. Word is that he's gone downland."

"Shit, I was afraid of that. How're we goin' to gravel him out of there?"

"If you really want to know where he is, you're best off diggin' up Three-eyed Erzsi streetside."

"Curb-roller?"

"Half-gone," Lila affirmed, "but not all the way. She tends to hang in the slugwarrens."

"She would." Kipper said, grimacing.

"Never were one for the flatlands, were you, Kipper," Lila taunted, then added, "Word is she usually picks up her midday one-square at the Arry Street Dispenser. It's lunchtime now."

A suspicion had been nibbling at Gabriel. He said, "Sorry, but this spook—the one who was in here—did he have a name?"

"Have a hard time getting his mail if he didn't, stike," Lila snorted. Gabriel waited, and she said indifferently, "Izeki. Harridora or some-so. Friend of yours, long-lost?" Her teeth glinted suddenly. "Or are you the long-lost?"

"Lila, you're my queenie-queen," interjected Kipper before Gabriel could respond, "but it's time we went pattyfoot."

"You haven't had your drink," replied Lila, beckoning to the bartender. Something in her manner had changed and Gabriel could feel the sudden tension in Kipper. "And maybe your friend wants to step into the INworld for a time. We do have special one-time-onlys for the first-time visits, stike. What'll your knock-'em-back be?" The bartender stood poised.

"Time we haven't, Lila, time we haven't." Kipper grinned, sidling away from the bar and heading for the door.

"Another time maybe," said Gabriel, following.

Lila watched them pensively, her bottom teeth nipping at her upper lip.

"Hey, newboy!" she called suddenly. Gabriel paused by the door. "I'd be careful about smiling with someone else's eyes!" She chortled. "Or getting mad with someone else's fangs!"

Kipper was careful to make sure that Gabriel was first out of the door and he was swearing as they emerged. Lila's evicted client was nowhere to be seen.

Quickly they hustled down the alleys and Halls until they had put a safe distance between themselves and Big Lila's.

"You can trust Lila . . . till you can't," grumbled Kipper. "Trust is business and you get what you pay for."

"Somehow I think she was feeing shortchanged," replied Gabriel drily.

"Took her ten minutes to start thinkin' it over, though" said Kipper. "Don't snook a ten-minute freebie from Big Lila. She must have liked you." He hissed to himself with satisfaction. "You know what the giveaway is with you, stike?" he said happily. "You get mad at the wrong things."

"Don't count on it," growled Gabriel.

The slugwarrens started on the western edge of Bugout Plaza, a maze of loading facilities, warehouses and storage bins, quarantine labs and customs security enclosures. Everything that moved in or out of Kyara passed through the slugwarrens: shipments of single-crystal circuitry outbound for Denube and Las Palmas; Walk-Vs,

V.T.s, INworld tanks arrived from Ho Chi; nicotine root, lysergic gum, fabiana and acrovak from Ikaat and Other-life pills from Mars; culinary delicacies like Elbany gum-wads and tekkelblossom, vinefruit and reddigab plums.

Aside from the legal goods trade there were the tram-liners, smugglers dodging import and export taxes, or dealing in goods either restricted or outright banned. There was only one route out of Kyara, for goods and people alike, and in the case of goods, either licit or illicit, that route led through the slugwarrens.

The Arry Street Dispenser was located, with standard bureaucratic logic, not on Arry Street itself, but in McGarret Hall, leading off from the northern end of Arry Street. Like all Free Dispensers the food it dis-pensed consisted of quickfarm-pulp nutribricks, perfectly vitamin- and mineral-balanced and with all the flavor of a damp sponge. Not that this seemed to bother the curb-rollers and bugheads gathered around the dispenser and squatting on nearby doorsteps. Fifty meters further up the street a police robot stood sentinel, surveying the tableau dispassionately.

Gabriel felt Kipper's finger giving him a reassuring poke in the ribs as they approached the dispenser where a half dozen figures were squatting around an old V.T. someone had set up in a disused doorway, watching a roundup of the past week's news.

"Erzsi?" said the first man they addressed, sucking nutribrick crumbs off a greasy thumb. "No Erzsi here. No Erzsi nowhere. None."

"Mm-hm." Kipper nodded. "No Erzsi, eh?"

"No Erzsi."

Kipper leaned in close and poked a finger in the direc-tion of the Police robot. "How 'bout I ask my toyman friend over there to ask you?"

"How 'bout you do?" snorted the curb-roller. "Mighty Mickey got no grip on me."

"Mighty Mickey got a grip on all and everyone, stike, so how 'bout you tell me?"

"How 'bout you give me one good reason?"

"How 'bout I show you how much you may not like my reasons, dilly-dill?"

The curb-roller considered this and shrugged. "Round

the corner, alley, second doorway, 'cept as she's finished her one-square," he grunted with a jerk of his head.

They found her squatting in the second doorway, a tiny, sparrow-boned woman of who-knew-what age, face framed by graying hair and a gypsy shawl. She glanced up from her meal at their approach and the origin of her nickname was immediately apparent. In the center of her forehead a prosthetic eye gleamed, a silver orb complete with surgically constructed browridge and eyebrow.

Her gaze shifted furtively right and left, considering her chances, before she settled down resignedly and resumed her meal.

"Erzsi?" Kipper hailed her.

She ignored him.

"We're looking for Three-eyed Erzsi."

"Dunno. Nobody here like that," she muttered, not looking up.

Kipper squatted down before her. He said coolly, "Dilly, dilly, dilly, never muck with a mucker. Now, unless you got a fourth headlight stashed in pocket someplace, I reckon we've got your label rightly-right. What d'you net through that thing anyway? You see infrared like the toymen?"

Erzsi fixed him with a fierce stare and Kipper swayed back on his heels. "I see a lot more than that, stike. I see you in the upland, hangin' three-points fast. I see Thor's ghosts in the streets, bringin' on the hammer. I see the ghosts on every shoulder."

"Well, we're not lookin' for ghosts."

"You lookin' for ghosts!" she cackled. "He know!" A twiggy finger was aimed at Gabriel. "I got the sight. I got the third eye. I see!" Then she was scouring for crumbs in her carton again, lips smacking as she licked her fingers.

Kipper was showing signs of irritation, so Gabriel eased him to one side and crouched in front of her. "I reckon we're all of us spending most of our lives looking for ghosts of some kind or another, hey?" he said softly. "You leave your childhood the day that you start looking for ghosts that aren't there, instead of seeing the ones that are."

Erzsi glared at him suspiciously.

"What's *your* story?" he pressed.

She spat. "I got no story! And I sure got no ghosts! I got nothing! I don't want nothing!"

"So what brought you to Bugout Plaza?"

Erzsi fell silent.

"I knew an old man," Gabriel continued. "He could see a thousand kilometers over the desert. He could turn into the eaglehawk and fly around the world in an afternoon, or become like the gecko and crawl invisible over the sand. He knew the songs that sang the world to life . . . all the worlds. There's still a few of them left, the ones that can see . . . but you know that, don't you. You've got his eye."

Erzsi grunted.

"We're looking for someone," Gabriel said. "Thought maybe you could help us."

"I don't know no one."

"I thought you had the sight."

"No sight. No nothing."

"He's an old man," Gabriel said patiently. "Another old man. Calls himself Old Mac. We need to talk with him."

There was a pause whilst Erzsi nosed for invisible crumbs in her carton. "You got sweet things on you?" she said abruptly. "You got something that tastes? Dispenser blocks don't tongue nothing. They could give them taste, easy, but Mighty Mickey like people to *pay*. Make the free bricks taste and everyone's going to want it free. I want something that *tastes*."

Gabriel looked helplessly at Kipper, who drew up his shoulders. Erzsi eyed him greedily.

"I'm sorry, we've got nothing," Gabriel told her regretfully.

"Then Erzsi got nothing!" she pouted.

"And if we get your something, something you like?"

"Erzsi still got nothing. Got nothing. Know nobody."

Kipper was looking disgusted. Gabriel thought for a moment. "Could you give Old Mac a message for me?"

"Don't know him. Can't remember messages."

"Fine. 'Cos I've got a message I want you to forget to give to nobody you haven't met anytime and nowhere, okay?"

Three eyelids blinked slowly in unison.

Aha! Got you!

"Now the message is . . ." Gabriel broke off. *Shit. This is good. What am I supposed to tell this person?* At length he said, "Tell Old Mac I've got a message from . . . Louise . . . from the woman who came back as Louise. Tell him . . . tell him she told me about the *Far Cry*. Tell him . . . I'm trying to find the people who killed Louise." Suddenly he remembered something else that Louise Daud had said to him. It was worth a try. "No. Tell him Ellis meets Louise in that park every night. And Louise met Elspeth Kylie. And Louise has a message for him. My name is . . ." He hesitated. "Gabriel Kylie. You got that? Gabriel Kylie."

"I got . . ."

". . . nothing, I know," Gabriel interrupted. He reached out and grasped her by the shoulders, ignoring her feeble squawk of protest and forced her to meet his gaze. A tiny reflection of himself stared back out of her third eye. "Erzsi, *please!* Do this for me. If you know where he is, I'll meet him anywhere, anytime, his conditions. I'll . . . meet him here, tonight, after dark-down. I'll be here. Midnight. Right here. Alone."

"Stiiiiike . . ." Kipper began in a wheedling tone.

Gabriel silenced him with a glare and a raised hand. He turned back to Erzsi. "Alone," he repeated.

Erzsi was still for a moment. Then she gave a wriggle and Gabriel released her.

"Don't know nothing," she mumbled almost inaudibly, rubbing her shoulders where he had gripped them. "You hurt me."

Gabriel sighed resignedly. "Sorry. Forget what I said if you want. But *remember* to forget it, okay? You'll do that for me?"

A whisper, defiant. "Don't do nothing."

"No, of course not." Gabriel rose to his feet.

Suddenly Erzsi stiffened, her witchety nose sniffing the air. "Spooks," she hissed. Before they could raise a hand to stop her she had dropped her food carton and was darting away down the alley into the slugwarrens.

Kipper made as if to pursue her, but Gabriel held him back. "It's alright, leave her. We're not going to get anything else out of her."

Kipper protested, "There's no rule says you've got to be so shagging polite, dilly."

"We're not the spooks."

"Shagging curb-rollers," Kipper muttered contemptuously. "They're halfway long-dropped anyway."

"She may have been right about the spooks, though, don't you reckon?"

"Hm," Kipper grunted. "Meet me on the corner at midnight." He snorted. "Where'd you think that one up, dilly?"

The police robot had disappeared when they returned to McGarret Hall. The eddy of bugheads around the Free Dispenser had thickened, clogging the Hall. The V.T. watchers had moved a little further down the street in apparent response to the overcrowding around the dispenser itself. It was as Kipper and he were pushing their way past the V.T. huddle that something made Gabriel freeze in his tracks. He swung around and shouldered aside watchers amidst a mutter of protests.

"What did that say . . . review it!" he exclaimed, pointing at the V.T. display. "Review that last bit!"

"Don't you lay hands on me!" growled one voice.

Another cackled. "You think some dill would have slung this vitty streetside if it could still review?"

"Shit!" Gabriel swore. But he did not really need to have the fragment of news broadcast reviewed; he was certain of what he had heard. He spun back to face Kipper, his eyes glazing . . . *the murder of seventy-three-year-old Louise Daud, which, according to TARC sources is connected to roofrunner activity. The window of her tenth-story apartment was shattered, apparently by a device delivering an infrasonic pulse . . .*

Kipper was already backing away from him, his eyes narrowed.

"Kipper!"

Kipper turned and began running up the Hall. Gabriel sprinted after him, slamming people aside right and left regardless.

"Hey, bugsucker!" A roar and an arm thudded into Gabriel's side.

"Kipper, you've been lying to me!"

Kipper darted in and out of view, amidst a forest of gray figures, vaulting over a prone eth-head and then ducking sideways into an alley. People flinched aside as Gabriel uttered a wordless roar, charging toward the alley. Rounding the corner he saw Kipper six meters ahead of him, fumbling at his chest as he ran. Gabriel knew what that meant. He increased his speed to close the distance between them. As he did so Kipper reached the alley's dead end and arrowed straight up the wall in one grasshopper bound.

Gabriel threw himself into the air, his arms closing around Kipper's right leg. Instantly his head and shoulders were pounded by vicious stamps from Kipper's free foot as they swung against the wall, forcing an audible grunt from Kipper. "Let me go!"

"Come dow . . ." Kipper's heel caught Gabriel a numbing blow in the mouth, but the worst of it was cushioned by the latezine mask. Kipper had not had time to get his slaphappy slippers on, so their combined weight was hanging from his gloved hands.

"You lied to me, you son of a bitch." Gabriel succeeded in grabbing Kipper's belt and pulling himself up until he was hanging from Kipper's waist. "Now let go!" Kipper's legs lashed about, scrabbling for leverage. They hung from the wall like a web-trapped beetle, two limbs stuck fast, the other four thrashing for freedom. "Let go!" Gabriel repeated.

"I can't! You let go!"

"Let go!"

"I *can't*!" Kipper panted, "Slap them down . . . peel them . . . up . . ."

"I'll peel you up, you little pillock!" Gabriel's arm was around Kipper's neck now and the little man was choking and writhing about.

"Let me go . . . and I'll come . . . down," he gasped.

Gabriel hissed between clenched teeth. "You think I'd . . . trust you . . . you're going to tell me about . . . the old woman." He grabbed for Kipper's right wrist and managed to loosen the fastening of Kipper's slaphappy glove. Kipper's wriggling became more frenzied. Then his hand slipped free and he emitted a cry of pain as they swung out and around, all the weight depending from his left wrist.

"I'll bring you . . . back to the . . . soil, you . . ." Gabriel grabbed at Kipper's other wrist. Kipper jabbed his elbow into Gabriel's ribs. Then, as they swung back, he managed to snatch his lost slaphappy free of the wall. He gave one last convulsive kick. Somehow his foot found purchase and suddenly they were falling, twisting, the wall rushing past them. Smack! Gabriel's breath jarred from his body as his side and shoulder struck the pavement.

He hung on grimly, trying to pin Kipper to the ground. The roofrunner was hissing, "You scabsucking flatlander . . ." He was trying to use Gabriel's injured arm to his own advantage.

Ignoring the pain, Gabriel panted into his ear, "That's it . . . that's right, you're in the flatlands now . . . and if you don't stop, I'll break your skinny neck!"

Abruptly, Kipper went limp. For a brief instant Gabriel thought that he had indeed given over. Just in time Gabriel felt Kipper fumbling in his leg pocket. A gnat-whistle rising. He seized Kipper's right wrist as the other brought up the buzz-knife to slash at the arm locked around his neck. The two men rolled over and over, sparks crackling, spattering, winging hot against Gabriel's bare neck and wrist as the buzz-knife scored the surface of the street, the air flinty with acrid fumes. A backward wrench of Kipper's wrist and the buzz-knife went skittering away across the ground. His weapon lost, Kipper collapsed.

Releasing his choke hold on Kipper's neck, Gabriel threw his opponent to one side and staggered to his feet, coughing as he bent to retrieve the buzz-knife. When he turned back, Kipper was on his hands and knees, breath wheezing. Feebly he picked up his fallen slaphappy and pawed at it like a sick child seeking solace from a favorite toy. He was mumbling to himself.

Gabriel glanced down the alley, but no one had followed them. People minded themselves in Bugout Plaza. He flicked off the buzz-knife and straightened up.

"Tell me about it, Kipper. And no more lies."

Kipper turned on him a gaze of pure venom.

"Who's been lying to who, dilly?" he rasped. "Mighty Mickey got you in his pocket, or you always play double-spiked?"

"Don't screw with me anymore, Kipper." Gabriel

strove to keep his voice calm. "I want some truth. Tell me something."

"I'm losing you, stike, what can I tell you?"

"A lovely, mad old lady called Louise Daud! Tell me about Louise Daud!"

"Flock it, you diddled my wrist rightly," Kipper muttered sullenly. "Shagging flatlander . . ."

"Tell me how she died, Kipper."

"I don't know how she died."

"Yes, you do, Kipper. You killed her. You or Lazarus or one of those shagging roof monkeys of yours . . ."

Kipper's face registered shock, but if it was real or put on Gabriel could not tell. "You're beating rags in a dry bath, dilly, nobody killed her . . ."

Gabriel's temper snapped. "She's *dead,* Kipper!" he shouted. "She's *dead*! People are *dead,* for Macca's sake! You and that flockin' psychotic playing half-assed coroboree on the shagging rooftops and people, *innocent* people, are being *killed!*"

"For Macca's sake, damp it!" Kipper hissed in alarm. "You want the flockin' toymen . . ."

"The toymen? You're worried about the toymen?" Gabriel seized Kipper by the lapels and shoved him backwards toward the mouth of the alley. "You're worried about the flockin' toymen? I'll give you flockin' toymen! Here . . ." Each repetition of the word "toymen" was punctuated by another shove, sending Kipper reeling off-balance.

"You've lost your bloody rags . . ." Panic was starting to show on the little man's face.

"You have *no* idea," Gabriel breathed, death bright in his eyes. Another push and Kipper fell sprawling.

He cried out, "Alright! Alright! Alright! Just stop!"

Gabriel stopped, breathing heavily, his voice shaky with anger. "So, tell me the story, Kipper . . . and don't even think it," he added, as Kipper's eyes flicked toward the wall.

Kipper climbed to his feet and held out his hands, his grin shaky. "It's the upside truth, stike, we didn't do it!"

"Oh, no?" Gabriel advanced on him again. "She lived on the tenth floor! Who else apart from an uplander doesn't know the difference between a front door and a tenth-story window?"

"You think . . . ?"

". . . These freaks around here? The TARCs? They don't need to!"

"You think uplanders are the only ones know how to put on a pair of slaphappies?"

Gabriel paused. "No, of course not . . ."

"No, of course not," Kipper sneered, pressing his advantage. "You never hear of a setup, dilly-dill?"

Gabriel examined Kipper's face, then his mouth twisted into a grim smile. "No, Kipper, no setup; you people were there. Oh, Mr. Toyman!" Gabriel called out, over Kipper's shoulder.

Kipper flinched, then shook his head defiantly. "No. You do that, stike, you'll be losing more than me if spookland gets the grip on us."

"Wrong, Kipper," replied Gabriel pleasantly. He mimicked the curb-roller patois. "I got nothin'. Don't got nothin', no, dilly. Mr. Tooooooyman!"

Kipper was genuinely frightened now. "I didn't kill her . . ."

"*Step* this way . . ."

"We didn't kill her!"

"You were there. Helloooo . . . ?"

"*Yes!* We were there, *but she was already dead!*" Gabriel halted. "She was already dead!" Kipper repeated. "She was lying on the floor, by her desk. We didn't even twenty-twenty her till after we'd blown the window inways. She was still warm." Gabriel studied him. Kipper seemed genuinely miserable, but . . . "We wanted to net the place, floor-t'-ceiling, that's all. We knew your sister'd spoken with her one time. We figured, after you spoke to her, that it might be worth a look."

"Who's 'we'?"

Kipper's mouth drew a straight line.

"Who's 'we'?" Gabriel repeated.

"Toh and me."

"And what were you looking for?"

"What do you think?" Kipper's eyes rolled heavenward. "You have yeast blocks in your ears all last night?" The slaphappy glove slipped from his fingers. "Shag it," he mumbled, bending to retrieve it.

"I listened very well last night, Kipper—" Gabriel broke off with a gasp as Kipper's foot struck him in the

groin. Reflexively he had doubled over and so escaped
the full force of the blow, but the pain of it still caused
him to gasp. There was a blur of celerity before his eyes
and Kipper was no longer there.

Slap! Slap!

Gabriel flung himself back, but it was too late, Kipper
was already two man-heights up the wall, skipping crab-
wise with his two slaphappies and spitting curses over
his shoulder.

"Kippeeeer!" Gabriel cried out.

But the roofrunner had disappeared over the first
parapet.

"Shit!" Gabriel struck the wall in fury with both fists.
He reached for his own slaphappies, but immediately
gave up on the idea. It was not even worth trying.

Stooped over with both pain and anger at himself,
Gabriel rested his face against the wall and closed his
eyes, a keening growl emerging from his throat. *You
stupid, stupid, stupid, bloody . . .* He was unsure what
hurt most, his own foolishness, or the sudden shame he
felt at having attacked the little roofrunner in that way.
And yet again he had been lied to.

Stupid, stupid, stupid . . .

Gabriel opened his eyes. A couplet of long-dead graffiti was barely visible against the wall's surface. He
pulled his head back to focus.

> *"There was a young dill from Clandinnish,*
> *Who left all his limericks unfinished, . . ."*

Abruptly dizzy, Gabriel turned his back on it and let
himself slide down the wall until he was sitting on the
ground. Only then did he become aware of the stench
in the alley; apparently even the cleaning pods seldom
ventured here.

He squeezed shut his eyes, desperately trying to recall
the burnt-glass scent of the dust around Landing and
with a swell of fear realized that he could not. It was
as if a deadness had descended on his guiding senses.
Everything he reached for seemed to crumble at his
touch. Since the moment he had arrived in Kyara he
had stumbled about, like a sun-drunk Sunday hunter,
trampling the delicate trail of his prey. And into this

morass Gabriel had dragged the one person who had believed in him unquestioningly.

"Iz," he whispered, and stood up.

Through a gap in the structure above him he could glimpse the domes of the city and the bars that caged the sky. He crushed the rising wave of claustrophobia and forced himself to concentrate. *Watch out for danger with the back of your neck, listen with your skin, but never take your eyes from the trail.*

It was time that he spoke to someone he should have confronted a long time ago. Fingering his mask to see that it was still in place, Gabriel strode out of the alley.

under the skin

Elspeth's journal:

> *I got word today that Grandmother Lalumanji's
> died. I knew that anyway. I wonder how Gabby
> found me here. Zuleika's a long way from Earth. Ev-
> erywhere is. I won't forget, Gran. I won't forget.*

Edom Japaljarayi was less than pleased to hear from
Isadora. It took intervention from Izeki, wielding Municipal Police authority, to breach the phalanx of secretaries
and bring him to the phone and when he did appear on
Izeki's home-phone viewplate, his manner was guarded.

"I'm not certain I'll be doing myself a favor by receiving you, Ms. Gatzalumendi. What is it that we can't discuss over the phone?

"I'm sorry, but it's important that I see you face-to-
face at your office," Isadora persisted. "Please."

"You know I had to endure an hour of grilling from
Targeting, Apprehension and Remand Central. That is
not a pleasant experience at the best of times and I am
not grateful for being associated with an escaped criminal and suspected murderer."

Izeki, sitting just out of sight behind her, shifted impatiently and Isadora held up a cautioning finger.

"You deceived me, Ms. Gatzalumendi," Edom
continued.

"Nobody deceived you, Mr. Japaljarayi," stated Isadora firmly.

"The TARCs intimated that Mr. Kylie was not
even . . . Mr. Kylie. Apparently there are grounds for
believing his name to be an alias."

"There are no such grounds. Look, Mr. Japaljarayi, did the TARCs mention something called the 'blue box'?"

Edom hesitated. "Yes," he said. Izeki straightened in his chair.

"Did they tell you what it was?"

"No, they didn't," Edom admitted.

"Did you ask them?"

"Yes, I did, and before you continue I should like to point out that the TARCs are in no way obliged to give out information concerning an investigation."

"But they grilled you for an hour and I'll bet they seemed more interested in this blue box than they did in Mr. Kylie himself."

Edom fell silent.

Isadora pressed her advantage. "And they treated you like a criminal."

"Yes."

Well, that's what they've been doing to Gabriel Kylie, from the day he arrived. Now, please, I need to see you. It's important. Please." Isadora put all the urgency she could muster into her tone.

Edom seemed to consider for a moment. "Some policeman pulled rank on my secretaries to get you this call. Is he going to pull rank on me if I refuse?"

Isadora paused, then sighed. "No," she said, hoping that he would believe her. She was less than certain herself. "But I'd like to bring him with me if I come. This is off-duty work for him."

Edom smiled faintly, without humor, "Come in an hour; I'll have a pass waiting for you at the main entrance. Phone off."

The image flicked out before Isadora could say goodbye. She heaved a sigh of relief. Izeki raised his eyebrows and gave her a nod of acknowledgment.

Edom was waiting for them himself when they arrived and he guided them to his private office on the ground floor.

When they were settled, Isadora and Edom with a cup of coffee and Izeki with nothing but a glower, Edom said, "Well, why don't you tell me what it is that is so important."

Isadora glanced at Izeki. "Mr. Japaljarayi . . ." she began.

He interrupted her. "You might as well call me Edom." He sighed. "Or we're going to be here all day."

Slightly flustered, Isadora continued, "When I was here the day before yesterday with Gabriel, we brought a map of Rainer Park with us. We downloaded it into your computer system. Do you still have the file?"

Without hesitation Edom put his palm on the desk-plate, and said, "Daedalus, computer on. Pass priority one-one-seven, code . . ." His voice faded as an audio-dampening field surrounded the desk. They could see his lips moving as he recited the access code. A blue sphere appeared over his desk, indicating that the computer was on and ready. The next minute his voice became audible again. "List all files downloaded from outside sources within the last forty-eight hours. A list comprising a dozen or so files replaced the sphere. Edom reached up and "pinched" one of them between his thumb and forefinger. The next instant the map of Rainer Park was floating above the desk.

"Ste*rike*!" Isadora exclaimed delightedly. She had been right!

Izeki walked over to the desk and examined the map curiously. "This what all the fuss was about?"

"This is it," Isadora replied, a little breathless.

Edom was waiting expectantly. At length he asked, "Well, having found 'it,' what now?"

"The file size," Isadora said. "It's too big. For the map. Too big for the quality of resolution."

Edom's expression remained puzzled, but he said, "Daedalus function: show file size." He studied the numbers that appeared over the map and his frown deepened. "Yes. It is too big. Actually, it's a great deal too big."

"Which means there's something else in this file, something hidden . . . or something that we just don't know how to access."

"All we have is this map; there's nothing else."

"Could there be a way of enhancing the level of detail? All this shows is architectural detail, rooms, access tunnels . . ." Isadora's voice trailed off as Edom shook his head.

"No, out of the question," he said. "Any increase of detail and you'd be getting into the actual technical stuff, generators and so on. The only person, apart from Mr. Rainer himself, who has access to that is me. Frankly, I'm surprised she managed to get ahold of this, although it's not impossible through normal bureaucratic channels."

"And you haven't given this to anybody," Iseki said.

"No, and I couldn't if I wanted to." Edom smiled and tapped his head. "Force-conditioned mental block. It's voluntary, but legally compulsory for anybody involved in Icarus Field grid construction. Since the park grid needs to be synched-up with the city grid to avoid Field turbulence at the point of joining, that means I have to know the precise gridpoint layout at the city's edge, and so that means me. I couldn't tell you if you set fire to my gums with a dental laser."

Isadora allowed herself a smile and went on. "You say it's not impossible to get ahold of this map through bureaucratic channels, though."

"No, of course not. The Central Construction and Safety Bureau has a copy of it."

"Mm-hm." Isadora pursed her lips.

"If this is significant," Edom said, "then I think that I'm obliged to turn this over to the authorities."

"What do I look like," Izeki growled, "Sammy the San-Man?"

"Well, no," Edom conceded doubtfully, "but it was Targeting, Apprehension and Remand Central that . . ."

"Oh, you want a repeat visit?" Izeki drawled. "Seems like a lot of people prefer their company to mine these days." He shot a sardonic look at Isadora.

Edom grimaced. "You have a point, Officer."

Isadora had been thinking. "What," she mused, "if we have an onion?"

"Onion? Aah, in that sense . . ." Edom considered, a spark of interest lighting up his face. "That does seem a little more likely. *This* is certainly not much use to anybody."

"Hello? Onion? What am I missing here?" Izeki looked perplexed.

"This is just a front," explained Isadora, indicating the Rainer Park display. "The real file is at the core. We

have to peel this off to get to it. Possibly even several
layers."

Edom elaborated. "It's a generic term, quite straightforward. With something like this I would guess that
you'd have to be somewhere in the map—be in one of
the rooms—and then enter a codeword to get you further in to the core, to the real file."

"How many rooms are we talking about searching
through?" Izeki asked.

Edom gave a rueful grimace. "Hundreds. And that's
not including corridors and access tubes."

"And then we'd still need the access code," added
Isadora glumly.

"That's just upside," growled Izeki.

"Unless . . ." Isadora was thinking now. "It may not
be as bad as all that. I've sat with that journal of hers.
It might make a difference if she hid it in order to hide
it, or if she intended for it to be found."

"You mean by the right person." Izeki's eyes gleamed.

"Right."

"Assuming that there is a hidden file at all," Edom
interjected. "And that's still a rather optimistic
assumption."

"Would you have a look through the display . . . just
to see if there is anything that's . . . I don't know . . .
out of place. Please," she pleaded when the little engineer hesitated.

"Very well, I can have a cursory look," he agreed.
"As long as you realize I have a *real* park to run. I can't
spend all day on this."

For the next twenty minutes Isadora sat restlessly as
Edom flitted from detail display to detail. Izeki was
slumped, unmoving, the chair he was seated on seeming
far too delicate to support his massive frame. His eyes
were focused on a point far beyond the confines of the
office. Only the nicotine root between his chubby lips
twitched occasionally, like some extended facial tic.

Isadora still wondered about the Municipal officer.
Sometimes he was there, in force, alert, prickling with
contrariness, yet grudgingly capable. At other times it
was as if he had curled some inner part of himself
around a thorn and was pressing himself deliberately
into the pain. She had placed her trust in him, as earlier,

she had placed her trust in a stranger from a distant world. Why did trust sometimes seem in itself a deception, offering the balm of certainty and the ache of doubt on two tines of the same fork?

Abruptly Izeki came to life. He surveyed the office speculatively, the 2-D photographs festooning its walls. Heaving himself out of his chair, Izeki sauntered over to examine one of the nearest photographs.

"Arranda," he read.

Curious, Isadora went over to look. Izeki acknowledged her with a grunt. The photograph showed four naked, bearded men sitting on the ground in a dusty landscape, like solemn gargoyles. Isadora immediately recognized them by their features as Native Australians.

"Aboriginal tribal elders. Long gone," murmured Edom from behind them. "Pre-Plague. Same tribe as Gabriel Kylie as it happens."

At the mention of Gabriel's name Izeki seemed to stiffen. Isadora snatched a glance at him. His eyes had lost their focus for an instant. Something was not right with Izeki, a Pavlovian twitch brought on by any reference to Gabriel. Disturbed, Isadora looked away before Izeki could notice her attention.

To distract herself she pointed to several long, flat wooden boards lying in the dirt in front of the seated figures. "What are those?"

"Tjurangas. Tribal totems," Edom added by way of explanation. Seeing from Isadora's expression that she was none the wiser, he levered himself to his feet and crooked his finger at her.

"You can see them better in that one." He indicated a photograph on the opposite wall and hobbled over to it. Isadora followed.

This print showed another group of men, as solemn as the first. The boards here were clearer and Isadora could see that they had been painted on one side.

"These are tribal tjurangas," Edom explained. "They represented the heritage of the tribe, its spiritual heritage. Its land. Of course, not all tribes had them. There were individual tjurangas, too, representing a specific man's or woman's totem. Every tribesperson had a personal totem—a lizard, a bird. They measured conception from the moment that the mother felt the totem spring into her womb. That could be anywhere, anyplace."

Edom went on, "I suppose you might also say they were the repository of the soul. To lose your tjuranga to lose yourself." His eyes twinkled. "But that's . . ." He looked at the photograph a little wistfully. ". . . long gone." He fingered one of the short staffs underneath the spears, tapped it. "Woomera. Spear-thrower. They're still used."

"On Earth?" Isadora said in astonishment.

"On Octavia. It's a sport among the Zimmers there," Edom replied mischievously, then added, "*And* on Earth. There they use them for real. No, not everyone. But there's still a few tribal people there. My mother was one, so were her parents. And my father and his parents."

Izeki was incredulous. "You mean there are still primitive people on Earth?"

"Primitive?" Edom said sharply. Isadora looked at him in surprise.

"Watch yourself," she murmured to Izeki. "I think you just nudged a raw nerve."

"There aren't many," said Edom, a little grumpily, "A few thousand. Of us, anyway. There are Maoris, Inuit, even Native Americans, despite the wars and the Plagues. But Native Australians are one of the last tribal people left there whose traditions go back unbroken to prehistoric times. Tribal elder to tribal elder, still trying to keep the vision alive. 'Course there's no real reason why they shouldn't . . . damn." He spilled a few drops of coffee on the floor and a teapot-sized cleaning pod darted out of its niche. "They managed for fifty thousand years before technological civilization intruded . . . thank you, I'm alright." He smiled at Isadora, who had taken his arm, gently prying the coffee from his hand before he could scald himself. "These little spasm attacks . . . sometimes even my harness can't compensate. They don't last long." He stood clutching the table, his body racked with shudders. After several seconds the trembling lessened and he maneuvered himself into his desk chair. He said, a little breathlessly, "You seem a bit surprised, Officer. There are plenty of people on the Seventeen Planets who've gone back to a low-tech lifestyle. On Earth they live by their own laws, laws that they've reclaimed. Not the easiest of tasks."

He leaned back and waved a hand at the Rainer Park display. The image sprang inwards to reveal the ground plan as a whole. "I'm sorry, Ms. Gatzalumendi, I really can't stay here all . . ." The sentence trickled away as he focused upon the display, head cocked to one side.

"Tch, of course," he tutted at himself. "There it is. So simple."

"You have it?" Isadora asked in excitement, shooting a triumphant glance at Izeki.

"It's obvious when you see it. Not so obvious if you're not looking for it . . . here. The microlife chambers"— Edom indicated a row of minute octagons lined along a narrow access corridor—"they breed soil life, phyolites, worms, beetles and so forth and monitor the overall balance of the microecology. The microscopic life released into the soil is genetically neutered. Unless it's constantly fed with new life, the soil will go sterile. If there's too many, they stop the feed. It's just monitoring the balance."

"Right, right. So?"

"Well, there should be eleven chambers, see? 0.1, 0.2 and on through 0.11. There are twelve. *That* one shouldn't be there."

"O.Z.," Iadora read, "Z, no number. . . . huh."

"Rather nicely done," Edom conceded admiringly. "If you're not looking for it, you won't find it. If you are, it's obvious . . . provided you know the park."

"But that still leaves us without a password," Izeki pointed out.

"Not necessarily," said Isadora.

"Figures."

"If . . . if . . ." O.Z. This rang a bell. Gleefully she exclaimed, "It's child's play." Chuen would have been proud of her.

"It would be," muttered Izeki sourly.

"It is. It's not O.Z., it's Oz, a place. It's a mythical kingdom from pre-Plague literature!"

"Um . . . I . . . don't follow," said Edom, puzzled.

"I was right, we're looking at the psychology of the person who set up the file. Or, more specifically, we're looking for the identity for the person who was supposed to find it."

"Her . . . brother?" Edom queried.

"Gabriel Kylie," rumbled Izeki.

Isadora said with conviction, "Enter 'Tin Woodman.' "

Edom seemed perplexed. Then he gave a little shrug. "Tin Woodman . . . Daedalus function: enter passcode capital T-i-n, space, capital W-o-o-d-m-a-n?" He looked to Isadora for confirmation. "Vocalize: Tin Woodman. Confirm."

The display rippled once and then flashed, "Passcode invalid."

Izeki remarked annoyingly, "Just how mythical was this kingdom?"

"Why . . . 'Tin Woodman'?" Edom inquired.

Isadora was scowling. She had been so *sure*! "Well . . . it was supposed to be . . . to signify Gabriel," she replied.

"I see. Well, why not keep it simple?" Edom suggested. "Daedalus function: enter passcode capital G-a-b-r-i-e-l, vocalize: Gabriel. Confirm."

The desk display rippled again . . . and again and then Rainer Park was gone and its place taken by a ream of colored file folders.

Isadora breathed. "KISS. Keep It Simple, Stupid," she added by way of explanation.

Izeki was circling the display, examining it intently. "One day, lady, you're going to be wrong," he said grudgingly. But there was respect in his voice.

Edom flicked open one of the folders. The space above his desk was filled with columns of names and figures. "Interesting," he said after a moment's perusal. "Looks like books . . . financial records, maybe share sales . . . or something of the like. Not my area of expertise of course."

Isadora tried to reach up and turn the page, but the display did not respond.

"Palm-keyed," Edom said gently. He flipped the folder shut again. "I wonder . . . no—" He interrupted himself. "Perhaps I shouldn't inquire further . . . no, perhaps not."

"I do appreciate this, Edom," Isadora said earnestly.

They downloaded the file into the Notebook that Isadora had brought along for just that purpose. As Isadora was pocketing it Edom asked, "If the TARCs should return for a second visit, what should I tell them regarding this conversation?" His remark was directed at Izeki.

Izeki was blunt. "Tell them what you like."

Edom's lips twitched. "That would indeed be a pleasure," he said speculatively. "But I will be obliged by law to tell them what they wish to know should they ask . . . however"—Edom turned back to his desk—"Daedalus function: erase current file, including all copies. Level one override, codeword: capital V-a-n, space, capital D-i-e-m-e-n; vocalize, VanDiemen. Confirm." The display rippled and was no more.

Edom turned back to Isadora and his expression was dry. "What I don't have"—his shoulders rose and fell—"I can't give them." He looked a challenge in Izeki's direction, but Izeki simply gave a sharp nod of his head. "I wish I could do more for you, Ms. Gatzalumendi," Edom said regretfully.

"Isadora. Courtesy goes both ways."

"Isadora. I don't think we should meet again unless this is resolved in some way."

"I understand." She let her gratitude show in her face and turned to go.

They rode back from the Rainer Park control center in silence. It was not until they were in the corridor outside Izeki's apartment that Izeki unexpectedly paused in the act of palming his front door open, and asked, "The mythical kingdom. What was this . . . mythical kingdom?"

"Myth . . . oh. It was an old story in pre-Plague literature. About a little girl who got blown by a storm over an uncrossable desert surrounding a kingdom full of strange creatures and magic," Isadora explained. "The story was about how she was trying to get back to her family."

"Hm." Izeki stared at her for a second, then turned back to the door.

It was then that Isadora felt something brush ever so lightly against her hair, a touch, a *breathing*. Instinctively she jerked around.

The scream froze in her throat as she found herself

staring at a stranger's face, less than a palm's width away
from her own, an eerie, bogey face that was somehow
all wrong. As their eyes met, a gloved hand materialized
out of nowhere, a finger pressing against the lips for
silence. Only then did Isadora realize that the face was
upside-down.

Caught in a spasm of vertigo she stepped back, staring
upward uncomprehendingly as a ragged figure strode
across the ceiling toward Izeki. Like an observer of a
surreal shadow play she watched Izeki turn back from
the open doorway. Just too late Izeki saw him. His reaction mirrored Isadora's own as he froze, his jaw slack-
ening, for the merest fraction of an instant. By the time
he grabbed for his stunner, it was too late—the figure
on the ceiling had reached him. Black-gloved hands
seized Izeki's weapon arm, then the assailant was no
longer standing on the ceiling but falling, twisting in midair, twisting Izeki's arm with him as he landed feet first.
Izeki gave a sharp cry of pain and fell to his knees,
arching backwards onto his back.

"Chuen!" Isadora shouted.

The attacker rolled across the floor, a shine in his
palm—Izeki's slumbergun. He came to his feet, then,
unbelievably, he was a cockroach scuttling straight up
the wall. Isadora caught a glimpse of Chuen running
toward her through the open doorway, then Izeki was
blocking her view as he swarmed up from the ground,
his face livid.

"Stop! Or I'll drop you where you bloody stand!" The
figure was once again standing on the ceiling, only this
time Izeki's slumbergun was in his hand and drawing a
bead straight through Izeki's chest.

Although his eyes never left the figure on the ceiling,
Isadora could feel Izeki searching right and left with his
peripheral vision. Just inside the doorway, out of the
gunman's line of vision, Chuen stood, silently mouthing
something that Isadora could not read. Isadora was less
concerned with Chuen, however, than with their assailant. Hadn't she heard that voice before? He was tall
and thin and dressed in what she now recognized as
roofrunner garb.

He spoke again. "I need to talk with you, Officer."

Izeki gave a downward jerk of his head. "Alright, let's

talk. You come down here, you give me the gun, and we'll talk."

"Right," said the roofrunner. He perused the weapon in his hand critically, his aim not wavering, "Is . . . er . . . is this thing set for stun or nerve-shock?" he inquired conversationally.

Izeki licked his lips and Isadora understood that a point had been made.

The roofrunner said, "I'll give you back your weapon, but I want your word that we talk and I leave when I want, no tricks."

"You've got my word," said Izeki. Too quickly.

The roofrunner shook his head slowly from side to side. "No, I want your *word*."

Izeki seemed to be trying to chew his own gums. Then he gave another of his head jerks. "You have it." He was hating this.

The roofrunner visibly relaxed, his manner giving an impression of overwhelming fatigue (although Isadora was uncertain how she could judge that on a man currently imitating a fruit bat). With a puzzling ineptness he climbed down the wall. Halfway down he lost his hold and fell awkwardly on one knee. "Shit."

Isadora no longer had any doubt; the face was a stranger's, but that easy lilt in the voice could only be one person. "Gabriel?" she approached him.

"Iz"—Gabriel picked himself up—"strewth. If that had happened ten floors up . . . Officer." He held out the slumbergun to Izeki, who accepted it with bad grace, glancing at it as he did so.

"Safety's on," he said sourly.

"I've never found much profit in shooting police officers. Got somewhere I can sit down?"

Questions were flooding Isadora's mind, but she restrained herself and guided Gabriel into the apartment, where Chuen was still waiting, her expression veering from annoyance to confusion.

"Chuen, this is Gabriel. Gabriel, Chuen," Isadora felt foolishly uncomfortable.

Chuen subjected Gabriel to hostile scrutiny. "He doesn't much look the way you described him."

"I photograph better. Can I use your shower?"

"You want to talk there?" Izeki inquired. Then he gave a dismissive sweep of his arm.

"I'll show you," Isadora said, leading the way.

In the bathroom Gabriel peeled back the mask from his face and tossed it aside, a discarded skin, returning himself to himself. For the first time in a day his own reflection stared back out at him from the mirror, yet it seemed no more familiar than the face which now lay crumpled on the bathroom floor.

"Welcome back," he tried. It didn't help. He winced and keyed the water in the sink.

"It's an improvement," said Isadora from the doorway.

"I'm wondering," Gabriel replied through splashes of water. He raised his head from the sink and turned to her, face wet, droplets running over his eyes and from his chin. A hand brushed at his eyelashes.

"Iz . . ." What was there to say? In the alleys of Bugout Plaza it had seemed so clear, but now the ambivalence had returned.

"There's a clothes dispenser there," she said gently, indicating the wall. "You look a little frayed around the edges."

Gabriel grinned wryly, relieved. "I could use a wash."

Isadora closed the door.

Gabriel spent more time than was strictly necessary under the shower. He let himself be dried off and dialed himself a fresh coverall. The roofrunner garb he threw into the disposal slot, except for the filamented body stocking. He would need to walk the streets again and there was no sense in making things any easier for any police robots that he might meet.

When he emerged from the bathroom, Isadora was waiting with a plate of fresh fruit. He ate ravenously. As he ate, Isadora talked.

Chuen sat behind the terminal, rummaging through a display of what appeared to be folders full of documents.

The Asian girl was fascinating to watch, communing with her terminal as if with a lover, her beautiful, shaved head moving with minute jerks, birdlike. He did not resent her apparent animosity toward him; as a male in the presence of a Sister of Tanit he could expect little else. One of his favorite drinking companions back on

Denube had been a Sister: Guinevere Bly, or Bley, he had never been certain. It had always taken a beer or two to take the burr off her hostility; by the third four-grain Starshine, a more delightful font of tolerant humor and bugle-voiced bonhomie would be hard to find.

There seemed to be more to the animosity that he was experiencing from Chuen than straightforward adherence to Sisterhood precepts. But he let it lie. These things had a way of bubbling to the surface eventually.

Izeki's attitude was more troubling. Up until now, he had been as communicative as a cactus plant. The inner conflict which Gabriel had felt from him on the first day seemed to have grown more polarized. Every once in a while he would smolder his way over to the drink dispenser and retrieve another glass of atovar. Then he would settle back into his chair, observing, listening, communicating in snaps and grunts.

And Isadora. In forty-eight hours she had changed, wearier perhaps, but the lynx in her was alive, intoxicated with fear and excitement, more alive than she herself realized. So far she and Gabriel had done most of the talking. Occasionally Chuen would interject to clarify a point or Izeki some caustic comment.

They spoke around each other's presence, of forgotten voyages and long-lost ships.

Far Cry.

Twenty years ago a small ship had journeyed to an island in the stars and returned laden with . . . what? *Spices?*

Twenty years. The ghosts of Thor were awakening.

Gabriel shook himself.

"When I got attacked the first time," he ventured, "they wanted to know where something was, they wouldn't say what."

"The blue box?" suggested Isadora.

"What else?" snapped Chuen impatiently.

Gabriel spread his hands out and gave a tight grin. "Ah-heh, they didn't say, they referred to 'that which was stolen.' "

Iseki said drily, "Your little sister got about a bit. I wonder if it's genetic?"

Isadora said, "So we reckon that, whatever it was, maybe the blue box, she stole it from KV 99, is that it?"

"Yeah . . . no!" Gabriel shook his head, "No. She didn't have any access to KV 99 . . . or maybe she did, but we don't know, okay? We *do* know that she had access to Byron Systems, or at any rate Calaban Transport—she was in and out of there like a weasel in a rabbit hutch. Now, what occurred to me . . . I know she's blinded some of the cleaning pods on the roof, by getting into the central brain and throwing in a program that blinds them to anything human-sized or human-shaped."

"Yeah, well, that's standard." Izeki looked disgusted. "Roofrunners do that a lot. At least they don't kick 'em off the roofs anymore." He took out a nicotine root.

"So where would she have done that?" Isadora asked.

Gabriel shrugged, "Where would they have stashed the blue box?"

"In Calaban Transport's Central offices?"

"In a warehouse," suggested Chuen.

"Under the bed," said Gabriel.

Chuen frowned. "What's the point of that? You'd see it as soon as you retract the bed."

"Never mind. Low-tech joke."

Izeki spoke around his nicotine root. "There's always a problem with storing something precious, particularly if you don't want anyone else to know that you *have* something precious. You boost your security too high and everybody knows that you've got something to hide. Almost better to have none."

"Yeah, but a secret cellar . . ." began Gabriel.

Chuen snorted. "What secret cellars? Kyara's an enclosed environment. There is no unaccounted-for space in the whole city."

"The Icarus generators," Isadora pointed out.

"They're built into the foundation; they were on the ground plans. Anything below ground level is service tunnels, sewage recycling. And anything else is taken up by downlanders; they know every damn nook and cranny down there."

"Remind me to ask you about your nooks and crannies," drawled Izeki. Chuen almost bit at the bait, but visibly restrained herself.

"So they can't draw any attention to themselves," Gabriel continued.

"Right, right," Isadora said. "I reckon if I were them, I'd stick it somewhere inconspicuous, with a standard security system. But where I could keep a good eye on it."

"So what do you call a standard security system?"

Isadora looked at Izeki expectantly.

He pursed his thick lips, showing little enthusiasm at the prospect of being helpful. "Hm.Weeeell, retina locks, maybe backed up by palmlocks . . ."

"Touch-sensitive floors," put in Chuen.

"Yeah, but you get that anywhere. For sure movement detectors and maybe infrared Eyes."

"Security robots during the night?" asked Gabriel.

"Right."

"Security robots? Now you're talking," Isadora jumped in excitedly. "That'd be the easiest of all if you've got a security robot."

"*If* you've got a security robot," mused Chuen.

"Why not?" said Gabriel. "In this town?"

Chuen agreed. "No, you're right. Particularly if you've got the same kind. You don't have to mess about 'blinding' the system, it's already blind to the robots. You've just got to change one digit. If the place has got ten robots, you tell the brain that there are eleven. As long as you know what to tell the robot to find and where it is, you get in, you get out."

"How to get in is the point."

Izeki removed his nicotine root, wielding it lazily, like a conductor's baton. "Na-ah. No, breaking in is the easy part of any break-in. Most people get caught when they're jerking about inside. Here the hard part would be getting to the central brain. We can assume that your Elspeth managed that."

"We know she did from her own records," put in Isadora.

"Yeah, but what about the robots?" Chuen said. "The roofrunners don't have any security robots."

Gabriel sighed. "You know what? I keep hearing the phrase 'roofrunners don't have any . . .' Is it me or is someone somehow missing something somewhere?"

"Maybe the roofrunners don't, but KV 99 would," Chuen pointed out.

"Aaaah . . ." Isadora lit up.

"Aaah, right, exactly, Aaah . . ."

"Corporate espionage."

"Corporate espionage."

"I was right."

"You were right."

"I was right, I said so yesterday, corporate espionage."

"I know, you were right, we *all* know."

"I don't," muttered Izeki.

"Waitwaitwaitwaitwait." Gabriel ran a hand across his eyes. "Just a second. *Where* would KV 99 have found out about the blue box in the first place?"

"Wake up!" Chuen snorted. "Look, Xaaron Corporation owned the *Far Cry*. Cross Star Shipping owned Xaaron. Eighteen months ago Cross Star Shipping is sold by Byron Systems to Kyaran Ventures 99, lock, stock and hardware. Let's say, for the sake of argument, that someone was careless. They didn't clean out their software properly. Someone else runs across an old file referring to the *Far Cry* expedition . . . no, wait! Wait! I've got a better one! We start with Louise Daud. Elspeth meets Louise in the park . . ."

"Louise . . . ?"

"Oh, come on, that's *so* flockin' obvious," Chuen exclaimed in exasperation. "She was *crew*. Look." Chuen swiveled round on her chair and called up the *Far Cry* crew list on Izeki's terminal.

Jean-Claude Barr
Ellis Quinn Macintire
Maria Delaney
Philip Mwabea
Sian Harewood
Kam Fong
Heloise Amiée
Jaap Esterhuis
Chao Gan Tai

"Okay," she went on, "this is who there was. Now, we scratch Jean-Claude Barr, Maria Delaney, Chao Gan Tai, Philip Mwabea and Sian Harewood—they all died on the second trip out. Next . . . I spent half of last night checking all the shagging obituaries over the last twenty years . . . Jaap Esterhuis. He died three years after the first expedition, of a stroke. He was at home, alone, and they didn't find him for two days, so that takes care of him. Then we scratch Kam Fong . . . remember him?" she said to Isadora.

"The . . . Loki file?"

"Right."

"The what?" Gabriel interjected. His head was beginning to spin.

"Never mind, we'll come back to that," Chuen said brusquely. "Now, Kam Fong, that one is a bit unusual. Suicide . . . they thought. Again about three years after the first expedition. Fabiana overdose."

"Hm." Izeki gave one of his grunts. "There are a lot of other painless ways to take the long drop. Fabiana's kind of flockin' expensive."

"So, where are they going to send the bill?" Chuen observed tartly. "Anyway, that leaves us with two: Heloise Amiée and Ellis Quinn Macintire."

"Louise Daud." Gabriel wondered at his own slowness.

Chuen grinned tightly. "I checked up on the name just to make sure. There's a psychology to aliases. People always need to take a little piece of themselves along. John Potter hardly ever becomes . . . I don't know . . . Albrecht von der . . . Smith, or whatever. Louise—Heloise, that's obvious. I had to go back to pre-Plague languages for Daud and Aimée. Daud means 'beloved' in old Arabic, Aimée means almost the same thing in old Français. Now, both Heloise Aimée and Ellis Quinn Macintire faded from sight a couple of years after the first expedition. There's no record of an official name change for Aimée . . ."

"Wouldn't that be covered by the Privacy Laws?" Isadora asked.

"Maybe." Chuen considered. "Frankly, love, I don't know. My guess, though, is that she headed off-world . . ."

"And came back Louise," Gabriel muttered. *Strewth!*

"What about Macintire?" Isadora asked.

Chuen raised her shoulders helplessly, "No idea. However . . . let's backtrack to my original point." She took a deep breath. "Louise—or Heloise—meets Elspeth in the park. She tells her about the blue box. Elspeth goes to KV 99 with this tidbit and gets them to let her clean up Cross Star's filework. She hits the jackpot!"

"And Elspeth agrees to steal the blue box *from* Byron Systems *for* KV 99," finished Isadora.

Chuen added, "Except that KV 99 never got it."

"Exactly."

"She double-crossed them. And now they're pissed."

Gabriel realized that his eyes were glazing over and shook himself awake. With mild annoyance he noted that Isadora had noticed and enjoyed the fact.

Izeki, who had remained silent for some moments, suddenly rolled to his feet and headed for the drink dispenser in the kitchen alcove. "You know what you've got here?" he said, turning back, a glass barely filling his massive paw. "The biggest pile of conjecture and self-generating bullyshag I've ever heard. You've got no proof, no concrete evidence, no nothing that has any existence without enough givens and assumptions to fill a quickfarm yeast tank . . ."

Both Isadora and Chuen burst out indignantly, Chuen's more strident voice triumphing. "What does He mean conjecture? It fits! Everything we've said fits! It all fits! Doesn't it fit?!"

"Yes, it fits," Isadora affirmed.

"So," Izeki replied belligerently, "did my father's dick! But I wouldn't hang my washing on it . . ."

"What the flock is that supposed to mean?" Chuen snapped.

"It means," said Izeki calmly, taking a sip from his glass, "that I don't trust a situation with too many right answers coming too fast too easily."

"*Easily?*" Isadora spluttered. "The only reason they're coming easily is because Elspeth Kylie got there first and was neighborly enough to keep a record of what she was doing!" Before she could continue Chuen suddenly interrupted.

"He's right."

"Hey?"

"He's right . . . no . . . he's right. It's too easy." Chuen leaned back, chewing on her lip. Isadora stared at her speechlessly.

Then Izeki leaned over them, and said, "Except . . . that people have tried to kill you"—he rested his eyes on Isadora—"and attacked him." He jerked his head in Gabriel's direction. Gabriel had retreated into watchful silence, allowing the discussion to wash around him. "And," Izeki continued, "then there's me. I know when something is wrong. I know . . . I know." Gabriel wondered exactly how many glasses of atovar Izeki had had. The big officer straightened, and said, "This is not right. This is all not right."

"So you believe us," Isadora said, relieved.

Izeki drained his glass and did not answer.

"I'll tell you what fits even better," Chuen said slowly, as if Izeki's interruption had never taken place. "If Byron Systems found out that it was Elspeth who took the blue box."

There was a pause.

"They'd be pissed," said Isadora at last.

Chuen agreed. "They'd be pissed.'

"The question is, how pissed?"

"How precious is the blue box?"

"We know the answer to that. *Very* precious."

"So they'd be *very* pissed. I wonder if they'd be pissed enough to . . . ?" Chuen broke off.

"Shit." Isadora stole a glance at Gabriel, but he was just nodding slowly.

He mused, "If you've got KV 99 and Byron Systems pissed at you . . . that's a lot of pissed people."

"I'd put my bets on whoever has the most to hide," replied Chuen grimly.

"A bunch of flockin' amateurs," growled Izeki indistinctly, "just a bunch of flockin' amateurs."

Chuen bridled. "If you mean we're not getting paid, right. But at least we're trying and not sulking around, working at an excuse to urinate."

Izeki went white. "A bunch of flockin' *amateurs*," he hissed, and Gabriel realized with concern that Izeki was very drunk indeed. He had been an idiot not to have noticed it. "Flockin' amateurs!" he said again. "You come here . . ." He sought out Gabriel. "You come here . . . you . . . start looking . . . start digging. You want to play shaggin' detective. Heh," he snorted. "You go to the flockin' park . . . I mean . . . d'you go to where she lived? Talk to her neighbors? Talk to . . . find out who her friends were? Huh? Who *she* was?"

"Did you?" Isadora asked carefully. Both she and Chuen had by now realized that Izeki was close to cracking.

"Yes!" Izeki shouted. "Yes! It's my flockin' *job*" He mumbled. "Or it was until they pulled me off . . . You know who your sister was?" Izeki's glass was now pointing at Gabriel. "The good flockin' neighbor! The good . . . flockin' . . . neighbor."

"I'm glad . . ." Gabriel began.

"No!" Izeki spat. "No! There *are* no good flockin' neighbors! Not anymore. Never. There's only the . . . dillies next door. Huggin' their shaggin' privacy and . . . shag it." The big man slumped. "Diggin' up the old dirt. Shag it."

At another time Gabriel might have sat with Izeki, taken a drink himself, shared whatever visions they happened to find in the dregs of their respective glasses, brought Izeki back that way. But there was no time for that now.

Moving with care he stood and made a move toward the front door. Instantly Izeki was barring his way, his expression saying, *"Where the flock are you going?"*

"You gave me your word," Gabriel said, his expression blank.

Izeki gave voice, "Where are you going?"

"I'll be back."

"Where?"

"You gave me your word. Or did I read you wrongly?"

Behind Gabriel Chuen's impatience expressed itself in a hiss. "Why doesn't He tell him where He's shaggin' going, stike!"

"I think I know where the last survivor of the *Far Cry* crew is." Gabriel heard Isadora's intake of breath and Izeki's eyes widened slightly. "He was in the park the night Elspeth died. But," he addressed Izeki directly, "I need to go. Now. I *will* be back."

Izeki looked away. He did not move, but it was enough. Gabriel edged around him and opened the front door.

"Gabriel," Isadora called after him in voice full of worry, "you're traveling with your own face now . . . if you meet a toyman, keep walking and watching your shoes."

"Thanks." Gabriel wished that he and she had had one moment alone, when he could truly thank her, thank her for her gift of faith in him. He wondered if there ever would be.

Thanks.

The door closed behind Gabriel and, as if loosened from bonds, Izeki walked over to the Denube Window and looked out on its pristine valley. Chuen made a study of busying herself behind the terminal. Isadora walked over to stand just behind Izeki, reaching out to touch his arm and then changing her mind. His shoulders were trembling.

"Can I get you something?" she asked awkwardly.

Izeki grimaced. "Mythical kingdoms," he mumbled almost inaudibly.

"What?"

"Mythical kingdoms." Izeki stared out into a Denube morning.

Isadora understood. She found herself reflecting on something that Gabriel had said about Elspeth and upon the little girl's last words in the story, the ones that had carried her back over the desert:

"There's no place like home, there's no place like home, there's no place like home . . ."

the ghosts of thor

Elspeth's journal:

> *I've found a longtime lover in Kaitja. He's traveled far with me. Warms my cold bed. Fills me with the fire. Gives me the pain I need. I am Molonga, carrying the dance of vengeance in my womb . . .*

Patience is a virtue, and Gabriel's virtue was ebbing fast. He had been waiting in the alley off McGarret Hall in Bugout Plaza for over two hours. Midnight had come and gone and he had seen the last life drain from the streets and vanish into a thousand doorways and burrows. The few exceptions still roaming the walkways were of the sort Gabriel was just as happy not to encounter.

His back against a wall, Gabriel pulled himself into the stillness which had allowed him to stand amidst a herd of forest deer unseen. A stillness which was growing increasingly difficult to maintain. The alley was dark, Plaza lighting was sporadic at best. Here and there vivid graffiti greens and reds and golds momentarily scarred the darkness.

Another dead end, he thought wearily, *another bug-sucking, lizard-licking, wombat-buggered, three-credit, dilly-bag-sniffing, Mac-all-flaming-mighty dead flockin' end!* It had been a long shot at best, but he had hoped . . .

A fragment of orange graffiti bobbed around the corner and approached him like a luminous street cat.

How long's it going to be before one of the Bogy's little

killers finds you and licks you up into its metal gullet, he thought at it amiably.

It glowed back at him, "WALK THIS WAY"

"That's what I'm doing," he whispered, *just like you, my friend, trying to find my way through the woods and hoping the big, bad Bogy'll be looking the other way when we meet.*

The words slipped away from him, mindlessly heading for the heart of the slugwarrens.

Mindlessly?

Gabriel frowned. *Walk this way?* Wit was not a term he would have applied to most of the graffiti he had seen in Kyara so far, but it was hard to imagine anyone with the inclination to deface city walls wasting their time on a nonmessage like this. Most of it at least had some point. Might this not also?

Gabriel glanced up and down the alley, hope and unease rising in him in equal measure. The graffiti was disappearing around a far turn. He must decide quickly.

Walk this way.

There seemed little to lose at this stage, so Gabriel peeled himself off the wall and padded softly after it, following its cryptic message into the maw of the night. The glowing words crept along the wall at a slow walking pace and Gabriel had to restrain himself from bounding on ahead of them.

Just as he was beginning to feel that he had started down yet another false trail, he reached a T-junction and found himself face-to-face with another message:

"Who clips the locks on the lip-sealed clown,
    Like clockwork clockwise slaps the ground."

A graffiti-killer had found this one and was nibbling at the "d" on the word "ground." Even as Gabriel watched the little pod slathered up the whole message. If he had arrived a moment later . . .

Who clips the locks on the lip-sealed clown . . . Like clockwork clockwise . . . The passage curved gently away from him in either direction, which made clockwise . . . left. He felt a grudging admiration for whoever had created the message, unless you knew what you were looking for you would never suspect that it had any meaning.

Unless there really was no meaning and he was creating imaginary tapestries in his mind. Gabriel was seized by a sudden doubt. He thrust it to one side. Sometimes you had to go with it, or you'd find yourself like the legless scorpion in one of Dig-Dig's nastier little games, stinging itself to death in a madness of futility.

Gabriel followed the passage, senses alert, until he arrived at a cross point; two alleys running at sixty degrees to one another. Several pieces of graffiti, a couple dimmed and almost lifeless now, circled one another on each of the four corners. Once he had found what he was looking for there was no doubt that he had found the right one:

"Beloved heart, when youth gives way to fallow days.
Her pale wrist, bitten by the serpent's tooth,
But still her beacon lights the way."

Beloved . . . the serpent's tooth . . . "Beware of the snake in the desert." And how had Heloise died? An injection to the wrist. Gabriel grimaced with satisfaction. *I'm with you now.*

The beacon lights the way . . .

High up above a long ribbon of sky was visible between the buildings, the Twist a bright sliver to Gabriel's left. And in the center of that sliver, the Beacon. A quick check to ensure that he was not being trailed and Gabriel began following the alley in the direction of the star. Again timing seemed to have been on his side, half an hour later and the twist might no longer have been visible from this point.

The only real trepidation that Gabriel had seen Kipper display was at the mention of the slugwarrens and he was beginning to comprehend why. To someone used to gazing out upon the Anvil from the crown of Kyara, entering the slugwarrens would feel like slipping into the mouth of a lobster trap. Certainly Gabriel's own latent claustrophobia was creeping up and squeezing his windpipe, making it necessary for him periodically consciously to stop himself from hyperventilating.

The alley down which Gabriel was now padding had almost become a tunnel, but up ahead he could see another T-junction and, beyond it, a wavering brightness, like a mass of hot coals seen through an upright letter box.

When he reached the junction and stepped out, he found himself facing a vast wall. It ran for over fifty meters to his left and right and towered so high that he had to bend over backwards to see the top. It was entirely without windows and graffiti covered every inch of its surface in a brilliant, writhing mass of luminosity. It shone, it pulsated, like a molten cliff face, a thousand hues of light, letters, scrawls, symbols swimming through and over and under each other.

"Bloody flamin' strewth," Gabriel whispered, awe-struck. Stumbling with shock he made his way along the wall, hands flat against its surface, head craned back. *Bloody flamin' strewth!* Someone must have worked overtime to keep Bogy's hungry little graffiti-killers away from this banquet.

—"Mighty Mickey up on high,
Dipped his fingers in the pie,
Downland dillies heard the lie,
Poked Big Mickey in the eye."

—"Motherland Boys"

—"Flock the snitches,
Scab their riches!"

—"Atsek Warriors"

—"Fight fire with fire, torch spookland to the flockin' ground!"

Bloody hell. How was he supposed to find anything in this mess? The answer came to him like a block of ice in his innards.

He wasn't.

I've been had! Gabriel whirled around to run back the way he had come, but it was too late. The first figure was already blocking the alley, his face aflame with graffiti light. It flickered and glowed red, yellow, green, the shadows of his features crawling about his shaved skull. His smile was a gash, point-filed teeth glowing white

with their own light. Behind him a square of pavement
yawned open and a second man was clambering out, a
silhouette with a filed crimson grin.

Downlanders. They had to be.

A scrape of slipper against pavement behind him told
Gabriel that he was trapped.

The first downlander began advancing on him, chillingly relaxed, unhurried. "You take a wrong turning,
flatland? You lookin' my wall?"

Gabriel's pulse hammered in his ears. "I'm not looking for any problems," he said, willing his voice steady.
He could not show any intimidation. *Yeah, no flockin'
worries.*

"But you lookin' my wall, flat," the first downlander
repeated. "This the Motherland Boy's very own wall and
you lookin' it."

"Your wall is your wall, mate," Gabriel replied levelly, "and I'm not looking." Even as he said it his eyes
flicked toward it involuntarily. *Shag it.*

"You lookin' right now." The figure stopped a couple
of steps in front of him. Gabriel could feel at least three
people behind him. His fists tightened.

"What do you reckon I just go on my way and don't
look at your wall again?"

A sneer. "Now flat doesn't like my wall."

Oh, boy.

"You goin' lookin' but you don't like . . ."

A silver ribbon uncurled from the downlander's fist,
straightened and went rigid. A roll-blade. Blades dripped
like threads of oil from the hands of his companions.

What frightened Gabriel the most was the idea that
his opponents did not want anything. There was nothing
with which they might be appeased. Gabriel was a distraction from boredom; the slip of blade and grind of
fist on split flesh adding welcome spice to an otherwise
dull evening. He rolled forward onto the balls of his feet
and prepared for the pain before the darkness.

It never came. Instead a familiar and welcome voice
croaked, "He the one. He the one got free pattyfoot."
Erzsi's third eye bloomed rainbows as she slipped past
the assembled downlanders. Gabriel tried to stifle his
sigh of relief.

The lead downlander did not move. "Surewhys, you?"

"Surewhy's you got GenTec rim-worm for a pecker, boy-boy," Erzsi snorted.

Gabriel flinched, but the downlander did not seem to react. Instead he shifted his weight slightly, a gesture of grudging dismissal.

"Follow." Erzsi pinched at Gabriel's arm. The downlanders had not budged and Gabriel was forced to press between them, his flesh twitching as their blades drifted, tracking him like the tines of a deadly compass. His relief was so great that Gabriel did not even shy when Erzsi dropped into the hole in the pavement, one witch's claw reemerging to beckon him below.

Ten minutes later Gabriel's claustrophobia had returned with a vengeance and the tunnel walls felt as though they were crushing the breath out of him.

"You followin' fine, stike?"

"I'm right here, no worries," Gabriel answered hoarsely.

"You bring somethin' to eat?"

"Eh? No. No, I didn't bring anything. Sorry."

Erzsi sniffed loftily. "Don't want nothin'. Just askin'. Here . . ." They rounded a corner into another passageway, dimly lit by pale green glow-coils in the floor. There Erzsi halted and gave a low whistle. "Mac," she hissed, "we here. Motherland Boys got eyes clearin' the flatside."

A gray, bent form stepped out of a hollow in the wall. His face was wrinkled, scored with cross-hatched lines, hard and coil-lit green like malachite. His eyes were rheumy and his nose and cheeks veined with the broken blood vessels of a full-time drinker. He was clutching a drinking pouch and as he spoke he expelled a great wave of gin-laden fumes. "Far enough, flatlander," he rasped. "You bin' lookin' for Old Mac, here he is."

Gabriel studied him cautiously. "I'm not looking for Old Mac. I'm looking for Ellis Quinn Macintire. Have I found him?"

The old man swallowed. "If you're spookland, the Motherland Boys're goin' be serving you up for protein blocks."

"They'd be doing spookland a favor if they did."

The old man took a nervous pull from his gin pouch

and wiped his lips on the heel of his hand. "Tell me about this message."

"Tell me if I'm talking to the right person."

The old man looked scared. He took another pull, licked his lips and then nodded sharply. "I'm Ellis Quinn Macintire."

As if by a prearranged signal Erzsi turned and started creeping back the way she and Gabriel had come. "I'll be waiting," she said. "Safer not to know, hey?" She gave Gabriel a knowing look and disappeared around the corner.

"The message," Ellis repeated.

"The message was . . . find the people who killed me," Gabriel said.

Ellis looked at him uncomprehendingly.

Gabriel took a deep breath and said, "Twenty years ago a survey ship called the *Far Cry* went on a privately sponsored Survey expedition to the Twist. She found something there and brought it back, something that's stayed hidden for twenty years and that a lot of people are going to a lot of trouble to keep hidden. They're so desperate to keep it hidden that they've killed to do it, starting with every member of the original crew . . . except you. You're the last survivor." Gabriel watched Ellis hopefully, waiting for some hint of recognition.

When none came he said, "My sister was one of the people they killed. I think that Heloise Aimée told her something that cost her her life. And later it killed Heloise."

No response.

"Listen, I've got every flaming TARC in this town looking for me. If they find me, I'll never leave this place except with a one-way ticket to Retreat. I'm asking you to help me find the truth. And the truth has got something to do with the blue box. *The* blue box," Gabriel repeated. "I'm asking you to help me."

The pause was long. Then Ellis gave a sigh. "So the name stuck, huh?"

"You know what it is!" Gabriel exclaimed with rising excitement.

Ellis nodded. "Em Delaney called it that." He sighed again and looked away. "It was an artifact, of course. Wasn't really a box, it was more like . . . I dunno, two tetrahedrons fixed together at the bases. You've gotta imagine a chair-sized sapphire, ocean blue . . . deep ocean blue . . . it was . . . you could look into it for hours, it seemed to change without your moving. It was Em that figured out it was symbols that we were looking at. 'Course we didn't have a clue what they meant. You couldn't even see them long enough to focus on them clearly.

"Have you ever had something floating on your eye? A dust mote or something? It seems like it's just at the corner of your vision, but then when you turn your eye to focus on it it always seems to keep just floating out of our line of sight?"

He looked to Gabriel for acknowledgment. "Right. Well, it was like that. Sent you the bugouts if you kept trying long enough. We all tried it on the trip back if we were off watch. Em called it 'box-watching.' "

Ellis took a pull from his pouch, grimaced and deliberately sent a threadlike stream of gin shooting out from between his two front teeth. Beads of gin sparkled off the wall. He regarded Gabriel reflectively.

"Reckon you know what the Beacon is?"

"It led me here," Gabriel affirmed. "A pulsar, no?"

"Yah. It's all that's left of Beacon's Mother, a G-class star. Beacon's Mother went nova about eighty thousand yeas ago and that's what the Twist is, most of it anyway. Expanding gases and dust from the explosion. Not all of it, mind you. Mother was at the center of a thick interstellar dust cloud before the explosion . . ." Ellis broke off, seemingly aware that he was beginning to ramble. It was as if the floodgates to Ellis's past had suddenly been breached in a dozen places, creating eddies and whirlpools of memory that vied with one another for release.

The old man took a moment to reorganize his thoughts. "Anyway, she had a planet in orbit around her, a little smaller than Earth normal and nothing but frozen ash, heh." He grinned, gin-soaked caries gleaming. "Anyway, that's what it looked like to me. Phil Mwambea, he loved it. Geologist, he'd been sitting with both thumbs up his ass for a month and suddenly, glory! Phil gets to go digging! The only person with less to do on board was Fong. Kam Fong. Flock, the man had just spent six weeks catching grains of interstellar dust, hoping to find something organic, *anything*!" Ellis shook his head, marveling.

"You found the blue box on the planet?" Gabriel prompted at length.

Ellis looked at him as if hoarding some guilty delight in the midst of a famine. "Oh, yes. Heh. We picked up a signal on our . . . I think . . . fifteenth or sixteenth orbit. Fong had had all his instruments trained on the surface the whole time and Phil was kicking shit five ways for Jean-Claude Barr to land and we pick up . . . radio signals, if you can believe it, actual radio . . . *a* radio signal. Just a 'pip', a steady 'pip-pip-pip.' Shag it, we were pissing ourselves! I mean, it was so weak that we could have stayed in orbit for a year and not picked it up if we hadn't been exactly positioned."

Ellis drew a long, unsteady line through the air with his finger, down to the floor. "We follow, land . . . shag it." His gaze grew distant, as if after all these years he still doubted himself. "It was a cave, a whole cavern complex, huge, we never got to the end of it . . . and it was filled with bodies." He let out a long breath.

"Not human," said Gabriel.

"No," Ellis averred, "not human. Flock. You know how long we've been looking for life, stike? I mean, intelligent life . . . or, not intelligent just, but technologically sophisticated, advanced, at least as far as we are. Lookin', lookin', lookin'.

"And there they were, right on our doorstep, all this time. And all dead. All of them."

Ellis went on. "The whole complex was one big cold-sleep facility, kilometers below the surface. But, well, time . . . who knows how much time? We never got that far either." Gabriel had not thought that it was possible for even more bitterness to seep into Ellis's disappointment-scarred features. But he was wrong. "We never bothered, because we thought there'll be another trip. We'll be coming back. Shag!" Ellis broke into a fit of coughing that lasted several minutes. Gabriel restrained himself from reaching out to the old man kneeling before him, hacking out his life on the tunnel floor. He knew Ellis would not tolerate his sympathy and would find no balm in his compassion.

When Ellis had recovered and eased his throat with several more pulls from his gin pouch, he continued.

"Have you ever had someone close to you die? And seen them. Up close?"

Gabriel swallowed. "Yes," he said hoarsely.

Ellis nodded. "Maybe you've seen the way the pain leaves them. All of a sudden they're ageless. Seven, seventy, seven hundred, none of it applies. They've kind of moved beyond the arithmetic. It was like that. Oh, they weren't pretty! Believe me, a freeze-dried, mummified alien corpse is *not* going to brighten up your living room. And these weren't pretty to start off with. But they *were* beautiful? I don't know how to explain it.

"The blue box was at the center of the central chamber. We took it with us when we left . . . I suppose because it stood out, I don't know why . . . no," he corrected himself, "I do know why. It stood out because it was alive . . . in some weird way."

"But," Gabriel asked, somewhat baffled, "why did you leave?"

Ellis's expression turned scornful. "Why, dilly," he said, "do you think? The only reason. Mo-ney. The Xaaron grant had allowed for a survey of eight weeks. Every day over that was going to cost the company a whole pile of cues. Jean-Claude did what he had to do. He pulled us out of there after four days . . . ho, stike." Ellis chuckled at the memory. "Phil and Eloise and, hoooo . . . Fong! Aw, did they go the bugout! Jean-Claude had to lock up the oxygen tanks for the suits, it was the only way to get them back aboard. But, dilly, if any of us . . . me, too . . . if any of us had been able to figure out a way of breathing vacuum, we'd be there now.

"So, we came back. Nearly got killed on the home trip . . . sterike. You should have seen them . . . *us*. We held it together." For an instant a glint of pride came into old Ellis's eye. "I had plenty to do, and Jean-Claude. The others, it was all make-work. Staring the Anvil in the eye and Em Delany's measuring Doppler shift on stars near the horizon, Sian's got everyone monitored for vital signs and is broadcasting the second-by-second results up to Orbit 3 so that they can record the effect of a smack-on how-de-do with Thor's surface on the human anatomy. As if there's some doubt." He snorted. "Kan Fong's got all his instruments on—and I mean *all* of them. Shag it. We came within three klicks of the surface. Unprotected. But everyone held it together," he marveled.

"Anyway, we get back and . . . well . . . the fun begins, dilly. Security, like you've never seen. We hadn't broadcast ahead, we didn't want to start a rush, but . . . stike, this was something else. I was going, 'Hang back, dillies, we're civilians here!'

"No . . . ach, it was stupid. We should have known better. They had us cold-wrapped tighter than giddy-ship ration blocks. Everywhere I went, there they were. Threatened us . . . not like a threat, no, like . . . a loving reminder. Said they'd enforce the confidentiality clauses in our contracts to the letter. Dropped the flockin Privacy Laws on our heads like a fifteen-ton rail-sprung hangcar. I was checkin' my flockin' underpants for Xaaron security personnel when I got up in the mornings. 'Course this was whilst they were still being nice."

"But why?" Gabriel asked, aggravated at his own obtuseness. "I mean, a mausoleum? Worn out cold-sleep booths? That's something for archaeologists. What else was there?"

Ellis regarded him with an expression of grim humor, masking triumph.

"What are you? Last of the innocents? You haven't picked it up yet? The corpses. They were *Querin*!"

For a long moment Gabriel found himself staring blankly at the old man, then the implications began to slot into place.

"Aaaah." Ellis's triumph blossomed. "Now we're home! This was six months before the first C.S.S. vote on the status of Querin. Kyara was the spearhead of the dillies wanting to open her up for exploitation, with Byron Systems at the head of the pack. You know what this would have done to their chances? Here we come back with proof in pocket that the Querin were the remains of a starfaring civilization, regressed into barbarism. No cul-de-sac there. And we figured that the boys in boardroom would be *glad*? How flockin' stupid can you get? How naive!

"Well, okay, we get the picture. Then, after the vote,

when the C.S.S. decrees a twenty-year moratorium on interference with Querin, we think. Fine! That's out of the way.

"But no, again. Byron Systems. Byron Systems wouldn't be what they are without a long-term *plan,* without *vision.* You think ahead. And Saxon Rainer? We met him, y'know. There's a far thinker. That's the man who knows his way through the labyrinth. In it for the long term.

"D'you know what Kyara would be without Byron Systems? It wouldn't. It wouldn't *be.* Akash Chandra Levinson—kiss her almighty sun-don't-shine!—she may have laid the first administrative stone, but the Rainers and their type? They're what made Kyara. And kid yourself not, Byron Systems wouldn't be yeast scum without Kyara and her Privacy Laws. But then again, her Privacy Laws wouldn't be what they were without Byron Systems. The Kyara conglomerates need the Privacy Laws for their own protection, so . . . think about it. Old man Rainer, he's there on the conclave. We've got three High Court benchers that he and his side of the Conclave table put there. The president? Mr. Tie-break hisself? Kicked upstairs courtesy of the Saxon Rainer lobby.

"They were ready for defeat last time. And they were already thinking ahead. Twenty years." Ellis shook his head in amazement. "Until the next C.S.S. vote. And they were going to win that one."

Ellis rummaged around inside his coat. He emerged with a chunk of nutribrick from which he broke off a fragment and began to munch noisily. He licked his lips and examined a few crumbs stuck to his fingers. Meditatively he crushed them between his forefinger and thumb, smearing them back and forth until there was nothing left but a greasy stain.

"D'you ever wonder what it would be like to feel Thor's hammer?" he mused. "Forty gees pressing down on you." His expression went cold. "I've felt it. From the first morning after we got back I woke up with Thor's hammer on my back. We all did. We tried to fight back, we tried to talk to the guys upstairs. Shit, Jean-Claude even got them to finance another trip. I didn't go, I'd had enough by then. So had Jaap and

Heloise and . . . old Fong. Him they snapped in half. Real Slow. Kept him walled up. Never alone. Ears on the phone. Stuff people don't even think about! They chewed up the Privacy Laws and spat them out in pieces and none of us—*none* of us—even dared to complain. Shag, the number they did on him. Saw him just a few days before he killed himself. He was laughing to himself and saying how the joke was on them. He was goin' to be their Loki, how he had them. God, I'm sorry, Fong." The old man was now trembling with rage.

Gabriel interrupted, suddenly alert. "What did he mean about Loki? How did he *have* them?"

Ellis sneered. "Life sciences officer on the trip that discovers intelligent life, stike! And the joke was on them! Tch," he went on. "And then the second trip . . . JUMP-shield failure or some garbage. No, it was *fixed*! They *fixed* them. Would have fixed us, too . . . they did fix us.

"You know the irony? I agreed with them. Shag the Querin! They had their chance and they blew it. BIG-ways. Cro-Magnon kicked away Neanderthaler, Neanderthaler put the bug on Australopithecus. That's the way it is. Nobody ever talked about wiping out the Querin, but they've got more room than they can use . . ."

Gabriel shifted restlessly and Ellis peered at him warily.

"You bothering, stike? Something biting your balls?"

Gabriel explained with an edge of tiredness, "My . . . people. They were a Stone Age people when the first hi-tech civilization reached their lands. The newcomers didn't need much land either, after all, the natives had more than they needed. For more than fifty thousand years our holy men painted the walls of caves all over Australia, yet within a couple of generations the paintings stopped. I've seen some of the last cave paintings that were ever made. They showed pictures of European ships arriving from across the sea."

Ellis nodded understandingly. "Took a picture of the bullet that killed 'em, eh?" He hawked and spat. "Yah. Well, maybe that's a kind of luck. Not everybody gets the chance."

"You did."

"Yeah. Still lookin' at it a-coming," Ellis rasped. "But I'm here. Im here," he repeated, defiance coloring his whisper. "So maybe they weren't so lucky."

"You listen," he remarked unexpectedly. "You're a listener. What'd you do before you came here?"

Gabriel raised his eyebrows and allowed his head to waggle from side to side. "I . . . listened. It's kept me alive in a lot of strange places. You should try it sometime."

Ellis snorted. "Ach, you think I don't? What d'you hear if you listen now?"

Gabriel detected a challenge in the old man's eyes. So he shrugged, stepped back into the stillness within himself. "I can hear . . . the hangcar rails up above, crowds . . . other sounds . . . I don't know, they're not my sounds, so it's hard to tell what they are. There's a hum . . . too low to hear with the ears, you hear it here"—he tapped his chest—"and . . ." He hesitated, wanting to be sure. He smiled, unable to resist. "And I can hear Erzsi finding out a lot more than she says she does." An evil giggle echoed round the corner of the passageway.

"Tell me something," Gabriel said. "With all this happening, why didn't you leave?"

"Leave?" Surprise cracked the old man's features open. "Leave? Where to? Kyara's my home, stike," He snapped. "This is mine." His hands slapped the wall. "Mine. Everybody's got a place that's theirs, stike, somewhere where you can hear the voice of the place. I was born here. Where am I supposed to go?"

"Anywhere. There are seventeen . . ."

". . . balls of rock, I know. But none of them have got the Anvil, stike. You're talkin' to me about your people's land . . ."

"My people's land was not theirs. That's what no one else ever understood. The land was nobody's . . ."

"Bullyshag!" spat Ellis furiously. Gabriel flinched as he felt pinpricks of wetness strike his cheek. "This place is mine! I've seen the sun . . . I've seen it grow as Thor got nearer to it, year after year! When I was a kid it was hardly bigger than anything else in the sky, just a little point, like . . . like starlight on a woman's lip. Now it's like a quickfarm berry. Alight. It casts shadows. You know that when I was a kid I had no shadow? Now I do. I walk outside in the daytime and I look down and see myself, me, stained in the ground, a part of it. It's *mine* . . . and I love it. I belong to the Anvil. It'll never let me go. It kills anything it touches. But it's still mine."

Gabriel did understand. Did Elspeth look down one day and see her own shadow-self? The eternal pursuer. Was that what really killed her?

"Tell me about the night that my sister died."

Ellis looked discomfited. He hugged himself, avoiding Gabriel's eye. "Shagging TARCs," he mumbled. "I didn't see anything, I told them."

"But something happened to you."

"Yah. I got bullywhacked. I used to meet Heloise there after dark-down. She left Thor. Left for years. But she couldn't stay away," he said, lips pressed tight with dark satisfaction. "She came back and they snapped her in half, too. Killed her in the end."

He studied Gabriel narrowly. "I've seen you, too, once," he murmured.

"Me?"

"In the park. After dark-down."

"Yes. I spoke to Heloise there a couple of nights ago." Gabriel realized, with a chill, that he could not recall how many nights ago that was.

"No . . . this was . . . months back. You were lyin' on your back, naked, with a stone in your hand." he rubbed a hand across his eyes, as if confused.

"A stone . . . ?" Gabriel blinked. "Are you sure you're not talking about Elspeth?"

"I know your sister," Ellis said scornfully. "I used to see Heloise talking to her sometimes . . . never met her myself, y'know," he added defensively.

"I know that."

"Oh yes? How d'you know," Ellis snapped back furiously. "You think Old Mac's nothin', you think I'm too much nothing to have met her!"

"No." Gabriel tried to make his voice as soothing as possible. "No. I know because if you had, you would have told me so by now."

"Hm. Well, I didn't." Ellis appeared to be mollified. "But I'd seen her before . . . maybe once. From a ways. Anyway, I found the way downland in the park, into a couple of the maintenance shutes. Heh." He chuckled mischievously. "flockin' security system was shagged five ways. Ha!" Ellis shrugged. "Fell asleep kissin' the liquid lady." He held up the gin pouch and gleefully jiggled it, so that the contents sloshed about inside. "Woke up after dark-down. Had a watch then. Wasn't going to risk going upside, 'cos I figured the alarms might be working there, but the flockin' legs, stike, the legs. Heh. No circulation and I'd been asleep for hours. So I stand up and there I go, back and fro, back and fro, legs wakin' up and bitin' at me and then *bam*! someone jumps me and *bam*! I'm on the floor. Then I wake up and there's fairboys everywhere and . . ."

Gabriel interrupted. "But you said you listen. You didn't hear anybody coming?"

Ellis shook his head. "They were good. Didn't see nothing, didn't hear nothing. They were good. Nothing. All of a sudden they're landing on my back and the floor's lickin' up at my face and then . . . then . . . there's spookland, hands like big fat twigleggies, puttin' the grip all over Old Mac."

Ellis examined his gin pouch with a deliberate intensity. Gabriel kept his silence, waiting. There was a tremble in the old man's fingers that had nothing to do with the effects of the gin and his eyes were agleam with a wetness that he could not blink away.

"Sterike . . ." he whispered, "they killed her. For what? Sitting in that park every day . . . tryin' to get her own back on . . . Rainer and his . . . with old cartons and candy wrappers? . . . Flockin' TARCs." He spat. "You know what it's like to find out you're nothing. A grain of sand. The fairboys—the Municipals—they pick me up . . . give me the spook hard-arm, tryin' to get me to tell me something. Then TARC takes over and . . . shag. And I'm thinkin', 'Hey, they've finally got the grip on me, after all these years . . .' And then they let me go. No questions. No, 'Who are you?' Nothin'. They spit me out. Some old flockin' curb-roller got no-thing, he isn't no-thing." Another swig at the gin pouch and liquor dribbled down his chin.

"Time was . . . I was someone. I had ideas, I had . . . I counted. Sterike. You know what it is? . . . Suddenly one day to the next, you can't get a job, you . . . I worked in engineering since I was twenty-two! Served in . . . I don't know, in . . . shag it . . ." Ellis seemed to be trying to count off on his fingers. He sniveled, groping clumsily with a hand that seemed suddenly to be someone else's. "I don't remember how many . . . a lot of ships. And then, suddenly, I'm flat-bound. Can't get a berth . . . credit gets canceled . . . too high risk . . ." He trailed off.

"They put out the word on you," Gabriel said gently.

"You know," Ellis whispered in wonderment, "There comes a point when it opens up beneath you, like a big pit in the ground, and all you can do is slide with it. It's easier than fighting. The liquid lady, she keeps your throat warm, and your belly warm, and your head numb. You hit the bottom and you find out that . . . it's okay. It's okay. You look up and it's such a shagging climb, you wonder why you ever bothered in the first place." Ellis Quinn was weeping unrestrainedly now, the cracks in his old face a bright web of tears. "Now and again I still hit the flatlands . . . I could stay down here or in the Plaza, but . . . I got no shadow here, you know. Sometimes I've just got to get out and see my shadow, see if I'm still alive."

Abruptly he rubbed vigorously at his face with his grubby sleeve, and said in a steadier voice, "If you're interested in the blue box . . ." He paused. "They got some dilly in to try to decipher it . . . some ex-pert, I heard. That was some . . . nineteen years ago. Dunno if he did or didn't."

"Did he have a name?" Gabriel asked, hope dawning.

"Magnus Westlake."

"And he's still alive?"

Ellis grinned a tarry-toothed grin, "Halfways yes and no. Heard he made the move down to Actuality Alley."

"Where?"

Ellis shook his head pityingly. "You've got a ways to go, dilly. The Alley's IN. My word was that Westlake west INworld permanently years back."

"Strewth," Gabriel swore softly. If Westlake had gone permanently IN, it meant that he was also permanently disconnect. "Why? D'you know?"

"The Alley's a rich man's bolt-hole. You only go there if you've had enough, or you're terminally sick, or maybe if you're halfway bugout anyhow . . . or if you're scared."

"Scared? Scared of what?"

"Anything. Life. Death. There's nowhere safer than the INworld, dilly. Toughest security, exterminators workin' full-time to keep the twigleggies and chiproaches out of the circuits . . . that's why it's so expensive. Nothin' can touch you. Reckon Westlake had a rich family . . ."

"So it's what was he running away from," Gabriel affirmed. It was not a question.

"Maybe who," Ellis said. "*I* know." He spat. "Time to go pattyfoot."

He clambered to his feet and stumbled a few steps away down the passage.

"Wait . . ." When Gabriel rose, the old eth-head lurched about, his arm sweeping out, as if trying to wipe Gabriel away.

"Go your way, brother-man. Downland won't keep you well if you stay."

Gabriel called, "But where can I find you?"

"*Find* me?" Ellis choked. "Find me? You don't find me! You . . . don't . . . find . . . me! You listened to anything? Huh? You didn't get what you wanted?"

"Ellis . . ."

"Old Mac! That's him," Ellis hissed. "Ellis . . . there's no Ellis here! Never was!" He turned and staggered away. Gabriel could hear him mumbling, "He died. He died out on the Anvil . . ."

Suddenly overcome, Gabriel leaned back against the wall and squeezed his eyes shut. *He died out on the Anvil.*

And now Grandmother Lalumanji was dying.

Gabriel returned to Landing for the first time in the two yeas since his near-fatal heart attack. His fingertips brushed the back of Lalumanji's hand and her eyelids fluttered open; her eyes swam from side to side, caught him, held him, focused.

Her lips moved. Barely. "Gabriel. What you doin' here, Gabriel? I thought . . . I thought you wasn't ever . . . comin' home . . . you said . . ." A breath. "You bring her? You bring . . . Elspeth? Bin' wonderin' where she's bin' hidin'. Our Elspeth . . ." Her voice drifted like a cloud.

Gabriel hesitated, then swallowed hard. Even now he could not bring himself to lie to her. "She's walkabout, Gran, you remember that. Three years gone. Far gone now."

"Not as far as old Lalumanji," Grandmother whispered, smiling. "She left. She left her . . . life behind. All she took was that anger of hers. She was angry for such a serious long time, you know. Don't you be angry, Gabriel, not with me, not that way."

"Why should I ever be angry with you, Gran?" Gabriel asked.

"I gave Elspeth my anger, you know . . . gave her all my anger. I seen her carryin' it about in that heart of hers . . . Guess . . . guess that's what the old people do, y'know. They gather up all that anger . . . all that anger . . . stickin' to 'em like them ticks on them cheeky dogs of Ruud's. And then they pass it on to the young . . . for them to carry. So it's always growin' and it gets bigger . . . and bigger . . ."

"Ssh, Gran, ssh."

Lalumanji's eyes traced the path of an invisible butterfly. "We used to swim down in the pool . . . by Mackay's Rock . . . fishin'. Remember?"

"I remember . . ."

"And before that, before that . . . me and Bulla . . . when he and me were young. Just sprouts, we were, and he, the cheekiest bugger in whole Landing and abouts . . . He walked straight then. Had arms and shoulders and . . . a back like . . . polished wood . . . and a touch . . . God, he had a touch, Bulla did . . ."

Young, Grandma? But you've always been old.

"Is he still there, where they buried him . . . by that clearin' there?"

Bulla? Uncle Bull? You and Uncle Bull? You never told us. Gabriel's eyes would no longer focus and he felt cold on his cheeks. "Gran . . ."

Suddenly Lalumanji's eyes opened wide and she said, her voice suddenly clear, "He saved your life!"

"Uncle Bull?"

"He's saving your life. Old Man . . ." Her voice sank

to a whisper again. "It wasn't like . . . He was savin' your life . . . Old Man . . ."

"No, Gran, he tried to kill me . . ."

"No. It wasn't . . . it wasn't . . ." Her eyes closed, her voice faded to a labored breathing.

But when Gabriel left the hospital he found Old Man waiting on the far side of the road. Old Man didn't say anything, just watched. He crouched on the veranda roof of the hardware store, claws gripping, wings folded tight, his yellow eye staring at Gabriel.

Gabriel slowly backed away down the street, Old Man's eye fixed on him. Then he turned and ran.

He had never stopped.

Gabriel heard the stealthy shuffle and sweep of robes against the floor. He was unsurprised when he opened his eyes to see a bony finger pointing up the passage in the direction from which he had come.

"Alright, Erzsi," he nodded, rousing himself. "Downlands are no place for flatlanders, eh?"

Three eyes glinted out of the darkness. "I wouldn't know."

Gabriel had recovered himself somewhat now and he growled at her without rancor, "I know another old lady here in Kyara who's even nastier than you are. Better watch it, or I might just tell her where you live."

t.a.r.c.

Elspeth's journal:

Christ, Gabriel is such a flaming asshole!

*Him and Old Man are hardly speaking to one an-
other anymore. It's not enough for Gae that he goes
his own way, that he doesn't want to follow the old
paths. Most of us left the old ways centuries ago,
some all the way, some only partway. I reckon for
them it's always been the hardest, trying to walk in
both worlds at once, trying to live two lives in the
span of one. But that's not enough for Gae. No, he's
got to rub Old Man's nose in it every time, giving
him cheek at coroboree, letting him know, real quiet
like, in that quiet way Gae has.*

*It scares me. You can step outside the law, live
your life by the new laws, the laws that came from
across the ocean, long before the Plagues—Old Man
would understand that. But Gabriel hates the Law itself! It scares me that one day he's going to step over
the line.*

"This doesn't make any sense," announced Chuen,
holding up the Notebook.

Isadora jerked awake and found herself drowning in
a lake of alphabet soup. Chagrined, she withdrew her
head from the center of the terminal's holo-display and
squinted at the display's timepiece—01:56. Her mouth
tasted as if she had been chewing on a mildewed face
flannel. Where was Gabriel?

There was a thump as Izeki's feet slid off the wall-
couch onto the floor and a mutter of invective. The So-

berside pills had cleared the big man's head, but had done nothing for his mood.

Isadora winced as Chuen repeated jarringly, "This doesn't make sense."

"Now, what?"

"This"—Chuen waved the Notebook like a banner—"that mess of folders in Elspeth's file."

"Oh, no more, Chuen, please," begged Isadora, struggling out of her chair.

"I'm with you," Izeki grunted in agreement. They bumped elbows at the drink dispenser.

"Water, please," Isadora said.

Izeki retrieved two cups from the dispenser, handed her one, idly clinking his against hers before drinking. "Piss and vinegar."

"Piss and vinegar."

"Iz, would you listen to me? This is important." Chuen was still frantically wielding her Notebook.

Isadora was sure that whatever Chuen had to say she did not want to hear. She had already seen and heard too much and seven hours sleep in three days had taken its toll. But she steeled herself and sighed. "Alright, Chuen, what?"

Chuen ignored Izeki's resonant belch and said, "It's this. This is sales, this is shares. One company selling off its assets and buying others, alright?"

"Right." Isadora reeled back to her chair.

"Okay, now, I'm not an expert on this, darling, so don't quote me, but . . ." Chuen paused. "the company in question—as far as I can tell—is Byron Systems."

"Uh-huh. So Byron Systems are buying and selling assets; look don't spin it out, Chuen, I'm tired, I'm going to bite someone in a second . . . what? So?"

"Everything that they've been selling has been here on Thor, everything they've been buying has been off-world—predominantly on Helios."

Isadora looked skeptical. "You got all that out of there? You managed to work all that out?"

"No, no, no,' Chuen answered impatiently. "I'm not a money-person, I'm just following the notes in here—there's notes all over the place, I guess Elspeth put them all there . . ."

"Wait a second." Isadora was certain she could feel a

headache coming on. "This is Byron Systems. *Byron Systems* . . ."

"I know . . ."

"No! Byron Systems! Byron does not . . . why would Byron . . . wait, wouldn't someone have noticed if Byron Systems were selling off their Thor assets?"

Chuen shook her head adamantly. "No, it's been done slowly, over several years, with cardbord companies and you name it and they've kept their heads ducked under every Privacy Law in the statutes."

Isadora already knew where this was heading, but she was not sure she wanted to believe it. "No, this can't be right . . .'"

"Let her finish!" Izeki unexpectedly interrupted. He was sitting up straight on the couch, his eyes pinpricks of alertness.

Isadora gave in. "Alright, Chuen, tell us, how much have they sold off?"

Chuen hesitated and bit at her lip as if she herself could not quite believe what she was going to say. Her voice was subdued. "All of it, Iz. Everything. Everything," she repeated.

"Chuen, they can't have sold off everything! What about Rainer Park?"

"No! Don't you see, Iz, that's the point! Byron Systems didn't pay for Rainer Park. *We* did! The city. And the other conglomerates, you know that! Rainer may have put the thing together and they may have paid the lion's share, or at any rate the biggest single percentage. I remember . . . what's his name? Thing at the office . . . Gerold! I think he figured they paid maybe . . . seven percent of the total cost. It's peanuts. But their name goes on it and . . . well!"

"Sleight of hand," Isadora murmured.

"Maybe."

"Sleight of hand. Don't you remember, during construction, the slogan." Isadora strove to remember the exact wording. After a moment she gave up. "Something . . . 'An Investment in Our Future!' Right. Byron Systems invests in our future with one finger and with the other nine they're shoveling everything else off-world and making sure no one else knows about it."

"The question would be, why?"

"Alright, that does it." Izeki rose to his feet, his face set. "Look . . ."

Chuen asided to Isadora, "Hold your breath, darling, here comes another pearl of wisdom from the ethanol oracle . . ."

"Stop! Just listen!" Izeki rode her down. "Just listen. This isn't small-time anymore. Now, how far do you think we are going to get, sitting in this apartment? Hm? If you've got something . . . and I think you might!" He raised his voice to forestall Chuen. "And I think you *might*. Then it's time to go to someone about this."

"Halle-flockin'-lujah," Chuen breathed.

" 'Someone' being . . . ?" Isadora demanded. "*You* know someone we can trust?"

"Maybe." Izeki was breathing heavily. "Maybe. Look, you may not like the TARCs—*I* don't like the bugsuckers—but they're not all dirty. I may know a couple of people we can talk to. This? This is out of Municipal Police terrain."

"Fine!" Chuen exclaimed. "If He knows who to go to, then for Macca's sake let's go!"

"Wait, Chuen"—Isadora beckoned to Izeki and went over to the desk-terminal—"I want to show you something."

Chuen watched her with incomprehension. "Iz . . ."

Isadora ignored her. "Two things. The first is that I looked through media files for references to Gabriel's roofrunner friend, Lazarus Wight. Easy enough, he made every news report that day. He's a fabiana burn-out case. Thirty-five years back Mr. Wight was a scholar, Kyara University Web graduate, top 2 percent of that year. A double major in history and trans-System-economics. After graduation, he goes on the Grand Tour with a couple of his rich classmates: Denube, Helios, Earth, Merryweather, even Leviathan . . ."

"Grand Tour?" Izeki interrupted. "What Grand Tour?"

"School talk." Chuen sniffed. "Wouldn't apply to some."

"It's tradition amongst those that can afford it," explained Isadora. "You see how many of the Seventeen Planets you can visit in a year. Actually, it's a spurious question; some cliphead worked it out once and with the traveling times involved the maximum is nine. But, anyway," she resumed her narrative, "one night, six months after he gets back, the Red Sector spooks find him facedown in a gutter, raving from a fabiana overdose. Basically he was lucky to be alive. They clean him up, send him home. But . . ." She made a scrambling motion with her fingers against the side of her head. "Three months later he's arrested for trying to plant a homemade magnesium bomb in one of the Churches of Cornucopia. Apparently a voice called . . . Kil, I think it was . . . told him he had to bring the worlds of Humanity and Heaven back to the soil."

"Hm," Izeki grunted. "We get about three of those a week downtown."

"That's not the best bit," Isadora went on. "They also gave the names of Wight's graduating class. One of the other alumni was a young man called Saxon Rainer."

"They knew each other!" Chuen exclaimed.

"Did the Grand Tour together."

"Mac-all-flockin'-mighty."

"Fabiana burnout, huh?" Izeki mused. "Still, I don't see what your problem is with going to the higher-ups."

"It gets better," Isadora said joylessly, knowing that under normal circumstances she might have felt a sense of triumph at having got one up on Chuen, but feeling none now. "I found something about two hours ago, when I was looking through our files, something Chuen and I missed, so I checked on it. I was looking at the investigating committee into the Far Cry accident. It was a joint STC-TARC investigation. Guess who was in charge of the TARC arm of the investigation, the arm responsible for looking into the possibility of sabotage or . . . or . . . whatever! Read!" She flicked a key.

Izeki read, "Tamara Lennox."

"TARC *Commissioner* Tamara Lennox now," Isadora corrected.

Chuen's eyes went round. "Oh, flock me . . ."

"Why didn't you say something about this two hours ago?" demanded Izeki.

Isadora answered dully. "And what? I was hoping . . . I don't know, I was hoping I might find something that pointed somewhere else. I thought maybe Gabriel, or . . ." She gestured at Chuen and her Notebook.

"We're shagged," stated Chuen.

"No, we're not, not yet. Not yet." Izeki ran an unsteady hand back through his hair.

"We're shagged," Chuen repeated.

"Chuen!" Isadora muttered impatiently.

"Oh, and you're going to tell me we're not, too?" Chuen did not raise her voice. "They own everything, Iz. The Conclave, every business in town, now they own the flockin' TARCs."

"They don't own the TARCs" Izeki began.

"Can't you read?" Chuen shrieked. "They own the flockin' TARCs!"

Izeki's voice was arch. " 'You'? Not 'He'? You're finally talkin' to me?"

"Chuen, you just said Byron Systems don't own anything on Thor. They can't own everything and nothing at the same time. Even Byron Systems couldn't pull that one off! Which is it?"

Before Chuen could open her mouth to retort, there was a chime from the front door.

"Gabriel," With a surge of relief Isadora rushed to open it. Izeki's hand clamped painfully on her arm.

"'Wait! It's 2 A.M. for Macca's sake! Function! Exview door."

Three heads turned toward the terminal display, where Izeki's brother was staring back at them.

Izeki mouthed the one word. "Isaao," Fear had drained the color from his face. In two strides he was at the front door and slapping it open.

Isaao stood alone in the hallway, his back against the far wall, his face strangely perplexed.

"Isaao, what is it?" Izeki's voice was hoarse.

Isaao did not reply. He seemed not even to see Izeki. He blinked, ever so slowly, and his left eye glowed with a marigold light. Izeki's hand reached out for his brother's shoulder and closed on nothing as, in the same instant, Isaao grew transparent and faded, leaving only the firelight glow in his eye.

Too late Izeki understood what was happening. With a dull "pop" the glow vanished. Izeki leapt backwards, inhaling sharply. His nostrils were filled with a scent of poison honey and he realized, belatedly, that he had not understood at all. The floor and ceiling slid down between his feet and something smote his back and head, spinning him into darkness.

Frozen in horror, the two women watched Izeki strike the ground with a gentle "thwump." Before they could react a man was stepping through the doorway, carefully avoiding Izeki's prone body. He pointed his right fist at Isadora and Chuen and Isadora heard two clicks. With the second click something stung her breast. She managed one pace and to open her mouth, before her body was no longer her own and she was toppling facedown onto the ground like a felled tree. A second thump told her that Chuen had also fallen.

The paralysis was complete. She could blink, but barely, and she could not move her eyes. Consequently she heard, rather than saw their attacker walk over to Chuen and kneel down beside her. There was a sharp "pip." A moment later, her terror rising, Isadora heard him leave Chuen and kneel down behind her. His breath was cool against her neck, stirring the fine hair there. Hands turned her gently over so that she was lying on her back and could see him. His hair was ash, his skin pale oak brown, his features so without distinction as to be even more frightening. Isadora realized that she would never be able accurately to describe him, or even pick him out of a crowd. His green-brown eyes bore the lightly troubled concentration of someone peeling an apple. Fingers dipped into his breast pocket. With a lover's precision he fastened a narrow, smooth, transparent, plastine collar about Isadora's neck. It was sickeningly warm with his warmth and it tingled. Then something metal was touching her jawline. A second "pip" and another gnat-sting.

The man rose to his feet, deliberately staying within her line of sight. He spoke with quiet, clipped precision. "In about ten seconds you will be able to move. You will obey me. The collars at your neck induce paralysis of the vocal cords. The pellets under your skin are filled with statrecks. It acts directly on the heart muscles. Should you disobey me, I will press once on this." He held up what appeared to be a sea-smoothed pebble the size of a matchbox. "You'll be dead before you hit the floor."

We'll be dead anyway, Isadora realized hopelessly.

*   *   *

When Izeki opened his eyes the apartment was empty, the front door still open. He climbed to his hands and knees, the walls flowing and heaving like a billious sea.

"Agh . . . shit." He dry-retched and moaned. His skull was filled with molten lead. He needed to hold his wrist steady with his other to focus on his watch face. To his surprise only a few minutes had passed since . . . what?

Isaao!

Izeki staggered to the front door, grasping the frame with both hands as the hallway corkscrewed away from him. No trace remained of that suffocating blanket of molasses that had enveloped him. His stomach knotted at the memory.

It was lucky that his reflexes had sent him leaping backwards. Had he inhaled a complete lungful of whatever it was, he might yet have been unconscious. Or even dead.

He stumbled along tilting fun-house floors and walls that crawled, his heart hammering in his breast.

Isaao.

His guts gave a lurch as the elevator doors opened on the seventeenth floor to reveal that Isaao's front door was open.

Oh, Macca, forgive me, he thought, *forgive me for my stupidity! Just let them not be hurt.*

He reached Isaao's front door and almost fell to his knees with relief. In the center of the living-room floor a pajama-clad Isaao was kneeling, grasping his head in both hands and moaning. When he spotted Izeki he said plaintively, "My head hurts." Behind him Aysha was leaning against a table, clumsily rubbing at her face with the back of her hand, like a newly wakened child.

"Shit," Izeki gasped. "Shit. You're alright."

"No, my head hurts," Isaao insisted reproachfully.

"Why the hell did you open your door . . . ?" Izeki bit back the rest of what he was going to say. *Why the hell did you open your door to a perfect stranger at two o'clock in the morning?* His own behavior had not distinguished him by its intelligence. Izeki's finger stabbed out. "Get dressed, shut this door and don't open it or move from here until you hear from me! You understand?"

With Isaao's sealed front door solid against his back,

Izeki squeezed his eyes shut and held his breath for a moment. He let it out with a rasp. No more! It was time to do what he should have done hours ago!

An open door. If the door had not been open, the apartment would have looked perfectly normal. With mounting dread Gabriel took in the empty glasses on the table and armrests, the phantom words hovering over the terminal display, the Windows to a dozen distant worlds. There were no marks of a struggle, or even a hasty departure. But the door had been open when he arrived and Gabriel did not need to be a genius to know that something was very much amiss. In the next room he could hear Isadora's pets stirring, a trace of Helios weasel tainting the air and . . . something else. Something sweet.

I should have stayed! I shouldn't have left them! Not with Izeki drunk as a sun-happy gold panner like that.

He stiffened at the first sound of footsteps from out in the corridor, then relaxed as he recognized a familiar heavy tread. *Izeki.*

As Gabriel stepped out into the corridor Izeki was already wresting his stunner from his shoulder holster.

"Izeki," what happen—"

Izeki's burst of fire caught Gabriel in the chest and his world exploded into livid crimson pain. Gabriel's scream shredded to a hopeless, animal braying as his body went rigid and arched, his eyes rolling back in his head. The pain was so intense that he did not even feel his head impact against the ground. Razored ice slashing at exposed nerves, frozen knuckles crushed by stones, paper slicing under torn fingernails, not a burning pain, but a cold pain, searing through his entire body. His mind shrieked, *God, let it stop, please let it stop, let it stop, let it stop, let it stop!*

And it did. In an instant. He was prostrate on his back, the only cold the sheen of sweat coating his body. His limbs twitched, convulsing, flinching from a pain that was no longer there, but that still filled him with terror. As he returned to himself he felt a wetness along his legs and a sour smell of urine and he realized that his bladder had voided itself.

Izeki was standing above him, his face slack with

shock. His eyes were vivid circles and his jaw worked. The slumbergun, which was still aimed at Gabriel, trembled.

"I didn't mean . . . I didn't mean—" The words seemed torn from his belly. Abruptly he fumbled with his slumbergun; he appeared to be clawing the skin off the back of the hand which grasped it. Then Gabriel saw him slide the catch from "nerve-shock" to "stun" and understood that Izeki had only intended to render him unconscious. It was cold comfort.

"Why?" Gabriel managed to gasp.

"No!" Izeki's voice cracked and he caught himself. "No! No more! No more!" Izeki ran a feverish hand across his face, kneading the flesh as if he wished he could tear it from his skull. But though unsteady, the gun in his hand never wavered. His voice was distant, speaking to someone or something beyond the confines of this hall. "You've got to keep with your people. You've got to stay with the ones close to you, you understand? You've got to take care of your own, you know? Like you."

Gabriel whispered, "Izeki, where's Isadora? Where's Chuen?"

"You've got . . . ! No." Izeki reigned himself in again. "No." He pawed at his collar, activated his phone. "TARC Headquarters, Purple Sector, extension tee-six-slash-one-one . . ." He focused on Gabriel again, a pleading note in his voice. "It's not you. It's not them, not . . . the women, okay? It's not personal; I just don't have a choice, you understand . . . ? He broke off again as the phone squawked at him. "Yeah? . . . Get me Pelham Leel . . . Yes, I know what time it is, get him for me or give me his home number! . . ." Izeki reacted with surprise. "He's on duty? This late? Then stop wasting my flocking time and get him on-line!"

"That's alright, Lieutenant," a silky voice said. "That won't be necessary."

Gabriel followed Izeki's stunned gaze to the elevator, where Pelham Leel stood, fox-terrier smile bristling avuncular good humor.

His feet paced a slow, soft, line along the hallway. "Well, well, well, here we all are, the night owls," pewter gray eyes gazed down and sucked in Gabriel, "Mr. Kylie.

This is a surprise. I must admit I'd been expecting to find one Isadora Gatzalumendi and a colleague of hers, but not you."

Gabriel started at the mention of Isadora. "Where are they? What did you do with them?"

Leel feigned astonishment. "They, Mr. Kylie? Do you think I'd still be here if I'd 'done' anything with them, as you so delicately put it? They're the ones I came to find." He turned to Izeki. "My arrest, I think?" He waited for Izeki's grudging nod before gesturing at Gabriel with two fingers. "Up. If you'd keep him covered, Lieutenant."

Leel waited until Gabriel had gained his feet before making a little circling motion with his finger, indicating that Gabriel was to face the wall.

"Hands."

Gabriel placed his palms against the wall. His feet were roughly kicked apart. "Tch," Leel tutted, "we seem to have had a little accident, Mr. Kylie."

Gabriel flushed with humiliation. Then his arms were being wrenched behind his back. Something thin encircled them and tightened. "Individual limb restraints vary from world to world," Explained Leel helpfully. "These are plastine-encased razor wire. Pull hard enough and you'll cut through the casing and slice your hands off at the wrist. You won't have to pull hard." He added icily.

"Izeki, for heaven's sake . . . ugh," A brutal jab in the kidneys choked off Gabriel's speech. "Izeki," he managed to croak, "what happened to the women?"

"Sorry about that, Mr. Kylie," Leel said carelessly. "That was just a little . . . uh . . . caution. You can turn around now."

Gabriel did so, staring hatred at the Bogy leering back at him. He understood that he was fodder now, less than human. The Bogy had put its little rubber stamp on him again, its precious ornament, and now it owned him.

Leel did not blink. One hand went to his mouth to politely cover a yawn. "Excuse me," he said sheepishly. "It's been a while since I pulled bat shift. Considering the resources we've put into locating you, Mr. Kylie, I'm surprised you were so imprudent as to come here. But it seems Officer Izeki's hunch was right, although really"—he turned a pained expression on Izeki—"you

might have let me know that you'd already requisitioned
the two women as a lure; it would have spared me a
great deal of anxiety—to say nothing of an interrupted
night's slumber. For a moment there I thought you'd
gone back on our little accord."

Gabriel turned his disbelief and silent rage on Izeki,
who steadfastly refused to meet his eye.

"How'd you know they were here?" The Municipal
officer appeared to have found his voice.

Leel shrugged. "Hm? Oh, well that's one of the draw-
backs of allowing members of the media into your living
room, isn't it? They always take the proverbial arm
when offered the ubiquitous finger. I'd take a good perusal of your next Web-subscription bill."

Izeki's expression turned to disgust. "The Web. You
tagged something they were looking for in the Web."

"Tch-tch-tch," Leel remonstrated. "I didn't say that *I*
tagged anything, but it helps to have acquaintances in
the Cyberspace Crime Unit, no?"

"Listen, Leel . . ." Gabriel began.

"That's Officer Leel to you, Mr. Kylie." Leel delicately removed something from the inner corner of his
eye.

Gabriel clenched his teeth. *Come on, mate, don't go
baiting the Bogy.* He ground the words out, "Officer
Leel. If you haven't got Isadora Gatzalumendi and Lee
Chuen in custody, then it means that their lives are in
danger. Somebody already tried to kill Isadora. Now,
lock me up, do what you like, but please find them."

"I intend to, Mr. Kylie, I intend to. Once I have you
secured." The TARC officer beckoned. "Come along,
please."

Gabriel pleaded, "Izeki, please, don't do this . . ."

"Shut up!" Izeki's jaw was taut-strung cable, his eyes
fireflies that darted everywhere but on Gabriel.

"Listen to me . . ."

"No!" Izeki snapped. "I told you, I'm not listening.
I've listened. No more listening. No more."

Leel's hand clamped onto Gabriel's upper arm. "If
you would, Mr. Kylie."

Gabriel tried to jerk away. "Izeki . . ."

Leel's grip tightened, "Mr. Kylie, you can walk or I
can ask Officer Izeki here to drop you with his weapon

and I'll have my A.I. module come up and carry you out."

A.I. module. Leel had a toyman downstairs.

Gabriel said, "You do that and you'll never know where the blue box is."

This took Leel off guard. He shot a glance at Izeki and his tongue darted over his lips. Gabriel wondered whether Leel knew that Izeki knew anything about the blue box. He quickly pressed his advantage.

"You wall me up and you won't get anything out of me."

Leel looked thoughtful. "There are ways . . ."

"No, there aren't. Not legal ways. And you always play within the boundaries as much as you can, don't you, Leel? Once I'm inside the only way you'll get anything out of me is drugs or a psych-Probe and there's no way you can get away with using those on me *inside* without some kind of court order. You think I don't know the chances of your getting that?"

For a moment Leel appeared to consider, then he gave a chuckle. "Mr. Kylie, you don't honestly think that I'm going to enter into some Intervend-Bazaar haggling session on the terms of your freedom, do you? Here? In a corridor at two-thirty in the morning? And that's assuming you even have a chip to bargain with."

"I know where the blue box is."

Leel's amusement shone undimmed. "So you do, Mr. Kylie, so you do."

Gabriel realized that Leel really did not care. He pleaded. "It's not for me! Look, Lee . . . Officer Leel, all I want you to do is call for backup and find Isadora Gatzalumendi and Lee Chuen! I don't know how long they've been gone, but the more time you waste on me, the more likely they're going to turn up facedown in a gutter somewhere!"

"In my experience a few minutes seldom makes any real difference."

In the corner of Gabriel's vision Izeki stirred restlessly and sudden hope dawned. What if the women had only been gone a few minutes? There might still be a chance. He demanded, "Izeki, how long is it since they've been gone?"

"I think I've had enough, Mr. Kylie." Leel was finally

showing his impatience. His hands closed like talons on Gabriel's arms and Gabriel found himself being propelled irresistibly down the corridor. With his wrists secured by razor wire he dared not struggle too hard. He cried out in panic, "Let go! Izeki! Izeki!"

"Quiet!" Leel snapped.

Gabriel could find no purchase on the smooth floor, so in desperation he allowed his knees to give way and dropped into a kneeling position. Futilely Leel attempted to drag Gabriel back to his feet. It was clear that the TARC captain was on the verge of losing his studied cool. "Get off your knees, Kylie. Off . . . *off* your knees!"

Gabriel tried to twist his head around far enough to see Izeki. "Izeki, how long have they been gone?"

The wire around Gabriel's wrists tightened suddenly and Leel's voice was a sibilant rasp in Gabriel's ear, "Mr. Kylie, one solid jerk and I can have both your hands off at the wrist."

Gabriel felt something nip into the flesh of his left wrist. Leel was growing increasingly angry and he understood suddenly why. Gabriel Kylie was impinging on Pelham Leel's dignity. He was making the esteemed TARC captain look foolish in front of a Municipal subordinate.

"If you do, I hope you've got the medical facilities to keep me alive until you get back to the bureau," he jeered, putting as much insolence into his voice as he could muster. The restraint constricted momentarily and Leel's breath quickened, hissing through his teeth. Then Leel released his grip and reached for Gabriel's hair. That was what Gabriel had been waiting for. He threw himself sideways, twisting so that he landed on his back, and kicked out with both feet.

Leel groped for Gabriel's shoulder and received several kicks around the head and chest, forcing him back out of the reach of Gabriel's wildly flailing legs. The corridor was too narrow for Leel to get around Gabriel without receiving a well-aimed foot amidships. "Get up! Get . . . shit! Get off the floor!" Leel's face was red with suppressed fury. Gabriel did not dare take his eyes off him to gauge Izeki's reaction to this slapstick double act.

"How long have they been gone, Izeki?" Gabriel panted.

Izeki's contempt was audible. "Leel, they were abducted less than fifteen minutes ago . . ."

"You! Not a word!" Leel shouted, his finger jabbing out at the Municipal officer. He had by now completely lost his temper. "Kylie, I've had enough of this. I can get a dozen agents here in minutes . . ."

"That's what I've been asking you to do, you pinstriped pillock!" Gabriel taunted.

Leel took a deep breath, and said through clenched jaw, "Izeki, get him up."

"I thought you said it was your collar, Leel. You want to share it now?" Izeki's contempt had an even greater impact on Leel than that of Gabriel.

Leel barked into his collar phone. "Lobo, get up here." His breath was coming hard and deep. Leel tore his weapon from its holster and for the second time in less than five minutes Gabriel found himself staring down a police stunner. The knuckles grasping it were white. "Alright, Mr. Kylie," Leel spat, "it's your choice. Are you going to walk or do I shoot you?"

"That'll be helpful. You expect me to sleepwalk?"

"Get *up,* Kylie!"

Gabriel called past him, "Hey, Izeki, you told me you weren't as dirty as most. What d'you think it'll take to get you clean if Isadora and Chuen end up dead?"

"Alright, Mr. Kylie, that does it." Very deliberately Pelham Leel thumbed the catch on the side of his weapon to "nerve-shock." Gabriel's muscles convulsed involuntarily, and he heard himself say, "No, don't . . ."

Triumph blazed from Leel. "Second thoughts?"

Yes, more than I can count, Gabriel did not say. Instead he drew in a deep breath and closed his eyes. He whispered, "Just this: why don't you put your hands down your trousers and count to two on the world's oldest abacus."

Pelham Leel seethed. "As you like."

There was a spitting and then . . . nothing. Gabriel opened his eyes in time to see the look of astonishment on Pelham Leel's face as he pawed at the three crimson pinpricks that had appeared on his cheek. The TARC officer crumpled to the floor like an empty suit. Behind him Izeki's face twitched fly-twitches as he reholstered his slumbergun.

Izeki threw an arm under Gabriel's shoulders and hauled him to his feet.

"Come on, go." He hurried them back down the corridor towards the open apartment door.

"Careful, careful," Gabriel yelped as a sting and viscid coolness along his fingers told him that the razor wire was slicing further into his flesh. The elevator chirruped behind them and Izeki shoved Gabriel through the apartment door. There was no time to close it; Izeki was running back toward Leel's prone form when the elevator door dropped open and Lobo stepped out into the hall.

"North-end elevators, roofrunners, quick!" Izeki puffed, jerking his thumb over his shoulder. He dropped down beside Leel and made as if to feel for his pulse. Shoulders tense, Izeki deliberately did not look up as the robot approached. Only when he knew that the robot was standing over him did he raise his head.

The corridor drew bell curves in the toyman's blank, mirrored face. And at its center a tiny white spot that Izeki knew was the reflection of his own face.

"What has transpired here?" Lobo inquired.

"Stunner. Took a shot in his face, he'll be alright, now cover the flockin' north end *now*!" Izeki put all the authority he could into the order.

Lobo remained unmoving. In its burnished face something stirred. Izeki knew immediately what it was. Leel was awakening. Izeki did not dare look down.

There was a flash of corridor light and Lobo was gone, dashing off down toward the north-end elevators. Izeki chanced a glance over his shoulder and saw the robot pause outside his open front door. He prayed that Gabriel was wise enough to have concealed himself. Then the robot's footsteps were thudding into the distance. One more close-range burst from Izeki's stunner ensured that Leel would be unconscious for several minutes yet.

Gabriel was trying to key open a kitchen drawer with his knee and swearing with frustration when Izeki entered.

"Come on, come on, come on!" Izeki reached out for Gabriel's arm but Gabriel twitched away.

He exclaimed angrily, "No! Stop grabbing me! I'm sick of being grabbed!"

Izeki held both hands up, palms out, sweat shone on his brow. "We've got about half a minute to get out of here. Leel's on duty, which means they're monitoring his vital signs back at Central. By now they know he's down and every TARC in the shagging sector is converging here for a jamboree. You want to argue?"

"Shit!" Gabriel twisted around and extended his wrists. "Then get this flaming thing off me, I can't run with it!"

"I can't, it's codelocked and only Leel's got it . . . unless you want to wait for Lobo to get back."

Gabriel pounded frenziedly against a drawer with his thigh, "Then *cut* them off me!"

"I *can't*! You can't cut razor wire with a knife!"

"*Shit*!" Gabriel cast about in despair. Then he remembered. "Buzz-knife!"

"Buzz-knife?"

"Here! Here! Buzz-knife! In my leg pocket!" Gabriel turned it toward Izeki. The policeman pried it gingerly out of Gabriel's damp pocket.

"A one-man hardware store." He grunted. There was a whine and Gabriel felt the fastening around his wrist loosen. He knew better than to jerk his hands apart, but waited until Izeki cleared the wire from his wrists and flicked it to one side.

"Now let's *go*!"

They hurtled down the corridor, Izeki slapping at the elevator palmplate with all his force. The elevator door remained closed.

"Aw, you've got to be joking!" Izeki's voice rose in a wail. "Who else is *awake* at this hour!"

"Did you break the doorplate? Maybe you broke it."

"No, I didn't flockin' break it! I don't *believe* this!"

Behind them Gabriel heard a steady pounding against the carpeted floor. Lobo. The robot must have discerned the deceit and was returning.

Then the elevator door was dropping open and they were inside. "Ground floor." Izeki fumbled with his I.D. card and slapped it, facedown, against the palmplate. Police override. It would prevent Lobo from freezing the elevator and trapping them in here.

"Isadora . . . Chuen . . ." Gabriel panted.

"One thing at a time, we're not out of here yet!"

"Wait . . ." The elevator door had dropped open on the ground floor, but Gabriel held Izeki back. His wrists left dark, sticky stains on Izeki's jacket. "Izeki, they're going to be killed."

"Let go of me! Look, we've got time. They may want to question them . . ."

"No! You're not understanding! They're going to be killed! They tried once already."

"For Macca's sake. . . . shag it!" The elevator door tried to close and Izeki blocked it with his body. A calm, sexless voice purred, "Please clear the door. Police emergency. Please clear the door."

Gabriel bellowed, "Izeki, they're going to be killed! I know it! You know it! They're taking them somewhere where they won't be found! Now where?"

Izeki stared back blankly.

"Clear the door. Now. Police emergency." The automated voice had hardened.

Suddenly Izeki's eyes widened. "The quickfarms," he breathed.

The quickfarms? It took an instant before Gabriel got it. The quickfarms were not only the central food supply, they were also the only utilizer of fertilizer, both chemical and organic. All of the city's organic waste was disposed of there to be recycled.

Including human remains.

"Oh, strewth."

The two men spun as one and bolted for the building's front entrance.

watchmaker

Elspeth's journal:

I lay with my ear to the ground amid the spinyfex today and listened. In the beginning the Ancestors walked through the world and sang the Universe into being. The Paths of Song they walked are there still, every step a note, every ridge a phrase, and we call them Ancestor lines. The Elders sing life into them every time they walk them, every day. I fell asleep in the shade among the spinyfex, with my ear still to the ground, and I dreamed my hair became roots, sucking moisture from the cool dark places, down deep.

I could hear the heart of the rainbow snake, the mother of all. Boom, boom, boom. Lately she comes back to me at night, slipping into my dream. Sometimes her heart beats in the streets of Kyara, boom, boom, boom. And sometimes when it gets too loud I go to the perimeter of the city and look out over the Anvil and wonder . . .

The quickfarms were ahiss with life, GenTec-altered life, that grew a hundred times faster than normal. In a day a cabbage could grow from seed to ripeness, a tomato from verdant bud to ruddy, skin-split sweetness. Here Jack's magic beanstalk had become a reality, touching heaven in a morning, laid low by night. And all the while that low hiss, filling Isadora's ears.

She had reached a place within herself that was beyond fear. Terror had knitted itself into a knot in her chest, freeing the rest of her to reflect on her present position with a giddy detachment.

Their assailant had forced them to walk in front of him, out of the apartment and through the deserted dark-down streets to the outer perimeter of the quickfarms. There a card pressed against the palmplate of one of the doors had granted them egress to the vast complex.

A police override card, Isadora wondered absently. *Now where did he get ahold of an override card?*

They had passed through several synth-vat hangars, the stench of the yeast cultures almost overwhelming. Isadora had attempted to make some sound, but the band around her throat had rendered her utterly voiceless and she could barely manage a whisper.

Beside her Chuen tottered, brittle-limbed with rage and humiliation. Dog-collared, silenced and imprisoned to the whim of a male, she was being forced into a position of servility, forced to march to her own doom. Terrified as Isadora was, to a Sister of Tanit like Chuen this was all but rape.

Isadora's greatest worry was that Chuen would do something foolish, like making a break, or tearing off her collar. The man had not indicated that his little device was selective; if one went, they would both go. She knew where he was taking them, there could be no doubt, and every door that slid shut behind them chopped off a fragment of hope.

Suddenly her life, which hitherto had been a pool of quiet resignation, of ambitions abandoned, hopes sadly left to wither; suddenly it had become pregnant with such promise, such cherry-bright promise. It was as if impending death had suddenly freed her to dream of possibilities.

And then there was Gabriel, that strange man with his need for truth. He had instilled in her such feelings of aliveness. That, along with the dizzy lure of the unknown. In five short days the walls of her snail-like existence had been breached by the thousand terrors and it felt . . . comfortable.

Another door opened before them to reveal yet another huge, multilevel quicklife hangar, brightly lit with a full-spectrum lighting system. She noticed Chuen staring rigidly at something next to the door. It was a map of the local area. Straight ahead of them, just beyond this greenhouse, were the organic waste-disposal tanks.

Isadora swallowed. Heedless of the consequences she reached out and took Chuen's hand. They linked fingers. Isadora felt a poke in her back. She squeezed her friend's fingers and Chuen squeezed back in a grip of desperation as they stepped through the doorway.

It's all right, Chuen, Isadora said silently, *it's alright. I'm here and I'll be with you until the end.*

Izeki and Gabriel tumbled out of the building's main entrance.

"Which way?" Gabriel demanded.

The police officer only hesitated for some three seconds, but Gabriel wanted to seize him and shake him until an answer rattled out of him and onto the ground.

"Jarrel Street . . . no, the disposal works . . . The nearest entrance is . . ."

Suddenly, over Izeki's shoulder, Gabriel saw the hangcars—five of them—appear around the far corner of the street, sparkling with light. They descended silently, like comets, their entire bodywork flashing.

Gabriel growled. "Don't look now, but your in-laws have arrived."

"Shag it! This way!" Izeki was off, charging down the street with a speed that belied his massive frame.

"This is the shortest way?"

"It is now."

They were running. Gabriel did not need to look back; the entire street was lit up with rainbow flashes, the silence broken only by the pounding of their own feet and a low, serpentine hiss as the hangcars gained on them.

A voice like thunder hammered at them, almost causing Gabriel to trip and fall.

"Halt! Now! Or bio-intrusive methods will be adopted! This is a TARC order!"

A glance back. The hangcars were less than fifty meters away, dropping like meteors ablaze. He found his gaze caught like a hypnotized rabbit and almost missed the alley that Izeki ducked into. Slumber-bullets strafed the sidewalk as Gabriel rounded the corner.

I've been here before. Then the walls of the alley were flashing, his own shadow darting ahead of him, appearing, disappearing, appearing again. The TARC hangcars had reached the mouth of the alley. As Gabriel rounded the far corner he caught a glimpse of shimmering radiance pierced by open hangcar doors that vomited a quicksilver rain of toymen and TARC agents.

Izeki led him through a wickerwork of forking alleys. It was like being trapped in a sounding box, the drum of dozens of pursuing robot feet echoing off the walls. They emerged into a broad street where the glowing cupolas of the quickfarms loomed over them. Izeki headed for a door marked "Last but not Yeast Enterprises" and slapped his police identification card against the doorplate.

"Police emergency. Lock override. Open!"

The door slid open and Gabriel gulped. There was no mistaking the fragrance of the synth-block yeast tanks.

The moment that the door closed behind them Izeki had the buzz-knife out and was slicing open the control panel. A shower of sparks and he pocketed the knife.

"Buys us some time," he gasped, bending over double and trying to regain his breath.

"Where now?" Gabriel wanted to know, unable to conceal his impatience.

Izeki glared at him in disbelief. "Would you . . . wait a second?" he wheezed. "I'm dying here."

Gabriel cast about. They were in an unlit reception area. A couch protruded from one wall, an empty frame affixed above it—a deactivated Window. The empty reception desk guarded the only other door out of the room. He sensed rather than saw the low coffee table in the center of the floor and gave it a wide berth. "That's the back way out of here?"

Izeki waggled a hand vaguely, "Yeah, that way, I'd guess . . . the quickfarms are just one big complex . . . everything is joined to everything . . . else."

"You know where the recycling area is?"

"My brother works in one of the farms here. Here, this way . . . yow!" Izeki yipped as his shins audibly struck the coffee table. Whatever the policeman's other skills, traversing a hostile landscape by night was not one of them.

Gabriel checked that there were no windows to the outside, then said, "Function. Lights on!"

"No!"

It was too late. That same instant they were blinded by the overhead lighting coming on. The empty window frame was no longer empty—it now overlooked a mountainous landscape that appeared oddly familiar to Gabriel. Somewhere on Denube's northern continent.

Izeki was cursing. "What are you? Stupid? You think I don't have a flashlight? Shag it!"

"Sorry, I thought you couldn't see . . ."

Both men jumped as a husky contralto voice spoke. "Good evening. Welcome to Last but not Yeast Enterprises. We are closed at this moment. Please state your reason for being here after hours or we will regrettably be forced to alert the police to your unauthorized presence here."

Behind the desk a handsome, yet curiously nondescript woman in her mid-thirties was beaming up at them. A good receptionist should put customers at ease, yet not intrude upon their consciousness. She waited until she had their undivided attention and then added as an afterthought, "You have ten seconds to comply."

"Congratulations," Izeki growled in an exasperated tone, then raised his voice, "Lieutenant Hitedoro Izeki, Municipal Police. This is a police emergency, we need to use one of your other exits. This is my I.D." His I.D. card clicked onto the deskplate.

"Palmprint confirm, please," trilled the receptionist.

Izeki gave Gabriel a look that could have wilted a daffodil at ten paces and placed his palm on the plate.

After an almost imperceptible pause the receptionist smiled again, and said, "Your identification has been confirmed and Municipal Police Green Sector Central Office officially alerted to your presence here. Please proceed. For your convenience the lights will remain on for another thirty seconds.

The moment they had emerged from the office into a wide corridor, one of the main quickfarm conduits, Izeki rounded on Gabriel, "Well, that's great! That's just upside!" Gabriel flinched back as Izeki waved his beefy forefinger under his nose. "Next time why don't you just send them a flockin' map with an arrow on it, 'Assholes this way'!"

Gabriel, who was feeling stupid enough as it was, had

had enough. His voice was low and cold. "I've got a
better idea, why don't you listen to *me*, Izeki! I've been
here on this one-ferret world for five days. In that time
I've been shot, razor-wired, imprisoned, kicked in the
bollocks, had my arm nearly broken, been kidnapped by
uplanders, mugged by downlanders, lied to by every rat-
buggering official I've met, including you . . . no, you
listen, you lard-witted pillock! There are two women
whose lives are in danger because of me. Two women
you were supposed to be looking after! You want to
help, then shut up and work with me. Otherwise, go
your own flamin' way and do what you do best: sitting
on your double D-cup backside, getting puke-eyed and
doing sweet, sorry *sod all*!"

Without waiting for a reaction, Gabriel pushed past
Izeki and headed for a color-coded map, projected onto
the far wall. He did not see Izeki's face pale, nor his
convulsive swallow.

The Organic-Residuum Salvage center lay on the far
side of the quickfarms. Gabriel deduced that he could
bypass the whole yeast-production sector by cutting
straight through the quick-growth greenhouses. Fifty meters further up the corridor he encountered the first
door—and his first obstacle. Although the quickfarms
were centered in one city locale, they did consist of dozens of independent businesses, each with its own separate security measures.

This is bloody perfect, he thought bitterly.

He was on the point of turning back when a heavy
tread and whistling breath signaled Izeki's arrival. He
reached past Gabriel's shoulder and slapped his I.D.
card onto the doorplate. The door slid open.

"Here," Izeki grumbled without looking at Gabriel.
He was holding out the buzz-knife. "Yours." Gabriel
accepted it. After a second's hesitation Izeki reached
into his jacket and withdrew a slumbergun. He fired it
experimentally at the floor. The "cling" of stun-pellets
striking metal echoed around them. "Good. Targeting
are a paranoid bunch of bugsuckers, always thumblock-
ing their weapons." He grunted with satisfaction and
handed it to Gabriel, "Leel's." One corner of his
mouth twitched.

Gabriel accepted the weapon without enthusiasm and hefted it. Then, as one, they took off through the door.

Pelham Leel's head was pounding and his cheek itched where Izeki's shot had struck him. A double dose of slumber-bullets would do little for anybody's disposition and the flashing bodies of the police vehicles were not helping. Brilliant green afterimages flared up on the inside of his eyelids whenever he blinked.

"Lobo, for goodness' sakes, make them turn those lights out," he croaked irritably. "The whole shagging sector must know we're here by now."

Lobo turned to comply, then froze. His head swiveled back toward Leel and the TARC captain came suddenly alert.

"Green Sector Municipal Headquarters report Lieutenant Izeki using official police overrides to gain egress to and passage through Last but not Yeast Enterprises offices on Highbourne Street at precisely oh-two-twenty-six."

The quickfarms!

"That's it!" Leel exulted. "Kahn! Over here!" A young man came hurrying over. "Kahn, our targets are in the quickfarms. If we move fast, we may be able to box them in there. I want all police-override capabilities canceled for the whole complex. Do it!"

Kahn seemed taken aback. "Er . . . sir," he ventured cautiously, mindful of his captain's mood, "there's a couple of hundred separate businesses in there. They've all got their own separate security systems."

Leel exclaimed impatiently, "For Macca's sake, I know that! But there's got to be a central shutdown point where all the doors can be opened or sealed. Now find out where it is, wake up whoever's in charge, and get that override capacity *shut off*!"

"That could take . . ."

"Ten minutes. You've got ten minutes."

Kahn hurried off and as he did so the police lights ceased their flashing.

Thanks, Lobo. Gratefully Leel rubbed at his eyes. It could have been worse. The quickfarms had too many exits to cover each and every one adequately, but if they could seal every security-locked door in the complex, then he and his people could start chewing through the place, chunk by chunk, until they nailed Gabriel Kylie.

And Izeki, he thought to himself sourly. He'd certainly misjudged that one. But, then again—and he smiled—so had Municipal Officer Hiterdoro Izeki.

They ran through aisles lined with verdure. The accelerated-growth greenhouses operated on a double six-hour light-up/dark-down shift system and most were in the first daylight shift of their twenty-four-hour cycle. Had he been alone, Gabriel could have traversed the distance to the Organic-Residuum Salvage center in half the time. The other man was fleet of foot for someone of his size, but by the time they reached the last quickfarm before the Salvage center his breathing was resembling the last gasps of a leaky kettle.

"Côtes des Kyara, vineyard," Gabriel read the sign on the doors in disbelief. "You've got to be flocking joking!"

Izeki gasped, "At a . . . hundred . . . twenty clips a pouch . . . they'd better not be." With a trembling hand he placed his I.D. card against the doorplate. "Police . . . over . . . override," was all he managed to get out. It was enough.

The door slid open upon a vast hangar. Gabriel gaped in astonishment. Set in long, curving rows, vines squeezed up out of black, mineral-enhanced sim-soil, twisting, knotted and grasping at the ceiling. Along the ceiling, bright, new shoots flowed across the plastine panels, trailing leafy fronds back to the floor. Everywhere tumescent clusters of purple grapes swelled from behind leaves and under overhanging branches. Here and there burnished, three-armed spiders the size of cats clambered amongst the vines, selecting, then slurping down bunches of grapes, occasionally descending to empty their juice-filled bellies into little plastine spigots that lined the edges of the soil beds. The air was thick with the honey-bitter smell of vineleaf and fruit and astir with the sound of growth, an inward sigh, a single endless inhalation, expanding, expanding unceasingly.

That, and something else. Gabriel put out at hand to stop Izeki, who had started forward. The Municipal officer looked at him questioningly. There it was again, soft as dewfall, from the far side of the hangar, a pad of feet. Hurrying.

"Iz," Gabriel whispered.

Isadora heard the purr of the door opening, the same door through which she had come a few moments before. She did not need to be told to stop.

Their assailant put his finger to his lips, staring at Isadora and Chuen in turn. He was wearing contact lenses, she noted for the first time, perhaps to hide his eyes' true color.

Feet ran, there was a rustle of vineleaves from near the far door. Sudden hope surged and Isadora's fingers itched to tear off the band around her throat, but she controlled the impulse. She glanced at her friend and saw, to her horror, that Chuen's tear-stained face had developed a tic, her hands clenching spasmodically.

Please, Chuen, she willed her friend, *please, don't do it.*

The man drew his hand across his many-pocketed chest, so deftly that the little gray control box seemed to vanish from his fingers. Instead a handgun sprouted in his hand like a greige orchid. In his other hand he held his override card ready.

"On," he murmured. He hustled the two women ahead of him, toward the door at the near end of the row, glancing over his shoulder as he walked. The row's gentle curve prevented them from seeing to the far end of the hangar. Isadora held her hands to her chest, praying.

Suddenly a figure appeared some twenty-five meters behind them. Izeki. Isadora's heart leapt. The assassin's arm rose, gun extended, even as Izeki dived to one side.

Pop! Zzziiiiii!

The sound was so soft, so innocuous. Then something bit a chunk out of a distant vinetrunk.

"Not a move," a voice said behind them.

Isadora's heart leapt. *Gabriel!* Their kidnapper's response was instantaneous. Before she knew what had happened Isadora was jerked forward, between the assailant and Izeki, whilst her captor fired a series of bursts over his shoulder, without looking, at Gabriel.

Gabriel saw the man's right hand appear over his left shoulder. Unable to get a clear shot past Chuen and

afraid of hitting Isadora, he had no choice but to duck
to one side.

Pop! Pop! Pop!

Vines shuddered spasmodically around him and Gabriel had a vague impression that the gun's projectiles
did not follow a straight line, but seemed to curve
toward him. Even as he ducked the man melted backwards into the growth and at the same time, to his horror, Izeki fired a fusillade of random shots, striking first
Isadora and then Chuen. As Chuen crumpled to the
ground a brief ripple of furious indignation passed across
her face. Gabriel hit the ground, rolled back up onto his
hands and knees and scrambled through two more vine
rows before finding himself face to face with Izeki.

"Are you out of your mind?" Gabriel yelped. "Is
there anyone you don't shoot? No flamin' wonder you've
got no friends!"

"I saved their lives, what more d'you want?" Izeki
was trying to peer through the thick growth, his head
weaving, ducking nonexistent bullets.

"Well, do me a favor and don't save mine."

"Done," Izeki growled. "Slumberguns and hostages
cancel each other out. The baddie knows it doesn't matter if you hit the hostage."

"Bloody strewth," Gabriel whispered, knowing that he
was being unreasonable and not caring in the slightest.
Something moved to his right and he swung his weapon
that way. Before he even realized it he had fired off
three shots. A snowfall of shredded leaves fluttered to
the ground in front of him, marking the slumber-bullets'
passage. He flushed at Izeki's scornful look.

"Shaggin' amateurs," the policeman muttered.

Gabriel jumped as a series of dull pops rang out and
a wave of thrashing vines worked its way along the vine
row toward him, strands of young growth whip-tailing
out and spitting chunks of foliage. Gabriel threw himself
flat just in time as the leaves in front of him, erupting
outward, revealed the path of a projectile from the assassin's weapon. He recoiled as a chunk of wetness slopped
against the side of his face, splattering sticky fluid into
his eyes.

Izeki. "Oh, god," he gasped. Nearly retching, he

slapped at his face, his hand closing on a wet, pulpy mass. "Oh, god."

"Shh!" Izeki's voice hissed at him from nearby. In that same instant Gabriel tasted sweetness on his lips and the heavy scent of ripened grapes filled his nostrils.

Grapes! Gabriel let his head fall back against the ground and closed his eyes for a moment, striving to calm himself.

Izeki was panting heavily, not with exertion, but with fear.

"Old-fashioned hunting weapon," he panted, "Solid . . . projectiles with heat-seeking capabilities."

"You mean he can shoot around corners." Gabriel groaned.

"More or less."

"That's alright. That's alright. It's alright," Gabriel was speaking more to himself than Izeki. *Come on, Gabriel, pull it together, mate. Use the knowledge. Use the knowledge.*

He rolled over onto his stomach. "Keep still," he said to Izeki.

"Why?"

"Just . . . shh." Gabriel listened. Izeki breathed like a hydraulic triphammer behind him. From all sides there was a constant scratching of leaves and ceramic clicks as the grape-pickers clambered about, obliviously carrying out their tasks. *There.* A whisper of fabric.

Gabriel fired in the direction of the sound. Silence. Nothing fell. No movement.

"He's . . . very professional. Knows a laser would start fires and set off the smoke alarms," Izeki remarked, face set in a lemon-drop scowl. The moment the words had left his lips another pop sounded and the foliage next to him shuddered. "Sha . . . aagh!" Izeki squawked.

Pop! This shot was followed by a *crack!* and Gabriel found his eyes stung with wood fragments. He gave an involuntary gasp of pain.

Pop! A rustle of leaves and for a fraction of an instant something breathed against the side of his face. *Strewth, he's targeting the sounds we make,* Gabriel realized, *and bloody accurately.* Managing to blink the fragments from his eyes, Gabriel sought out Izeki. The policeman was grimacing, but appeared unhurt.

Gabriel mouthed silently at him, "He's targeting our sounds; don't make any noise."

Izeki's lips moved, forming the one word, "What?"

Oh, for crying out loud! Gabriel thought in exasperation. Hardly daring to move, Gabriel inched over the ground until his face was next to Izeki's. As quietly as he could he whispered, "Targeting sound."

"I know that!"

Gabriel nodded and made to move away, but Izeki grabbed his shoulder. "Heat-seeking bullets. Useless unless he can get a clear shot."

Gabriel swallowed and glanced up and down the row they were lying in. Fortunately the rows curved, so their opponent would have to get to within twenty-five meters of them in order to get a clear shot. If only he could work out exactly where those previous shots had come from. As carefully as he could, Gabriel raised himself up into a low crouch.

Come on, Gae, he said to himself, *you're in a forest. Use it. Nobody can get past you in a forest.* Shooting glances over his shoulders he waddled backwards slowly in a squat position. He had spotted an opening in the vines through which he could creep silently.

"You stay here," he instructed Izeki, and hunkered down onto his belly.

"Stay . . . alrigh . . . wait! Why?"

"Bait."

Gabriel did not wait for Izeki's indignant exclamation. With barely a whisper of leaves to mark his passage he slipped between the vines. With grim amusement he heard Izeki grumble, "Bait? Bugsuck that. You can be the flockin' bait!"

Their opponent had not fired at the sound of Izeki's movement, which could only mean that he was otherwise preoccupied. This did not bode well. Gabriel paused and listened, disciplining himself into stillness. He could hear Izeki's rubber-footed efforts to creep silently through the undergrowth; somewhat further off he fancied he could make out Isadora's and Chuen's steady breathing.

Twenty meters further up the row he was crossing a vinestem stirred. Gabriel froze and brought up his weapon. A grape-picker?

The assassin spun out of the vines, his fist stretched

out and bright with metal. It did not even occur to Gabriel to fire back. He was diving headfirst into the next row of vines and barely heard the *pop!* above the shredding of leaves and splintering of twigs. A tuck and roll brought him back to his feet, lengths of young vine draped over his shoulders and left ear, his vision blocked by the leaves caught in his hair. He slapped the leaves away from his face, just in time to see his assailant emerge from the row.

Pop!

Gabriel was crashing nosefirst into the next row as something went *thock!* next to his ear, a bullet striking wood. Then he was in the open again, lurching to his feet.

Pop!

This time he remembered his weapon and managed to get off a couple of shots in no particular direction as he went diving into the next row of vines. His left shoulder and the side of his head struck the earth at the same time and his skull rang like a tuning fork. At the same time his arm struck a vinetrunk and the next thing he knew the slumbergun was no longer in his hand. His tuck and roll was more of an uncontrolled spill and twigs clawed at his face.

Pop!

Something smacked his left heel and there was a sudden burning.

"Gabrieeeeel!" Izeki's distraught voice was distantly audible above the static of splintering undergrowth.

Pop! Pop! Pop!

Gabriel and his attacker followed parallel courses through three more rows of vines, Gabriel just managing to keep a fraction of a second ahead. His face and hands were scratched and spattered purple with grape juice, soggy clumps of grape meat and skin oozing stickily down his neck and he was so bedecked with leaves and lengths of vine that he was starting to resemble a drunken reveler from a Dionysian festival. Plunging headfirst into the third row, he found himself aimed directly for a knot of vinetrunks and tried to bring himself up short. His shoulder collided with a trunk as he hit with a force that jarred his spinal column and sent agony down to his fingertips. He hooked his other arm around a branch to keep himself upright, shoulders hunched as he waited for the next shot.

Instead of a shot there was a dull click from the row beyond the one Gabriel was in. *He's reloading!* Gabriel's heart leapt. With one convulsive gesture Gabriel shrugged most of the shrubbery from his shoulders and dropped down onto his belly.

Pop!

The leaves above his head chuckled at him. Someone was making his way down the row toward him, but Gabriel was wriggling through the brush on fingers and toes, ignoring the burning in his heel and shoulder, his only aim to put distance between himself and his attacker.

At length, satisfied that he had lost his opponent, Gabriel stopped behind a dense tangle of brush and allowed himself to sink to the ground. A quick examination of his foot revealed that a bullet had grazed his heel, slicing open the shoe material and laying his heel bare to the bone.

As for his shoulder, whatever good had been done by Sharry's healing net had now been firmly undone. He felt like someone had taken an axe to it. Rolling over onto his back, he flexed his arm experimentally, breath hissing through his teeth as he inhaled sharply.

Christ, couldn't, just for once, someone else get hit?

A crack of breaking wood identified Izeki's location. The big man must have wondered what the hell had happened to him.

Forcing his attention away from his wounds Gabriel took stock. *No weapon, smashed-up shoulder, buggered heel and a sharpshooting opponent with heat-seeking bullets who can move almost as silently as I can. Brilliant,* he reflected. *At least things can't get much worse.*

Three seconds after that thought passed through Gabriel's mind the overhead lights went out, plunging the vineyard into darkness.

In the few moments that it took Gabriel to recover from the shock his eyes adjusted and he became cognizant that the darkness was not complete. Regularly spaced pinpricks of green light along the aisles edged the rows of vines in an eerie emerald glow, the leaves transforming into shadowy claws and the twisted stems into intestinal knots. The grape-pluckers were also lit, one tiny, orange light on the foot of each limb and a larger one on their body. They were designed to continue their labors during both day and night cycles of the quickfarms and so continued to clamber about undeterred, a twinkling dance of three fireflies around a minute candle flame.

This isn't so bad. Gradually Gabriel discerned that he might just have gained an advantage here. The lighting was now more or less the equivalent of a moonless night in the Stonypine Mountains in northern Denube, not impossible for someone who had followed Stonypine deer trails over dew-spun grass with no light but that from a starlit sky.

Except, another nasty, niggling little voice inside him queried, why would this man have turned the lights out? There could only be one answer to that.

His opponent could see in the dark.

Gabriel went ashen. "Bloody, flamin' strewth, we're up against the bloody Pungalunga man here," he whispered, remembering the home-fire tales of the cannibal giants that haunted the Dreamtime. A fat lot of good a buzz-knife was going to be against that. He had to find his weapon and fast, before the assassin found either him or the two unconscious women. That, at any rate, was one relief. Izeki had been right. As long as Isadora and Chuen remained unconscious they were no threat and so would be relatively safe.

Isadora opened her eyes and for one dreadful moment thought that she had gone blind. Then a glint of light in the corner of her eye told her that she was not blind, but lying on her back in a darkened chamber. Filled with . . . leaves? Black leaves edged with luminescent green and, here and there, orange sparks spinning bright coils in her aftervision as they darted from point to point.

She closed her eyes and faced Izeki down the shaft of a slumbergun. And Gabriel. And behind her . . . something else.

Her throat itched and, reaching up, her fingers closed in on a thin band of plastine.

She remembered. Izeki firing, firing, almost blindly

and the sting of slumber-bullets in her leg. Where was Gabriel? Izeki? What had happened?

She tugged and felt the band stretch and tear loose. Beside her someone stirred. Isadora reached out and touched hard flesh; the top of Chuen's hairless skull.

"Chuen?" she managed to croak.

Gabriel stiffened. *Isadora? Oh, no. Please, don't move, don't say anything.*

For the last few minutes he had been trying to back-track through the plant life to locate his slumbergun, following his own trail back by touch and scent and the occasional glimmer of artificial light outlining the vinework.

"Chuen?" Isadora's voice repeated faintly and this time Gabriel was able to pinpoint the direction from which it came. *Macca, if I know where she is, then he's going to know and he's going to make straight for her,* his mind chattered at him. Gabriel abandoned any hope of retrieving his weapon. Even if the killer could see in the dark, the vines offered floor-to-ceiling cover and he would have to track them down by sound first. Right now he must be making a beeline for the two women.

Gabriel raised his head and opened his mouth to shout, but was preempted by a burst of tearing foliage some distance away and a loud roar that could never have been mistaken for anyone but Izeki. "Isadora! Chuen! Don't make a sound!"

Gabriel ducked back down again in anticipation of a burst of sound-guided fire from the assassin. *What the flock was that?* Officer Izeki might be a stupid, bilious bastard, but there was no disputing, Gabriel thought with wry admiration, that he was a courageous, stupid, bilious bastard.

Izeki, however, was not through yet. "Come on you prize-assed piece of GenTec chug-monkey turd! I'm over here!" Gabriel traced the sound of his passage as he blundered through several meters of growth, letting off indiscriminate salvos of slumber-bullets. Gabriel hesitated, in an agony of indecision as he waited for the *pop*! of the assassin's weapon and an answering scream from Izeki. He would be a fool to give his own position away, but he could not just stand by and let Izeki barge straight to his death.

Gabriel leapt up. "Over here! This way!"

Izeki's crashing stopped. "Gabriel? What are you doing?"

Stooped double, Gabriel worked his way along the row. "Me! Try me! You want to shoot somebody, try me! I'm the one you're after!"

"Shut up, you idiot!" Izeki bellowed at him, much to Gabriel's surprise.

"You shut up!" he replied indignantly. "I'm not talking to you!" Then he realized what he was doing and dropped down onto his hands and knees, his arms shivering with the strain. *Shag it! What's wrong with us? Why not just paint a target on your backside and moon the bugger while you're at it, Gae?* Sweat stung his eyes and he wiped his face with a sim-soil-caked hand.

Use the knowledge!

Apparently Izeki had also thought better of sacrificing himself on the altar of misguided chivalry, because he also fell silent. For a long moment Gabriel waited. In every direction the rustle of the grape-pickers and the movement of the vines themselves as they grew made it impossible to tell if the assassin was moving anywhere nearby. And that was clearly what he planned. He had every advantage and was in no hurry whatsoever.

Gabriel fought down his fear and tried to think. There must be some advantage that he had over this assassin. Actually, there mustn't, but he determinedly ignored that possibility.

He can see in the dark, move as quietly as I can, shoot a lot better, he has a weapon, I don't. Shag! The way things were looking, mooning the bugger might just be a real option. Gabriel considered climbing the vines and ambushing the assassin from above, but he dismissed this immediately. Even he could not manage that without some noise.

Then he remembered his slaphappies.

In seconds Gabriel had them out of his pocket and was slipping them over his hands and feet. "Let's see how you like this," he said under his breath.

He was in an area where the vines grew all the way up to the ceiling, so he would be well covered here.

Using a knot in a fat vinetrunk to help himself up, he
leapt. His hands struck the ceiling and stuck, a swing of
his legs and he was four-points secure.

Heads up, mister spider, he thought smugly. *This fly's
just grown a scorpion's tail.*

From someplace on the far side of the greenhouse
something clapped softly and Gabriel felt the ceiling vi-
brate beneath his fingers. Immediately leaves crackled
under a hail of slumber-bullets as somewhere off to Gabriel's right Izeki fired blindly at the source of the sound.

But Gabriel had recognized the sound of a set of slaphappies striking plastine. He knew that Isadora and
Chuen had no slaphappies and he knew Izeki had no
slaphappies and would probably bring down the ceiling
if he ever tried using them. Which left . . .

"Oh, shit."

For a long moment Gabriel remained frozen in his
spread-eagle position on the ceiling. "Oh, shit," he repeated. And then once again, "Oh, shit." Perspiration
trickled back across his face behind his ears. This was
like swimming up a river with a drag-chute bound to his
feet. Every time he thought he had gained a length he'd
glance at the shoreline and see that he'd lost two. He
raised his head, desperately searching the floor above
him for some kind of answer. There was as much growth
on the ceiling as the ground to shelter behind, but
sooner or later the enemy would spot him. Except that
the enemy would be searching the floor. If only he had
some bait. The only bait he had was himself and there
was only one of him . . .

Yes!

He released his hold on the ceiling and dropped to
the floor, then made for the densest area of growth and
crouched down.

He was known to his clients as the Watchmaker, for
the precision with which he effected his commissions,
and to himself as "I," an island of one. There was himself and there were the assignment cases, which one
could reach out and move, alter, divert or eliminate. His
briefs tended to be broad in aspect, and included sales,
purchases, removals and, on occasions, disinfection. He

did what he did and, although it raised no passion within him, he prided himself on doing it well.

Tonight's commission had proven more irksome than he ever would have expected. Clearly he had been too complacent in his choice of the manner in which he had planned to dispose of the two female cases. With the quickfarms in such close proximity, how could the pursuers have avoided coming to the correct conclusion? It was doubly unfortunate that they had caught up with him in an area where his long-range tools were of such limited use. In a word: messy.

But there would be no further errors. This regrettable contretemps had already damaged his reputation considerably and he intended to see that the damage spread no further. Having dealt with the lights, the infrared feature in his contact lenses would allow him to see, whereas the cases were effectively blinded. Of the four cases, he had already pinpointed the location of three by their sound alone; the two females and the bigger of the two males. The second male case was of greater concern. The Watchmaker had been certain that he had had him nailed down, that he had even laid target on him and yet, somehow, the case had vanished in the three seconds that it had taken to reapplicate his tool. It was significant and unsettling.

A moment ago, the same case had shouted, apparently in some absurd attempt to distract him from the two females, but the Watchmaker had no doubt that he had moved on again.

No. It was imperative that that case be located and removed as quickly as possible. The others could wait. His brief called for the disinfection of the two female cases—which is to say, for them to vanish without a trace—so he needed them alive, long enough for them to walk under their own power to the disposal site. They were awake and moving now and they might, in fact, prove a useful distraction.

There was a momentary crackle of twigs and the Watchmaker knew that he had found his prey. Eyes alert and searching, the Watchmaker started to creep along the ceiling.

After crossing nearly a third of the length of the hangar his progress slowed. He was near the source of that latest trace of movement—the case must be nearby, unless he had vanished yet again. No, there he was, less than ten meters away. His heat signature was a faint glow, obscured by the dense growth crowding that section of the hangar. He was crouching, unmoving, as if waiting for an ambush. For a fraction of a second the Watchmaker's hand drifted to his gun. No. A rustle of leaves told him that the other male case was approaching and that one might just get lucky if he had a weapon report to draw a bead on. There had been enough sloppiness for one night. He double-checked the precise location of his target case, swung his feet down, dangled from his fingertips and dropped silently onto the floor of the next aisle over.

He hit the ground at a low-crouching run, a close-range tool glittering in one hand. A prick was all that would be necessary. As he drew level with his target his hand snaked out through a gap in the vine leaves . . . and met no resistance.

His shock lasted for the flutter of an eyelash. *Deceit!* His supposed target was nothing more than a self-heating, filamented body stocking, of the kind usually used for disguising a body's signature, draped cleverly over several branchlets.

The Watchmaker was already moving, his right elbow jabbing inward, when a heavy weight slammed down onto his back and dislodged the tool from his grip.

The elbow in his ribs nearly dislodged Gabriel and prevented him from gaining a proper grip around his opponent's neck. Already winded by the drop, he choked and clawed for breath as he was battered by a frenzy of blows to his ribs. He managed to croak Izeki's name once before a shoulder butt to his chin snapped his jaws shut on the tip of his tongue. He yelped and tried to bring his legs up around the Watchmaker's waist. Then he was being smothered by leaves, his spine crushed against a vinetrunk. Grape juice slopped against his face. A rush of leaves and he was in clear air again. From out of the gloom a gleaming, hollow-pointed spike arced inward and instinctively he released his choke hold to fend it off. The Watchmaker writhed in his grip like an oily serpent, twisting round in Gabriel's clasp to bring them face-to-face. Gabriel managed to jerk his head back, but his opponent's head butt still split his lip open and the next thing he was aware of the quicklife was splintering about him and the ground was hard against his back and an inky figure was towering over him, raising a gleaming tusk to strike at his belly.

Gabriel raised his arms in a feeble attempt to ward off the blow. But, instead of striking, the wraith spun away. The next instant a black mass of vines erupted, roaring, outward to envelope the Watchmaker, carrying him out of Gabriel's line of sight. A gleam of metal drew a slow circle through the air and vanished.

Barely sensible, Gabriel struggled to his feet. The Watchmaker was locked in combat against a roaring mass of vegetation with Izeki's voice and face. The police officer had apparently lost his weapon. Even as Gabriel stumbled forward the Watchmaker's foot rose and connected in a glancing blow with Izeki's cheekbone. The policeman's head snapped back and then forward as he lunged wildly, his fist swishing through empty air. *Smack!* Another kick and Izeki was tumbling backwards. As the Watchmaker turned to meet Gabriel's attack a goblin figure launched itself out of the undergrowth and impaled itself on the Watchmaker's fist. With a shriek Isadora fell, bent double and clutching at her abdomen.

The momentary distraction allowed Gabriel to grab the Watchmaker's right wrist in both hands. Before he knew it a sledgehammer blow almost stove his ribs inward. Twin meteors exploded in front of Gabriel's eyes. Before he could even gasp, his opponent was thrown bodily against him and Izeki's snarl was in his ear. The frenzy of limbs that was the three men reeled sideways. Gabriel could do little except hang on. He had no idea where he was anymore; his existence was divided into pain and numbness. Foliage tore at his hair and somewhere Isadora was screaming Chuen's name.

Suddenly, his enemy's wrist was twisting round . . . and round . . . and round, impossibly, and then he was falling, still clutching the wrist between his hands, but the wrist was no longer connected to anything. Stamping feet tripped over his legs and lost their purchase. Roots tore out of the sim-soil as the Watchmaker and Izeki toppled to the ground.

The detached hand was in front of Gabriel's face, fingers wriggling. Before his disbelieving eyes the skin in the fingertips split open and shining claws stabbed out.

"Holy flamin' strewth!"

With a howl of fright he threw it away from himself. As it flew through the air it coiled insanely, righting itself like a cat, hollow needles shooting out of every pore. By the time it landed it resembled some glistening, nightmare porcupine, twin eye stalks rising out of the center knuckles. Then it was coming for him, scuttling ratlike over the ground. Isadora's eyes stared wildly out of the gloom, shouting incomprehensibly. Izeki was still prone and the Watchmaker was rising from the undergrowth like a tsunami. But Gabriel had no time to pay them any heed. He scrambled backwards on all fours until his back connected with a vinetrunk. In one, convulsive leap he was climbing the trunk. A glance down turned his entrails to ice. The claw had not even slowed down, shining up the vine with the ease of a squirrel. Gabriel sprang at the ceiling. His slaphappy fingers brushed its surface, failed to find purchase. Back he fell, grabbing wildly at anything. His fingers closed on a branch. There was a deafening tearing and the entire vine ripped loose from the ceiling and crashed to the ground, carrying Gabriel with it.

Blinded by the mass of leaves he flailed out with his arms like a swimmer drowning in a wash of vine tendrils.

The Watchmaker struck out. Isadora flopped like a rag doll and Izeki rolled away from a kick aimed at his chest.

In the sea of shattered vines, something crackled invisibly toward Gabriel. In a panic he struggled free, lurching backwards, eyes wide, trying to pierce the gloom around his feet.

Through the corner of his eye he saw Izeki lift his outstretched arm with the Watchmaker's gun in his fist. The Watchmaker's mouth opened. Wide, as if to scream. Instead he spat. But he was off-balance and a dozen shiny pellets struck Izeki's chest instead of his face. Izeki flinched. Then his pudgy lips tightened. Izeki was a policeman. Wearing standard-issue light body armor.

Pop!

The impact sent the Watchmaker arching back to land in a storm of breaking foliage.

A bundle of claws and needles cannoned out of the undergrowth, straight at Gabriel's face. He ducked sideways, felt a breeze against his ear. He spun around, fell to one knee, rose again, with a length of branch in his hand.

"Gabriel! Look out!" Isadora screamed, struggling to her hands and knees.

It came straight for him, in a rain of claws across the floor. Gabriel hopped backwards, swinging at it with his improvised cudgel. The stick connected with a *thuck!*

And stuck fast on the needles.

Before Gabriel had time to fathom why his stick had suddenly become so heavy, the claw gave a convulsive wriggle, came free and dropped to the ground, righting itself as it fell. It landed and was again arrowing straight at him. Gabriel hop-skipped backwards as best he could, trying to keep it at bay with clumsy swipes of his cudgel.

"Hold on!" Izeki was back on his feet and limping toward him, gun outstretched.

"I can't bloody hold on!"

Suddenly Izeki gave a cry and went sprawling, face-down on the ground and, like an incubus, the Watchmaker was leaping forward to retrieve his gun. A fraction of a second later Gabriel's cudgel made contact, sending the claw spinning away into the darkness. He raised his eyes in time to meet those of the Watchmaker, glowering at him down the barrel of the gun. Over the Watchmaker's shoulder Isadora was still on her hands and knees, mouth agape with horror. Gabriel gathered himself to spring aside, knowing that it was too late.

And then the sun came out.

Gabriel shut his yes against the surge in the overhead lighting. He heard a pop and a hiss as the Watchmaker's shot went wide. When he opened his eyes the Watchmaker was waving his weapon wildly from side to side, his other arm thrown protectively over his eyes. The sudden change in lighting had sent his night-vision lenses into momentary overload.

Gabriel was barely able to stay on his feet. A sullen blackness nipped at the edges of his vision, tightening with every second. He focused. Two steps forward and he brought his cudgel down on the Watchmaker's gun hand, knocking the weapon to the floor. He raised it again, but, before he could strike again, a fist in his chest sent Gabriel hurtling back again and the Watchmaker was bending for his weapon once more.

From the shadow of the vines a bright thing sprang out at Gabriel, claws outstretched, hollow needles slurping. In desperation he swung his branch two-handed. A clang of wood against metal and an unearthly yipping followed. The sound of a body hitting the floor, even the Watchmaker's gun popping, was barely audible above the tearing of foliage as Gabriel collapsed.

For a long time he heard nothing.

"I got the lights." Chuen's voice broke the silence.

Gabriel opened his eyes and struggled out of the wreckage of vines.

Izeki was standing over the prone form of the Watchmaker, gun in hand. A couple of meters away the Watchmaker's claw lay on is back, its quilled surface marred by a bullet hole at the juncture of the wrist. The fourth digit twitched rhythmically.

"Shag it," Izeki was muttering. "Shag it." He looked up, the side of his face already visibly swelling, a thin line of blood trickling from one nostril. "I didn't know," he said stupidly. "I didn't know he was wearing body armor, too. You're not supposed to . . . civilians aren't supposed to . . ."

Isadora swayed to her feet, still hugging her abdomen.

Chuen was standing some distance away. "I got the lights," she repeated pleadingly.

Aghast Gabriel looked down at the body of the Watchmaker. He did not need to see the needle scratches on the man's cheek to know what had happened. The claw had pounced at him. He had struck it in midair. Sent it flying.

The assassin died by his own hand, he thought perversely. The nervous giggle turned into a half sob in his throat.

"Oh, God," he whispered. He felt a touch on his arm. Isadora was examining him worriedly, her soft features smeared with sim-soil and plant sap and a cut on her forehead, hair a mess of leaves and twigs. She reeled back from the desolation in his face. "I didn't mean it," he said helplessly.

"Nor did I," Izeki murmured.

Gabriel repeated, "I didn't mean it." His vision was blurring.

"Nor did I." Izeki was not talking about the Watchmaker.

"Gabriel, it's alright . . . it was an accident. He would have killed us," Isadora implored.

Gabriel's lips were pulpy, wet, tongue dry with the salt of his own blood. He wished that he could feel sick, that he could feel something aside from this hurt. Not just the agony of his wrists, the burning in his foot, the bruises along his battered body, the glancing pain of cracked ribs every time he inhaled. It was the hurt inside, deep inside. The hurt that squeezed his throat, crushing his windpipe like the soft stem of a reed, silencing the moan of grief that ached for release.

Isadora shook him. "Gabriel"—her voice was soft, but urgent—"we can't stay here, we have to go. Gabriel, come. Come."

Gabriel looked about dazedly. Did it never end? Even after all these years? Was the strength that was needed to give in really any greater than that which was needed to start running again? He pressed his fingers against his forehead. Things were not connecting. "They're making assassins of us all," he managed to say.

"Got it!" Chuen announced. She was standing by the Watchmaker's body, holding up the little gray control box. The hatred oozed from her pores as she hovered over his face, hands and feet twitching. Gabriel thought briefly that she was going to plant her foot in the lifeless features, but instead she turned to Izeki and said, "You shot us."

Izeki looked confused. "I had to."

"You shot us. You left us helpless. I woke up in the dark . . . and I couldn't see. I didn't know where I was. D'you know what that's like? You *left* us like that!" Tears of anger were pouring down her cheeks.

Izeki looked to Gabriel for support. "I had to," he stammered.

Taking a shuddering breath, Gabriel attempted to pull

himself together. "Izeki. We have to go. Isadora's right. They're going to be looking for us."

Izeki was still staring down at the body.

"Izeki," Gabriel repeated.

"My name's not Izeki," Izeki said tightly. The other three looked at him in surprise. His expression was a barren field. "Nobody calls me Izeki. I don't call you Kylie. Don't call me Izeki. You want to call me something, you call me Officer Izeki, or you call me Lieutenant Izeki, or *Mr.* Izeki. Or you call me Hitedoro. Not Izeki."

Chuen seemed about to come back with some acerbic riposte, but, oddly, appeared to think the better of it and held her peace.

Gabriel acquiesced in an even voice. "Okay. Alright. Maybe . . . uh . . . I think maybe we should go now? Okay?"

Izeki nodded his assent. Isadora pulled Chuen away from the Watchmaker's prone form and they made their way through the rows of vines to the door. Izeki pressed his I.D. card against the doorplate, his fingers leaving brown smudges.

The door did not move. Frantically Izeki tried again and again and again, but the door did not move. "Shit-shitshitshit*shit*!" he muttered.

"What is it?" Gabriel asked.

"They've found us," Izeki said.

another fine tribe

Elspeth's journal:

She comes to me at night, saying end it! End it now! Bring the bastards down! And I tell her, wait, wait a little longer. Her love lies buried under the mulga, but her anger lies buried in my breast, so much a part of me for so long now that I wonder what the rest of her felt like now.

"Found us? How?" Isadora demanded.

Izeki grimaced. "They must have put a call back to Municipal Central and found out about the override I used at the yeast tankers'." Gabriel felt a twinge of guilt at that, but there was no accusation in Izeki's tone. "And now they've canceled the police overrides, probably for the whole quickfarm area till they pinpoint our location. Bugsucks their style, too, though, they're going to have to override the override cancellation one door at a time while they work their way through the whole complex."

"But we're still trapped!" exclaimed Chuen fearfully.

"Maybe." Gabriel pulled his buzz-knife from his pocket and thumbed it on with more confidence than he felt.

Izeki looked apprehensive. "Let's hope they give us the time, stike. The one thing we've got going for us is they don't know exactly where we are."

The instant the buzz-knife bit into the door's surface, however, they were all deafened by a piercing shriek.

Isadora's words were drowned out by the alarm, but the expression on her face was eloquent enough. "They do now."

Izeki bit his lip and jerked his head toward the door on the far side of the quickfarm hangar through which they had originally entered. Gabriel understood and gestured for Isadora to take the buzz-knife.

"Just cut it big enough for us to get through," he bellowed. She nodded. Izeki seemed to be occupied with his collar phone, so Gabriel selected a thick vine and gingerly hauled himself up it until he could make out a corner of the far door.

He waited tensely, casting occasional glances back to monitor Isadora's feverish progress. Chuen was hovering nervously over her, shouting, and above the din Gabriel could just distinguish the words, "Big enough for *all* of us, nitwit! How's Mr. Officer Lieutenant Fatso supposed to get though that?!"

Gabriel's foot and arm throbbed agonizingly, and he felt himself weakening from the combination of exhaustion and loss of blood.

Not now, sport, just keep it together a little while longer, he whispered to himself. *Just a little while longer.*

At last there came a triumphant cry from Isadora. Gabriel dropped down and hobbled to the door. Isadora had already dived headfirst through the orifice she had made and Chuen had made the mistake of trying to go feetfirst and was now yanking her leg back out and following Isadora's example.

Izeki swore as he saw the hole. "What do I look like, a flockin' chiproach?" He gestured abruptly for Gabriel to go first.

The edges of the hole were razor-sharp and Gabriel felt his already tattered leggings rip still further as he fell through it. He was lying in another broad, rib-walled corridor, dimly lit and leading in a gentle curve in either direction. Isadora was clutching at her ribs—her head-first dive had demanded its price—and Chuen was feebly trying to close up a tear in her sleeve with her fingers. Izeki squeezed through last, losing a strip off his coat and skinning a knee as he did so.

They moved a little way down the corridor until they could converse normally.

"Okay, listen," Izeki panted. "They're going to be coming here direct through the corridors and Halls. The place we need to get to is Unilyfe Farms. I think I know how to get there but we're going to have to cut through a couple more doors."

"And then?" Isadora asked apprehensively.

"Cross your flockin' fingers they don't have the outside entrance covered. There's hundreds of exits and they can't cover every door in a whole section of city. We might get lucky if they think they've got us trapped in there."

Gabriel shrugged. "Till they find the hole in that door."

"They won't until it's too late," said Isadora, mouth tight with determination. Her eyes met Gabriel's, held steady, and he felt a wash of admiration for her. *The soul of a Helios weasel.* The other two wondered why he was smiling as they started off down the corridor.

Izeki led them through the corridors, searchingly but with increasing confidence. The next time that Isadora had to cut through a door she made certain to do it at ground level so that they could slip through without injury. Their progress was painfully slow, each of them were sporting bruises, cuts and more serious injuries; Gabriel felt at times the desperation of a sprinter caught in a web of molasses and was increasingly conscious of the extent to which his gouged heel was impeding their progress. At one point he was forced to call a halt in order to remove his shoes, so that he could proceed on bare feet without the chafe of material against an open wound. As he ran he tried to ignore the trail of damp smears he left on the gleaming floor.

During the next ten minutes they sliced their way through three more doors, proceeding through one yeast-block farm and two quicklife vegetable hangars, each time setting off fresh alarms. There could be no doubt that their pursuers were homing in on them, impeded only by their own cancellation of the overrides.

By the time they found themselves outside a mauve, unmarked emergency door, only sheer force of will was keeping Gabriel upright. Izeki looked little better and Chuen appeared as one of the walking dead, moving on autopilot but barely conscious of her surroundings.

"Just this one," Izeki rasped as he tried to stifle a hoarse cough. "Last one . . . Unilyfe's on the other side."

"Good," Isadora replied tersely, as the buzz-knife

crackled a wavering line across the door's surface. "The power in this thing's running low."

The circle of door fell inward with a clatter and Isadora started through. She had barely gotten her head inside when she stopped and withdrew it again with a sharp exclamation, "I thought this was supposed to be a quicklife farm! This is a yeast-tanker's!"

Izeki gaped. "Wha . . . it can't be!" He dropped to his knees and shouldered her aside.

"Can't you smell it?" she demanded.

Chuen leaned her face against the wall, eyes closed. Her murmur of, "Oh, sweet Goddess," was scarcely audible.

Gabriel watched Izeki's feet vanish into the hole. A moment later they heard him call, voice heavy with relief, "It's here! It's here! Just one more."

They scrambled through the opening and found Izeki signaling urgently from the far side of a yeast-tank chamber. He was excitedly slapping a door marked "Unilyfe Farms Inc." Isadora was halfway through making an opening, the buzz-knife now flickering as the last of its power drained, when Gabriel, who was standing guard at the first doorway, felt a faint tremor through the soles of his feet. He put his head to the hole and caught the first echoes of voices and the jackhammer reverberation of myriad running feet. He caught Izeki's eye, whose face tightened. Seconds later Chuen's panic-stricken expression revealed that she had heard the sounds as well.

There was a splintering of brittlefoam and Isadora's rising cry of triumph, "Got it!" Gabriel followed the others through, the rumble of pursuit dredging up previously unlocated reserves of incentive.

This quickfarm hangar was the vastest yet, in its night cycle and sporadically lit by vertical shafts of light—a bilevel construction with a cleft in the ceiling running the entire length of it that allowed one to see up to the next level. Rows of beach ball–sized cabbages unfurled out of sim-soil troughs, flanked by dead white fingers of meter-high asparagus, snaking melon vine and a floor-to-ceiling, Gordian tangle of tomato plants, pepper and beanstalks.

They hurtled down the central aisle towards a flight of steps on the far side of the hangar.

Hardly had they passed the halfway mark when Gabriel heard a cacophony of bangs and shouts behind him, one voice rising above the others, "There they are!" He risked a glance back and saw the door spew a bile of TARC toymen, erupting out of the cut orifice like greased eels.

"Scatter!" he yelled. The four fugitives dispersed right and left, abandoning the main aisle to seek shelter amongst the vegetation. The pounding of toyman feet rose like a rush of arterial blood in Gabriel's ears as he vaulted green, creeping tendrils of melon vine that clawed out at him, threatening to ensnare him with every step. Behind him a dozen toymen and TARC agents had fanned out, fingers outstretched and tracking him. Slumber-bullets flailed through the leaves on either side of him and he could hear Chuen wailing with terror as she ran. They had almost reached the steps, but the hunters were gaining on them with every step, flashing in and out of the gloom as they splashed through pools of light.

Gabriel veered to his right until he was abreast of Izeki. "The squirt! Give me the squirt!"

"The what?"

"The shooter! The gun!"

"Wh . . . you can't shoot TARC agents!"

"I'm not going to bloody shoot them, just give me the bloody gun!"

Gabriel managed to catch the Watchmaker's weapon with both hands as it spun from Izeki's fumbling fingers. Then they had reached the steps. Chuen had got there first and was already halfway up, with Isadora hot on her heels. Izeki clawed his way up on all fours with Gabriel bringing up the rear.

"*Halt!*" the magnified voice of the Bogy resounded off the hangar walls. "*You are ordered to halt!*"

Gabriel took the steps four at a time, the zip and trill of slumber-bullets nipping at his feet. At the top of the steps Gabriel shouted for the others to continue and turned to one of the armchair-sized cauliflowers rearing like cumulus clouds on every side. A point-blank shot blew apart the thick stem and sent the cauliflower head rolling into one of the aisles. Gabriel threw his weight behind it, guiding it toward the steps, and managed to roll it off the top step just as the first toyman gained the foot of the stairs. He bolted toward the elevator, where the others were waiting for him, pursued by a squeal of metal against metal. A ringing crash followed and a confused and irate babble of voices. Gabriel reeled into the elevator and Izeki released his hold on the door.

The first toymen were already catapulting out of the stairwell. Four breaths were held, four silent prayers uttered that the elevator would arrive before the TARCs overrode the controls.

The door froze halfway through the act of dropping open. Izeki thrust his body into the gap.

A by-now-familiar voice purred, "Please clear the door. Police emergency. Please clear the door."

They squeezed past Izeki, emerging into another quicklife hangar. Isadora and Chuen headed for the exit indicated by Izeki. Gabriel drew his gun again.

"Where's the next elevator they can use to this floor?"

"Not far enough," Izeki answered shortly. Sweat ran in rivulets along the clefts and dales of his ruddy face.

"Shag it! Gabriel!" Isadora's desolate wail from the exit drowned out the increasingly insistent robotic demands that the doorway be cleared. "The knife's power's out! We can't get through!"

"You go!" Gabriel rapped.

Gabriel took Izeki's place in the doorway and the policeman ran to see what could be done. Gabriel took the opportunity to catch his breath. Agony lanced up from his heel, through his shoulder. He examined his razor-wired wrists, leaking life and scabbing black already. His breath hissed through clenched teeth.

Shag this! How easy it would be to give up now, to stop running. No more pain. No more fear. Leave the running to the adrenaline junkies of the universe. Already he could taste the relief, like honey on his tongue.

Gabriel shook the perspiration from his eyes. This was no time to be losing it. Strange that the lights seemed to be growing dimmer.

Isadora had succeeded in cutting nearly a complete circle when the buzz-knife gave out, leaving only a last fifteen centimeters uncut. When Izeki arrived both women were hammering away at the door with their shoulders.

"I can't break through," Isadora cried in despair. "It just . . ."

"Move," Izeki elbowed her aside. He lay down on his back and started to pound at the center of the cut piece with both feet held together. "C'mon, t'gether!" he puffed. Both Isadora and Chuen picked up his rhythm, putting their whole weight behind each blow. With each assault the brittle plasfoam gave a little before springing back into place.

Creak! A hairline fracture appeared in the surface of the door.

"Gabriel!" Isadora cried over her shoulder. "Come on! We've got it!"

Gabriel roused himself, forcing his eyes open. He found that he had slumped into a squat in the doorway. The warning voice of the elevator appeared to be losing patience. "This is a Targetting, Apprehension and Remand Central warning, please clear the door. This elevator is being commandeered for official purposes."

"Gabriel!"

How did the elevator know his name?

You've got me at last, Old Man, he thought with dull amusement. *It's taken you nineteen years, you old bastard, but you've finally got me. Be just like you to use the flamin' Bogy on me. What did you need me for, anyway? You had Dig-Dig and Billy and the others. Why couldn't you have just let me make my way?*

But such questions always come too late. And Old Man, who had been dust for ten years, reached out, as he had so many times, out of the Dreamtime to the present, to sit on Gabriel's shoulder, bone in hand. And pointed. Pointed.

"Once more!" Izeki gasped. There was a splintering snap and the circle of doorway broke off and flew inward.

"Gabriel! For Macca's sake!" Isadora screamed.

Through the plant growth Gabriel glimpsed Isadora rising and starting back for him. But if she did that . . .

No. Gabriel tottered to his feet. "Coming!" he croaked.

He stumbled away from the elevator, tripping over writhing reddigab shoots. Izeki and Chuen were already out of sight and he could barely make out Isadora through the vegetation, standing next to the door and gesticulating frantically at him. Gobbets of bitter-sour juice splashed against his cheek as he charged through a row of ripening tomato plants, causing him to flinch and run for a few steps with eyes closed. When he opened them again Isadora was gone as well and he was only a few meters from the door.

Above the pounding of blood in his ears he heard the elevator opening behind him and threw himself forward in one final effort, charging at the last row of plants as if they were a rice-paper wall. As the first slumber-bullets whipped the leaves behind him to ribbons, he exploded out of the growth in a hail of cherry tomatoes that splashed onto the wall in front of him like shrapnel wounds.

He dived for the hole and slid through it on a mire of crushed leaves, sim-soil and tomato juice. On the other side hands seized his from both sides and hauled him to his feet and to one side as slumber-bullets rained through the opening. They were at the end of a tightly curved corridor.

"Nearly there!" Izeki snapped.

Nearly where? Gabriel wondered wearily, but he was left no time to ponder the question. They had just left the door behind them out of sight when the first of the TARC robots clattered through the opening. Ahead of them another door appeared, sealed like all the rest. Gabriel wanted to laugh at the futility of it all, to mock his companions in the way they ran with such benighted hope toward that dead end. Old Man had had the last laugh, thigh-slapping with the Bogy.

"Halt! There is no way out." The walls shivered with the voice of the Bogy.

And still Izeki did not slow his pace. Instead he seemed to be fiddling with his phone. "Isaao! *Now!*"

And, by some miracle, the door opened before them and Isaao was standing on the other side, gob-eating grin on his face. Then they were all spilling out onto the darkened street, Izeki bellowing, "Close it, Isaao! Close it, close it, close it!" And Isaao palmed the doorplate and shut it, with the panache of a latter-day prophet, just as the first burnished robot faces bobbed into view.

"I work here," he declared proudly. "See?" He held up his palm.

Somewhere in Gabriel's spinning mind, it clicked into place. The TARCs had shut of the police override functions, but Isaao was an employee with standard access to his place of work. That was what Izeki had been doing on the phone, back in the vineyard.

Gabriel was not even surprised to see a hangcab waiting patiently on the far side of the street, with Aysha peering worriedly out of the passengers' cabin, although Izeki seemed less than pleased by the sight of the cabbie, leaning against the nose of her vehicle, yawning.

"For Macca's sake, Isaao! I told you to get one without a driver!"

"She was the only one I could find!" protested Isaao.

The cabbie scowled as they approached. She had a face like an angry carp. "You have a problem with the service, stike?"

"No, you do." Izeki's card glowed in his hand. "Police emergency; I'm commandeering your vehicle."

The cabbie's jaw dropped as she took in the group of tattered individuals scrambling into her pristine hangcab interior. "Hey, dill, I just had my mover cleaned. I get recompense for this?"

"Take it up with the TARCs. They should be along any minute." Izeki's eyes gleamed wickedly. "The dilly you want's called Leel. Pelham Leel. Cleaning's a specialty of his. You can tell him I said so," he called, as the hangcab rose and started up the street.

As soon as Izeki was confident that they were well away he stopped the hangcab and had them all pile out and into another, this time driverless, hangcab. By this time the TARCs would have gotten the first vehicle's registration from the cabbie and be busy pipping the locator that was a standard fitting in every hangcab. Ten minutes later they changed hangcabs again.

Finally even Izeki appeared satisfied that they were in the clear and the big man seemed, all at once, to cave in on himself. His eyelids drooped and he passed a chunky hand across his face. He regarded Gabriel expectantly.

"Now where? You got any ideas?"

Gabriel blinked, a little taken aback. Over the last few

moments he had gained the impression that Izeki had a clear plan in mind, but the same expectation was written in the face of each one of his companions. Bereft of any real ideas, he stumped for the most obvious option.

"We need to get some sleep. Do you know of anywhere where we'll be safe for a while?"

Izeki looked vaguely surprised, but he shrugged and leaned forward to give the control panel the necessary instructions.

Gabriel let his gaze rove over his companions. No one had escaped uninjured. Skinned knees and elbows poked out of ragged clothing, blotched with mud, grape and vegetable juice. Sim-soil and plant fragments littered cabin upholstery. Chuen sat rigid, her Sisters of Tanit tattoo black against the paleness of her tear-stained face. Izeki's bruised cheekbone was swelling like a pomegranate, his upper lip was streaked with dried blood from his nose where he had rubbed at it. His coat hung in tatters. Absently he patted his pockets and emerged with a bedraggled end of nicotine root, which he placed between his lips. Aysha and Isaao, understanding very little of what was going on, but comprehending that things were well amiss, had shrunk into a corner, clutching each other's hands and observing pensively. Only Isadora seemed somewhat alive. Gabriel's midnight eyes met hers as she picked quickfarm residue from her hair. She held his look for a while before turning away.

And all at once it felt strangely worth it.

Gabriel had arrived on Thor alone and yet, in the few days that he had been here, he had gathered unto himself this small and motley tribe.

"You could have done worse, Gae," he murmured to himself, "you could have done a lot worse." He treasured the feeling even more so because he did not know how long it would last. But just at this moment he knew that he was right where he should be and with the people with whom he would most rather be. That alone was surfeit.

He could have done a *lot* worse.

The Fried Arm'n Leg Hotel was part of a stubby architectural pockmark at the northeast edge of Bugout Plaza. Entirely automated, without even holographic

staff, its rooms were little more than shoe boxes with
garret-type windows. Its clientele were made up of footpads, tramliners and those bugheads still far enough this
side of complete bugout as to be willing to invest the
few cues it cost to spend a night within secure walls
(after all, what did a roof matter in a domed city?). The
Fried Arm'n Leg's single virtue was its barnacle-tight
adherence to the Privacy Statutes. A client knew that he
could sleep safely here for at least the time it would take
to process a client list request through the lower courts—
roughly three days. As Izeki pointed out, Thor wouldn't
be Thor without its Fiscal Privacy Statutes. Indeed at
this point not even Gabriel's credit account had been
frozen yet.

They managed to secure five rooms on the same floor.

Gabriel sat on his bed and surveyed his room listlessly.
Fleabag establishments like the Arm'n Leg obviously
never bothered with shutout subscriptions—a tracery of
images danced against the window—but the genera of
consumers found in the Plaza were apparently not worth
the cost of hol-projector maintenance either. The images
were so faint as to be barely visible and Gabriel had an
all-but-unobstructed view of the street below. The switch
to change the wall coloring was broken as well, so he
was stuck with the pastel cud green for the night. Not
that that mattered either. Who would be looking?

He caught something darting across the floor and into
a crack in the ventilation grill. A cockroach—he recognized that furtive scuttle with astonishment.

And yet, why should he be surprised at the presence
of Humanity's oldest and most hardy traveling companion here on Thor? Official History relates that the first
living creature to transcend the tenuous boundaries of
Mother Earth's atmosphere had been a dog called Laiza.
But unofficially, who knew? Perhaps the humble
cucaracha.

Life seeks and finds its niches, he thought idly, *and
Elspeth spent her last years taking you and your mates
out for a living.*

The clothes dispenser dispensed nothing but one-piece
overalls, but Gabriel was beyond caring at this point. He
sloughed off his soiled and shredded clothing, which he
stuffed into the disposal slot, and spent about a minute

in the shower booth until the pain of needle jets of scalding water lancing into open wounds became too much for him. By the time he limped back over to his bed, the blast of hot air from the drying vents having finished the work begun by the water jets, Gabriel cared little if Leel and the combined personnel power of both TARC and Municipal authority came pounding at the door, as long as they did it in the bloody morning.

Shag it, how was it possible for *everything* to hurt?

Gabriel had barely closed his eyes, when there was a chirp from the door. *What now!* he thought with annoyance, levering himself off the bed and hobbling over to answer it, not even thinking to check who it might be. As it happened it was Isadora, holding a small, plaspyrus packet in her hand.

"I got some first-aid stuff out of the dispenser in the hallway. I figured you might not have thought of it."

"Er . . . well . . . no. Thanks."

She inspected the bloody drops on the floor with concern, the streaks on the bed. "For Macca's sake, Gabriel! Come on, sit down!" Gabriel allowed himself to be guided to the bed.

"Hang on, what about you?" he objected feebly.

She snorted, glinting amusement through exhaustion-ringed eyes. "You think I didn't take care of myself first?" She busied herself with his wrists, whispering apologies every time he flinched. Then she applied anesthetic to the wounds on his face, keeping up her running commentary. "Flock, stike, what did you do to your lip? It looks like someone strapped a synthfurter under your nose."

When she reached the wound on his foot she showed real concern. "Shag-a-lackey, Gabriel, that's nasty, I never realized it was that bad." After anesthetizing it she started clumsily to apply seelskin, trying to smooth its edges with her thumbs.

"Here, can I . . . ?" He gently eased her hands away. "I've maybe had more opportunity to do this kind of thing than you . . . Strewth." All of a sudden his fingers had turned to wet noodle.

"Maybe if we both . . ."

Awkwardly they administered the seelskin, Gabriel

muttering as they got in each other's way. "I should be able to manage."

Her ministrations completed, Isadora dropped the left-over anesthetic and seelskin back into the packet. But she made no move to leave.

"What do you think will happen to us?"

Gabriel shrugged. "I don't know. I think maybe Izeki . . . he's a spook, he may know some people. Fix up a tramline somehow. Get you off Thor that way."

Isadora did not miss the telling pronoun. "Me?"

"And Chuen and himself. They've got nothing on his brother or his wife, so . . ."

"They had nothing on us."

"No," Gabriel replied flatly.

"You didn't mention yourself."

"No," Gabriel said. "Iz, you remember the second time we met? I told you, that they'd gotten me angry?"

Isadora shook her head uncomprehendingly. "Angry's not enough, Gabriel. Where's that brought you so far?"

He said quietly, "Are you sorry? Are you sorry you got involved?"

"Of course I'm sorry!" she exclaimed testily. "Shit, Gabriel, how could I not be sorry! Look around!" She indicated the bare hotel room. "Look at this! Look at us!"

Gabriel nodded understandingly. "Then why did you do it, Iz? You didn't have to be a part of any of this."

She stared at him as if he were stupid. "Why? Because it matters. Because . . ." Her voice became constricted. "Because . . . *I* matter. I thought . . . I thought I would matter."

You had to get nearly get yourself killed to know that? Gabriel thought sadly. *Sweet Iz.*

Isadora threw up her hands and gave a light little laugh. "More fool me, what's your excuse? Just angry?"

"Elspeth."

"Yes. Of course."

"No, not of course. I wish it were that simple. I thought of Elspeth a lot before I came to Kyara . . . traveling. And since I got here. I keep asking myself, why?"

Isadora said understandingly, "Of course, that's natural . . ."

"No, not why she died," Gabriel said impatiently. "But all the rest. Why this? Why this . . . *mess*? Why would she care? Why did she leave home all those years ago to come to Thor? Locked in this . . . *jar,* with nothing but a thirty-seven-gee hammer outside the door, far as the eye can see! I mean, strewth, Iz, Elspeth had her feet on the ground—*in* the land! The living land!— deeper than I ever did. And she let us know. A flamin' proselytizer of the first order. Got to get back to the old laws, no more compromise. If she'd been a man, she'd have revived the Molonga ceremonies and . . ."

"The what?"

"Molonga ceremonies. They were ceremonies performed by our people centuries ago, when they still thought they could drive the European invaders back across the sea. Except"—he shrugged—"who's there to drive back now? The damage was done when the bombs fell and made the Glass Deserts during the Plagues and before. Things have changed; it's not the way it was centuries ago. There's . . . respect now." He murmured, almost to himself, "Uncle Bull used to say we were all tribal people . . . whether we knew it or not. Said *we'd* won the contest and no one had noticed."

Abruptly Gabriel pulled himself back and regarded Isadora. "We were brought up together by my grandmother. If you were to go back into ancient tribal law, our official guardian would have been my father's sister. But he didn't have a sister. So it was Grandmother Lalumanji. *That* was a lady."

"What about your parents?"

"Ah." He shrugged. "They were there. Mum was city folk, but Dad tried to return to the tribe . . . and couldn't. Neither fish nor fowl. It's an old story. Things have changed, but still . . . I guess what's changed since pre-Plague is that you're freer not to fit in anywhere. Even if it kills you. Our people's culture was always inclusive as opposed to exclusive. It means nowadays you've got Aborigines in parts with hair as blond as straw and blue eyes. Tribal people. All keeping the old magic alive.

Isadora regarded him curiously. "You don't really . . . believe in . . . things like that, do you?"

Gabriel replied, "Don't you? You non-Sol'ers talk about Earth and Sol System in whispers . . ."

"We don't!"

"Well, alright, but it seems like it sometimes. We had an old man, *the* Old Man. He was neck-deep in the old magic. Could disappear, turn into an eaglehawk, fly over the land and . . .

"Wait, you *saw* this? You saw him turn into an eagle?" Isadora was incredulous.

"Eaglehawk. I saw him *in* the eaglehawk."

"That's not . . . the same thing."

"Isn't it? Oh, I see. Yeah"—he held up one hand—"I know. But, you know, there's always been one assumption amongst proof-seekers and that's that anyone who can prove anything actually wants to. It's not always . . . it's hard to explain . . . it's not always: 'Oh, there's the nicotine root in the flashtray and there it goes, gone! And now we take it apart and that's how it works. Presto!' Before your very eyes! That's just tricks, carnival stuff."

"Car . . . ni . . . val?"

"Special effects. Illusions. Illusion is the lie you see. Truth can hide. Your eyes see a trail of dried rocks. The next fella sees a riverbed. You die of thirst because your truth says the river, by definition, flows above the riverbed. He sticks a reed half a meter into the ground and gets a cool drink. The old magic's no more magic, no less magic than that."

"And you? Where do you fit into that?"

"Me? Ach . . . yeah, well, the old laws and me never got on too well. And Old Man was the keeper of the law. He had a brother—we called him Uncle Bull—pissed as a newt half the time, mad as a March hare the other half, and lot of fun for us. When Grandmother was away doing woman's stuff—especially later when she was teaching the business to Elspeth and they'd go up to Katatjuta, a woman's djang place, taboo for men. I found out after she died that she and Uncle Bull had been lovers once. They say he spread the benefit of his company about quite a bit at one time . . . Anyway me and my mates would follow Uncle Bull around the bush around Landing. Taught me how to hunt, track, trap birds. Play hide-and-seek with the little trapdoor spiders, hiding under the sand. We had a game, fly-snatching. See how many flies you could snatch out of the air with one snatch. Even taught us how to chase down kangaroos . . ."

Isadora broke in excitedly, "Kangaroos! I know about them . . . but," She looked doubtful. "They're fast, aren't they?"

"And endangered, some of them." Gabriel nodded. "But, you see a 'roo'll always run in a wide circle, so one man chases behind him to keep him moving. The other cuts across the arc. You wear him down that way. Can take days sometimes. 'Course, then you've got to let him go again, 'cos they're protected." Weariness was settling down on him again.

"Uncle Bull was killed that way, by offworld poachers. They were probably after red kangaroos and they got . . . Uncle Bull instead. I'll never forget the look on Old Man's face when they found him. Nothing. Just . . . nothing, like an empty field. He was always a malevolent old bastard—hated me, me him—but *this* time . . . that look. I only understood it when I heard that Elspeth had died. When Uncle Bull and then, later, when Grandmother went, it was like someone took away the roof from over my head. When Elspeth died . . . that was something else. That was more like the thread with my childhood, like it had been broken. Till I was about eleven, her memories were my memories." Gabriel swallowed. "And now they're just mine."

"I'm . . ." Isadora searched for something to say.

"Nah." Gabriel managed a grin. "They're good memories."

Isadora was silent for a time, smoothing invisible wrinkles in the bedcover with the palm of one hand, over and over. At length she said, "Gabriel . . . I thought I was going to die tonight."

Gabriel nodded understandingly. "So did I."

"You thought . . . I was or you?"

He smiled, "First you. Then me. When those lights went . . ."

"Yeah. Were you scared?"

"What d'you think? I was flocking wetting myself."

"You never seemed scared. You never seemed like it was really scaring you, any of it. You just went on."

"We all just went on . . ."

"Yeah, but . . ." Isadora shook her head.

Gabriel said gently, "You know, dying doesn't scare me. Dying doesn't. It's the fear of dying that does. That moment when you stare it in the face, before you accept its presence. You know? Just that last few seconds when you're still fighting it and you panic . . . and lose your humanity. That scares me. Like there's no way out.

"Two times I've nearly lost it. Once was tonight, the other was . . ." He shuddered. "In the lockup. They could have split me open like a turtle's egg, spilled me over the floor if they'd only known it. I would have said anything to get out. Anything. It's like that nightmare of crawling into a pipe to escape and the pipe slopes down so there's no crawling back up, and, ever so slowly, the pipe gets narrower and narrower and you don't even realize it until you're too far ever to get back out. Shit. You know, not being able to stretch your arms out, or your legs out. Nothing scares me more than the idea of hearing myself screaming."

He looked at her bleakly. "If they catch us, there's no way I'll ever survive a spell in Retreat."

"You're tired," she said soothingly. "You're just tired."

"Yeah, I'm tired. I'm tired. Aren't you?"

"I'd blow Pelham Leel for a good night's sleep."

Gabriel gaped at her in surprise, "Um . . ."

"Sorry." She looked embarrassed, lips trembling.

Gabriel gave a snort of laughter and she joined in with relief, a cascade of madcap giggles spilling out of her. It was not long, however, before sheer exhaustion smothered their laughter. Gabriel let out a groan. "I'm too flockin' tired to laugh."

"Yeah," she agreed, wiping her eyes with the heel of her hand and checking the bandage on his foot one last time. "Me too."

Something tickled Gabriel's nose and he noticed suddenly that her bowed head was close enough to his for a stray hair to be touching him. Beneath the smell of quicklife and grime and fear on her clothing, he was aware of her own personal scent, musky like hazelnut with a tang of citrus. Very her, very right. Realizing that his breathing had gone shallow, he inhaled deeply, slowly, weariness vying with the desire to touch her, lay hands *on* her.

Come on, Gae, he chided himself. She had in no way invited his attentions in this way. Or had she? Women were so damned inscrutable. Then her head was raised and their eyes locked. There was no mischief in her gaze now and he could feel the heat of her face against his own. Yet she made no move toward him. She had come to him and so the last few centimeters were his to cross. As he teetered on that edge, so familiar to men of every persuasion, the demands of the heat in his belly wrestling with his natural, puling cowardice, he could feel the moment slipping away and knew he must act.

Their lips met and he winced with pain. Then their smiles melted into one and he caught a wisp of cheap, hotel deodorant soap and wondered how the hell she had managed to strip and wash herself that fast.

I've been had, he thought contentedly, as she molded herself against him like warm clay. It was happening to him a lot these days.

He was not gentle and neither was she. But the sleep that followed was and, when he awoke in the morning, the smell of her had permeated the pillow and she was there.

actuality alley

Elspeth's journal:

> *We parted in anger. Show Gabriel a line and tell*
> *him he's not allowed to step off it and he'll step off*
> *it just 'cos you said so. Not loud, but quiet. Guess he*
> *was born like that. There's always one. Gabby just*
> *sent me word that he's in hospital. Says he'll be*
> *okay. I've been crying anyway. I told you so, Gae. I*
> *told you so.*

The receptionist at Paraline Cyberspheres Inc. eyed
Gabriel through rainbow-hued eyelashes. Even had he
not been able to smell the lavender-heavy scent she was
using, Gabriel would have been able to distinguish her
from a projection by her air of mild disapproval. He
could hardly blame her. Despite Isadora's best efforts
this morning with the cosmetics, he still looked like a
refugee from a drunken dustup at a post–jockeypuck
bender.

"Westlake, Magnus. Could you spell that please?"

"Er . . . W-e-s-t-l-a-k-e," he guessed.

She spelled out loud, "W-e-s-t-l-a-k-e"—fingers
nipped at the keyboard—"Magnus . . . function, vocalize:
Westlake, comma, Magnus . . . Right. That's all in
order."

Gabriel threw a nervous glance over his shoulder to
the waiting lounge, where Izeki, Chuen and Isadora were
attempting to appear inconspicuous. Whatever had possessed him to agree to them all coming? But Chuen had
been in a state of near panic when it was suggested that
they all split up again and Izeki had aquiesced with sur-

prisingly little resistance. Apparently it was not unusual for people visiting INworlded family members to come in groups, often treating it in a way that, in low-tech societies, could be equated with a visit to Grandma. Izeki had insisted, however, in leaving Isaao and Aysha at the hotel with strict instructions not to move until he phoned them.

"Your name, sir?" the receptionist repeated politely. "For the records."

"Hm? Oh, I'm sorry . . . um . . . I'd prefer privacy." Gabriel held his breath.

But the receptionist just nodded. "Of course, sir, you are under no obligation and your privacy will be respected. Please confirm your credit rating." She indicated a palmplate. Once Gabriel had done so, another smiling attendant seemed to appear out of nowhere. She was a gray-haired woman in her late fifties, with a somewhat regal bearing, a white, form-fitting coverall outlining a well-kept figure. Her eyes were pale hazel, her face only lightly lined, and if she had undergone any cosmetic regen treatment Gabriel could not see it. The receptionist said, "If you would go with Technician Mia here, she will attend you and answer any questions you might have."

"If you'd step this way, sir," Mia invited him to follow her. In contrast to the receptionist, Mia's manner was one of brusque but courteous efficiency. She led Gabriel into a carpeted hallway, lined on both sides by identical doors. The color scheme was keyed to neutral pastels, the air filled with ambient music. Soothing perfume overlaid stress-reducing pheromones. Gabriel did his best not to limp. Isadora had all but drenched him in anesthetic spray before they left and his left leg was numb from the knee down.

Somewhere in this building the permanent INworld residents lay in their individual tanks, paralyzed, fed intravenously, blood oxygenated through a complicated recycling system, monitored, guarded day and night. Over one-third of the Actuality residency budgets went toward the army of highly paid exterminators and cyberspace surgeons whose sole job it was to guard the inhabitants' INworlds against the incursions of chiproaches and twigleggies. Here a thousand individuals lay side by side, untouchable and unmoving. All except their minds. They were elsewhere.

"Have you experienced Actuality before?" Mia inquired.

"Uh, no," Gabriel admitted. "I've gone V.R., but . . ."

She glanced at him quizzically, but she must have noted his privacy request at the desk, because she simply nodded and went on, "Of course, well, I'll explain the procedure to you."

They entered one of the doors and Gabriel found himself in a small, womblike chamber. Its walls, floor and ceiling were softly rounded, flowing seamlessly into one another. At its center a knee-high form-adjusting bed rose from the floor. Gabriel felt the first twinges of discomfort. Although constructed in such a way as to make its occupant feel at ease, the room's crampedness reminded him far too readily of the cell in the TARC holding tank.

Mia showed him the cubicle where he could hang his clothes, or dispose of them and dial up new ones, should he wish, then said, "Once you've undressed, just lie on the bed with your head facing the inner wall. You have simply to say the word 'activate' and the rest will be done automatically.

"When the tabs, eye and earpieces and olfactoric nerve stimulators are in place, you will be paralyzed from the neck down. This is an entirely safe procedure and done to prevent you from inadvertently injuring yourself through involuntary muscle spasms. You will be given ten seconds warning before you enter the INworld. Once you are INside you may leave at will by uttering the words, 'heading OUTworld.'

"In the unlikely event that you should find yourself in a position where you are unable to talk, this will present no problem as the apparatus registers subvocalizations and the conscious intent will be sufficient. In any event the program will end precisely two hours after commencement. We have a full staff to assist you with any physiological and psychological difficulties incurred as a result of your INworld visit, but I must add that your agreement to our liability waiver was registered when you paid."

The last sentence was delivered in the same lilt as the

rest of her speech, so that Gabriel barely noticed when she ground to a stop.

"Thank you, I'm sure I'll be fine" he said, trying to conceal his trepidation. But the INworld technician made no move to leave.

She said slowly, "Since this is your first INworld trip, there are a few things that you might find useful to know, particularly about the man you're visiting—and I'm not breaking any privacy codes by telling you this. You'll of course be aware that all our Actuality residents are entirely and permanently disconnect as a result of the length of time they've spent IN. Where they are is real and—should we rewire their nervous systems and bring them OUT—they would react to *this*"—she gestured at their surroundings—"as some kind of waking dream. Or nightmare," she added with an attractive dryness. Gabriel decided at this point that technician Mia was alright.

She continued, "Residents will, however, recognize you as not-of-their-world and have the means to banish you from that world with a single predetermined word or gesture. The word or gesture is individual to the resident in question and we are not permitted to reveal it. So, if you suddenly up-toes and find yourself back here, whatever he said or did last? That was it. Should you be banished, you will not be permitted to revisit that resident ever again, unless that resident verbally requests your presence. Furthermore, visits to any other Actuality residents will also be prohibited without appeal to the Lower Court. This is to discourage day-tripping by strangers and protect the privacy of legitimate guests like yourself, you understand?"

"I understand." Gabriel's impatience was growing.

"Okay," she went on, showing no sign of having noticed Gabriel's restlessness. "This brings us to Mr. Westlake. Before going IN, Actuality applicants are permitted to restrict visits to their world by outsiders to a minimum of one visit per six months. Most opt for a token restriction. Mr. Westlake opted for the maximum."

"You mean if someone had visited him within the last six months I wouldn't be allowed in now?" Gabriel asked in astonishment.

"Precisely. So"—Tech. Mia's eyes glinted—"if you

didn't know Mr. Westlake before he went IN, the fact that he chose that minimum should tell you something about him."

In other words, Magnus Westlake is an antisocial bastard. Out loud he said, "What you're telling me is that he might sling me out on my ear before I even have a chance to wipe my feet."

"Thereby seriously restricting your Actuality access for the future."

Gabriel considered. "Can you tell me what kind of a world he inhabits? It might be helpful."

Mia shook her head. "I'm sorry, I can't help you. Privacy prohibition."

"But I'll be there in about five minutes."

"Then that's when you'll find out. I'm sure that as a traveler you must be used to this kind of thing anyway."

A chill went through Gabriel. "What did you say?"

"Well, you're not from Thor, are you? Not with that accent," Mia observed easily.

"No, I'm not." Gabriel forced a smile. "I'm from Helios."

"Welcome to Thor," she replied. "Now, if there's nothing else?"

Gabriel made a careless gesture. "No worries. Thanks a lot."

The INworld technician shrugged, tight-lipped. "Have a pleasant visit. This room is completely secure. If you need anything else, just call. Enjoy the fishing," was her parting shot as the door slid shut behind her.

Enjoy the fishing? He puzzled as he lay back on the bed, feeling it adapt automatically to his shape. Now that he was looking up at the ceiling he noticed what appeared to be an inverted coffin, which, presumably, would shortly lower and cover him, enclosing him completely. "Oh, strewth," he whispered in sudden angst. "I'm not sure if I can do this." His hands were clammy with sweat. Squeezing his eyes tightly shut he took a deep breath, and said, "Activate." His voice came out constricted and far too high-pitched.

Wide open plains, he told himself, *think of wide-open plains and broad valleys. And woods and mountains and oceans and blue skies . . .*

Which you may never see again, another voice inside him replied.

At once he sensed the lid of the INworld tank covering him, then he was being smothered from head to foot in a feather-pillow embrace. His ears were cupped, silencing every sound but the hammering of his heart; a mask covered his face, leaving his eyes clear. There was a slight pinching at the back of his neck and he knew without trying to move that his lower body had been paralyzed.

Oh, God!

All of a sudden a gentle voice spoke in his ear. "Are you in distress? Please reply 'no' within five seconds or the program will be stopped."

Yes! Bloody, flocking hell, YES!

"No," he managed to croak out.

"The program will be resumed as soon as heart and respiration have returned to normal levels," purred the voice.

Oh, for crying out loud, just get ON with it! Gabriel willed his breathing to slow. Inoutinoutinoutinout, in, out, in, out, in . . . out . . . in . . . out . . . in . . .

Out.

In.

Out . . .

Abruptly Gabriel was up to his waist in freezing water. He gasped with shock and felt his testicles retract and shrink to the size of peanuts. In the same instant his eyes snapped open and he found himself standing in a slow river of limpid water, clad in nothing but a soft leather loincloth. He was bent almost double, his arms outstretched and up to their elbows in the river.

"My," he said, a little breathlessly. "Oh, my."

Without moving a muscle he glanced about him. From the length of the shadows it was clearly late afternoon. The banks of the river were red sand, lime yellow grass springing up in thigh-high clumps. But it was the trees that caught his attention. *Red river gums,* he thought in amazement. Red river gums, of the kind that lined the waterways of Australia, with their papery white bark, curving multiple trunks and drooping branches. But as he continued looking he realized that those were the only familiar elements. The olive trees on the hummock fifty meters inland certainly had no business in the Antipodes.

A little further upstream a lean man stood poised near the riverbank with a thin, fire-sharpened spear in his hand, his attention rapt upon the water in front of him. His skin was bronzed and curly gray hair with a few streaks of red in it cascaded over his shoulders. Gabriel could see muscles tensing under his taut skin as he gathered himself to strike. The man lunged suddenly, his spear thrusting downward and emerging unblooded a few seconds later. Hardly surprising from Gabriel's point of view, considering the clumsiness of the thrust. Apparently the hunter himself shared this opinion, for across the water there came an audible grumble. "There are some days when it simply is not worth getting up in the morning."

At that moment Gabriel felt something tickle the back of his hand. Being careful not to move he peered down into the water and caught a glimpse of quicksilver syrup. The tickling returned for an instant. It was almost too easy. Gabriel let his awareness descend into his fingertips, waiting . . . waiting . . . waiting. A feather touch. His hands snapped together, closing on the slippery body, fingers automatically searching for and finding the gill openings as he heaved the trout flapping out of the water and over his head.

Gotcha.

He stared in delighted bemusement at his catch, savoring the atavistic joy of a successful hunt. He noticed the man's attention on him. He was fingering a flat stone pendant around his neck. Gabriel waded toward shore brandishing the fish, calling cheerfully as he passed, "I reckon that should take care of dinner. You've got good fishing around here." He tossed the trout onto the bank and shook the water off himself. The late-afternoon sun ran warm fingers down his back.

The man observed drily, "I've spent fifteen years trying to master that little feat and I haven't managed it yet."

"Fish are like those little flecks of dust you get in your eye. They're never where you think they are," Gabriel observed, seating himself on a large white boulder to dry off.

"I'm well versed in angles of refraction between air and water," the man said sourly, his eyes downcast as he scrutinized the pendant he was handling with an studious air. "Do you have any other recommendations?"

"Silence and invisibility," Gabriel replied genially, closing his eyes and basking in the sunshine.

"Really," grunted the man.

"The honest crafts of the backwoodsman."

The man broke off his contemplation of his pendant and climbed up onto the shore. "Craftiness is not always associated with honesty."

Gabriel opened one eye to find the point of the man's spear hovering less than a finger's breadth from his nose. A crystal droplet of water hung from the tip. Emerald eyes studied Gabriel with quiet amusement. "I wonder . . . where you came from," he mused.

Gabriel stared back mildly, betraying no hint of his inner tension. "I was born among a people who saw life as a waking dream and dreams as a reflection of the truer reality."

The man cocked a sardonic eyebrow. "Remind me not to ask you for street directions." The spearpoint did not waver.

Ignoring it, Gabriel reached down and plucked a stem of dry wildgrass, which he stuck between his teeth. "This"—his glance encompassed the surrounding landscape—"is all my dream. But I reckon where I come from would be a dream to you." He pointed at the shadow of the nearest tree. "Red gum trees like that one grow along rivers at home. I've seen spirits there called Kutji spirits, who come from the Dreamtime and live in the shadows of rocks, bushes. They appear to you as birds and small mammals and a wise man can read the message they bring." He grimaced. "Like most news, it usually stinks."

"So you're the harbinger of evil tidings, is that it?"

"Nope. I'm just a bloke with an appetite and few questions on his mind, who'd enjoy a little educated company round the fire."

"I see. Might I know your name?"

"Gabriel."

"Hm. Appropriately biblical, considering the circumstances." The spearpoint floated to the ground and the man stepped back. "My name is Magnus Westlake, although I *think* you know that."

"I know that." Gabriel smiled his easy smile and held his breath. Westlake's talisman flipped from finger to finger.

At length Westlake said, "Alright, tell you what, you get us back to my camp with your woodsman's skills and we'll have a little fireside chat. Since you've supplied dinner, I think you're deserving of a little hospitality." Westlake hooked the still-twitching fish on the point of his spear and gestured for Gabriel to walk ahead of him. Gabriel let out a long, slow breath.

Good on you, Gae, he thought. *Cadging a free meal is always a first step toward friendship.*

The trail was so clear a blind man could have followed it. Uncle Bull would have laughed and said a backpacker with a pack full of bricks had been playin' four-beer hopscotch. But perhaps that was to be expected. Gabriel had already noticed that there was something subtly un-subtle about his experience of the INworld, something that betrayed its nonsomatic origins. He noticed it mostly with the sense of touch; the water had been cold, but somehow not really wet, the pebbles on the ground looked less uniform than they felt under his bare soles, even the warmth of the now-reddening sun was not commensurate with what he was seeing. But it was very close and for moments at a time he would forget and accept it as being truly real. And he wanted to, longed to, accept it as real.

Westlake himself walked with a languid tread, a lazy man's walk, and a city man's—heel-toe, heel-toe. As they emerged from the woods near Westlake's camp he gave an approving grunt and took the lead.

Westlake's bark shelter was built on an escarpment overlooking a shallow valley. Below them a number of shelters were grouped in an untidy circle, ruddy in the deepening light. Black, shining figures in brightly colored wraps moved quietly about, performing the simple tasks consistent with a hunter-gatherer society. A tinkle of children's laughter echoed up to where Gabriel and Westlake were standing.

Westlake propped the spear with the fish on it against a sun-bleached log and strolled toward a dense clump of bushes further along the escarpment. "I need to take a pee," he drawled without looking back. "Why don't you get the fire going."

It took Gabriel but a moment to spot the thin, hardwood stick and its softwood companion, its surface pitted with charred holes. Sitting on the ground, he gripped the softwood piece between his feet, placed the end of the stick in one of the holes and began the work of creating fire, spinning the stick between his palms and pressing downward. As he worked he reflected that Westlake did not display the characteristics that he would have associated with someone who was—as Technician Mia had put it—permanently disconnect. It was also clear that Westlake was in the process of testing him. The little incident with the fish had undoubtably prevented him from giving Gabriel the size 49 boot without waiting for so much as a hello. In that, Gabriel had gotten lucky with the choice of environment Westlake had chosen for his INworld retirement.

Just for once things seem to be going my way. A feeling of well-being was stealing over him of a kind that he had not experienced for . . . was it really less than a week since he had arrived on Thor?

The wood was squeaking now, a thin wisp of smoke curling up out of the hole. Before long Gabriel had a fine blaze going and was gutting the trout with a sharp stone he had found next to the fire-making tools and deduced to be for that purpose, enjoying the crackle of unseasoned wood, the smell of the fire. High up above a flock of white birds, made pink by the sun, flew across an indigo sky. Things were as they should be at the close of the day. The fire, the stilling of the breeze, the smell of early dew. Gabriel breathed deeply.

He had just finished constructing a simple spit to roast the fish on when there was a patter of light feet over loose pebbles. Gabriel looked up to find a young boy watching him from the edge of the clearing, an expression of perplexity on his face. All freckles and flaming red hair, his resemblance to Westlake was striking. Did this man have *children* in the INworld? Gabriel kept his face impassive as the implications struck him. Of course, if a person could hunt or enjoy a sunset on the INworld, why couldn't he or she marry and raise a family as well?

Still, something disturbed Gabriel. After all, what would happen when Westlake died? At that instant his descendants, his family, creation itself as he knew it would die with him, vanishing, as if it had never existed.

Which it hadn't. At any rate, not outside of a single-crystal circuit board.

Gabriel shook himself. This was becoming too confusing. If he was not careful, he'd be going disconnect himself.

And yet, a part of him would not be stilled, *this place, those people down in the valley, this young boy. All these will have existed within the perception of one man. And in the memory of another. I'll remember it.*

And he found himself grieving for two thousand generations of a gentle people who had walked and sung life into the land where he had been born and now existed only in the memory of a precious few. And at last he understood the look in Old Man's eyes the day that Uncle Bull died.

All these things passed through his mind in an instant and when he focused again the young boy was still watching him, his expression unchanged. As casually as he could, Gabriel waved at him, and said, "Hi there. You've made it in time for tucker. Caught it myself." He gestured at the fish.

"Where's my dad?" the boy asked.

Gabriel jerked his head in the direction of the bushes and winked. "Went for a piss, but I reckon he got his dingle caught on a cactus."

"I know what you are. You're one of the bad people," the boy informed him gravely. "My dad told me I should fetch him if ever I saw one of you and he'd make you go away."

Oops.

Gabriel opened his mouth to reply, but changed his mind as a rustle of dried grass told him that Westlake had returned from whatever it was that he had been doing. Certainly not just communing with nature; he had been gone far too long for that. Probably another test: the fire, gutting the kill. Gabriel was also already fairly certain as to what Westlake's method was for getting shot of unwanted intruders: the little talisman around his neck, which he kept fondling.

"It's alright, Colm," Westlake said. "He can stay for a while."

"Mama wants to know if you're coming down to the village for supper," Colm said.

Westlake eyed Gabriel. "I think I'll be eating up here with my guest. Tell Mama I'll be home later. Come on, shoo!" he added, as his son remained, studying Gabriel curiously. Colm turned reluctantly and was went running back down toward the village. A moment later a high-pitched whooping marked his passage. Gabriel found himself grinning fondly. Billy Halfpint had always done that. He'd never been able to go anywhere without letting the entire population of Landing know where he was off to.

Westlake threw himself to the ground, on the opposite side of the fire, sprawling languorously, one hand idly flipping a lock of hair from his face. "So here I am and here you are. Where does that put us now?"

"Waiting for the sunset. Looks like a fine one." Gabriel gave the fish a half turn. "This'll need a little time."

"More than I think you'll have if you don't state your business, supper or no supper." Westlake was tiring of the game. His fingers rubbed agitatedly at his little medallion.

"I came here to talk about dreams."

"Yours?"

"Yours."

"Ah. So you said before. A present dream?"

"A past one."

"My past."

"And mine. My sister was killed. She was murdered. I thought, perhaps, you might know the people responsible. I thought maybe you might help me find the truth."

"Is that all?" Westlake said archly.

"That's all I've got."

Westlake rubbed at his eyes for a moment and said, in a tone that was not unkind, "Now let me point this out to you, my fine fisherman friend. I do not know you, you could be anyone . . ."

"But I'm not. I'm a Native Australian from Earth. My sister came from Earth and she died on Thor. And I . . . I'd just like to find out why." And then he added in a subdued tone, "Before they kill me."

"Thor." Westlake's face had become rigid. Where his medallion had hung was only a clenched fist. Gabriel did not move. "Thor," Westlake repeated, and the muscles in his face and fist slackened. Then he grinned. "A past dream."

Gabriel shrugged and busied himself with the spit to hide his trembling hands. "When I grew up I was taught that the time of dreams, the Creation, was the true reality and the present just an echo of that past to which we're linked."

"Making us ghosts in our own reality," Westlake observed. The thought appealed to him. "Well, it's a not-unheard-of paradigm. There are echoes of that in spirituality all through history. Spirits in the material world and all that. But it always leads me to the question: what is the point? And I don't mean the sophistry after the fact, God's unknowable purpose and all that—although the Unintendo cult on Las Palmas does hold—in perfect seriousness, I might add—that we are all just peons in the Almighty's V.R. game. Which is why it all—all of it—makes about as much sense as your average five-year-old's 'Zark Zone' chip. Don't you think?"

"Um." Gabriel spread out the coals a little more evenly. He forebore to interrupt. Here was a city man living far from the city and missing city company. As long as Westlake was talking there was less chance of Gabriel being banished.

Westlake went on, "Quite. Frankly, I think we've allowed ourselves to be misled by prophets down the ages, not through any fault of theirs, but by our rigid insistence upon answers to a question that has been formulated incorrectly, to wit: 'What is the meaning of life? Had we had the insight, or indeed, the *courage* to reformulate 'What is the meaning of life?' to read 'What *is* the damned *point*?' We should have done ourselves, and indeed history, a far better service. At the very least we could leave the rest of this nonsense to the side and get down to the business of zapping computer-generated aliens out of our friendly skies."

Westlake pursed his lips and regarded Gabriel musingly. "Earth," he said.

"Australian," Gabriel affirmed.

Westlake nodded. "I've done quite a bit of reading on

Earth. You are aware that before they bombed it the Everest Plateau was once the peak of the highest mountain on Earth?"

"No, I didn't." Gabriel was quite surprised by this gap in his own knowledge.

"It was first conquered—how I love that term, 'conquered.' Nobody ever walks, climbs or swims across anything, they always 'conquer' it. At any rate, it was conquered by a Tibetan called Tenzing and a New Zealander called Hillary. Actually, their great achievement was not in reaching the summit of Everest, but in reaching it from the bottom up. Had they reversed their point of view and been willing to tackle the problem from the other direction, from the top down—by floater, for example—the whole exercise could have been completed with far less risk and effort by those involved. But then risk is the point, isn't it? What is there to admire in facility? Which," Westlake seemed to reflect, "perhaps answers the question as to what the point is. And it indicates a basic fault on the part of the prophets. If their fragile egos had not demanded the creation of a thousand-page tome to justify their existence every time, they might have saved us all a lot of debate by simply replying, 'Who the hell said it was supposed to be easy?' Don't you think?"

Gabriel was not sure what to think. The languid river of Westlakes' soliloquy had enveloped him in its music, diverting his attention from the content.

Westlake noticed this and nodded, a little disappointedly. "Yes, well, you didn't come here for that, did you? The art of conversation has few exponents these days, if ever it did."

"Fish?" Gabriel offered.

"Is it ready?"

In answer Gabriel sliced off a length, the succulent meat oozing through cracks in the blackened skin, and handed it to Westlake. They ate in silence, savoring the meat with the respect due an honorable prey. At length Westlake licked the tips of his fingers and let out a satisfied belch. "What do you want to know?"

"I want to know about the blue box. I know where it came from. I know about the *Far Cry*, I know what

they found out there. I know that it was some kind of
blue crystal . . ."

"Oh, it was more than that!" Westlake chastised him.
"Far more than that. It was . . . aah . . . it was beautiful,
beautiful! Almost transcendant in its simplicity. The
whole thing was solid-state. Shine a laser at its core,
directly at its core, and you were rewarded with a holographic projection out of its opposite face. A symbol, a
picture. Change the angle of approach—even by a micro-
degree—and you'd change the display. Change the wave-
length and again you'd change the image. In fact it even
ran the gamut of simplicity to complexity of ideation as
you moved along the ROYGBIV scale of visible light.
The further toward red, the simpler the concept presented. Sublime! Sublime!

"Now, of course the problems of translating an alien
language—a truly alien language!—are far greater than
that of cracking a lost tongue from the history of our
own species, and those are, at times, insurmountable
enough, unless one is lucky enough to stumble across a
Rosetta stone. Or in this case, unless—and this was *the*
thought key—unless the crystal were created, not as a
missive per se, but for posterity, should the creators not
survive. The symbols were constructed to be understood
by *anybody!*"

"An epitaph."

"As it happened. And more. A repository of the sum
total of their knowledge and culture. Anyway, take on
that assumption and start looking for the system, the
order, a methodology of some nature. Basic Newtonian
geometry might be the most obvious instance. There are
still pitfalls. Even if it was made to be understood, did
there, in fact, exist a common frame of reference? Their
solmization of the wavelengths of visible light demon-
strated that—at the very least—we shared the same
range of visible light—I suspect that their spectral range
of vision might even have been a little narrower than
ours."

"So . . . what happened to them?"

"Ah, a war. A war and the ultimate in Pyrrhic victo-
ries. Imagine"—Westlake leaned forward—"a spacego-
ing culture and all that that implies. Encompassing half
a dozen worlds. A level of technology . . . oh, far beyond

our own—I couldn't even begin to describe the marvels barely hinted at—*except* . . . ! Ah, yes, *except* . . . for one thing."

Westlake paused for obvious dramatic effect.

"JUMP drive. The ability to transcend the speed of light in travel. Somewhere down the line, somewhere these wondrous people—and I do call them people— chose a fork in the technology road that led them away from Skimzone Dynamics and left them stranded in Einsteinien space-time. And yet . . . and yet . . . they crept outward, crawling from star to star, building new worlds, until they met the Other. On a frontier world, on the leading edge of a nebula called the Twist, they met another race, another *people* . . . whose purpose mirrored their own, but with whom there could be no dialogue, no compromise, no common understanding. At least from their own point of view."

Westlake shook his head and poked at the fire with a stick, sending a little flurry of sparks crackling heavenward. "I never got as far as discovering the why of it. It lasted years . . . and they lost. Faced with annihilation, the last few thousand made the choice of Pyrrhus. They buried themselves in coldsleep, far below the ground . . . and detonated their sun."

Gabriel blinked. "Excuse me?"

"At the touch . . . of a button"—Westlake withdrew his stick and blew gently on the glowing tip—"they wiped out the Other, whilst at the same time sending a message to their homeworld. All that remained of their sun was a rapidly expanding cloud of gas with it, at its center, a pulsar, the last ember of a great flame, flashing on and off, on and off, like a beacon."

Gabriel was breathless. "Then, the Beacon really was a beacon."

"An unmanned lighthouse dutifully flashing its message . . . to no one. It's funny that no one else— apart from me, I think—ever worked out that the Beacon's plane of rotation precisely intersects where Querin's star would have been 350,000 years ago. Does that number mean anything to you?"

Gabriel replied at once. "Van Straten's theory about the Querin says that they've been stranded at their present level of culture for 350,000 years."

"Precisely. How could those last, forlorn survivors out there have known that all was not well on the home-world either."

"They sent out a distress call which nobody ever saw."

Westlake nodded bleakly. "Another civilization passes unmourned, another spirit dies unheard."

There was a long silence. A droplet of fat fell hissing from the spit into the embers. On the horizon the mountains drowned in a dying twilight glow and a ribbon of newborn stars climbed the heavens. Gabriel's eyes followed them upward and there, directly above them, he saw the Twist glowing and, at its tip, a tiny, blinking pinprick of light.

"Jesus," he whispered.

"I brought it as a reminder," Westlake said softly.

Gabriel's eyes widened with sudden understanding. "You're not disconnect at all."

"Well, that took a while, didn't it." Westlake twinkled, and jerked a thumb upward. "How could I resist the opportunity to bring my own slice of heaven from the Old World to the New?"

Gabriel laughed softly and Westlake raised a quizzical eyebrow.

"Care to share the source of merriment?"

Gabriel shook his head disbelievingly. "The only person I've met connected with all this who knows where his place is, isn't anyplace at all."

"To be frank, the disconnect phenomenon has more to do with being unable to distinguish between so-called reality and so-called computer-generated reality. The dream is real enough at the time, at the moment it's the only reality. The difficulty is in trying to step across and having to choose which is the dream and which not."

Gabriel looked at Westlake. "Why did you do it? Why did you . . . come IN. I mean, this is all very nice, but there's Seventeen Planets to choose from. There are some with low-tech cultures on them, places you could have chosen to go."

Westlake paused. Then his mouth twisted up in a sad and bitter little smile. "Courage, my friend, or the lack of it rather. I didn't have the guts to face the difficulties that a low-tech lifestyle might induce. All the mud and . . . have you noticed any biting insects since you've been here?"

"Uh, no."

"Well, there we are already. To say nothing of the weather! The darling eggheads do their best with weather control, but, oh dear, oh dear. And my family was wealthy enough for me to be able to choose. Besides, I'm a lazy fellow, and why break the habits of a lifetime? Supreme indolence is not achieved without single-mindedness of purpose and a steadfast commitment to excellence in one's chosen calling."

"I don't know that you're making headway there." Gabriel looked around him. "Seems you couldn't keep this going just by indolence."

"Quite. You have a point." Westlake looked vaguely troubled. "But then I've never claimed anything greater for myself than to have successfully reached the pinnacle of mediocrity."

"Congratulations."

Westlake shrugged. "As far as the OUTside world is concerned I'm as good as dead, but for me it's still to come. So why not enjoy an aperitif of heaven before facing sweet oblivion. Or my just deserts."

Gabriel chuckled, but shook his head "It still doesn't tell me why."

"To survive, my friend."

"Survive!"

"The blue box is . . . power. Of course it's power. But secrecy is essential to its power, and how long do you think I would survive, knowing its secrets? I was recruited by Saxon Rainer personally to break the code, as it were. It took me a year and a half. By that time it was clear to me that the day I handed them the key, they'd hand me back my head on a platter. So I put them off for six months, made my preparations and, the same day I submitted my analysis, I came IN.

Westlake smiled again, still sad. "Dying scares me as much as anybody, so I embraced the paradox and died to survive."

"Perhaps not that much of a paradox," Gabriel observed. "In most cultures when a tribal boy is initiated into manhood, he dies, some say symbolically."

"Some say?"

"Most, but not all."

Westlake beamed. "Something tells me that you number one of the few."

Gabriel thought for a while before replying, "In our way death is ever-present. A moment must die to be reborn and the passing of time is just a cycle of death and life intermingled. A woman lives to give life and gives life to truly live. A man, a warrior, lives not to kill, but to die, and must die to be reborn as himself. Maybe that's the power of women. A woman dies each and every time she gives life. We have to choose our own moment. I guess that's what makes it so hard."

Westlake chortled. "My friend, take it from someone who knows"—he ran his finger through the ashes at the side of the fire—"it's just a line. You believe that you're standing on one side of it and not the other, but can you ever be sure? Can any of us? Does it matter? The line is the fear, is the terror, is the grieving. It's the first step and the hardest step. The terror's never of what lies on the other side, but in the crossing and I've always wondered why. After all, you can never be sure of which side of the line you've started out on and onto which side of the line you're stepping."

Gabriel agreed. "Maybe not."

"So what's your real reason for coming here?"

Gabriel gazed down on the valley where the fires of Westlake's village flickered, breaking open the night with a message of warmth and comfort. Someone was singing, a faint, but haunting melody that sent the hairs on his neck a-prickling.

And Gabriel knelt amongst the mulga and cradled death in his hands. Gabriel did not know what had brought him here . . . no, Gabriel did know what brought him here. Or at least what had sent him stamping through the bush. Billy Halfpint, still knee-high to a wallaby, despite his eighteen years, flashing his manhood scars and joining Dig-Dig's jeers and taunts. Nobody else seemed much minded, even Old Man seemed impassive, but Gabriel knew. Old Man was the Law and Billy Halfpint and Dig-Dig had adopted the Law and what came at Gabriel out of Billy's and Dig-Dig's mouths was put there by Old Man.

So Gabriel had marched out of Landing, ignoring

*friends' entreaties for him just to ignore them, and had
found himself here, in a clearing of rounded stone and
mulga brush. He knew immediately that it was a djang
place, that every stone here, every twig was steeped in the
power. On any other day he would have backed away,
left it. But not today. His anger needed release and he
began scrabbling amongst the rocks and bushes, searching
for he knew not what.*

*Until he found it. Under a smooth stone. A tiny bundle
of feathers and tobacco leaves. Gabriel knew what it was
at once. In awe, for he had never seen one before, he
lifted the bundle up in both hands, peeling off the leaves
until he found the bone, its sharpened tip covered with a
wad of dry clay.*

Death.

*So simple. Within that bone rested someone's soul, their
life's essence, sucked in and trapped by that little lump of
clay. One day the bone and leaves would be ceremonially
burnt and someone would pass from this world. Gabriel
had a sudden urge to pull off the clay, break this token
of the Law, scattering it across the brush in a frenzy of
defilement. Cheat the stealer of another person's life.*

*With a convulsive twist he tore the clay loose and stood,
breathing hard, both euphoric and appalled at what he had
just done. His attention was momentarily distracted by a
galah's cry. He glanced up in time to see the pink-breasted
cockatoo burst out of the trees, soaring in a tight arc toward
him. He ducked instinctively as it passed over his head and
vanished into the brush on the far side of the clearing.*

*And where it disappeared, Old Man was standing, still
as a burnt shrub. Gabriel went cold, unable to move. Old
Man stood, empty-handed and naked, but for his green
shorts and the dilly band round his waist, full of clever
things. His phone gleamed on his wrist and his eyes were
all a-glitter.*

*And in that moment Gabriel knew that the death he
held in his hands was now his own.*

*He could not move. All he had to do was crush the
spell between his fingers, crush it to dust, and he would
be free. But the bone slipped from his nerveless fingers
and vanished in the crack between two rocks.*

*Old Man held out his hand. "Gabriel," he said in a
voice that was so mild.*

"No! Not yet!" Gabriel screamed. *He turned and ran into the bush, choking with terror.*

He ran.

Three days later Gabriel suffered a massive heart attack. The doctor pointed out quite acidly that if it had not been for tribal restrictions, the congenital defect that had led to it could easily have been detected and treated at birth. Now, however, Gabriel would have to make do with a MemPlas heart. He might even have won on the deal, provided he survived the night.

The singer had fallen silent. Westlake was still waiting. And at once Gabriel heard his own voice saying, "I came here to die."

"So be it," said Westlake, and before Gabriel could react he had calmly scooped a handful of sand from the ground and thrown it into Gabriel's eyes.

Gabriel clawed at his eyes with a cry of pain and he heard Westlake's voice whispering, "Dream of life." Westlake's words echoed strangely, and the pain in Gabriel's eyes suddenly lessened and he understood.

"No!" he cried. "Not yet! Not yet!"

He forced his eyes open, was blinded by brilliant light. Blurred faces rippled, congealed. Westlake laughing with the sun behind him, Isadora speaking to him with lips that became those of Pelham Leel, teeth snapping like a bear trap, the Watchmaker's hand reaching for his eyes.

God, he was dying! He had to wake up. *Wake up!* He screamed at himself. None of this was real.

He could still hear the singing in the valley, but the voice was Technician Mia's and she was saying, "He's gone disconnect! Code white!"

"It's not real!" Gabriel shouted, trying to strike out, but his limbs would not respond.

And then, with a clap, he was in the Actuality room, lying on his back with the pastel walls and ceiling curving softly over him. His body was still paralyzed. Technician Mia was hovering over him, peering anxiously into his eyes.

"Are you alright? Do you recognize me?"

Another face jointed hers and Gabriel gasped, "No, wait, this isn't right."

Pelham Leel smirked. "Oh, there's no mistake, Mr. Kylie. *This* is the real world."

conversation

—It's over.

—What, precisely, is over?

—Don't be obtuse. We've made the sale and we've got possession.

—I see. What about . . . the other matter? We just landed him!

—Even he can't do anything now. It might be better just to cut the strings, this whole thing is on the verge of breaking out.

—You're worried about the media? That's just background noise.

—It's loud background noise. The clashing of swords wakes the neighbors and we don't need that now. The rest doesn't matter anymore.

—So what was the deal?

—What they asked for.

—You did it.

—It was a legitimate sale.

—I know that . . . but I thought we wanted to wait until we were clear.

—Let's face it. If it wasn't for Kylie, we would have had the time to do this with a little less fuss and a little more *savoir faire*. Still, we've discussed this contingency and the whole thing might work out in our favor. We've got the last tramline in place; by tomorrow none of it'll matter anymore.

—I'm not arguing, it's about time.

—Good, I'll want to talk to you tonight; there's a few things to discuss.

—I'll be there.

the grip

Maximum.

Security.

Whose security? The point was debatable. Three by three meters of floor. Soft. Not pillow-soft, but belly-soft. Walls identical to the floor. Ceiling identical to the walls. Belly-soft and impermeable. No prisoner could beat out his brains against it in a frenzy of despair. No window, no furniture, no visible exit, the only light source a fuzzy glow in the ceiling. Metal bands around wrists and ankles. And silence, absolute silence. No ripple of sound to mark the passage of time.

Maximum security.

Gabriel knelt on the floor, gripping his head in his hands, fingertips digging into skull.

*LETMEOUTLETMEOUTLETMEOUTLETMEOUT-
LETMEOUTLETMEOUT . . .*

He would do anything to get out. Anything to get out. *No!* He wouldn't let them break him. Except . . . how much time had passed?

Anything.

There was a movement of air, a change of lighting against his closed eyelids. His fingers released his skull, clenched into fists. He looked up. In one of the walls an orifice had formed through which light was shining. He heard a whisper of movement beyond.

Let me out.

Gabriel tottered to his feet, unsteady on the soft floor. Shielding his eyes, he pogo-stumbled up the corridor of light and stepped through the orifice. More power tricks: the orifice was just too low to walk erect, a prisoner

would step out, head bowed to the minions of authority
waiting in the room beyond.

Pelham Leel was sitting at a small table, an empty
chair facing him. The room was octagonal, a TARC
robot standing in each of four corners. Four fingers
pointed at Gabriel, tracked him as he moved into the
room. Gabriel took the empty chair, still squinting
against the unaccustomed brightness. Penal ergonomics:
the table was just too wide for Gabriel to reach Leel
without rising to his feet.

Leel regarded him silently for a time.

Tell him anything he wants to know, the voice inside
Gabriel chattered, *anything he wants, anything he wants!*
But the Bogy did not believe the truth, what the Bogy
wanted was lies. Yet the Bogy had ways of recognizing
lies and would reject them, demanding more. The truth
was of no help. A court could choose to reject the results
of a cerebral Probe as invalid. The truth would be seen
as a lie, the lie would be seen as a lie.

And this was Pelham Leel. Gabriel's fury reawakened
and he nursed it, feeling it grow.

"This has a riveting familiarity about it, Mr. Kylie,"
Leel said softly.

Gabriel twitched, then drew back.

Leel's lips parted, exposing white, white teeth. "Oh,
do, please, Mr. Kylie. *Exacerbate* the gravity of your position, expedite the wheels of justice."

Gabriel clamped down on his anger, conscious of the
robot fingers still pointed at him.

Leel looked mildly disappointed. "No? Ah, well. Your
Actuality visit? That was clumsy. A serious underestima-
tion on your part. And it still leaves us with a chasm,
Mr. Kylie, between your wants and my needs. Would
you care to bridge that chasm?"

Stillness.

"No? Oh, dear. You came to Kyara, Mr. Kylie, less
than a week ago. Your name . . . may be your name.
Your claimed motives for being here . . . grow unlikelier
by the minute. Your actions . . ." Leel spread his hands,
"Well . . . there we are: One murder—*alleged,* of
course"—he smiled apologetically—"one *alleged* escape
from a TARC detention center, allegedly assisted by two
alleged roofrunners and allegedly witnessed by . . . oh,

let's see, two, four, sixteen, twenty . . . forty-three alleged bystanders. Well, the escape charge on its own
breaks down into several dozen individual charges . . .
um . . . alleged assault on bystanders, alleged damage to
private property, alleged theft of a hangcab and so on.
And then, oh yes, alleged accessory to alleged assault
on an officer of the law . . ."

"*Alleged* officer of the law," Gabriel murmured.

"Ah, no, that's proven and on record," Leel demurred
regretfully. "Well, and then we come to, heh, another
escape, resisting arrest, damage of private property,
more damage of private property, *more* damage, assault
on law-enforcement A.I. units, *another* murder, hangcar
th . . . well . . . Ad nauseam." Fingernails clicked against
the formica tabletop. Leel seemed to be evaluating Gabriel. His manner became brusque, "You, Mr. Kylie, are
a professional. You were sent here, I don't know by
whom. You're from Earth, so we're going to have a hard
time checking. But I will find out. You are a professional
and you will be treated as such. We've applied to the
High Court for permission for a psych-Probe examination of you and, all things considered, this time I think
we stand a fair chance of getting it. Probably within the
next seventy-two hours."

"If you're going to probe me anyway, what's the
point?"

"Convince me, Mr. Kylie, convince me not to."

"I can't convince you. Nothing's going to convince
you, 'cos you'd have to be smart and you're too blind
and you're too bloody dirty and you're too hungry for
what you're hungry for to let anything like intelligence
get in your way."

Leel got up. "I'm leaving you a brochure on the Retreat correctional center, which is where, if you are
lucky, you will be spending the rest of your natural life.
It includes details of all the rehabilitation facilities there,
including . . . well, read it yourself, Mr. Kylie."

"What about the others?"

"Others?"

"You know what I'm talking about."

"No, Mr. Kylie, *you* know what you're talking about.
I know very little as yet."

"The others. Officer Izeki, Isadora Gatzalumendi and Lee Chuen."

"The . . . others. I'm afraid I'm not permitted to disseminate any information on our other clients. But I will say that they are all presently examining brochures identical to yours. That should be good news to you. Misery loves company." His hand was raised, gesturing politely toward the open orifice of Gabriel's cell.

Gabriel froze. There was no way that he could go back in there. He could not! Frantically, he tried to think of something to say that would delay Leel, keep Gabriel in this laughably relative freedom for a few moments longer. Four robots stepped forward as one.

Contemptuously, Leel turned his back on Gabriel and walked out of the room and Gabriel found himself being herded back into his cell by four faceless turnkeys. The orifice contracted, vanished. In the center of the floor now lay a single, tissue-thin piece of plaspyrus with the legend, "Retreat Correctional Facility" heading a column of fine print.

The voices began their shrieking again.

LETMEOUTLETMEOUTLETMEOUTLETMEOUT-LETMEOUTLETMEOUT . . ."

Maximum security.

It's white and the size of an astonished "ooh!" Who can resist an edelweiss in the wild, and how many have seen one? Gabriel knew that to see one growing one had to ascend to where nothing else could grow. Go where there is no life and behold! So he had ascended Mont Rosa and there it was, poking out of the snow beside a skull-shaped stone. His mittened finger stroked its woolly petals and the marvel of life cast its spell on him once more.

He was half a world away from home, but he knew that it was not far enough. In three weeks the starship Thule *would depart for Las Palmas and carry Gabriel too far for Old Man ever to reach him.*

This was the lie that Gabriel chose to live on that day.

Bright light awoke Gabriel. The orifice had opened again. He rubbed at his eyes. How long had he been asleep?

"Come on, Kylie, out of there," a curt voice said.

Gabriel egressed, blinking, from his cell, to find two toymen and a TARC agent waiting for him.

"Come on," the agent beckoned.

"What . . . what's going on?"

"You're going for a walk, stike."

Memories of his last walk out of a TARC cell came flooding back, but with the toyman honor guard stepping into place before and aft of him Gabriel had little choice but to obey. His bare feet smacked across the floor as they led him through several corridors lined with identical doors, all eerily bare, giving no indication of what was behind them. With the exception of one door, where the word "**Detention**" glowed copper-bright. As they passed, the word dissolved and re-formed into the word "**Interrogation**" and the meaning became chillingly clear. Every room was multifunctional and, at the moment when he had happened to be watching, that particular room's function had changed.

Gabriel decided that he preferred the doors plain.

Yet another identical portal opened before them, emitting a wash of murmured conversation that muted and died as Gabriel was led in, aware of three TARC green uniforms and two garish splashes that indicated civilian presence. Five pairs of eyes studied his approach as if he were some genus of insect, trapped on a microscope slide, which, in a sense, he was. Another of the Bogy's dehumanizing little tricks. Remove a person's clothes, hand him a gray coverall, reducing him to a monochrome cipher in a world of color.

The room was dominated by a broad oval table. On the far side of the table a nervous young man who looked like he had just crawled out of bed was sitting, flanked by an elderly woman, plainly, sensibly clad, with intense hazel eyes. Her hair was close-cropped and spiky, silver chains running like trimming through multiple holes in her ears—a lone concession to vanity. She had the air of an absentminded and benevolent grandmother and leaned back in her chair as if seeking shadow, superficially subordinating herself to her young companion. But Gabriel recognized the stillness of a predator there.

Pelham Leel sat to one side of the table, his face

blank. Behind him stood two uniformed TARC agents.
By the door, burnished toyman faces, carved jade senti-
nels that missed nothing.

Still in a daze, Gabriel took the chair indicated. His
hands were placed on the arms and Gabriel felt the
bracelets around his wrists stick fast. Similarly his ankles
were jerked against the foot of the chair by inbuilt mag-
nets. Simple, but secure.

Even through his disorientation he could feel under-
currents in the room; Leel was agitated in a way that he
had not yet witnessed. When the TARC captain spoke,
his tone was expressionless. "Mr. Kylie, I would like to
ask you to identify this man."

Gabriel turned his attention to the young man, who
squinted back, his eyes dilated more than looked
healthy. His clothes looked like they had been slept in;
even his eyebrows appeared to have apparently been
brushed the wrong way. He was biting apprehensively at
a thumbnail.

Gabriel shook his head slightly. "I can't," he mumbled. "I don't . . . no."

Wrong answer! Leel seemed relieved. "He is, therefore, not your legal representative."

The young man's stare intensified, as if he was trying
to tell Gabriel something. What was more important to
Gabriel, however, was that Pelham Leel was doing the
same thing.

At length he nodded. "Yes, he is."

The young man heaved a deep sigh of relief. "Right,
Captain," he said, wiping at his brow with the heel of
his hand. "Now that we've gotten through the
formalities . . ."

Leel snorted. "I don't think so," he said scornfully.
"He doesn't even know who you are."

"I said I couldn't identify him," Gabriel interposed.

"And it's irrelevant anyway," the young man said with
a rather unconvincing gesture of dismissal. "He has now,
on the record, accepted me as his counsel. Mr. Kylie,
I'm Kynan Christmas. I'm a friend of Isadora
Gatzalumendi."

"Pleased to meet you," said Gabriel.

"I'm sure you are," muttered Leel. "Look, Mr. Christmas, shall we get to . . ."

". . . The point?" Christmas said brightly.

"If there is one."

"Oh, there is . . . er . . . yes, look, Officer, we do have the right to private consultation with our client. We are prepared to exercise it."

"Then why haven't you?"

"You know why, Officer. Why waste time? Look"—Christmas appeared to be enjoying himself—"Mr. Kylie, I've asked Claudia Ernst here to act as adviser and second counsel, if you're agreeable. I . . . *hope* you're agreeable."

"Yeah, alright," Gabriel said cautiously.

"Please, if you'd state your agreement for the record."

"I agree to her being adviser and second . . . what is it? Counsel?"

"Excellent." Ernst sat forward. Her voice was surprisingly deep and husky. She laid her wallet on the table, touching Christmas's elbow as she did so, and he subsided with obvious reluctance. For a moment she peered shortsightedly at the wallet, fiddling with its controls. Finally she gave a grunt of satisfaction. "Now, Officer Leel, for the record, we'd like to review the charges against my client."

Leel sniffed. "I was under the impression that you were in a hurry."

"Well, no . . . not *all* the charges. Just the first, the initial ones, preceding my client's alleged escape."

Leel's face clouded with suspicion. "You've already seen all the charge displays."

"I just . . . ah . . . wanted to hear it from you, personally. You know, for the record." Her eyes twinkled.

After a brief hesitation Leel shrugged and leaned back in his chair. "For the record. The main charges are assault, possible murder of a person or person*s* unknown in the plastines industrial sector. There's also a secondary charge of complicity in the murder of Louise Daud."

"Thank you, Officer." With apparent difficulty Ernst activated the hol-display on the wallet and rummaged through several screen-pages of text. "Let's have a look . . ." she muttered to herself. "Um . . . Now, as far as I can see, his connection to the Daud murder appears to be . . . well . . . *is* circumstantial. He . . . spoke to her less than an hour before she died, is that right?"

"I've not charged him with the murder itself. But there are good grounds for thinking roofrunner gangs may have been involved and, as we both know, Mr. Kylie here escaped with the aid of two roofrunners."

"Quite." Ernst smiled good-naturedly. "But Mr. Kylie also claims that he was a rather reluctant escapee. He was removed from his cell by men masquerading as TARC officers and only decided to go along with the escape attempt after the alarm had been sounded."

Leel matched her smile, incisor for incisor. "A claim is not proof."

"You would know."

Touché. Gabriel was impressed, but baffled. He was at a loss to see where this was leading, but a touch of predator had just glinted through Claudia Ernst's matronly facade.

She cocked her head to one side, sending the tassels in her ears dancing. "The point I'm getting at here, Officer Leel, is that without the initial charges—and this is just a first impression—um . . . without the initial charges, you have no case against my client."

Leel gaped, then threw back his head and laughed. It was a silent laugh, symptomized only by the twitching of throat muscles.

"I have more than a case . . ." he said at last, adopting a slightly paternal air.

"Not as far as I can see."

"Counselor Ernst, do not imagine that a mere declaration on your part makes it so."

"But, you have no case," Ernst declared implacably.

"Excuse me, but do you take me for a fool?" Leel's tone remained patronizing. "You've seen the charges against this man. I have a list of charges against him the size of a carpet, of which breaking out of a state incarceration facility is only the third."

"After the fact of initial false arrest by your bureau."

"Bullyshag, Ms. Ernst."

"Oh, really, Officer, without that initial charge, the rest is so much chaff and you know it. You should also know the courts tend to take quite a broad view when there is evidence to suggest that police harassment had led directly to subsequent crimes and in this instance we even have a case for suggesting that Mr. Kylie's escape

from incarceration was not entirely of his own volition."
The twinkle in her eyes had been replaced by a hard
sheen.

Leel frowned. "You'll have to prove harassment."

"I don't have to. The implication will be enough."

"Try it and I'll have you for slander."

"You'll have to fight off a claim of deliberate false
arrest first."

"False arrest?" Leel was starting to betray some irritation. "I'm sorry, Counselor Ernst, but I think we're talking at cross-purposes here. The fact is that we have a
case against Mr. Kylie and a good one."

"We're not talking at cross-purposes. I'm simply
pointing out that it'll have to be good for the rest of the
charges to stand up."

"That goes without saying!" Leel snapped. "The fact
is, however, that we have your client over the proverbial barrel."

"So you concede the point."

Leel blinked. "What point?"

"That without the initial charges, considerable doubt
is thrown on the rest."

"I've conceded no such thing!"

"Shall we review the recording?"

The look that the TARC officer shot Ernst was that
of a man who has just found a scorpion setting up
housekeeping in his sock drawer. "I think I've had
enough of these games," he said coolly. "If you've got
nothing else to offer . . ."

"Just one more thing," Ernst said amiably. She turned
to Gabriel. "Mr. Kylie. For the record, I'd like you to
identify this man," she said. She touched her wallet and
a hol-projection of a man's face appeared over the table.

Gabriel started. "That's one of the men that jumped
me the second night I was here . . ."

Ernst cut him off smoothly. "Good." She turned back
to Leel and the glee she displayed would not have
looked out of place on a barracuda, "The man in question is called Dana Sotack. He is a security guard with
Kyaran Ventures 99. He's prepared to testify, as are two
other witnesses, that he was with my client between
twenty-three oh-five and twenty-three fifty-seven on the
evening that the woman . . . Louise Daud . . . was mur-

dered—making it impossible for my client to have been anywhere near her residence at the time of her death. You will find that his blood matches the samples found on the site where the assault took place."

There was a long silence. Leel looked stunned. Gabriel's mind was awhirl. What the hell was going on here?

Leel managed a thin smile. "The assault on whom? Mr. Kylie claims that the assault was on him."

Christmas interjected. "My client is not intending to press charges against Mr. Sotack."

I'm not? Gabriel wondered in surprise.

"Any more than Mr. Sotack is intending to press charges against Mr. Kylie," Ernst continued, hazel eyes flashing.

"An illegal weapon was been found . . ."

"Belonging to Mr. Sotack and he is quite prepared to plead guilty to possession of an illegal firearm, Mr. Leel. You don't have a case against my client!"

There was another pregnant silence. Then Leel moved his head slowly from side to side. "I'm not biting."

"You're not biting? I'd think twice, Officer Leel, because you're about to bury your unpleasant self in more writs and claims forms than you'll be able to dig yourself out of in a lifetime!"

"Is that a threat?"

"Gangsters threaten. Lawyers render assessments of a person's legal prospects."

"Then"—Leel made a sour attempt at passing the whole matter off lightly—"I don't respond to assessments."

"Fine, in that case imagine I have your health at heart and look upon it as a prognosis, because you're going to need a surgeon with a buzz-blade to saw you out of this one. You know who I am, Officer Leel, you know whom I represent, you know that I will make good on my legal assessments, you know that if I say I will have your tongue stapled to the wall, then I will *have* your tongue stapled to the wall and have you *thanking* me for it if I demand it! Now, you have falsely arrested my client, as a direct result of which he suffered grievous injury and not only his life, but the lives of several other people were placed in serious jeopardy!"

"The quickfarms . . ."

"Oh, spare me! You took those pellets out of Ms.

Gatzalumendi and Ms. Lee's necks! You know as well
as I do that what you found there was the corpse of a
cyborg-boosted hit man . . ."

"That's an assumption."

"You'd have to be neck-deep in assumptions to come
up with the kind of allegations that you have against my
client. Now, stop wasting my time! He has an ironclad
alibi and you know damned well that there isn't a court
between here and the Clouds of Magellan who wouldn't
release my client on his own recognizance."

"That's as may be, but they haven't done it yet!"

"No, but I swear to Æsir, if I have to go to court to
get my client out of this tank, I'll flocking see to it that
you spend the next ten years picking lint out of your
navel in the rubber-romper-room, I diddle you not!"
Ernst rolled the words off her tongue with the casualness
of a butler reading out a list of groceries. As for her
companion, it was clear that Kynan Christmas was enjoying himself hugely at the furious Leel's expense. At
one point he even made as if to put his hands behind
his head, but caught himself just in time.

Gabriel was by now even more dazed than when he
had entered the room.

"Allow me to spell this out for you," Ernst went on.

"You needn't," Leel said icily.

"Oh, but I must," Ernst insisted. "And I really would
pay attention, Officer. Should my—*our*—client not leave
this room with us when we depart, I intend to press a
deliberate wrongful arrest and departmental harassment
charge against you! In fact, I am going to come down
so flocking hard on you, personally, Officer Leel, that a
jog across the Anvil is going to seem like a paid INworld
vacation to a Las Palmas diving resort. And if you think
that Remand central's going to thank you for the kind
of scrutiny this is going to bring the department from
the media ticks and every fringe-dwelling, reactionary
pencil picker in town then, *please,* wake up, Officer Leel,
feel the heat and *smell* the fat of grilled *scapegoat*! In
other words, Officer Leel, you, not-to-put-too-fine-a-
point-on-it, are going to be *FINISHED*!"

Gabriel listened to this in a state of semidelirious awe.
Leel, to his credit, did not even blanch. His eyes darted
to the wallet on the table, recording this exchange, and

he licked his lips, very aware of the presence of his two
subordinates and the toymen by the door.

"Counselor Ernst," he said carefully, "if you imagine
that Remand central is going to drop its charges against
Mr. Kylie . . ." He trailed off.

Claudia Ernst's smile was as winning as a double row
of flint-edged bread knives. "Of course not, Officer, but
Remand have the option to waive bail-court proceedings
and release my client at their own discretion, providing
that he agrees to and adheres to the legal precepts bind-
ing him under the specific circumstances of that release."

Leel locked gazes with her. The pause was long. Gabriel's nails bit into his palms as he waited. At last Leel
muttered something under his breath.

"I beg your pardon?" Ernst said, "For the record."

Leel rasped, "On my authority Remand waives bail
court and releases Gabriel Kylie on his own recognizance pending review of the charges to be brought
against him."

Kynan Christmas could barely contain his ebullience.
He leapt up and came round the table to help Gabriel
up as the chair released him. Ernst gathered up her wallet and nodded pleasantly at Leel, who ignored her and
stalked out of the room.

"I'll meet you outside," she called to Christmas, and,
with another affable cock of her head, she took her
leave.

"Think yourself lucky," Christmas beamed at Gabriel,
keeping his voice low. "You've just seen the best of the
best at work. Claudia uses prosecuting attorneys to dunk
in her coffee. I could not be*lieve* it when she turned
up here . . ."

Gabriel could not quite accept what was happening.
"I don't understand . . ."

"Chicken, stike," replied Christmas.

"Chicken." Like Snapper on the rooftop, Leel had
blinked first.

"Come on." Christmas's elation was already evaporat-
ing. "We should get out of here before he changes his
mind."

"Wait a second." Things were moving just a tad too
fast for Gabriel. "What about Isadora . . . ?"

"She's out," Christmas placated him. "Both she and Chuen are out. There're no charges against them."

"And Hitedoro?"

"Izeki?" Christmas ran an uncertain hand through his bed-swept hair. "That's a different story, there's nothing we can do for him for the time being. He's up for assault on a TARC officer during said officer's performance of his duty. Look," he went on hurriedly, his voice sinking to a whisper, "they're not letting you out because they've got nothing on you; they're letting you out because you've got something on them."

"Me? I don't . . ."

"Ssst." Christmas cringed and glanced over at the toymen still standing in the doorway. "This is really not the place. Can we get you out first, then discuss the rest?"

Gabriel acquiesced reluctantly.

It took almost an hour to process him. Forms were palmed, ret-printed, and his belongings were returned to him, including—at Christmas's insistence—those confiscated from his hotel room. The weight of his mountain coat around his shoulders was like the embrace of an old friend. Even his slaphappies and the phone card Kipper had given him were returned. And his knife. He wondered how they'd managed to pull that one off. Under Christmas's eye and in the presence of two TARC officers, he went through his possessions to confirm that nothing was missing. An unfamiliar plasper envelope caught his eye. The moment he picked it up, he knew what was inside it. He turned to Christmas.

"Listen, have they got a public toilet I can use here? I'd just . . . like a minute or two to myself."

"You've just spent twenty-two hours in solitary. That wasn't enough for you?" Christmas said in surprise.

Gabriel touched the lapel of Christmas's jacket. "There are two things in life no man can escape," he explained gently. "One is death, the other is the occasional need for a good piss."

"Well, if you can't hold it in," Christmas grumbled.

Once ensconced in a cubicle, Gabriel sat and rested his head in his hands. Just a few moments alone, with the lock on *his* side of the door for a change. This was wrong, it was all flocking wrong! They'd wanted him and they'd had him and now they'd let him go and it was all too shagging easy. He smote the door of the cubicle with the heel of his hand.

Something's changed between then and now, in the last day something—some THING—has changed! Something's altered the landscape, but what?

Out of his coat he took the envelope that he had brought with him, and thumbed it open. Carefully he poured its contents into his lap, using the end of his coat as a catch net.

Elspeth. It was all there: the red pebble, the carved jacinth fish, her little pocketknife. The final fragments of her last self. Gabriel held up the transparent envelope containing the tiny parakeelya seed.

"Why?" he whispered, "Why?"

And then . . . it clicked. And he *knew*.

He slumped back against the wall, Elspeth's knick-knacks trickling unnoticed from his lap onto the ground. For a long moment he even forgot to draw breath.

"Oh . . . oh, strewth," he gasped.

He was still frozen, in exactly the same position, when Christmas came banging on the cubicle's intercom ten minutes later.

"Hey, are you still alive in there, stike? I thought you wanted to get out of this place."

Gabriel came to. "Uh . . . yeah, yeah," he stammered, gathering the bits and pieces off the floor. "Be right there."

Isadora and Chuen rose to meet him as he emerged into the reception area. They both looked worn and disheveled, Chuen especially. She was chalk white, fingers entwining nervously. Without a word Isadora wrapped her arms around his rib cage and buried her face in his neck. She was warm.

"You alright?" he whispered.

"I'm fine." she pulled away, absently straightening the collar of his jacket. The gesture surprised and discomfited him slightly. "There wasn't much they could say after they got those pellets out of our necks." She stroked his cheek worriedly, "You look terrible."

"I've looked nothing but terrible since you met me. I'm so glad you're okay. I really am."

He reached out a hand toward Chuen, saw her stiffen,

and contented himself with a pat on her shoulder. "You alright, too?"

Christmas interposed before she could reply. "Stikes, what speak we get ourselves out of here? We're in Mighty Mickey's waiting room here; I don't know if it's the best place to be chatting."

"I want to see Izeki," Gabriel said.

"Izeki . . ."

"They didn't tell you about him?" Chuen queried in surprise.

"Tell me what? Wait, you told me"—Gabriel turned to Christmas—"you told me he was still in lockup."

"He is."

"That's just it, he won't see you," said Isadora despondently. "He doesn't want to talk to anybody."

"He doesn't want to see *anybody*?"

"Well, no, look, that's not actually true," Christmas corrected Isadora. "I just talked to him and his lawyer. Under the circumstances, his lawyer advised him not to go talking to you or Gabriel. He's willing to talk to you." His finger pointed at Chuen.

"Me?" Chuen's jaw dropped. "Me? I don't even like him!"

"Oh, come on, Chuen," Isadora muttered.

"Look . . . well, what does he want to talk to me for?"

"I didn't say he wanted to talk to you; I said he was willing to talk to you," Christmas clarified impatiently.

"Well, golly, I'm flattered."

"I'm just telling you what he told me! He said he was willing to talk to you and just you and then he told me to shag off."

"Yeah, well, that's how he makes friends," Gabriel put in. "Look, Chuen . . ."

"IknowIknowIknow!"

"Just talk to him, find out if he's okay."

"I will, I'll do it."

"Hey, hello there, is this a picnic?" Christmas was scrubbing fretfully at his mussed-up hair with one hand. "The whole point of my being here was to get you people out. I'm sure the entertainment director in there'd love to have you back . . ."

"No, you're right, we'll go." Gabriel had spotted Clau-

dia Ernst waiting pointedly by the exit. As he caught
her eye she approached him.

"If I could have a minute of your time . . ." she said
gravely.

"Sure . . . yeah . . . listen, I didn't have a chance to
thank you . . ."

"It's not over yet. Officially they're only reassessing
the charges. They haven't dropped them yet. You won't
be permitted to leave Kyara."

Gabriel made a resigned gesture. He'd known it.

Ernst continued, "My motives for taking on your case
were not entirely altruistic. My employer would like to
speak with you in private. There's more privacy out
there"—she indicated the main exit—"than in here."

Your employer? So that's it, he thought. The last time
that somebody had informed Gabriel their superior
wanted a word with him, they had referred as that superior as "the One." Fervently he hoped that this character, whoever it was, was not "the One" as well, since
that would make "Two." And one "One" was already
plenty.

The situation became clear the moment he stepped
out of the building. On the far side of the Hall a hangcar
was parked. The door slid open and a woman stepped
out. It was the same woman who had attempted to kidnap him the night he shot Dana Sotack.

"I might have bloody known." He had gone from
being a prisoner to a hostage. He turned to Isadora.

"What is it?" She'd read the look on his face.

"Welcome back to the flockin' circus. Iz, I have to go
for a little ride here."

"I'm coming with y—"

"No! I need you to do something for me. I need you
to call up Jael Nyquist at Rainer Park. I want you to
ask her to find out how much debris was gathered up in
the park the day after Elspeth's death. I'm sure they
keep records of all that stuff."

Isadora looked confused. "How much debris? I . . .
don't understand."

"*Please.* I'll see you later." He gave her arm a
squeeze. "I'll be okay."

"Be careful."

"I intend to be." He eyed one of the toymen standing

guard on either side of the TARC headquarters' entrance. "Which is why I want to have a word with Brilloface over there."

Rule 1: Use everything you've got. Rule 2: When what you've got is nothing, use that.

Gabriel approached the TARC robot. "My name's Gabriel Kylie," he said cheerfully. "You see that woman across the Hall there?" He poked a thumb in the direction of the hangcar. "She works for Kyaran Ventures 99. Now, I want you to remember her face, 'cos if anything happens to me, that's the first person Captain Pelham Leel is going to want to talk to. Alright?"

Then, with a wink at Claudia Ernst, he crossed the Hall and stepped up to his erstwhile captor. She eyed him without warmth.

"Greetings." Gabriel smiled his easy smile. "Take me to your leader."

a veil of whispers

Izeki looked incongruous in the gray prison coverall, like an overripe pear bursting from its skin. His face was drawn, the canny glitter in his eyes had withdrawn behind a dull, cobweb stare that seemed to focus only occasionally and, even when it did, take in nothing at all. Occasionally he fingered the surface of the table, leaving little smudges of sweat that congealed almost immediately.

The expanse of tabletop separating him from Chuen was wide enough to prevent their touching one another. The Privacy Laws covering visitation rights prevented any kind of barrier being placed between a prisoner and his or her guest, but there was no law against the sticky strip in the center of the table to prevent anything being slid or rolled across. The Privacy Statutes also guaranteed that no one would be listening in on their conversation. Of course, who believed that? Chuen might have a week ago.

Not anymore.

"I want you to go . . ." Izeki's voice was like clay. "I want to ask you . . . or one of the others . . . if you'd look after my brother and . . . Aysha."

"Yes, of course," Chuen replied stiffly.

"Just . . . you know, they're still sitting in that flockin' hotel, they're . . . probably scared. Just see that they get home."

"I'll see they get home."

Izeki rubbed at the tabletop with his thumb. "They . . . I told them, the TARCs here, that Isaao . . . he didn't know anything about it, about anything. He didn't know anything . . ."

"Of course he didn't . . ."

"He just did what I asked him. He didn't know."

Chuen realized that Izeki was talking as much for the benefit of unseen ears listening as for her.

"I'll look after it. I'll see they're okay."

"The TARCs are going to want to talk to them and somebody's . . . I don't want them losing their jobs. If anything can be done."

"I promise."

"We did saw their boss's office doors full of holes."

"I promise."

Izeki said nothing further, neither did he look at her. Flickers of expression darted over his sagging face, as if he was remembering . . . things. Chuen made no move to leave. The events of two nights before replayed themselves before her mind's eye. A fleeting spasm of anger shook her, but it was not directed at him. There were things she wanted to say to him, but something held her back.

"Izeki . . . Hitedoro," she said hesitantly. He did not react. *"You saved our lives and I just . . . I just wanted to thank you,"* she did not say, *"I just wanted to say that to you."*

"I know," he did not reply. *"It's alright."*

She did not continue, *"I also wanted to tell you . . . that I was sorry. I said some things . . . I didn't mean them."*

"Yes, you did." He didn't smile.

She didn't shake her head. *"I know, it seemed that way. I did. I know I did mean them. I'm just . . . sorry."*

He didn't say, *"So am I. I didn't mean the things I said to you. You and your Sisters, I've never been able to much abide you. I'm sorry I had to do what I did."*

"It's alright. It's all alright."

None of these things were said. Instead they both sat in uncomfortable muteness, each wondering about the other. At length Chuen stood, resenting his silence and her own inability to express what she felt to him. Well, it wasn't his brother's fault and she would do what she'd promised.

"Good luck," she said without warmth.

He nodded absently. He had not moved from his chair when the door closed behind Chuen. She found herself thinking, *For the first time Izeki is living in a cell without Windows.*

They made the trip in silence. Claudia Ernst declined to accompany him, so Gabriel and his ex-kidnapper climbed into the hangcar together. She set the hangcar on automatic and sat facing him, studiously intent on everything but him. Gabriel tried gently baiting her, to no avail. Apparently her vocabulary had reached its limits with, "Get in," "Get out," and "Tell us where it is, or else!"

So they made the trip in silence and Gabriel had time to reflect. It was obvious that his reprieve was temporary and would remain in effect only for as long as he remained useful, which might be for only an hour or two. Yet, still something did not make sense. Like his present companion, Claudia Ernst had represented Kyaran Ventures 99, which meant that her threats had the weight of the second most powerful multisystem conglomerate on Kyara behind them. That was a lot of muscle, but was that enough to get him free? No. Somewhere in all this there was still a vital piece missing.

The building in front of which the hangcar halted was a vast, tiered construction, topped by a dome, ornate even by Kyaran standards. "Kyaran Ventures 99, *in touch today with your tomorrow!*" glowed above the doorway, rippling just enough to attract an involuntary glance from anyone passing the building. His companion guided him wordlessly inside, bypassing the reception desk and showing him into what turned out to be the private elevator to the penthouse suite.

The woman did not step into the elevator herself. Instead, as the door closed between them, she spoke for the first time, speaking with a kind of joyless menace. "Enjoy your trip up; you might meet me on your way down."

A few seconds later Gabriel stepped out of the elevator into what appeared to be a broad living room. There was no one present. The walls were pale pink and the gleaming floor inlaid marbeline, forming an abstract mosaic of fractal spirals. The furniture consisted of little more than four form-molding couches standing like pearl-colored puddings around a central coffee table in

the form of a gilded male figure, lying curled up in a
fetal position. The transparent tabletop was supported
by his shoulder and hip. Two pointed-arch doorways facing one another in opposite walls were hung with semitransparent spider silk. A coruscation of light against the
one to his left betrayed the presence of a pool of some
sort in the room beyond. He could hear a fountain and
the air was bright with the singing of birds.

What caught his immediate attention, however, were
the peacocks. There were three of them, one blue, one
deep wine red, and one yellow, trimmed with gold. They
circled the room slowly, tails fanned out in a regal display. Gabriel's visceral dislike of all things GenTec was
briefly overcome by the sheer beauty of them. They were
less like birds and more like living pieces of fine jewelry,
gilded and feathered with flakes of precious stone.

With some difficulty he tore his eyes away from them
and walked to the center of the room. He could hear a
voice somewhere.

"Hello?" he called out. "Anybody home?"

His voice echoed strangely. A violet-and-pink bird
burst out of one of the silk curtains and Gabriel's eyes
followed it as it soared up. And up.

And up.

"Whoa," he whispered. Gabriel had assumed that he
was beyond surprise, but this . . . was something else.

The walls of the room were nothing more than three-
meter-high partitions, forming a series of open-ceilinged
apartments, all contained within the vast dome that
formed the roof of the building. It must have been almost thirty meters high and from its center an extraordinary mobile seemed to defy gravity. A transparent
amber globe, over a meter across, hung from the ceiling,
encircled by rings that rotated through and in and about
one another. Ivies and other hanging plants draped the
entire construction and birds of rainbow hues flitted
from perch to perch. From the ends of some of the plant
fronds water trickled downward to fall somewhere beyond the partition.

An ocean green–and-turquoise bird dropped down
toward him and instinctively he held his arm out. In a
reaction that seemed Pavlovian the bird backwinged and
came to perch on the back of his wrist. It sang brightly.

There was no question that the little creature was Gen-Tec-designed and he sensed that its responses were pre-programmed, to land on an outstretched wrist and begin singing. The form was that of a nightingale, although no nightingale had ever displayed the tropical coloration that this one displayed. Nightingales rarely wore jeweled chokers either.

He noticed that there was also something odd about the bird's beak. At no point did it move. Gently he covered the bird with his hand, trapping the humerii between his fingers until he had it immobilized, then he examined the beak carefully. It was no beak at all, he realized. The mandible was fused into the skull to form a tube-shaped construction, immobile and impossible to open or close. With a sick feeling he flipped the bird over; it was still singing hysterically. As he had suspected, it had no anus. Then how . . . ? Of course, that was what the collar was for! The bird was fed directly, intravenously.

Right, he thought bitterly. *Wouldn't want to get bird shit on our precious furniture, would we?*

Gabriel heard footsteps approaching and loosened his grip on the bird. It gave a wriggle and broke free, fluttering upward into the dome. At no point during his examination had the bird stopped singing.

"Mr. Kylie, I'm sorry to have kept you waiting. I see you've found our wildlife already."

He turned to find himself facing a petite, dark-skinned woman. She was clad in high-society, northern-continental, Helios fashion: a long, brocaded robe of sky-blue, flecked with silver and yellow and topped by an ornate headpiece, with a veil that cast a fine mist across her features. The skin on her hands was ebony and baby-smooth, but the cautious precision with which she moved spoke of accumulated years of experience and Gabriel suspected that she was far older than her regen-treated skin revealed.

"You *are* Gabriel Kylie . . . or have my people dragged some innocent passerby off the street?" Her voice was musical and tinged with amusement.

Gabriel's stomach was still soured by his examination of the GenTec nightingale and he did not feel disposed to any great friendliness. It was with an effort that he burred the edge of curtness in his tone to something approaching civility. "No, you've got the right bloke." He did a slow 360-degree pivot on one heel, surveying the dome, then let his face slip into a lopsided grin. "So, this is how the cream lives."

"The cream of the cream." An ivory smile shone out from behind the veil. "Naomi Sol. I'm pleased to meet you." Her hand swept out to one of the puddings. "Please, take a seat. May I offer you something to drink? Are you hungry?"

"Either or." Gabriel sat down uneasily, found himself enveloped by a liquid touch that firmed up against his back and supported his shoulders.

"Which is either and which is or?"

"They fed me in prison. They're obliged to."

Naomi Sol observed him intently, then sank back into the couch opposite him. "Yes," she said sympathetically. "You haven't really had the usual tourist-bureau introduction to Kyara, have you?"

"You saw to that," Gabriel said easily.

Naomi Sol's eyes appeared to narrow behind the veil. "Did I? I see."

Before she could continue, she was interrupted by the sound of a throat being cleared. A man was standing in one of the doorways, dressed in a one-piece green uniform with a Genes-"R"-Us insignia on the lapel. He was carrying what seemed to be a pure white lyrebird in one hand.

"Sorry, I don't mean to interrupt. Ms. Sol, I've netted this one all in-out and I'll have to replace it, it's a dud. Both lungs are faulty and there's a glitch in the diaphragm as well. I'll bring the new one round myself later this afternoon, if that's convenient."

"Yes, that's fine, Allard, just see that it's fresh. I don't want it dying on me the first time I have guests."

"I'll make sure." The man disappeared into the elevator and Naomi Sol turned back to Gabriel.

"I hadn't realized that maintaining this aviary would be as much work as it is. We tried to set up the simplest possible ecosystem in here, but a week doesn't go by without a casualty, invariably due to something which could have been avoided if it wasn't for the legal design restrictions on anything GenTec. You know how it is, you have to get everything approved through about fifteen independent tech-approval committees."

"Well, they have their reasons, I reckon," Gabriel said lightly.

"Oh, of course, I'd be the last to dispute that. But one can wish. Last month one of the midget egrets went into some kind of seizure and managed to get itself tangled up in the ivy. I was having a dinner here and we hear a crackling sound. The next thing Judge Weller has an epileptic egret splashing around in his soup. He didn't turn a hair. He looks up, and says, 'Could you tell the cook mine is a little rare?' " Sol laughed gaily and Gabriel forced a bitter smile.

After her laughter had subsided, Sol sighed happily. "Well, there it is. They used to say that a camel was a horse designed by a committee. Nowadays that's literally true." With a graceful gesture she raised her veil to reveal a face like a polished African sculpture. Her eyes were half-lidded, proud and steady. Her skin smooth, but hard, like mahogany; beautiful but without true character. Cosmetic treatments might serve to restore a semblance of cotton-candy youth, but you could read the story of a person's life in her or his face and regen inevitably stripped that story away. Gabriel wondered what the point was of having lived if one was going to rob oneself that way.

"Have you ever seen a real nightingale?"

Sol raised one finger upward.

"No, not that. A real nightingale. The real thing's rather dull. Brown, you know, with . . . a little light blue? It raises itself to grace by the beauty of its song. It has to sing, you understand, to make itself special. That need . . . is what gives it its dignity."

"Hmm." The amusement was back in Sol's face. "Why do I feel like a V.T. program-maker who's just gotten a bad review?"

Discomfited, Gabriel slipped off the chair to the ground, crossing his legs and folding his coat about him. He was aware of how pompous his words must have sounded. Annoyed, he said, "Look, why don't we talk about why I'm here."

"Ah." There was a tinge of mockery in her voice. "So you don't much care for games."

"I'm big on caber-tossing."

"On . . ."

"Never mind. No, I'm not. I've had more games than I'm used to recently."

"Alright." Sol made a gesture with her right hand. The center of one of the spiral mosaics detached itself from the floor and rose on a double helix of unfolding MemPlas coils until it was level with the arm of her chair. From the resulting spiral-shaped tabletop a long-stemmed glass emerged, containing something pink and transparent. She put the glass to her lips and took a delicate sip.

"I suppose I owe you an apology," she said, without a hint of remorse in her tone. "I wanted to see you the other night and some of my employees got a little overzealous."

"If you'd wanted to see me, you could have just asked."

"As I said, my people went a little over the top. I'm a businesswoman, not a gangster."

"Oh, so you were waiting down in the industrial plastines sector that night with the champagne glasses and welcome mat, were you?" Gabriel snorted sarcastically and knew instantly that he had gone too far.

Sol's fingers tightened imperceptibly around the stem of her glass. With her other hand she flicked her veil back down. "You're not making this very easy."

"Why should I?"

"Politeness, maybe? I don't see why courtesy and honesty should be incompatible."

"They're not, so why didn't you just come up to me and ask? Why send the flocking goon squad? You know . . ." Gabriel preempted her reply and pointed at Sol's glass. "Maybe . . . some herb tea would be good. Mint and licorice root. It's a good combo. Or if you don't have that, just a glass of water'll do."

Sol gestured with her hand again. "Denube Assam," she said. "I think you'll find it a bit more refreshing than herb tea at this time of the day."

A section of the coffee table in front of Gabriel opened and extruded a delicate teapot with a mother-of-pearl finish and a matching teacup. A thread of steam rose from the spout, bringing with it a scent of tarry pungency. Gabriel poured, reflecting with mild chagrin that Sol was probably right. Herb tea would have sent him into a doze.

"Anyway, what am I doing here?" he asked, taking up the teacup and blowing softly on the tea to cool it off.

"I thought we could do a little business. We both have something to sell."

Gabriel paused. "Oh, yeah? What have you got?"

Naomi Sol lifted her hand regally. A blur of ruby red plummeted out of the dome and alighted on her outstretched fingers. Whispering endearments, she lifted the songbird to her lips. Her eyes met Gabriel's. "Your ticket out of Kyara."

Gabriel took an experimental sip of tea before answering.

"No. I . . . don't . . . think . . . so," he said thoughtfully. "I don't think there's any legal way that you can get me off Kyara. Your little pet piranha there got me out of the lockup, but . . . no . . . I don't reckon you can get away with that. There's a lot of folk who're fairly enthusiastic about keeping me here."

A wisp of a smile stole from behind Sol's veil. "I don't think you're looking at this on the right scale, Mr. Kylie. Let me tell you a story. It's an anecdote from before the Plagues, in which a leading businessman once observed that, if you're there at the right moment, a small war can be a very profitable venture. Then, when somebody pointed out that you couldn't always be sure that a war was going to start in any given place at any given time, he replied that the solution to that was simply to organize one."

She waited for a response from Gabriel and when none came she continued didactically. "The kind of nationalistic war that he was talking about then isn't really possible anymore—hasn't been for centuries—it's much too hard to contain, but . . . the point is, you've just got to change your sense of scale. Your sense of what is and isn't possible will alter to match."

"Maybe. But if even Byron Systems don't have the clout to keep me in the lockup, then you sure as hell don't have the clout to get me out. Not legally anyway. If you had the kind of clout, I wouldn't be sitting here, would I?" Gabriel deliberately put a note of scorn into his voice. Naomi Sol had just flexed, not only her muscle, but her vanity. And vanity was not only attractively human, but handy.

Sure enough, there was an edge of pique in her tone when she replied, "I think you're underestimating me, Mr. Kylie."

Gabriel looked unconcerned. "Oh, yeah? Okay. Well, now we know what you've got, what have I got?" She said nothing, so Gabriel waggled a finger at her and said mock-scoldingly, "You're not going to say the blue box now, are you?"

She stiffened. "You have it?"

Gabriel sighed. "No, I don't have it. I don't, I never have. I've never seen it, never touched it. In fact the first time I even heard about it was when I took a little hangcar ride with a couple of your cronies. Now"—he held up his hand—"you don't have to believe that—nobody else has—but that's the truth. You want to know what I am? I'm a tourist. And that's all I ever was. You know," he went on with a laugh, "it's amazing to me. Does everybody here live in a vacuum? Nobody here has a family? Or friends . . . well, *one* man . . . one man I've met does! But when I turn up here, nobody believes that I could be anything as simple as a grieving brother. Oh, no. Nono. But that *is* all I am. Now, what are you going to choose to believe?"

Naomi Sol leaned back in her chair and Gabriel felt her gaze dissecting him. He suddenly felt the might of this woman, the urbane ease with which she wielded it. At last she said, "You know, I don't think you're lying."

Gabriel threw a grateful glance heavenward.

"In fact . . . I think you really are what you've been saying you are."

"That I am."

She rose to her feet. "In other words," she went on, "you're nothing."

Gabriel feigned a hurt expression. "Well, I wouldn't quite go that far . . ."

"You're nothing," she repeated in a sort of inward-looking awe. Her manner changed like the snap of a mousetrap. "I don't think we have anything else to talk about."

And with that she turned her back on him and walked toward the doorway.

"Whoawhoawhoa! Wait a second!" Gabriel scrambled to his feet. This was not going the way he had intended.

"I don't think so. I think you've wasted enough of my time," she drawled over her shoulder. The spider-silk curtains billowed around her as she passed through the doorway and hid her from view. Right and left sections of the floor were coiling upward to reveal slumber-weapons pointing right at Gabriel.

"What if I told you I had something more valuable to sell?" Gabriel shouted.

"I doubt it," she called back mockingly.

A metallic voice spoke so close to Gabriel's ear that he jumped in surprise. Directionally focused sound. It said, "Walk directly to the elevator door. Do not attempt to move in any other direction or you will be rendered unconscious and prosecuted for unlawful presence in a private residence. You have five seconds to obey, starting . . . now."

Gabriel called frantically, "Doubt's what you're going to be living with, unless you hear what I have to say!"

He waited, counting off the seconds in his mind, not moving from where he was. He had little to lose at this point. At least half a minute passed and still the slumber-weapons fired no shot. Gabriel stepped gingerly toward the doorway through which Naomi Sol had departed. When this produced no reaction he continued walking. The spider-silk curtains parted before him. His skin twitched as they brushed the knuckles of his outstretched hands. Somewhere on Grayscape, the only world whose laws were lax enough to permit it, fist-sized GenTec spiders, eyeless and legless, had spun this silk, producing almost half a kilo each day.

Gabriel found himself standing at the edge of a round pool, almost eight meters across. It was clear and bright with turquoise light that sent ripples dancing about the walls. Beneath its surface blue-gray shapes darted past Gabriel's feet. At one end a rocky waterfall cascaded into the pool, itself partially fed by water trickling down from the hanging plants in the dome. Naomi Sol was standing on the far side of the pool, veil raised.

"So, tell me what you have to sell," she said coldly.

"Supposing," Gabriel said, "that I was to tell you that the blue box is sleight of hand."

Naomi Sol looked away contemptuously. "The blue box is very real."

"The blue box may be real," Gabriel allowed, "but it doesn't matter."

"It matters to me."

"Why? Why does it matter to you? Have you ever seen it? Do you know what it is?"

"An artifact. And a key to a great deal of power."

"Who told you that? Elspeth? My sister?"

"I don't know your sister."

"Yeah, right."

Something broke the water at the center of the pool. Miniature blue dolphins the length of wine bottles arched up out of the water, skittering across the surface on their tails before falling back. There were over a dozen of them, their tiny squeals so high-pitched that they were almost out of the range of human hearing, piteous, like the whispers of a baby.

GenTec dolphins? Gabriel thought aghast. But nobody messed with dolphins; dolphins were *sentient!* He hoped to hell that these weren't. Sol was still waiting for an answer.

"I'll tell you what the blue box is," Gabriel said a touch breathlessly. "The blue box is sleight of hand."

There was a pause. The dolphinettes drew bright circles in the water.

"That's what you have to tell me?"

"Let me guess," Gabriel replied. "You want it 'cos Saxon Rainer wants it. And if he wants, ooh, it must be good! Is that it?"

Sol was losing patience with him again. "Mr. Kylie. It has cost me a great deal to get you out of prison. I suspect that Dana Sotack would just as soon withdraw his confession as accept the money we're paying him to voluntarily risk two years on Retreat for possession of an illegal firearm."

"Then why don't you educate me? What has Saxon Rainer got that you want?"

"Kyara, of course." A savage look passed across Naomi Sol's face.

Gabriel snorted. "Sorry, I don't get it. What is he?

King? He's on the Conclave, but so are you! Byron Systems is only one of *hundreds* of conglomerates centered in Kyara."

"It's a little more complex than that. Kyaran Ventures 99 is a fine company. We were originally based on Helios and then . . . oh . . . about forty years ago, we moved our center of operations here."

"Because of Thor's Privacy Laws."

Sol averred, "Among other things. A company is a living thing, that's KV 99's philosophy. It has to be nurtured to survive and Kyara is the most vibrant center of business in the C.C.S. A company has to grow . . ."

"Aah." Gabriel's voice was heavy with irony.

"You disagree."

"No. But nothing grows forever, without strangling itself."

"What's strangling KV 99 is not itself, but Byron Systems!"

"Byron Systems? Just them? I thought there were a couple of hundred multisystems here! None of them have anything to do with it?"

"What I'm talking about here is a level playing field. Byron Systems is not like the other conglomerates. Byron Systems *is* Kyara."

"So I've heard."

Sol's expression darkened. "There is not *one* thing on Kyara that Byron Systems does not in some way control! The Orbit stations? They're owned and leased to the city by Byron Systems. The seismological watchdog setup. Byron Systems. There hasn't been a proper survey of the surface for half a century and why? Because Byron Systems controls anything to do with Thor itself and Byron Systems can't be bothered to authorize one. None of these things are important in themselves, but they do have a symbolic importance. Make no mistake here about Saxon Rainer. We're talking here about a man egomaniacal enough to enter a hunter virus into the Kyara Web to track down and wipe out every copy of an unauthorized biography that someone wrote about him. No one's ever been able to prove it, but I know for a fact that he did." This last was said with such deadly earnestness that Gabriel nearly burst out laughing. Sol must have noticed, because her tone abruptly hardened,

and she said, "Now the next thing you say had better
pique my interest or this conversation will be at an end."

"Alright." Gabriel spoke slowly. "Supposing I was to
tell you that Byron Systems, *your* Byron Systems,
doesn't own a thing on Kyara anymore. Nothing. Supposing I was to tell you that it's spent the last twenty
years slowly selling off all its nonmovable assets here on
Thor and moving the rest off-world, without anybody
noticing."

Sol oozed superciliousness. "I'm afraid, Mr. Kylie, you
know very little about how these things work . . ."

"Very little? I know bugger all! I have no conception
whatsoever, *but* . . . there are those who do! I could
show you a record with an analysis demonstrating precisely what I've just told you. Byron Systems owns almost nothing on Thor. I don't even think it owns that
building it's sitting in anymore."

"That's impossible."

Gabriel said urgently. "Anywhere else but on Thor,
yes. But with Thor's Privacy Laws, yes, you might *juuust*
get away with it. Providing everybody's looking somewhere else!"

"At the blue box." Sol kept her tone neutral.

Gabriel spread his fingers like the rays of a dawning
sun. "Sleight of hand."

For a moment that seemed to Gabriel to go on forever
Naomi Sol gave no reply. He was very conscious of the
crackle of wings echoing down from the dome, the rustle
of hanging ivy. The fountain was a roaring hiss and, high
above it, the dolphins still whispered.

"Might a person inquire as to why Byron Systems
would go to all that trouble to give up its holdings here
on Thor?" Sol inquired at length.

"That's where I need your help to find out."

"Hm," Sol mused. "I'd have to check on what you're
saying, of course."

"Oh, it's all checkable . . . although I reckon it's going
to take you months to go digging back up the trail."

"You're going to offer me that record, though."

"I have a price."

"I'll meet it."

"It's not what you think."

"I see. What is it then?"

Gabriel counted off on his fingers. "Two things. One, Isadora Gatzalumendi and Lee Chuen. I'd like to get them safely off Kyara and I want Hitedoro Izeki fished out of jail by that pet lawyer of yours."

"That's three things already."

"Are we gonna be picky?"

"I can't guarantee that I can get Izeki out of jail. I will have Claudia Ernst do what she can for him."

"Good enough," Gabriel agreed. "Now, tell me something else. The cream meet the cream, don't they?"

Naomi Sol said quizzically, "I'm not sure I follow, but, yes."

"You meet Saxon Rainer, face-to-face. To discuss . . . business." Gabriel gestured vaguely. "The . . . well, you don't discuss the weather . . . maybe you compare jewels. Whatever."

"Yes, of course, we meet for business sometimes," Sol allowed.

"Intuition doesn't always work over the phone."

"No, it doesn't."

"Good. Number two: I'd like you to pop round for a drink, tonight . . . with a couple of your lawyers."

Naomi Sol regarded him steadily, comprehending precisely what he was suggesting.

byron systems

The Byron Systems Works Building stood in austere contrast to the sugar-frosted Gothic of the rest of Kyaran architecture. A ninety-story obelisk, it thrust upward like a knitting needle from the center of the city, almost touching the spun-diamond domes and dwarfing everything around it. Upon the unveiling of the plans for the construction of Rainer Park, the Bugout community had instantly redubbed the Byron Systems Works Building "Rainer's Pecker". Within a matter of weeks the name had stuck and spread into general usage, despite some pundits' pointed objections that a man of Saxon Rainer's reputed vanity might just find the comparison flattering. The great man himself was said to occupy the slim pyramid at the summit of the obelisk, overseeing, from that vantage point, the life of the entire city.

The single security guard at the armored reception desk on the ground floor of the Byron Systems Building had long since ceased to speculate on the doings of the upper eighty-nine stories. If this was Rainer's Pecker, then he, personally, was Rainer's Bollocks. This meant that, as long as he did his work properly, he could leave the business end of things to someone else.

Tonight was a steady night, no undue surprises. One of the seventy-second-story security robots had developed a directional glitch, a giddy mob of the Church of Macca had done a merry conga past the front doors, celebrating Meal-day Weekend, and he'd split a nail whilst cleaning them for the third time. Still, one shouldn't complain. There was a time when chronically boredom-inducing labor did not, by law, merit extra pay.

The only point of real curiosity on this dull evening was the impending visit of Naomi Sol and even that guaranteed no more than a minute and a half of passing interest. Her visits were rare; it was a known fact that she and Rainer did not get on. Moreover, ten o'clock after dark-down was an odd time either to be doing business or making social calls. Still, the security guard reflected, what the upper echelons did was, quite literally, none of his business.

That attitude was what had gotten him his job.

On the stroke of ten Naomi Sol's hangcar drew up outside the main entrance and the head of Kyaran Ventures 99 swept in, punctilious as always.

And veiled, as always.

The security guard scanned the case she was carrying for weapons (a futile but symbolic exercise, since Sol herself was never subjected to a scan), checked her bodyguard's slumbergun to make sure it really was just a slumbergun and then returned it (another futile but symbolic gesture), and checked the identities of both the bodyguard and the accompanying lawyer. Their palm and retinaprints both matched those lines in from KV 99 Central earlier this afternoon.

"Nice to see you again, Ms. Sol," the guard said, with as much conviction as he could muster. "The executive elevator's waiting for you."

Hadn't she put on a little weight? he wondered to himself as the three of them disappeared into the elevator. Her two companions excited no interest on his part at all. For obvious reasons KV 99 had an extraordinarily high number of Sisters of Tanit employees and as for the bodyguard, the only thing odd about him apart from the limp—and a face that looked as if someone had been practicing timpani rolls on it with a rubber mallet—was the fact that no one had ever known Naomi Sol to tolerate scruffiness amongst her employees.

As the elevator door closed, "Naomi Sol" slumped back against the wall and rubbed at her face in a most uncharacteristic gesture. Her hands were shaking. Lee Chuen glared over the top of Isadora's head at Gabriel, her scalp glistening with sweat. "This is the most stupid shagging exercise I've ever heard of in my life!" she growled.

"Nobody forced you to come, Chuen." Isadora tried to set her veil straight.

"Guilt is a mighty sword, darling," Chuen retorted, then muttered, "The last hurrah of the quickfarm pickers. Much as I hate to admit it and with all due respect to those present, I'd feel a lot safer if Lieutenant Fatso was here."

"No offense taken." Gabriel kept his face steadfastly turned away from the Eye in the ceiling. The swelling in his lip had gone down, but he still looked badly used. His eyes were black pits, his usually wayward hair was tied back tightly. Every time he moved his head, the silver earings in his left lobe winked, like teardrops on ebony.

What was it Ellis Quinn Macintire had said? *Saxon Rainer's a man who knows his way through the labyrinth.* The monster at the heart of the maze usually did, Gabriel reflected. Expectation pulsed like a living weight in the pit of his belly.

On the other hand it might also have been the dinner he'd had at Chuen's apartment. Chuen herself had spent all evening complaining that she was starving hungry, but the state of her nerves was such that the slightest nibble sent her retching into the toilet. She had eventually given herself a shot of LieGestive to kill her appetite. Chuen had had the right idea, Gabriel reflected morosely.

He downright envied Isadora who, typically, had devoured anything that stayed still long enough to be classified as edible and seemed none the worse for it. Moral certitude seemed to give her courage—you could see it in the way she moved, weight snug against the floor. To Gabriel moral certitude had always been something that shackled your limbs and narrowed your vision, sent your emotional center of gravity reeling off at unwanted angles.

Or gave you indigestion.

Gabriel raised a warning hand as they felt the elevator stop. Unconsciously he rolled his weight onto the balls of his feet. He was ready.

The small anteroom that they entered was but a cou-

ple of meters wide. Directly before them was a second
door. Gabriel was sure that there must be Eyes watching
them, but they were well hidden. He gave Isadora's arm
a surreptitious squeeze and touched Chuen's shoulder
briefly, then he palmed the doorplate. The door slid
open.

They stepped out into an immense, dimly lit chamber
that took up the entire ninetieth floor of the building.
The walls and ceiling formed the inside of the five-story
pyramid that crowned the apex of Rainer's Pecker,
climbing and narrowing until they were swallowed up in
the darkness above. The stark floor space was punctuated only by the odd, freestanding pillar and a three-
meter cube that was the anteroom. Lack of any partition
walls was made up for by blur-fields that prevented one
from clearly seeing far into the gloom, thus preserving
privacy. Although completely different, it was every bit
as impressive as Naomi Sol's residence.

A single window ran all the way around the entire
building, providing a 360-degree view of the night sky,
except where the blur-fields canceled the effect. The
view was peculiar in a way that Gabriel could not quite
put his finger on.

Once the initial impact had worn off Gabriel found
his eyes drawn to the only source of illumination in the
chamber. Two hovering lamps created a pool of light
some fifteen meters away to his left, in the center of
which was a beautifully crafted, wooden desk. A man
and a woman were sitting at it, studying a hol-display.
As the three entered, they looked up without surprise.

The hol-display evaporated and the man rose from his
desk, standing solid as a granite block.

Saxon Rainer.

"Hello, Naomi, you seem to have put on some
weight," he said in a voice that was deep, mellow as the
brown of an oak casket. The smile he flashed was craggy
and rather magnificent. He was not overly tall, but his
frame was broad and he moved with the grace of an
aging athlete. His hair and close-cropped beard, once
deep mahogany, were now almost entirely slate-gray. An
aquiline nose clove the shadow of his brow in two like
a scimitar. His eyes were deep-set and very dark, with
luminescent flecks of red gold around the irises.

Isadora lifted her veil and Rainer's eyes narrowed. Then he gave a bark of delighted laughter. "Let me guess . . . Isadora Gatzalumendi!" He strode around his desk, his hand outstretched. Isadora took it in confusion. His grip was gentle, but with a might behind the gentleness. "I'm Saxon Rainer. I'll call you Isadora, if I may. Formality's for working hours. And you must be Lee Chuen." He beamed at her. "I won't insult you by offering you my hand, Sister. May your Goddess keep you." There was no hint of mockery in his tone. Then he turned to Gabriel and studied him with an expression of unbegrudged respect. "And you are Gabriel Kylie, if I'm not mistaken."

They stood taking each other's measure, Gabriel's face dark and unreadable. Abruptly Rainer turned, one hand sweeping out toward his companion, his other settling on Isadora's shoulder, urging her forward. "Please, I'd like you to meet TARC Commissioner Tamara Lennox."

Lennox gave a brief tilt of her head. She was angular, thin almost to the point of emaciation, mousy-haired, with pale, translucent skin and large, oval eyes, her features a filigree of fine bones.

Rainer went on blithely, "Tamara . . . well, you know all these three, Tamara. Please, take chairs, we have a lot to talk about. Anybody want a drink?"

Chuen looked at the other two for guidance and when none came, raised her finger. "I'll have a crème de menthe." Isadora shot her a bad look and Chuen shrugged. Gabriel did not react, he was studying Rainer, who was at the dispenser, a beautifully carved, free standing rosewood cabinet. The head of Byron Systems hesitated before removing the glass from the slot.

"Do you stick to Sisterhood precepts all the way?"

"He can touch the glass, I'll accept it," Chuen said courteously.

Rainer let out another booming laugh. "Good for you. I admire strong principles, even if I don't agree with them. But I admire even more slinging them out of the window when the drinks are good. Here." The glass changed hands. He noticed that Isadora was staring out of the window, mouth agape. "Ah," he said in satisfaction, "you like the view? Come and have a good look."

He guided them all to the window and it was only now that Gabriel understood what was wrong with the view. Kyara was gone. He was looking straight out onto the black face of the Anvil and it was as if the Byron Systems Building were standing alone on its surface.

Isadora was similarly impressed. "Where's the city?"

"It's not a projection—not entirely, anyway," Rainer explained with obvious pride. "The view's real enough, it's just enhanced, the city's removed using the information we get from the Eyes around Kyara's perimeter. Everywhere . . . here . . . where the city is actually standing, that's all based on the original terrain surveys." He scrutinized the vista with barely suppressed excitement, as if taking in the magnificence of it for the first time. "I can see the Church of the Æsir's point sometimes. Keeps one vital. Looks back at you like a challenge, don't you think? I always think so. And we rise to it, we beat it, daily, daily, we beat it."

There was something very grand about Rainer's every gesture, his pose, the angle at which he held his head, the light, balanced contact his fingers made with his listener's elbow; all spoke of an immense self-confidence, a belief not only in his ability, but his ordained right to inspire and lead others. His energy was infectious and Isadora and even Chuen seemed to be rather overwhelmed by him.

A part of Gabriel wanted to be swept up in the tide of Rainer's charisma. But another voice kept whispering, *Don't trust a man who doesn't value his own privacy.* Three complete strangers had just invaded Saxon Rainer's private premises under false pretences. By rights, and at the very least, Rainer ought to have called for his security personnel. Yet here was the president of Byron Systems behaving as if he was host at a long-planned social gathering, chatting away with Isadora and Chuen, pointing out landmarks visible on the black plain before them.

Gabriel let his gaze roam around the immense chamber. He could not help but receive the niggling impression that this place was very sparsely furnished . . . or, rather, not so much sparsely furnished as *unadorned*. It was the subtle difference between a room with little furniture and a room from which a great deal of furniture had been removed. The empty spaces were not natural and Gabriel thought he recognized the signs. This was a man ready to travel.

This was confirmed by the presence of a pair of packing containers that he spotted, standing just outside the circle of light. They were surrounded by what appeared to be several statues of animals.

Unable to resist, Gabriel made his way over to them, very aware of Tamara Lennox's eyes following him. The commissioner reclined in her chair, milk-pool eyes taking everything in with studied dispassion.

Bending down, Gabriel picked up one of the figures. It was no statue, but a stuffed rhenea, a cat-sized quasi-mammalian from Denube. He ran his fingers over its soft hide. Whoever the taxidermist had been they'd done a good job, avoiding most of the stiffness and awkward-ness of pose usually associated with stuffed animals.

A tingle along his spine told Gabriel of someone's approach.

Saxon Rainer was standing just behind him. "I shot it five years ago on Denube," he rumbled.

"Up in the Lorentien Mountains," Gabriel murmured, "during the second half of winter."

"You've been there!" Rainer was delighted. "But how did you . . . ?"

Gabriel brushed the fur gently backwards. "She's still got her winter coat, but you can see the summer growth coming up here. She'd have been approaching her estrus, ready to breed as the snows melted."

"I hadn't realized that you were that much of an out-doorsman. Here . . ." Rainer strode around the container and beckoned to Gabriel. "Maybe you've seen one of these." He drew Gabriel's attention to a low-slung, six-legged, reptilian beast with a crest running down its back, twin incisors hanging from its mouth like the blades of a hunting knife.

"A Bekker's beaver," exclaimed Gabriel, disturbed at seeing this particularly unfriendly predator residing in a Kyara business office. "But . . . they're protected."

Rainer replied airily, "Mm, yes, usually, but the La-land authorities waived the ban in my case as a personal favor. This was a sick one, it was going to have to be culled anyway. See? It was missing one eye to cancer—

although I put it back when I was stuffing it—you can actually see the scar a bit . . . here." Rainer ran his finger along a ragged edge just under the beast's left eye.

"You stuffed this yourself?" Gabriel let his surprise show in spite of himself.

"Well, that's part of it, isn't it? Trying to recapture the sense of life and movement in a single pose." Rainer gave the Bekker's beaver a fond pat on the head. "Led us on one hell of a trek. I think we must have tracked him . . . oh, forty miles, something like that. Took us the better part of a week. Right up above the tree line."

Gabriel touched the deadly incisors. "I have to say I've never seen one up this close before."

Rainer grinned. "You wouldn't be here if you had."

Gabriel nodded in appreciation, taken for a moment by that intimate bond shared by fellow hunters. "Had one chase me up a tree once. I think I must have sat up there for three flockin' days, freezing my balls off."

"Yeah, they're persistent devils. Smart. See, I nailed him . . ." Rainer indicated a small patch of scorched hide—"right there. Through the frontal lobe. He was coming straight at me."

"Laser?" Gabriel frowned.

Rainer chuckled. "Not what you think." He rose and reached into the nearby container and drew out a finely carved, wooden rifle case. He flipped it open to reveal a slim, lightweight laser rifle. "You might appreciate this. Lovely, very light." He hefted it. "Catch." He threw it to Gabriel, who caught it one-handed and inspected it closely. It was an antique Mayburn of a model that Gabriel had not seen before. According to the date on the stock it was over a century old. As far as Gabriel could see, however, it was little more than a frame, without any kind of power pack or firing mechanism.

"That's a gentleman's hunting weapon," Rainer explained, retrieving it from him. In his free hand he was holding an oversize and very primitive power pack. With a practiced movement he slotted it into the frame, checking the safety catch was on as he did so. "Power pack and firing mechanism in one. Good for one shot. You miss, you've got to take it out and put a new one in. By that time your prey's probably halfway across the continent and not coming back. I play by the rules." His eyes twinkled mischievously. "Everything deserves a fair chance. And I like a gamble, don't you?" He tossed the loaded rifle back to Gabriel.

It was the last thing that Gabriel had been expecting and he nearly fumbled the catch. He covered his confusion by examining the rifle again. None of this was going the way he had expected. The interest the Byron Systems' chairman was now displaying seemed to be altogether genuine. He was clearly enjoying the opportunity to share a passion with a kindred spirit. Deliberately Gabriel returned Rainer's weapon to him.

Rainer stood caressing it, his gaze distant. "I think you've never really understood an animal until you've hunted it . . . hunted it properly, I mean. I'm not talking about those assholes who go cruising over barkon herds in floaters carrying cannons with banana clips full of heat-seeking bullets, where you can't bloody miss. Or even some of those sickos on Grayscape who hunt illegal GenTecs with so little wits they stand still whilst you walk up to them and blow their brains out. I mean real hunting, one on one . . . where you learn the creature's ways and you . . . build up a link between you and it. It's like a line of communication, made of . . . I don't know . . ."

"Respect," Gabriel suggested. Out of the corner of his eye he tracked the barrel of the rifle. But although it wafted slightly from side to side, Rainer kept is steadfastly pointed at the ground.

"Respect!" Rainer exclaimed. "Yes. Respect. You hunt out of respect, so that you've already met your prey, you've gotten to know him intimately before you've ever met him and the shot—the final shot—is just . . . a confirmation."

Gabriel nodded, discomfited. Despite his suspicions he was finding a lot to like in Saxon Rainer. Rainer leaned the rifle upright against the container, absently checking the safety again as he did so, and walked back to his desk where Isadora and Chuen were watching and listening to their exchange.

"I must say, Gabriel," he observed, "you're not really what I expected. You don't feel like a professional troublemaker and you're certainly not the kind of bumpkin that Naomi Sol said you were."

Gabriel snapped abruptly out of his musings. By the desk Isadora had come similarly alert and Chuen was standing with her glass of crème de menthe arrested halfway to her mouth. Tamara Lennox's translucent skin glowed with a cold light.

For a moment nobody said anything. Rainer himself broke the silence.

"Oh, come along." His grin was broad as ever, but there was suddenly something faintly chilling about it. "You didn't honestly think that Naomi was going to risk your being a professional hit man or something of the like, did you? With dastardly plans for me, and thereby setting herself up as an accomplice to something? I can't believe you're quite that naive. And you don't think my security's so lax that perfect strangers could stroll in here as easily as you all did this evening, do you?

"Look," he continued apologetically, "I didn't mean to deceive you, but when Naomi called me this afternoon I have to say I couldn't resist. It's a bad habit of mine, I have an ill sense of humor sometimes." He paused, then gestured at a chair. "C'mon, Gabriel, sit down."

Gabriel sat, cursing himself inwardly and trying not to let it show in his face. Rainer was wrong, he *was* a bumpkin. They must have laughed long and loud at him.

As if reading his thoughts, Rainer waved a dismissive hand. "Hey, she's a sick cow. You've seen that chamber of horrors of hers, with the GenTec dolphins and those poor, bloody birds." Rainer screwed up his face in disgust. "Anyway, when she called me, I couldn't resist meeting you face-to-face."

Isadora broke in uncertainly, "But . . . you use Gen-Tec. I've seen them in the park.

"Hm?" Rainer blinked. "Yes, of course. I had a burning, flocking row with Edom Japaljarayi about it, but you couldn't honestly expect me to have a pride of *lions* running about a public place, restraint collars or no restraint collars! You'd have an all-sirens alert every time some mother lost her five-year-old. GenTec has its place, if you use it appropriately. The lions and the other beasts we've got in the park are harmless, but they're happy and healthy enough. All we did was a bit of genetic claw-clipping.

"Anyway, Naomi told me she suspected that you were nothing but a victim of circumstances here on Thor. Any truth to that?"

Gabriel considered before answering. "If you mean by that that I just came here looking to say good-bye to my sister and not looking for any trouble from anybody, yes."

Rainer ran a hand through his beard, thumb and forefinger pulling outward from under his nose, along his moustache, before the flat of his palm dragged back over his chin and down his neck. "Well, you seem to attract trouble like bugheads to a free acrovak shipment." He chuckled again. "My, my, my. And here I was thinking that you were some kind of professional troublemaker sent here by . . . well, I don't know who by. Maybe some Earth authority. More fool me." He shook his head in good-natured rue at his own folly. His expression set and the red-gold flecks in his deep-set eyes appeared to glimmer of their own light. "Either way you've caused me and my business interests a great many problems . . . as have you two." He nodded at Isadora and Chuen. "Rather disloyal, considering you're employees of mine."

"We're journalists with an independently chartered news office," Isadora objected.

"Belonging to *me*. Still, news is a matter of consensus anyway, isn't it." Rainer reached for a slim silver box on his desk and lazily withdrew a length of nicotine root from it, which he popped into his mouth. The box rattled back onto the desktop. "My point," he went on, "is that, with all the best will in the world, I can't afford to have people running about the streets slandering both myself, personally, and this company and what it stands for . . . You do understand this. I mean, you *do* understand." For the first time a true aura of menace shone through Rainer's geniality.

Gabriel's weight shifted forward on his feet. He had consciously to loosen his shoulder muscles, which were as taut as a bridge cable.

"It's a pity." Rainer's voice took on a tinge of regret, as did his face. "Gabriel, at another time, we might have been friends. There's a lot to admire in you. Tamara?"

Without taking her eyes off Gabriel, Tamara Lennox spoke into her collar phone. "Yes."

Gabriel's hand was already reaching for his slumbergun when a rustle behind him told him that the door had opened and someone had entered. It was the twinkle in Rainer's eye that stopped him. He sagged and his hand dropped away from his weapon. Slowly he turned, already knowing what he would see. He was not disappointed.

He groaned. "Oh, no, not you again."

"I'm afraid so," said Pelham Leel. His slumbergun was already in his hand. "Mr. Rainer, Commissioner," he acknowledged each in turn.

The expression on Chuen's and Isadora's faces changed from shock to weary resignation.

Rainer explained unhappily. "It's not a personal decision of mine. You three made it yourselves when you decided to break into this building with these silly disguises. In legal parlance that's known as unlawful entry. It can fall under the Privacy Statutes and my legal department will do their best to see that it does. Tamara . . . well, I think the rest is up to you."

Saxon Rainer stood and strode into the shadows over by the window, standing with his back to them as if uninterested in any further proceedings. He cut a dark silhouette against the stars. With a twist of his heel he had banished them from his consciousness.

Tamara Lennox said softly, "They're all yours, Leel." Then she, too, rose and joined Rainer by the window.

Leel's tone became businesslike. "Mr. Kylie, Ms. Gatzalumendi, Ms. Lee, I have A.I. modules sealing off every entrance to this building. Mr. Rainer requested that I see to this with dispatch and without unnecessary violence, so I'm offering you the opportunity to come with me of your own free will. Personally I consider it's more than you deserve. Mr. Kylie, your slumbergun, please." He smirked. "I *think* you'll find it's inoperable anyway."

Feeling little more than contempt for his own stupidity, Gabriel retrieved the slumbergun that he had received from the KV 99 security chief and tossed it onto the ground. He had never even thought to check if it worked.

Twit!

"Ms. Gatzalumendi, please place your case on the desk, then move back." Leel continued down his list of formalities. Isadora hesitated and glanced at Gabriel. He frowned at her and shook his head slightly. There was no point any more in Isadora placing herself in any further jeopardy on his behalf.

"Place that case on the desk, Ms. Gatzalumendi," repeated Leel. The nose of the slumbergun remained pointed at Gabriel's midriff.

Isadora's nose tilted up in defiance.

Oh, no, don't do it, Iz, Gabriel's face betrayed some of his agitation.

With a saunter that seeped insolence with every step, Isadora obeyed and then backed away from the desk.

"I wouldn't open that, if I were you," she remarked sweetly, as Leel reached for it.

Leel's left eye narrowed slightly. Isadora's challenge was so transparent and yet . . . that transparency might in itself be a deception. Leel glanced down at the case.

"It's been scanned," Isadora added casually. "So it can wait until we get back to the bureau."

"Leel, is there a problem?" Tamara called from the window.

"No . . . no problem."

Gabriel's teeth were clenched so hard that his jaw ached.

The temptation was too much for Leel. Without taking his eyes off Gabriel, he thumbed the catch. The lid popped up with a chirp.

Then everything happened at once. In the same instant that Tamara Lennox cried, "Leel, wait . . . !" an olive green blur of fur and serrated teeth fastened itself to the TARC captain's fingers. Leel gave a yowl of both fear and pain, the one shot he managed to get off going wide. Then Gabriel's fingers closed on his wrist, twisting down and wrenching the slumbergun from his grasp. With his shoulder Gabriel knocked the TARC officer sprawling. The Helios weasel loosed its grip on Leel's fingers and scurried off into the darkness.

"Not you, Rainer! Not a move!" Gabriel had the slumbergun pointing at the figure of Saxon Rainer, who was already in a half crouch, set to flee.

the boatman's coin

Isadora cackled wickedly at Leel, who was clutching his fingers, hissing with pain. "What'd you think it was? My snake?"

"Flock it, you bitch . . ." Leel climbed to his feet, still trying to staunch the flow of blood.

Tamara Lennox walked toward Gabriel, hand held out, "Give me the weapon, Kylie. There's nowhere to go. Didn't you listen to what Captain Leel said? There are fifteen A.I. modules downstairs. It's going to take more that a pair of slaphappies to escape from this building."

"Chuen, check if there's a lock on that door," Gabriel ordered, and allowed the slumbergun to shift a few degrees in Lennox's direction. "Have you ever been hit with a nerve-shock, Commissioner?"

"Yes, it's part of standard TARC training," she replied calmly. "Now give me the weapon."

Gabriel could not help but admire her cool. He inquired. "Tell me something then. How many times in a row d'you reckon you could get hit with one before you're permanently drooling on your bib."

That stopped Lennox in her tracks. She shook her head pityingly, but the nervous dart of tongue over lips spoiled the effect slightly. "A threat against an officer of the law. You know, every time you open your mouth, Kylie, you add another year to your Retreat sentence. There aren't any extenuating circumstances this time. You entered this building of your own free will. That was unlawful entry; now you've made the grade to kidnapping."

Gabriel did his best not to react to what he knew was

the truth. "Hands where I can see them, all of you," was his reply.

He herded them all together into a sullen group near the desk. At which point he realized that he was unsure of what to do next. His hesitancy was evident to all. Leel smirked and Saxon Rainer and Tamara Lennox exchanged a knowing glance.

Rainer's eyebrows arched. "Well, here we all are," he said. "And I suppose we are all here for a reason. Was there anything in particular you wanted?"

Gabriel refused the temptation to let himself to be hurried. He perused Rainer, sought his own center of balance again. Isadora and Chuen were waiting expectantly. They had followed him this far, let him lead them down a dead-end Hall. Now was the moment for him to state his case and get them out. For an instant he allowed their faith to unnerve him, then got himself under control again.

"Well, yes, there is," he said at last. "I wanted to ask you why you killed Bulla."

There was a puzzled silence and everybody stared at him in surprise. Whatever they had been anticipating, this was not it.

"Who?" Chuen mouthed soundlessly to Isadora, who shook her own head in bemusement.

Saxon Rainer's, "Who?" was like an echo. Even Leel's face betrayed a hint of uncertainty and only Tamara Lennox remained inscrutable.

"Actually, 'why?' is more to the point." Gabriel reflected a moment more before continuing. "It's something I've kept asking myself ever since all this stuff began. Why? Why? I only . . . realized today—actually I was sitting in the toilet at your offices,"—he inclined his head at Leel—"and I only realized then that I'd been asking myself the wrong 'why?' I mean, it makes a difference."

"I can see that it might," Rainer said sardonically.

"Yes," Gabriel went on blithely. "Except for a couple of nights ago, when I was in a hotel with Iz here, I'd kept asking myself 'Why would someone have killed Elspeth?'. But then, when the answer to that started coming up, I wasn't really any closer to what I realized I wanted to know, which is why Elspeth would have given a toss?

Why would she have cared about all this? It was nothing
to do with her. And then I was on the loo and . . .
well . . ." Gabriel's hand rummaged through his pockets
for a moment. "It's . . . uh . . . hang on, here we go."
His hand emerged with the little bag containing the parakeelya seed. "Then I found this and I thought: Landing.
She brought this from home."

Rainer leaned forward and examined the bag dutifully,
as well as he could from that distance.

"Ah . . . sorry, you want to bear with me just for a
second. I'm sorry, I'm not very good at this." Gabriel
gave an apologetic, lopsided grin. "But it is worth your
time. You see, Elspeth caused you no end of bother and
that wasn't a coincidence. You know, you think, 'Why?
Why here? Why this place at this time?'—but, you know,
she came looking for you."

"For me?" Rainer looked blank.

"For you. Long ago she swallowed an old woman's
anger whole and wrapped it up in herself. She must have
dreamed you every night for over twenty years, all those
years she was searching. She'd never seen you, she never
knew who you were, until one day her Dreaming led
her here. And there you were. And it wasn't enough for
her to just get you—personally—she wanted to take you
down. *All* of you, everything you stood for. Everything
you were."

"And what is it that I am?" Rainer's tone betrayed a
certain amused fascination.

"Well . . . I'll tell you about an experiment they once
did, a couple of hundred years ago, with tropical fish."
With his free hand Gabriel brushed a strand of wayward
hair from his face. "See, they had two instincts, these
fish, opposite instincts. One was to swim to the center
of the school of fish and follow the other fish and the
other was to swim away in search of food. You'd get a
fish that would swim away from the center of the school
and some of the other fish would follow him. Then, as
they got further away from the center of the school,
some fish would turn tail and fall back to the center until
the lead fish would be almost alone and then he'd turn
back. The school would kind of fluctuate as some fish
pulled away and then fell back to the center. Then the
experimenters took one of the fish and removed half its

brain—the half with instinct to follow the other fish in it. So what happened? This one fish would swim out of the school to look for food . . . and just keep going. And the other fish would all follow him. Thousands of fish all following the one fish, and why? 'Cos he's got half a brain. The prerequisite of a tyrant."

"I'm sorry, Gabriel." Rainer's mouth was twitching. "Let me get this straight. You're comparing me to a half-brained tropical fish, is that right?"

Tamara Lennox emitted a snort of laughter and even Leel betrayed faint amusement. Beside him Gabriel felt Isadora attempting to suppress a wave of nervous giggles and studiously avoiding Chuen's eye.

"You're calling me a fish?" Rainer repeated, biting his lip to contain his mirth.

"No." Gabriel smiled his easy smile. "I'm calling you a callous, lying, thieving, poaching, poison-blooded, plague-pissing, murdering bastard."

The atmosphere of jocularity in the room vanished in the snap of an eyelash. Gabriel's eyes were blazing with fury. He could taste it now.

Leel took a pace forward, but Rainer waved him back. "Really," he said blandly. "And how do you come to that conclusion?"

"You ask Ellis Quinn Macintyre, who right now's dying in some Bugout Plaza sewage service tunnel, or . . . what's his name? . . . Magnus Westlake, who had to run INworld to get away from you, or the crew of the *Far Cry,* who never made it home, or those that did, like Heloise Amiée, who you had killed as well, just as you tried to have Iz here killed, and Chuen . . . and Elspeth. And you ask Lazarus Wight."

Rainer glanced at Lennox, then leaned forward, frowning, "Lazarus? Lazarus Wight? I haven't seen Lazarus in twenty-eight years. The last I heard he'd been institutionalized."

"Sure. Where you put him. My guess is that he was with you that day near Landing, when you and he were doing the Grand Tour together, and started threatening to crack once you got home. Unlike you, he had a conscience. So you served him a fabiana punch and fried his brains. And you did a good job, 'cos I've met him and the bloke's two fuses short of total disconnect."

"He was a friend of mine," Rainer said quietly. "We studied together." He paused. "Are you finished now, Mr. Gabriel Kylie?"

"Finished?" Gabriel's voice was trembling. So far Rainer had given nothing away. Gabriel knew how tenuous the thread he was spinning was, but he could *not* be wrong! He extended the slumbergun so that it was pointed right between Saxon Rainer's eyes. "Surely you jest! I'm just getting bloody started!"

"Alright, alright," Rainer held his hands up in a pacifying gesture. His gaze darted to Pelham Leel. "Alright. My, my, my."

Gabriel caught the look and smiled icily at the TARC officer. "I don't think so, Leel. You think I'm a murderer?—then believe this: one toyman sets foot out of that elevator . . ." He let the words trail off and snapped at Tamara Lennox. "And that goes for you, too. Because," he said tight-lipped, "it get's better. You see, the way it went was this: Elspeth hears of the *Far Cry* expedition from Heloise Amiée, whom she met in Rainer Park. Two people with a reason to hate you drawn to the same place. With this knowledge she goes digging through Cross Star Shipping, for whom she works as a freelance exterminator. Somewhere amongst the old cybertrash there she finds a reference to something called the blue box—it must have been overlooked when Cross Star changed hands from Byron Systems to KV 99. She shows it to KV 99, who enlist her to get it for them. And she does, with a little help from Lazarus Wight's roofrunners.

"Now, you couldn't go after Lazarus Wight directly—I don't think you knew at this point that he was involved—and you didn't dare go after him when you knew that he was, after all, he had what you wanted, *needed*. But you could go after Elspeth. Once you found out that she was also digging into Byron's Systems' books, checking through the shell companies that you had erected to disguise your real interests, you knew that you had to get her. So you set your little, one-handed assassin on her, the same friendly bugger that you later set on us. And then you stifled the investigation with the help of the snow queen here and her two-a-cue, pocket wide boys."

Leel bridled visibly, but succeeded in restraining himself.

"You needed Querin," Gabriel went on, his voice growing hoarse with the tension. "You would have settled for any other inhabitable planet, if one had been discovered, but Querin was the goal!

"Hoo, I'd love to have seen your whiskery face when the *Far Cry* turned up with the blue box and ten thousand mummified Querin corpses in a high-tech cold-sleep facility. *That's* a flocker of a secret to have to keep for twenty years, with StarrTX and the 'Hands Off Querin' lobby breathing down your neck. They would have killed your house-moving plans deader than a mummy's gums.

"So you saw to it that the *Far Cry* never made it back the second time around, and you squashed the few who were left behind like soft-backed beetles between your fingernails. Boxed them up, let them know that if they ever leaked a word they'd all go the same way. You fried Kam Fong's marbles with a fabiana o.d., just like you did Lazarus Wight when he became a threat. And then you killed Heloise Amiée . . . why? Because she spilled yogurt on your precious park lawn? And Elspeth. And *Bulla*?"

Saxon Rainer reached for his chair and sank into it, his face suddenly drawn with fatigue. "Alright, Gabriel," he said wearily, "alright. If I may say something here?" He waited until Gabriel had given his acquiescence, then continued. "Now, I've sat here . . . we've all sat here . . . patiently and listened to this exposé of yours. You'd dredged up this whole mad conspiracy out of some Bug-out Plaza gutter and now you—" He broke off and passed a hand across his face with a mirthless laugh. "Now, first of all, you want to tell me—and these good people assembled here—that somehow, out of . . . ah, twenty-two and a half *billion* people, I think the last count was . . . on seventeen *planets,* somehow you've come to the conclusion that I am the person your sister was sent to find . . . for some reason that's not quite clear to me? I'm supposed to be guilty of shooting some old man through the head in some benighted . . . *bush* thirty years ago . . . is that it?"

Rainer's face was bleak. "Look, you lost your sister.

That was tragic. Now, isn't there enough of that in God's own universe without creating more out of . . . ?" He made a gesture with his hand as if he were plucking something out of his head and casting it to the winds. "Hm?" His voice was calm, measured, inviting belief. He waited expectantly.

But Gabriel was momentarily bereft of speech. He had thought he'd known, sitting in the TARC toilet cubicle. He had been certain that he'd known. But he realized now that, until this instant, he had not truly *known*. Saxon Rainer had changed that.

"Tell me," Gabriel said when he could trust himself to speak again. "Do you know anything about Native Australian names?"

Rainer looked puzzled. "Aus . . . No, should I? Ayers Rock, isn't that Native Australian?"

"Uluru," Gabriel corrected him. "We call it Uluru. No, I was just wondering if maybe you'd picked up some knowledge from Edom Japaljarayi."

"We hardly speak. Not with much civility, anyway," Rainer added drily.

"Hm," Gabriel mused. "Well, it struck me, if you don't know anything about Native Australian names, then how did you know that Bulla was an old man?"

Nobody moved. For the first time Rainer seemed a little taken aback. "I . . . well, wasn't he?"

"Sure he was," Gabriel said sadly. "We used to call him Uncle Bull; he had a grin that could melt ice cream. Bulla was an old man and he was once loved by a woman who was old like a tree when I last saw her, when she died. She never forgave those who killed her Bulla and, to her own later shame, she gave the burden of her anger to her granddaughter to carry to the stars. But . . . I never said he was an old man before you mentioned it. For that matter, I never mentioned he'd been shot through the head either."

Isadora realized that her jaw was hanging open and closed it quickly. Saxon Rainer's left hand was resting on the table, clenching and unclenching slowly. At long last Rainer seemed to slump. "As a matter of fact," he said, "it wasn't I who shot him; it was Lazarus." He pointed to the laser rifle still leaning against the container. "I was using one of those. I'd just taken down a 'roo. My reloading charges were in my backpack, so I couldn't have shot him if I'd wanted to. He came out of the bush and saw the 'roo." Rainer shrugged. "Lazarus panicked and shot him before I could do anything."

Tamara Lennox broke in, "Mr. Kylie, have you finished? I'm still wondering if you really think you can get away with any of this."

"It's alright, Tamara"—Rainer laid a hand on her arm—"Gabriel, look, why don't you come to whatever point you're leading up to. So far, all anyone here has heard is the most convoluted conjecture . . . I mean, it's beyond me how you've managed to come up with any of it . . . just think for a second, alright? Just think. Now, the only thing you've got that is in any way concrete— which I think is where all the rest of this springs from— is this analysis? Which claims that Byron Systems does not own anything here on Kyara, alright?"

"Is it so?"

Rainer shrugged. "Yes, of course it is, why should I deny it? It's in no way illegal; it's not even unethical. As far as the fact that it hasn't been exactly publicized is concerned, well, that's simply good business practice."

"Good business practice?" Chuen burst out incredulously.

"Yes, good business practice," Rainer replied matter-of-factly. "In this day and age—for that matter in yesterday's day and age and the day before's yesterday's day and age—the one advantage one has as a businessperson is secrecy. You have to be secretive to stay one step ahead of the competition. Gabriel, you can't be any stranger to secrecy. I wouldn't presume to claim to know anything about the customs of Native Australians, but I'm quite sure that secrecy isn't unknown in your culture. The Elders have secrets from the junior members. Well, in this business, I'm the Elder. Of *course* I'm going to keep secrets! Wouldn't you? And being one place when everyone thinks you're another is quite a secret to have, don't you think?"

"Sleight of hand."

"More than that. Sleight of mind." Rainer's manner grew intense, one finger pressed against his forehead. "Up here. It moves. Watch it, watch it, gone! That's the trick. You want to muddle your metaphors a little further, then forget the goldfish and think shark. A lot of people have called me that, meaning that I've got a lot of teeth and an insatiable appetite. Small-time, small-minded." His detractors were dismissed with a flick of his fingers. "They've got the metaphor right, but they've missed the point. The shark . . . you're from Earth, I assume you know something about sharks?"

Gabriel affirmed, "I wouldn't tickle one's tonsils with a bare arm."

"Okay. A shark is dynamism incarnate. In certain respects it's very primitive, it has to keep swimming to breathe. If it stops, it asphyxiates and sinks, so it has to keep moving, moving, growing. That's the nature of society, it's the nature of business, the nature of what I do. We, as creatures, we're negatively weighted. If we stop, we sink. It's essential. You have to keep moving, you've got to keep moving, dynamic! dynamic! alive!" Rainer's fists punctuated his speech with short, quick jabs in the air. "It's the mistake we always make, we build something up, a society, a company, then we reach a certain self-imposed limit. Either we're too flocking scared or we're too flocking stupid to strive any higher, but we stop, we crystallize. Then we try to impose a permanence with laws or . . . who knows? . . . rules of some kind and bang! It's over. That's it, with the slap of a palm on a contract, we sign our own death warrant! We've stopped moving and we spend the rest of our lives— or the rest of society's life—sinking to the bottom of the ocean.

"For heaven's sake, d'you know how many . . . have you ever *looked* at the laws we have? Not looked, *read*? The Privacy Laws, the Proscribed Technologies Statutes? That's what's holding us back! That's what's killing us! You can't change the shape of a flocking urinal without Pros-Tech approval by seventy-seven law courts and subcommittees. 'Sorry, I've got a pecker the size of a hangcar, it doesn't fit.' 'Then grow a smaller one!' 'I tried, but you rejected my appeal for GenTech adjustment,'" Saxon Rainer gave a bark of laughter and leapt to his feet. He must have seen Gabriel's weapon hand twitch, because instantly he became very still and his expression turned sheepish. "My apologies. I get a little . . . carried away."

"No worries." Gabriel eased his finger off the trigger. His palm was greasy with sweat. That was the danger of a weapon, any weapon, that was so often overlooked. Once it was in your hand, it always took on a life of its own.

Rainer remained standing. "Gabriel. Look around you. Look at all this. My grandfather built all this. From nothing. He created Byron Systems from *nothing*. Isn't that something?"

"If we're right, darling, your something is nothing again, since you don't own any of this anymore," Chuen put in caustically.

Rainer betrayed his annoyance by ignoring her and keeping his attention on Gabriel. "It's time. The law of dynamism dictates it. Either we move on, either Byron Systems moves on, or it dies. I die. So we will move on! It's the nature of a man to build, to build things! To create! To pro-create! Co-create! You don't want to? That's your prerogative, but then move out of the way. *That*—" Rainer broke off apologetically. "Well, that's my little slice of armchair moralism, Gabriel. Perhaps it answers your question?"

Gabriel considered. "Hm. I keep thinking about a mate of mine back on Helios—Marvin. He ran a pub and used to make his own beer out of real hops that he had grown. Every batch was different, he kept trying all kinds of things, you know, adding cherries, more, less, importing water, whatever. Never tried to market it, just flogged it in his pub and he never made it the same way twice. Kept trying to find the perfect beer. As far as I know, he never did, but, boy, we drank some fine beers along the way."

Rainer looked nonplussed. "I gather there's some moral hidden in there about the best things in life being for free?" he sighed.

"Are you kidding? The bugger charged ten cue a bottle!"

Once again a smirk played around Saxon Rainer's mouth. "Well, *is* there a moral, Gabriel?"

"No, not really, at any rate not one you'd understand. Except that Marvin never had to kill anybody to get them out of his way."

"And I would . . . so *you* say." Rainer leaned his fists

on the desk. "Quiz me this, Gabriel, what if I would? What if I was the cyclops, with a big, lighted sign in my eye saying, 'Outta the way or get crushed!' And they didn't. Who's to blame? Me? Them? I'm clear about my intention *and* my shoe size. Isn't there a nonpareil honesty about that? Isn't that clean?" He laughed gently, deep, rippling laughter, and said ruefully, "It's a moral cleanliness we could all wish for. Instead, we've built our glass cage and we can't move without breaking off a few bars and being punished for it. But it would be a pleasant fantasy . . . I go my way . . . you go yours."

"Except I can't anymore, can I? Thanks to you."

"Ah, but that was your choice, wasn't it? You didn't read the sign."

"So I'm right."

There was a pause. "No."

"Then why?"

"Then why what?" Rainer sighed in exasperation. "Now what, Gabriel? I'm doing my best here . . ."

"Yeah, you are," Gabriel agreed. "But you still haven't told me why."

"Why *what*?"

"Why would you want to move everything off Kyara?"

"Look, if anyone else left it wouldn't make a blasted bit of difference, but if Byron Systems suddenly floods the market with its assets, the bottom of the market would fall out. We'd lose trillions, because everyone would suddenly get nervous . . ."

"No, no, not why the secrecy, I can see that. No, I mean, why move at all? With the setup that Byron Systems has here on Kyara, why move at all? Why move to Querin? Why move anywhere?"

Rainer took a deep breath. "*That* is a complicated question . . ."

"Oh, no, it's a real simple question."

"Alright then, it has a complicated answer . . ."

"No, no, answer's simple, too."

Rainer rolled his eyes heavenward, "And I suppose you've got the answer to that as well?"

"Yes, as a matter of fact," Gabriel said cheerfully. "You couldn't . . . stay."

"I . . . couldn't stay," Rainer repeated, scowling.

"The Loki file."

Rainer's scowled deepened.

"Sleight of hand again," Gabriel explained. "You see, you never gave a damn about the blue box. So you could destroy a world at the push of a button. We've been able to do that for centuries! You ever seen the Glass Deserts? Where's the profit in that—unless you manufacture Geiger counters? No-no. What scared you wasn't what the *Far Cry* brought back. It was what they found when they got home! Something that someone like you could never deal with because it goes against your humanocentric delusions.

"You see, the *Far Cry* passed over the pole at a distance of ten klicks with all survey instruments running. That's the closest thing to a survey this planet's undergone in forty years. And Kam Fong was watching and he found something that scared the living shit out of you and made you realize that you had to get the hell off this planet."

"Oh, yes?" Rainer said mildly. "And what was that?"

Gabriel held up the parakeelya seed. "Life," he said.

Rainer never flinched, but something deep in his gaze stirred. *Bull's-eye!*

Gabriel radiated his glee. "Oh, yes. That was Loki's trick on you and Kam Fong was your Loki. The last thing anyone would have expected to find on the surface of Thor. What kind of form it has, I couldn't say. I haven't seen the survey results. I couldn't even speculate on how Kam Fong recognized it. But I can take a guess that it isn't going to be friendly. Not to us, anyway. Look out of that window! Look!" Gabriel jabbed a finger out at the Anvil. "You tell me what kind of life's going to be born out of that!"

"But," Isadora ventured dubiously, "why wouldn't anybody have spotted it earlier?"

Gabriel laughed. "Flock, *how*? How? How long have we been on Thor? Less than a hundred years? Thor's year is eight hundred years long. When Ellis Quinn Macintire was born he had no shadow. Today the sun casts a shadow on the pavement. It's springtime! We arrived at the tail end of winter and now spring is here! How could we have recognized a dormant planet? But now the rains have come, and it's *glorious*!

"This whole flockin' planet is going to come alive—it's coming alive right now, right under our feet—and it scares the shit out of you, Rainer, because there's nothing you can do about it. Nothing. What are you going to do? Irradiate the planet? Ha! There's enough hard radiation hitting Thor's surface every second to kill any Earth life in a matter of minutes. Bet you Thor life'll just lap it up. There's *nothing* you can do.

"And where's that going to leave Kyara, *your* Kyara? You think any one of those four million people is going to hang about? Face it . . . well, you already have. Of course you couldn't tell anybody about it! Byron Systems has made damned sure that there hasn't been a survey of Thor in decades. The fact is that when this gets out nothing in Kyara's going to be worth anything! And Byron Systems *is* Kyara. Or, at least," Gabriel added acerbically, "it was."

For long minutes nobody said anything. Lennox sat like a salt-crystal statue, Rainer, expression thoughtful and fingers tapping the desk. Isadora and Chuen broadcast disbelief which gradually metamorphosed into realization as Rainer continued not to respond. Pelham Leel seemed oddly withdrawn.

At last Rainer shifted in his chair. "Gabriel, with all due respect, do you think it's likely that—if all this were true—I would have allowed you to be released from prison?"

Before Gabriel could reply, Isadora said, "Sure, if you thought that keeping us there would raise a bigger media stink than letting us go. And with KV 99 behind us and me being a wave-buzzard, it would be quite a stink."

"Besides," Gabriel picked up her thread, "you're on your way now." He gestured at the containers. "You're all packed and ready to go, now that you've got what you . . ." Gabriel broke off. *Now that you've got what you want.*

What WOULD you want?

"Now that you've got the blue box back," he finished. From the way Saxon Rainer's gold-flecked eyes narrowed, he knew that his guess was right. He mused. "And what would you have to pay in return . . . ? Who would have the blue . . . box? *Yes!* You gave Lazarus

Wight the plans to Rainer Park! That's what he wanted and *he* had the blue box!"

"Are you guessing here?"

"Am I wrong here? What did you give him?"

Saxon Rainer moved in his chair again, his unease growing. "Gabriel, are you going to keep this up much longer?"

"What did you give him?" Gabriel was losing patience and he let it show. Rainer's smugness was starting to gall.

"Nothing that wasn't mine to give."

"Rainer Park. You gave him the plans to Rainer Park."

At this point Tamara Lennox broke in. "Kylie, that's illegal, he wouldn't be allowed to do that . . ." She broke off at Gabriel's scornful look, aware of how patently absurd her words sounded. She didn't even need to add anything about mental blocks. There was no doubt anymore that Rainer could have avoided submitting to one if he had really wanted.

"Why would he want the plans?" Gabriel asked, still keeping his voice pleasant.

Laughing, Rainer threw his arms out helplessly. "Look, Gabriel . . ."

"Sure, Saxon," Gabriel drawled. "Why would he want the plans?"

Rainer reacted at the use of his first name, then conceded the point to Gabriel with a pointed finger and a mischievous wink. "Gabriel, in all seriousness, how am I supposed to know that?"

Gabriel wasted no more time on him. His weapon shifted a few degrees, until it was aimed at Pelham Leel. "Leel, I want you to call Edom Japaljarayi. Make it an official call."

"Forget it, Kylie, it's out of the question," Tamara Lennox said quickly.

Gabriel addressed Leel amiably. "Leel, you know how much I like you. Using that as a guide, maybe you can work out just how much it would hurt me to hurt you."

Chuen jumped in, "Oh, then can I? Please? Can I? Can I?"

Pelham Leel got the hint. Avoiding his commissioner's gaze, he reached for his phone.

"Ah, no," Gabriel stopped him. "Use the main phone; I'd like visual. Here, Chuen . . ." He handed the slumbergun to Chuen, who took it with evident delight.

Within a few moments Leel had circumvented Edom Japaljarayi's home receptionist and they were greeted by the sight of Edom's disgruntled face glaring sleepily out at them.

"Officer, do you know how late it is . . . ?" Edom's voice trailed off as Leel stepped out of the viewframe and Gabriel took his place.

"Edom, it's Gabriel Kylie."

Edom said plaintively, "I can see that. Why is it every time the police call I end up talking to you or Isadora Gatzalumendi? I'm not supposed to be talking to either of you."

Gabriel was in no mood for this. "Edom, why would somebody want the plans to Rainer Park?" he asked brusquely.

"Is this a riddle?"

"If somebody had the entire plans, all the technical specifications, everything from the floor up, of Rainer Park. What use would that be? What could they do with them?"

Edon said dismissively, "Nobody would have the plans."

"What if they did?" Gabriel insisted.

"Nobody would."

"But what if they *did*?"

"Look, Mr. Kylie, maybe I'm not making myself clear. There is nobody on Thor or anywhere else who would ever be permitted to have that information. I have it and Saxon Rainer has it . . . look, where are you calling from?" Edom peered out of the display suspiciously.

Gabriel ignored his question. "Edom, what could he or she do with the plans if they had them."

Edom yawned. "Well, anything they want? They'd have the plans."

"They could do anything to Rainer Park. Sabotage it, destroy it."

"Well, yes, they'd know the Icarus grid layout and the location of the generators . . . what is this about? In a couple of seconds I'm going to hang up and phone the real police."

"One last question," Gabriel said. "Just one. Why would it be inscribed in the law that all those with knowledge of the Rainer Park grid would have to undergo a mental block operation?"

Edom looked puzzled. "I just told you. They could sabotage the park . . ."

Gabriel tried to control his impatience, "Yes, I get that. And I can understand why Byron Systems would insist on it, but why *by law*? I mean, for the park. Why by law?"

"Ah, I see your point. Uh . . ." He hesitated. "Well . . . I don't quite know quite how to put this in layman's terms . . . In the case of the park, for instance, it was necessary for me to know the direction feed of the city grid at the point of contact between the park grid and the main city grid. You need to know that to avoid gravity fluctuations at the point of contact. This was incorporated onto the plans. If someone had the plans to the park, they could use that information to find the precise location of the city generators."

"Flamin' bloody strewth," Gabriel murmured, appalled. "Thanks, Edom." He broke the connection and turned ever so slowly back to Saxon Rainer. Their eyes locked. Rainer tugged gently at his moustache.

"You knew," Gabriel whispered, stunned. "You knew."

"Knew what?" Rainer inquired blandly. The half-moon whites of his manicured nails stroked at his moustache.

"Lazarus Wight is going to bring his people back to the soil," Gabriel replied. "He's going to bring Kyara back to the soil."

Isadora burst out, "Wait a second, you don't mean . . ." She had gone white.

Gabriel set his lips in a tight line. "He's going to blow the flockin' generators. He's going to bring the whole city back to Thor's soil and you"—he shook his head disbelievingly—"you knew. You . . . That would make it all so simple for you, wouldn't it. No more loose ends. At all. Four million voices silenced."

Saxon Rainer groaned in mock despair. "Gabriel, Gabriel, Gabriel, this is getting grander and grander. You start out by accusing me of killing one person, now you're going to accuse me of wanting to kill *four million*?"

"You already have," Gabriel murmured in awe. "You already have. You don't even see them when you look out of your window. You've already wiped them out."

"Just like that, huh? Like magic." Saxon Rainer leaned back in his chair. "Well, there we are, then. If this is what you believe . . ."

"Oh, I do."

"Good for you. Then what are you going to do? You've got me here . . . along with the commissioner of Targeting, Apprehension and Remand Central and one of her officers. The cast is assembled. Where does that leave us?"

"I'm not sure," Gabriel admitted. "The last time I had three people at gunpoint I got myself in quite a bit of trouble." He laughed uneasily and bit at his lip. "Um . . . Chuen, maybe I'd better . . ." Gabriel retrieved the slumbergun from her.

"Wise move." Rainer placed his fingertips together on the desk. "Look, Gabriel, if I may. Officer Leel, I hear you're an amateur magician."

Leel started.

Rainer continued good-naturedly, "The commissioner here's told me about it. You can make things disappear; rings, pebbles, small things, large problems. Aah, don't be shy, dexterity's a good thing to have. Do you know the story about the deaf and dumb magician, who stuttered whenever his hands shook?" Rainer chuckled at the blank looks that this elicited from everyone except Gabriel. In this day's society both blindness and deafness were all but extinct. "Never mind, I'll tell you, Gabriel, there's a fable you might like . . . Magnus Westlake wrote me a few lines of fatuous rhetoric before he went on the INworld . . . I didn't get it until I heard he'd gone IN.

"There was a great magician and someone once asked him, 'What is the difference between real magic and illusion?'

"And he replied, 'Nothing but the size of the rabbit.' "

" 'I don't understand,' she replied.

"So he said, 'Watch,' " Rainer held out his hands, palm up. His movements were careful and deliberate.

"No sleight of hand . . . nothing up my sleeves." He matched his actions to his words, tugging gently at each sleeve in turn. His eyes were soft. He held out his hands again, palms down and squeezed into fists.

" 'That you must believe.' Then the magician said, 'Because in order for you to believe in what you think of as magic . . . you've first got to believe that something cannot be, in order for you to think of it as magic when it does. But for you to believe only in illusion, you have to continue to believe that it cannot happen, even when it has.' The difference is just in the degree of doubt, or the strength of your initial belief."

Isadora glanced from Rainer to Gabriel. His weapon wavered uncertainly.

Rainer continued, "Real magic is in transcending the belief and transcending the doubt. Because when you do then nothing is magic"—his left hand turned, opened to reveal an empty palm—"Or everything is." Isadora watched the fingers of his right hand uncurl, one by one.

In the palm of Rainer's hand lay three silver hornets.

Isadora's cry of warning caught in her throat. Gabriel did not need to hear it, her description of the drones that had attacked her in her apartment had been vivid enough. A wasp scream filled the air and three sparks of light flicked from Saxon Rainer's palm toward Gabriel, Isadora, and Chuen. The slumbergun was already tumbling from his fingers when Gabriel stepped forward, without thinking, without regret, just noting ruefully that somewhere along the way death had crept up onto his shoulder and he hadn't noticed.

The prize had been a watch with an inbuilt phone and global positioning system, something all three boys had coveted and Uncle Bull had laughed at. "Never bin lost in my life," he'd chortled. "What d'yer need a G.P.S. for if you know the songs of the land? Y'know the trees, y'know the ground, y'can feel the nice places where the djang comes bubbling out o' the rocks."

But boys will be boys will be chrome-obsessed little sods and what could be more enticing than a toy to let you know where you were, when you were and one with the means to call and tell everyone why.

So they waited until a moment when the flies were thick in the air and they grabbed! Three tries each. Dig-Dig

*and Billy Halfpint had panned out at three flies apiece,
Dig-Dig on his third try, Billy on his second. But Gabriel,
ooh, Gabriel, that had been a day. Dig-Dig had com-
plained afterward that two of Gabriel's flies had been having a midair screw, but that was well within the rules,
Uncle Bull had wisely said. "Y'choose your moment,
that's a part of the game."*

*Gabriel's right hand had swept through the air,
snapped shut with buzzing life between his fingers and
when he had opened it there they were. Four flies, all
iridescent blue and bad-tempered.*

Three was a piece of cake.

Gabriel's right hand swept through the air, snapped
shut with buzzing death between his fingers. One, *click*!
two! The third was too far, darting directly toward Isadora's stricken face. *Y'choose your moment . . .* On the
other hand, if y'choose a bad moment, y'change the rules
of the game.

He reeled off-balance as his left hand darted out as
well, closed on metal and porcelein. There was no real
pain, just a mild sting as needles entered the palms of
his hands and a burning—did he imagine it?—that
flowed up his arms. Either way, it was all alright. The
room swept about him, Pelham Leel, Saxon Rainer, Tamara Lennox, Chuen and Isadora. Somewhere an Old
Man laughed with glee. And then the floor smote the
living breath from Gabriel Kylie.

thor's hammer

Isadora watched in helpless horror as Gabriel toppled to the ground. She did not even react as Leel leapt forward and snatched up Gabriel's weapon. She saw only Gabriel's still body, prone on the wooden floor, his onyx eyes staring blindly at the ceiling. Isadora's breath came in short spasms, as if someone had clamped a toothed vice to her lungs. Her throat ached, tears of rage flooded her eyes.

"Oh, Goddess," Chuen whispered next to her.

Leel was fiddling with his slumbergun, which seemed to be jammed, muttering epithets. Neither Tamara Lennox nor Saxon Rainer had moved.

"Damn it." Tossing the weapon aside, Leel turned to confront Gabriel. He stopped and his eyes widened. Cautiously he approached Gabriel's body until he was standing over him. "He's . . . dead."

Tamara Lennox spoke. "Search him. See that he has nothing else on him." Her words clanged in Isadora's ears, their actual meaning lost. She only heard Leel repeating, "He's dead."

Leel himself was slow in obeying. His expression was rigid as he knelt beside Gabriel's body, studiously ignoring the three silver beads that now lay as lifeless as Gabriel himself on the floor next to his outstretched arms.

"My, my, my, that was a trick," Rainer said at last, rising from his seat. There was admiration in his tone. "Quick hands. I wouldn't mind learning that one myself."

Isadora turned to face him, filled with hatred. She could no longer bear to watch Leel; his searching of Gabriel was like a defilement. He had reached Gabriel's

breast pockets and seemed almost to be staring down
into his face.

"Gabriel," Isadora said softly.

"Yes," Rainer replied complacently, "there's no question he was a brave man. Unfortunately, one fine quality
does not a living hero make. Now, as for you two . . ."

He got no further, for at that moment Leel gave a
grunt of pain. Isadora was just in time to see Leel apparently caught in a grotesque struggle with Gabriel's
corpse. Gabriel's hands were grasping him by the lapel
and he had apparently just kneed the TARC officer in
the testicles, because Leel's eyes were almost bugging
out of his head. With one wrench Gabriel threw Leel to
one side, rising from the ground like a black banshee
spirit, his ragged coat a pillar of smoke.

Isadora felt herself growing dizzy and squeezed her
eyes shut for a moment. When she opened them again
Saxon Rainer's face was a mask of dread and incomprehension. "But . . ." His mouth worked. "There was
enough statrecks in there to stop the heart of an
elephant . . ."

"Yes, but, you see"—Gabriel's smile was death itself—"I have no heart."

In three strides he was around the desk, moving like
a wraith. Saxon Rainer was too petrified to move,
ghoulie eyes wide as platters, a hare gripped in headlight
fascination. Gabriel watched his face grow bigger and
bigger, caught in his own fascination, watched it grow
until there was nothing else, until it was close enough to
reach out and hit. And then he did. Gabriel grabbed
him by the collar and drew his fist back, squeezed his
rage and his grief like soft cheese in his fingers. Mashed
a thousand memories that welled up into a tight, white-
hot clench. Uncle Bull, laughing at the world seen
through his beer-bottle telescope; Grandmother Lalumanji's old-worldly love and cactus giggles; Elspeth
chuckling threads of well-aimed water through her teeth
in the lake under Mackay's Rock . . .

Elspeth . . .

With the first blow he felt Rainer's nose turn and
break, the cartilage snapping like soft whalebone beneath his knuckles, and Rainer's head snap backwards.
Only then did the Byron System's chairman raise his

arms to ward off the attack, but by then it was already too late. Gabriel groaned like a dying tree, sobbed deep and heavy . . .

Heloise . . .

They saw that the one who gets in the first blow has won the fight and Gabriel had. With Gabriel's second punch Saxon Rainer's whole body spasmed, like that of a rag doll on a jerking string. Gabriel skinned his knuckles on the broken edges of Rainer's teeth, but he sucked in the pain like air, and rained blow after blow . . .

Uncle Bull . . .

Saxon Rainer whimpered, his body all ropey now.

You're sorry now aren't you? You're sorry now . . . and now . . . and NOW . . .

Gabriel's left hand clamped around Rainer's throat, his right hand grasped his hair. He drove forward, deliberately impacting Rainer's skull against one of the free-standing pillars. Rainer's eyes rolled back in his head and suddenly his full body weight was hanging from Gabriel's fingers. His beard and moustache glistened black with fresh blood, his breath bubbled out of his throat. And then something changed.

Perhaps it was the sound of the welling agony of his breath, but Saxon Rainer became a person again. Gone was the Bogy, gone was the killer, there was a man under his fingers. Gabriel was aware of his fury draining out of him and there was nothing he could do to stop it. God, he wanted to stop it. He pursued it, grasped at it, but it oozed from his grasp like melting butter. The world around him caved in upon him, roaring its presence—"We're here!"—drew him back from the brink. He realized that he had been screaming each name out loud, a vivid, bestial howl of rage, and his face was wet with tears.

As his own screaming stopped he was able to hear Isadora shrieking at him, "Gabriel! Stop! Stop!" She was clawing at his arm, trying to pull him away, pleading, "Stop, please, stop . . ."

Then another voice rose above hers. "Drop him, Kylie, *now*! Let him go!"

Pelham Leel was standing on the far side of the desk, Saxon Rainer's hunting laser shouldered and aimed at Gabriel's head. For an instant Gabriel thought of hurling

Saxon Rainer's body at Leel, using him as a shield. Then he realized how little he cared anymore. Death had left him and the bitter hopelessness he felt now was akin to a second death. He felt sickened at his own savagery, recognizing how much of himself he had had to hack away to achieve it. That had been the true dying.

He loosened his grip on Saxon Rainer's neck, let him slip and crumple to the floor, where he coughed feebly, dabbing at his face.

Tamara Lennox stepped forward. "Well done, Leel. Good work." She took a deep breath, considering. "Alright," she rapped. "Look, get these three out and into custody, send an A.I. with medic programming up here. I'll take care of Rainer till it arrives . . ."

"Not so fast." Leel's voice was granite. The laser rifle pivoted sixty degrees and came to rest on the TARC commissioner's chest.

For the first time true astonishment showed on the face of Tamara Lennox. "Leel? What are you doing? Have you . . . ?"

"No, Commissioner, not a step." Leel flipped his collar. "Hanna, get up here with two ranking officers, no A.I.s, repeat, no A.I.s! . . ." He broke off. "Don't even think it, Commissioner!"

Lennox's hand stopped halfway to her phone. "Leel, what do you think you're doing? What's it going to accomplish? You're in this as deep as I am."

"No, Commissioner, I beg to differ. A lot of what I've heard tonight, I've heard for the first time."

"That may be so, but it doesn't change a thing, Leel. Now you know, you're privy, there is no way back."

"No way back? What about the line, Commissioner. You remember the line? The one we weren't supposed to step over?"

Gabriel watched this exchange as if from a great distance, as if his only hold on the moment was through Isadora's grip on his arm. Chuen, whom he had completely forgotten about, piped up suddenly, "Excuse me, darling, I'm confused."

"Stay where you are!" Leel shook a droplet of sweat out of his eyes. His jaw was clenching and unclenching spasmodically. Gabriel had never seen the man in this state before. "Now, I know that line's a little flexible

when it comes to preserving social order. I fail to see
how any of what I've seen in the last half hour preserves
any social order. Would you care to explain it to me?"

"Leel," Tamara Lennox said carefully, "you're making a mistake if you think you can get away with this.
You know that, or you wouldn't have left the A.I. modules downstairs. You know damned well they'll take my
orders over yours."

"No mistake," the TARC Captain rasped. "None.
None. None."

There was a faint rustle of fabric and three figures
appeared in the doorway, two men led by a fair-haired
woman, whom Gabriel recognized as one of Leel's side-
kicks, Hanna Bork.

"What's this?" she asked in surprise, taking in the
scene before her.

Both Leel and Lennox spoke at the same time, each
attempting to shout down the other.

He: "I'm making an in-house arrest of Commissioner
Lennox for accessory to attempted murder and conspiracy to . . . to . . . damn it, I don't even know what to
call it . . ."

She: "Officer, arrest this man, now!"

Lennox was the more convincing of the two and one
of the TARC agents drew his weapon, presumably to
arrest Leel, as ordered. Bork stopped him with a curt
gesture.

"Pelham, what's going on? That's the commissioner."

"I know it's the commissioner!" Leel said impatiently.
"That's the whole point, that's why I told you to bring
those two. Now, take her!"

Lennox said calmly, "Officer, I want this man arrested
now, for conspiracy to murder, or it's going to be your
mark!"

"Bork," Leel said. "You want to arrest me, that's at
your discretion. But if you do, then make sure you arrest
everybody in this room!"

"Hey, just a second . . ." Chuen objected.

"I told you to stay where you were!" Leel snapped.

"I *am* staying where I am," Chuen replied sullenly.

Gabriel spoke up. "Maybe I can help . . ."

Leel shouted, "Kylie, you shut up as well!"

Hanna Bork moved forward, palms open. "Pelham,

put the gun down, stike, or I'm going to have to drop you."

The man who had originally drawn his weapon drew it once more, and said, "Hanna, I'm going to have to drop him anyway, that's a laser he's holding."

"Do it!" Lennox commanded. "Right now! I order it!"

"Wait!" That was Bork.

Isadora, brushing at her eyes with the back of her hand, attempted to intervene. "Officer, if you want to be here a few hours from now, you'd better listen to what we have to say . . ."

Bork pointed at him. "I don't want anybody speaking unless I tell them to."

Leel began, "Sergeant, listen to her . . ." Lennox tried to drown him out, but Leel raised his voice to a roar. "Right now there's a pack of roofrunners out there, who know the precise location of the main generators! Do you understand what I'm saying? They know it and they're planning to use that knowledge!"

"The Icarus generators?" Bork paled.

"Yes, the Icarus generators. Four million lives, Hanna, including yours."

Lennox began, "Sergeant . . ."

"Quiet!" Bork ran a shaky hand through her hair.

The trigger-happy TARC tried to speak up again. "Bork, we've got to drop him."

"You too!" Bork turned on him in exasperation. "Look, what is wrong with you? Huh? Just put it away, I need to think a second." She licked her lips. "Pelham, if I go along with this, you'll give yourself into custody?"

"Of course."

Lennox hissed, "Sergeant Bork, you're about two seconds away from a terminal career move!"

"Do you mind, Commissioner? I . . . Commissioner, if you're right and Officer Leel here is wrong, then there shouldn't be any problem with everybody coming with me."

"Sergeant, did you hear what I said?"

"Yes, Commissioner, I did." Bork took a deep breath. "Alright, let's get some A.I. modules up here. Arrest everybody."

"Arrest everybody?" The trigger-happy TARC gaped.

"Among the four of us, we outrank the commissioner. I'll take responsibility. We'll sort it out back at Central." The two other TARC officers were clearly unhappy with this, but after a moment's vacillation they obeyed, moving into the room and wielding their slumberguns like cattle prods.

"That, Sergeant, was a wrong decision!" Lennox was livid.

Bork looked troubled. "I'm sorry, Commissioner, but, under the circumstances, I don't have much choice."

Leel lowered his weapon slowly and held it out to Bork. Before she could take it Lennox was striding toward the door, snarling, "I've had enough of this! You can consider that as the last decision of your career, Sergeant!" The third TARC officer moved uncertainly to block her path. He was not needed. A shot from Hanna Bork's slumbergun sent the TARC commissioner crumpling in a heap at his feet.

"And that was resisting arrest, Commissioner," she announced coldly.

The door slid open and several toymen strode in. Under Bork's instructions they picked up Tamara Lennox and Saxon Rainer and took up posts next to each of the other prisoners. With an A.I. module's fingers encircling your wrist, restraints were superfluous.

Gabriel had finally managed to clear his head and called urgently to Pelham Leel, who was presently conferring with Bork. "Leel, I think I can help you get to Lazarus Wight."

"I don't doubt it. You'll get your chance; I have a few difficulties of my own." Leel was also being flanked by a toyman.

"Yeah, but there may not be a lot of time . . ." Gabriel's toyman guard started to steer him toward the door. "Leel, I can get you in touch with Lazarus Wight *right now*!"

Leel shrugged and glanced at Bork, who signaled for Gabriel's guard to halt.

"Let's hear it, Mr. Kylie."

Gabriel pointed at the floor. "There, on the floor, where you threw it . . . when you searched me. There's a safe-phone. I can use it to get through to one of his main people."

Bork retrieved Kipper's safe-phone from the floor. "This what you mean?"

"Yes." Gabriel held out his hand, but she withheld it.

"Uh . . . maybe we'd better wait with this until we get back to Central. Even if they know where the generators are, they don't have any of the codes or any means to get past the security systems."

"Leel, if you're going to stop them, you're going to have to know where the generators are. How long's it going to take you to get permission to know the location?"

Leel clicked his teeth together a few times as he considered. "Assuming that we can convince Deputy Commissioner Klagham—and assuming he isn't compromised himself—and then assuming that we can get High Court permission . . . Days . . . at best. There's no one person who has both the location and the codes. Hanna, give him the phone."

"I'm looking at Retreat if you're wrong about all this, Pelham, I hope you know that," she grumbled as she handed Gabriel the phone.

Gabriel touched the "ON" contact. After a moment a cracked voice spoke, "Show and tell."

Kipper. The little roofrunner was unmistakable. Gabriel allowed himself a moment of relief. He had been half-afraid that Kipper might have destroyed his own phone after they had parted.

As calmly as he could he said, "Kipper, it's me, Gabriel, I need to talk with you just for a second."

There was a pause. "Not a good moment, dilly."

"Kipper, I know what Lazarus is planning, I know what you think you're planning. I don't know what he told you . . . maybe blackmail, or some kind of ultimatum to the authorities. He's not. He's going to . . . Kipper, he's going to bring down the Hammer. He's going to blow the main generators. That's what he meant by bringing it all back to the soil; he's going to blow the generators, you understand? He's not going to be polite, or offer any choices, he's just going to do it."

Silence. Gabriel's eyes met Isadora's, held them. The air in the room was brittle with tension.

"Kipper, I . . . look, there isn't time to give you the whole story. Lazarus has got his reasons, but you can't

let that crazy bugger take four million people with him!
I need your help. What about Sharry and Kata? Little
Kata. You wanted a future for her, that was what it was
all about, I thought. Kipper, you're not a killer. I know
you didn't have anything to do with Heloise . . . Louise
Daud's death, now, for crying out loud, *talk to me*!"

No answer. Gabriel tried to make out what the sounds
in the background meant. A brief patter. Footsteps,
perhaps.

He said helplessly, "I don't know, he's not answering.
I know Kipper, he wouldn't take part in something like
this, but . . . it's still on . . ."

"It's on? He hasn't broken the connection?" Leel
plucked the phone out of his hand and listened. "You're
sure it was him?"

"Wha . . . yeah, I know his breathing."

"His breathing." Leel seemed skeptical. "Well, if he
leaves it on long enough we can trace it, safe-phone or
not. Have you any idea how it's been scrambled? Never
mind. Hanna, get Central on the line, have them pip it.
My authority."

"Er . . . Pelham, you're still under arrest," she
pointed out.

Leel shot her a withering look. "I know that, I'm here,
I'm not going anywhere, and if I'm wrong about any of
this, you're halfway to Retreat anyway. Now, trace the
damned thing before he hangs up."

Bork took the phone dubiously and called Central,
reading the number off the back of the phone.

"Why would he leave it on?" Gabriel wondered out
loud. "Unless something's happened to him . . ."

"Or unless he wants you to find him." Isadora's voice
cut through the general murmur like a shard of glass.

For the space of two long breaths it was as if someone
had thrown an aural-dampening field over the entire
room. Nobody moved as what Isadora had said sank in
and led everybody to the same conclusion.

"They're there already," Gabriel breathed. He could
feel himself breaking into a cold sweat.

"What do you mean, they're there? How could they
be there already?" Leel yammered, his face the color of
putty. "How could they get past the security system? All
kinds of alarms would have gone off!"

"Christ, he's had *thirty years*! You don't think that in thirty years someone couldn't have managed to find a key to the lock? The only thing he didn't have was the lock itself! Now he does! *He's there!*" Gabriel sought out, found Saxon Rainer, who was being supported by two toymen. His battered face yawned in terrified disbelief. "You stupid nitwit! You overestimated me and underestimated the person you should have been bloody watching. You didn't think it would happen this fast, did you? You thought you'd be well on your way!"

Leel was already on-line with his main office. Gabriel noted that the toyman guard was no longer securing his wrist. "Everybody! I don't care who! Every unit in the sector! The instant Com-line dep. has a bite on that phone, I want everyone to converge, you understand? Now"—he jabbed a finger at Gabriel—"I want him with me. Bork, you get on-line with Klagham and every pencil picker you can get five seconds airspace from! Tell Klagham he'd better start waking up every High Court judge he can get on-line with, the entire Conclave, and start phoning around Assembly members and come up with some override codes!"

Ten minutes later Gabriel was sharing the back of a TARC hangcar with Pelham Leel and another, younger TARC agent named Khan. Leel's pet toyman, Lobo, was at the controls.

Kipper had been right about a safe-phone being safe for only a short time. Within seven minutes from the time when Hanna Bork had instructed her colleagues in the Department of Communication to pip Kipper's phone, they had nailed it as being located somewhere in the northern end of the slugwarrens, in Kyara's oldest sector.

Kahn seemed both confused and exhilarated by all the excitement. Gabriel recognized the highly polished sheen of a young idealist, not yet tainted by the unpleasant realities of his job. Leel, on the other hand, looked physically sick. The ramifications of his actions over the last week (and probably years) were apparently just getting through to him. Gabriel was unable to summon up much satisfaction from this fact. The time was past for such

petty joys—although the knee to the TARC man's bollocks had felt pretty good.

"D'you think she's going to be able to get those
codes?"

Leel grimaced sourly. "Not a chance."

Gabriel had expected it. He gazed out of the window
and murmured to himself, "That's okay. It'll be okay."
He had died once today already. It hadn't been so bad
after all.

There seemed to be an extraordinary amount of traffic
on the hangcar rails for the midnight hour. Leel cursed
something about Meal-day Weekend for the Church of
Cornucopians and, indeed, many of the hangcars that
pulled over to the side of the rails to allow the police
vehicles to pass had people hanging out of the windows,
wearing hats and headbands embellished with the double
arches of the Prophet, and waving holographic flash banners. Hangcar windows, framing red-faced merriment,
zipped by, the occupants hooting good-natured insults at
one another. Little did they know, Gabriel thought
moodily.

As they neared their destination TARC and Municipal
Police hangcars converged from every direction, bodies
flaring with light. They dropped to a halt just over a
titanic warehouse with the words "Lone Chimera Prod-
ucts" stenciled on its flat roof. Like so many warehouses
in the slugwarrens it was built like a toybox, to be entered from above. Within seconds the roof was a tangle
of law-enforcement officials. TARC green–clad toymen
faced off against the dull gray of Municipal uniforms,
flashing hangcar bodies spat skinny, fleeting shadows in
every direction. Bursts of unintelligible spook-speak
leapt out of the general turmoil.

Pelham Leel was bellowing at a Municipal officer. "I
want a buzz-blade team effecting breach on the main
doors, and I want your people to establish a perimeter
in a three-block radius. Seal every street, Hall or passage. Any downlander or bughead that strays inside the
perimeter gets dropped and wrapped, you understand?
You understand?"

"You'd better have Privacy clearance for all this!" the
Municipal officer growled as he stalked off.

Leel jerked a hand at Gabriel. "Kylie! With me! You

stray, every A.I. on this roof has orders to drop you on sight!"

"It's inside this building?"

"It's *under* this building," Leel replied glumly, "which doesn't mean that the entrance is anywhere near here." Leel's phone trilled and he turned away. Gabriel watched three toymen with buzz-blades slicing a hole in a human-sized hatchway next to the vast, twenty-five-by-twenty-five-meter trapdoor set in the center of the roof. As he watched the three pink slivers withdrew in unison and a perfect circle dropped out of the hatchway. The toymen snapped erect as, at the same instant, Lobo stated, "Breach effected."

Leel's face was black with rage as he broke the connection on his phone. Bork hurried up, announcing unnecessarily, "Captain, we've got breach."

Gabriel responded to Leel's curt summons. "Flocking Klagham's on his way here!" the TARC officer spat as the three of them marched toward the hole cut by the A.I. modules. "Wants everything frozen until he gets here . . . shag it!"

They reached the hole where another TARC said, "Captain, we're in. It's empty, too. Completely. No storage, nothing."

"A warehouse this size? That's a great deal of floor space unused."

"And no alarms either."

"No alarms." Leel peered intently into the yawning pit below them. "That's not right. Have you ever heard of a warehouse without alarms?"

"A malfunction?"

"Spare me any talk of coincidences today!"

Everybody waited expectantly whilst Leel considered his next course of action. He had been ordered to halt all activities, but on the other hand, ten minutes might just be the difference between success and failure. Or, rather said, the difference between life and death for four million Kyaran inhabitants. Gabriel had an idea. He touched Hanna Bork's shoulder.

"The phone, have you still got it?" he asked softly.

"Hm? Yeah . . ." Bork surrendered it reluctantly. The line was still open and Gabriel listened, squeezing his eyes shut and plugging one ear in an attempt to close out all other sounds. At first he thought that there was nothing but the all-encompassing ambient hum, then faint sounds began to distinguish themselves, little scratches and twitters that gradually coalesced into . . . shouts . . . screams . . . feet running . . .

Oh, God . . . Something bad was happening.

He opened his eyes. "Leel, something's going on, it sounds like a fight . . . I don't know . . . people screaming . . ."

Leel screwed his nose up, sucking air in through his teeth. He snapped his fingers. "Okay, we're moving in. Wide-eyed and awake, everyone!"

The hatchway opened directly into an open-cage elevator. By the time that Leel and Gabriel's turn came two advance loads of toymen had already piled in and staked out the interior. Their first impression had not been wrong, the warehouse was completely empty, a single, cavernous space. The darkness was complete, broken only by the red beams of flashlights and the reflected twinkle off the heads and bodies of toymen. From the hole in the ceiling flickering shafts of hangcar light scrawled a pattern of luminescence on the matte black floor. Every movement or scrape of feet resounded off the walls. After the frenzy of the last half hour the anticlimax could not have been greater.

"This is perfect." Leel's disgusted voice resounded through the chamber. "This just about sums it up. Ten thousand square meters of empty floor. Any suggestions, Kylie?"

Gabriel, who, all this time, had been keeping one ear to the phone, shook his head in despair, "No . . . there's nothing, it's all gone quiet."

"Shag it." Leel sank to the floor and sat with his arms resting on his knees and his head bowed. "That's it . . ."

Hanna Bork said with some concern, "Captain, are you alright?"

Only the gleam of Leel's eyes was visible as he looked up at her. "Am I alright? I'm trying to . . . I'm just trying to think if there are any more . . . efficient ways of committing career suicide than what I've been doing this evening. Setting fire to a High Court judge springs to mind."

"Sir!" a toyman voice broke out of the gloom. "Your attention!"

Hanna Bork hurried over, followed by Leel and Gabriel. A four-meter-long crack had appeared in the floor, through which an eerie blue light was flooding.

"Attention here, all alert!" Bork rapped, drawing her slumbergun. Leel followed suit, after checking to see where Gabriel was. Toyman arms snapped out straight on every side, pointing at the crack like mannequin schoolchildren. As they watched it, the floor peeled back, deforming to create an oval, vagina-like opening, with a series of steps leading down into it at one end. Eldritch sounds, moans, wails echoed out of it, as if from a great distance, causing the hair to stand up on the back of Gabriel's neck. He was reminded of the dolphin pool in Naomi Sol's apartments.

Bork made to step forward, but was stopped by a hiss from Leel. Something was moving down in the opening, something that whimpered and scrambled on all fours. A Rumpelstiltskin silhouette clambered up the steps and out of the opening. It stopped and emitted an audible gasp as it was confronted by a circle of mirrored robot faces and TARC and Municipal uniforms.

"Stay where you are!" Leel barked. "Not a move! Police!"

The ragged figure shrank back, searching frantically about for an avenue of escape as two of the toymen closed in on it. As the toymen neared the opening, blue light from below struck their bodies, casting, for a brief instant, a reflection against their quarry's face.

It was Kipper Gibbons.

He gave a squawk of terror as the TARC robots seized him. The next instant the mass of law-enforcement officials, robots and agents swarmed forward, amid a cacophony of shouted orders and the brittle clatter of toymen feet, and poured into the opening. Gabriel tried to shoulder his way through the crowd and received a robotic elbow in his ribs for his trouble. He could hear Kipper yelping as they dragged him away.

"Leel . . . Bork . . . let me . . . I know him! I know him!" Gabriel yelled. He found himself confronting Hanna Bork. She flickered in and out of view as people passed between her and the light from the floor opening.

"You know him?"

"I know him! Let me talk to him!"

"Kylie! Where the fl . . . Kylie! Where are you?" Leel's shout rose above the din.

A moment later Gabriel was face-to-face with Kipper. The little man was in a dreadful state, babbling incoherently. Gabriel had to grab him by the neck and shoulders and twist him around so that he was forced to meet Gabriel's eyes, before Kipper would calm down enough for a coherent conversation.

"Kipper! It's me, Gabriel! What hap . . . look at me! Look . . . at . . . me! What happened? What happened down there?"

"It's a five-time downside, stike, it's the flockin' hammer-man, it's the . . . every . . . it's the flockin' bug . . . she brought the bug . . ." Kipper gibbered helplessly. "It was . . ." He held up his hands. In the blue light they appeared to be streaked black with something. Gabriel didn't want to guess what.

"Oh, no. Who did it, Kipper? What did she do?"

"It was Snapper . . . stike, I didn't know . . . I didn't . . . Sharry, even Monk . . . and then . . . and then Laz told us what he was going to do . . . stike, I tried to stop him . . . we tried to stop him, we did . . ."

"I know you did, I know . . . Kipper . . . Kipper, where is he, what happened?"

"It was . . . it was . . ." Kipper stammered. Tears were starting from his eyes. He lifted his restraint-bound hands pleadingly. "It was Snapper. She went the bugout . . . she . . . Lazarus is locked in there . . . and she wouldn't let us through . . . Gabriel, Toh's dead . . . she . . ." He broke off, unable to find the words.

Gabriel buried his face in his hands, aghast, dragging them back over his head, squeezing his eyes shut. *God . . . will it never end? Is there no end?* He remembered the protective tenderness with which big Toh had held his daughter, even as he whined and threatened and hung on the words of Lazarus Wight up in their rooftop cavern. Another casualty of someone else's misguided dreams.

Pelham Leel snapped him out of his reverie. "Let's move! Wide-awake!" he ordered. "Kylie, with me! Him as well!" A hand jabbed at Kipper.

Kipper gave a despairing cry of, "No, I can't . . . !"

Then they were moving again. Down the opening, into a long, rounded corridor, bathed in the same blue grotto light. Here and there fierce red pinpoints indicated the presence of active Eyes. The corridor was already lined with toymen, who fell in behind Gabriel, Kipper and the TARC officers as they passed. Leel seemed to be in constant communication with someone or some persons via his collar phone. This was confirmed when they were met by a toyman coming back down the corridor toward them.

"Lobo," Leel called. "Any more casualties?"

"No, sir, only the three," the robot replied, as it fell into step beside them. "There is an open area sixty meters from here."

Only the three? Gabriel thought numbly. *Only?*

They lay like ink stains, stamped in blue silk. The room was broad and low-ceilinged. In the wall opposite the one from which Gabriel and the others had entered was a black door, rimmed with orange light. Snapper lay against it, her black tresses spread around her head, beautiful turquoise eyes lifeless hollows in the milky pool of her skin. The thin line across her throat and the buzz-knife lying in the center of the floor told of how she'd died, as did the dark stain behind her neck. Next to her right hand was a projectile gun.

Toh and Monk were both sprawled a few feet from each other, Toh's face mellowed by a peace he'd never known in life. Each had a bullet hole in his chest.

As he caught sight of them Kipper let out a soft moan. It did Gabriel no good to close his eyes from the sight. Every time he did he was met with the sight of Uncle Bull and Elspeth as she must have looked the night she'd fallen. A night as blue as this.

After a cursory inspection Leel ignored the bodies and gave his attention to the black door. "You!" The toyman guarding Kipper jerked him across the room to where Leel was beckoning. "How did you get in?"

Kipper whispered something inaudible.

"How did you get in?" Leel shouted, his face barely an inch from the distraught Kipper's.

Kipper whimpered, "I . . . it . . . we had the codes . . ."

"D'you know them?"

"I . . . had . . ."

"DO . . . YOU . . . KNOW . . . THEM?"

Gabriel tried to intervene and found his way blocked by TARC Agent Khan. Kipper stammered, "I've got them."

"Open it." Leel grabbed Kipper by the shoulder and propelled him toward the door.

"I can't . . ."

"Open it!"

"I can't! Fair word, stike! Laz's locked himself in there; I can't override him from out here."

That Leel did not do something violent to Kipper was purely as a result of Bork calling his attention to some words that had appeared in green on the wall to the right of the door. "Captain, over here."

Leel read, "All access, standard security, on." He turned on Kipper. "What am I looking at?"

Kipper was wearing an expression of complete incomprehension. "I don't . . . I don't . . ." he began, then caught the look on Leel's face and pulled himself together. "He's gone. He's left."

"Gone? Gone where? If he's gone, where is he then?" Leel demanded.

"There are two other out-ways."

"Oh, *marvelous*!"

"But . . . I can get you in now."

"You can get us in? Then do it!"

They stood back whilst Kipper stuttered his way nervously through the surreal conversation that constituted the access code. The door folded back and Gabriel pushed forward. He was standing at the edge of a wide, low-ceilinged room, it must have been over a hundred meters across. Its center was dominated by three black pillars, each twenty meters thick, running from floor to ceiling.

Gabriel knew instinctively that he was looking at the Icarus generators.

the window above the sky

"I'd always thought they'd be . . . bigger," breathed Bork. Even Pelham Leel was enveloped in a kind of awe. As Thor natives they had been brought up with the ingrained knowledge that somewhere, in the secret bosom of Kyara, rested a living heart that kept all the wonders about them—the domes and spires, the milling crowds—in existence. And here, for the first time in their lives, they were faced with it and, for the moment, it was still beating.

It was Kipper who broke the stillness. "They're actually spread through the whole grid, dilly. This is just the nerve center. One alive and two backups." A note of defiant pride had entered his voice. Here the government minions were the greenies, experiencing for the first time something the knowledge of which he, Kipper, had lived with for years.

His words brought Leel into action again. "Deck the area." Two toymen peeled off in either direction to circle the room. Bork, Khan and another agent strode toward the generators. "Where is he?" He turned on Kipper again.

"I don't . . . he must have taken the other way out."

"Show me."

Kipper pointed across to the far side of the room, "There's two ways out, exits only, can't get in that way." Leel nearly jerked the roofrunner off his feet as he dragged him toward the far exits and Kipper gave a yowl of pain.

Gabriel protested, "Leel, give over, you've got him razor-wired!"

"Sir! Captain! You'd better have a look at this." Khan was beckoning from the generators.

Leel abruptly changed direction, driving another squeak from Kipper, "What is it?"

Nobody replied; Bork simply pointed. The sides of the generators seemed to be covered with a coat of freshly applied paint enamel—in the blue light the precise color was difficult to determine. Gabriel touched it. It was already hard. Two big spray cans were lying, discarded, on the floor. Leel tapped the enamel with his nail.

"Some kind of membrane explosive," Bork said quietly.

Leel replied hoarsely, "The detonator?"

Bork shook her head gloomily. "No. Wouldn't have to be larger than a sand grain. We'll need a couple of blow boys here with scanners to find it. Even then it'll take time," she added unnecessarily.

Leel turned on Kipper again. "How's he going to blow it? *How?*"

Kipper pointed at his forehead. "Up here, dilly. Next to his O.T.E. Oral trigger. Had it plugged in surgeon-wise. All he has to do is say the word and it's away-a-day."

"What is the word?"

A faint smugness stole over Kipper. "I am Vengeance Enthroned."

"Oh, flock," Gabriel groaned. *Lest there be any remaining doubt!*

Leel emitted a wordless snarl. "Which way? Whichwaywhichwaywhich*way!*"

Kipper cringed, all smugness vanishing. He looked appealingly in Gabriel's direction. "I . . . I . . . think . . . that one." He pointed.

Gabriel reached the door first. He slapped the palm-plate and the door slid open. Behind him Leel was shouting for six agents to take the other exit. Two toymen shouldered Gabriel aside and set off up the corridor at a speed he had no hope of matching, so he turned back. "Kipper! Where does this come out?"

"Parella Hall . . . I think."

Instantly Leel was on the phone. "All vehicles to assemble in Carroway Hall, suspect is Lazarus Wight; has that description come in yet? . . . Why not? Kylie, what does he look like?"

"Wait!" Gabriel said loudly. "Are you out of your bloody mind? If he so much as smells spook, he's going to do it. He'll bring the whole bloody hammer down!"

"Kylie, don't interfere. Just give me that description!"

"I know where he's going."

Leel's stare did not leave Gabriel. "Hold that last order. Stand by. Alright, where? Where's he going?"

A slow smile crept over Gabriel's face. Leel's eyes widened. "Oooh, no you don't, no, no, no, no, no!"

"Oh, yes, there're a couple of conditions."

"Ster*ike*! Kylie, there is no time for games!"

Gabriel nodded at Kipper, who was watching this exchange openmouthed, "First the restraints come off him . . ."

"No!"

"And, secondly, you let me deal with Lazarus Wight. Me and him."

"It's out of the question! Kylie, you're going to die as well if he goes through with this."

"They say it's easier second time round," Gabriel replied with open amusement. "Or is your memory that short?"

Leel's mouth opened and closed several times very quickly.

Gabriel continued, "It's the only way, Leel. He claps eyes on you or any of your wide boys and it's going to be over like *that*. I might have a chance."

Unexpectedly, Bork interjected, "He's right, Pelham."

"I know he's right!" Leel retorted. He touched his collar phone. "I want one vehicle in Carroway Hall fast! Do it! I'll talk to Klagham!" He broke the connection. "Alright, Kylie, I'm all ears."

Gabriel said, "It's simple. He's out for revenge. Where's the one place where a person could witness the whole of Kyara destroyed and survive, even for a few minutes? Somewhere with its own, independent, Icarus generators."

"Rainer Park," Leel growled. "Of course! Shag it!"

"You could have worked that out yourself."

Bork was already busy with Kipper's wrist restraints when Leel began to rap orders at her. "Sergeant, you're going to talk to Klagham. You're going to stall him until you're damned sure he understands what's at stake and make sure that *no one* goes near Rainer Park, that no one interferes with Wight in any way!"

"I'm already on it; you move now!"

"You, you and you, with me!" Gabriel, Kipper and a robot whom Gabriel took to be Lobo followed Leel through the exit at a dead run.

Their hangcar was just arriving as they emerged from the ground in an alley off Carroway Hall, sending one very surprised eth-head howling away in fright. Seconds later they were careening through traffic, Lobo at the controls.

The traffic at this point was, if anything, denser than an hour ago. Meal-day was obviously a misnomer. It had started two days ago and was showing no signs of letting up. From Leel's splenetic mutterings, Gabriel gathered that the penalties for dropping booze pouches out of hangcar windows onto the streets below were severe enough to deter even the most walleyed of revelers, but that did not stop them from hurling ceremonial nutri-bricks and sticky-bombs at other vehicles, and the hangcar's windscreen was soon caked with both.

It was not until they were nearing their destination, however, that Gabriel started to get concerned. The largest Church of Cornucopia was located a short distance from the entrance to Rainer Park and the number of hangcars on the rails seemed to be increasing the closer that they got to the park.

The torrent of adrenaline that had muted Gabriel's senses for the last few hours had petered out and all of his aches and pains were returning with a vengeance. He had his eyes shut and was trying to ease them away by concentration, when a loud curse from Leel jerked him upright in his seat.

They were on the final decline that would take them to the perimeter avenue on which Rainer Park's entrance lay. Up ahead a jumble of hangcars were massed, blocking the entire lane. It did not look like an accident—people didn't hold impromptu singsongs out of hangcar windows at accident sites—it was probably some kind of breakdown. Either way it was impassable. Although police hangcars were equipped to cross the block-stripe into the oncoming lane, they were hemmed in on both sides by civilian vehicles. A backward glance told Gabriel that their way back was blocked as well.

Pelham Leel was swearing under his breath as they shuddered to a halt, suspended thirty meters above street level, still too high for the hangcar's arm to lower them onto the ground and certainly too high to jump.

Leel slapped open one of the windows and they were immediately treated to a chorus so tuneless that Gabriel almost found himself overcome with admiration.

"A plutonium-testicled TARC,
Had a bite that was worse than his bark,
His scrotum had stashed, such a critical mass,
That his pecker would glow in the dark!"

"What the hell's going on here?" Leel shouted forward to the vehicle in front of them. One of the passengers answered with a marshmallow grin, and shouted back, "Double guidance-system failure! No fret, Officer, nobody hurt. What took you so long . . . ? *Oh, I believe in pollinogs and figs on Orbit One . . .*" she started caroling. A spatter of nutribrick from an unseen source caused Leel to yank his head back inside in a hurry.

"Shagging sociopaths," he seethed. "Lobo, call Central, find out why the flocking Municipals aren't here doing their job and clearing up this mess! They can't all be Macca-backs!"

In the midst of this Gabriel caught Kipper's eye. The roofrunner's goblin body was scrunched up in the corner of his seat. He made a single clapping motion with his hands and raised his eyebrows questioningly. It took Gabriel a fraction of a second before he understood what Kipper was getting at, then he was digging into his back pocket and pulling out his slaphappies.

Leel was still raving, "And if you can't get the Muni . . ." He noticed what Gabriel and Kipper were up to. "Hey! What d'you think you're doing?"

Gabriel patted his slipper fastenings into place. "You going to argue?"

"Slaphappy use is illegal."

"Then why'd you give them back to me?"

Leel was simply going through the motions. "It's not illegal to own them, just to use them."

Gabriel opened the window on his side of the hangcar. "Fine, arrest me."

"I already have. Three times," Leel said drily. "Here"—he pushed a phone card into Gabriel's hand—"that's a spare. I'll keep in touch. I'll make sure the Municipals cooperate with you and I'll get the Rainer Park people on-line."

Gabriel did not bother to reply. As one, he and Kipper heaved themselves out of their respective sides and clambered onto the roof of the hangcar.

"Just like olden times, dilly-dill," Kipper cackled grimly.

Almost, Gabriel thought, screwing his face up in pain. He had banged his heel against the rim of the window. It was funny how much harder the street surface looked when you were only thirty meters above it than when you were a hundred.

"Hey, stikes! Roofrunners!" someone exclaimed in delight. "We've got real roofrunners!" Shouted comments rained in from all sides.

"Shag-a-lackey!"

"Hee-hee, dilly, has the TARC budget gotten that tight?"

"There once was a roofrunner hangin' on the wall," somebody started to sing and was quickly joined by a gaggle of voices, *"From his ass to his elbow he was half a meter tall . . ."*

Bent double against the hangcar rail just above their heads, Gabriel and Kipper leapfrogged from hangcar to hangcar, pursued by hoots of drunken glee and increasingly crude comments. Word had spread throughout the pileup and everyone was craning out of their hangcars, hoping for a glimpse.

They were clambering over the fourth vehicle when some bright egg struck upon the notion of using them for nutribrick target practice. Within seconds Gabriel and Kipper were cowering under a salvo of nutribrick, sticky-bombs and the odd fresh vegetable (hurled by the more affluent revelers). Those out of ammunition aimed their holographic flash-banners at the two men and Gabriel found himself being accompanied by a garish jig of red-haired harlequins, spinning clusters of fruit and, at one point, a unicorn.

"A three-legged dilly with an extra thigh and fibula,
Had thirty-seven nipples that would twinkle like a nebula . . ."

Twice Gabriel nearly missed his step as a result of being struck in the face. Kipper was returning every hit with an insult, letting forth a nonstop verbal barrage without seeming to pause for breath, "Scab-pricked scum-suckers! Diddle your flockin' spleen, skaghead! Shit! Shit! Flockin' pecker brain! Shag it!"

Under any other circumstances it might have been funny.

It wasn't until Gabriel stumbled and rolled off the roof of one of the vehicles, as a result of being blinded by a flash-banner, only saving himself with a lucky slap against the hangcar door, that the bombardment let up slightly. Four hands reached out of the hangcar window and assisted Gabriel in pulling himself up, sending him on his way with good-natured slaps on his behind. He had a brief glimpse of several Gladland-bright eyes, a picket-toothed smirk and a slurred voice that bellowed a cloud of acrovak fumes in his face. "A fine time for it, stike; give my love to the bats."

Eat, drink and be merry, Gabriel thought wearily, *'cos tomorrow the beer and chips might run out.*

"You all upside?" Kipper asked with concern.

"Don't I look it?" Gabriel flexed his arm painfully.

Kipper chuckled, a little of his natural humor finally showing through. "You look like yesterday's one-square."

By the time Gabriel and Kipper leapt onto the last vehicle, three Municipal hangcars were arriving to deal with the mess. Leel had been true to his word and the instant they pulled up, a window opened in one of them and an arm beckoned to them urgently.

"This way! We're here for you!"

As Gabriel and Kipper climbed inside, another round of *"A three-legged dilly,"* was just starting up.

The policemen had no idea what was going on, but it had obviously been made clear to them that they were to cooperate with Gabriel fully, although being ordered about by roofrunners was something that undoubtably lodged firmly in their respective craws. At his behest they pulled the hangcar over a block from the Rainer Park entrance and proceeded on foot. To Gabriel's gratification, Jael Nyquist was waiting for him at the park entrance, leaning against a little lo-float and looking rather flustered. She gave a grimace of relief as she spotted Gabriel approaching at full gallop.

"What the flock is going on, stike? We've just had some raving spook on-line . . . oh, sorry . . ." she broke off as she noticed Gabriel's two uniformed companions.

" 'S upside, dill, allow me." Kipper turned gleefully to the scowling police officers. "We're going to be going pattyfoot. Your job, my laddibucks, is to put the spike in any of your follow graynoses and TARCs if they turn up wanting to get in here . . ."

Gabriel, meanwhile, gave Jael Nyquist a three-sentence rundown of the situation. She lost her usual florid complexion, but not for one second her composure. When he had finished she gave a sharp nod, sending her multiple chins wobbling. "He's here, the reeker you're after. We watched out for him after we got the call; he got here just a couple of minutes ago. I left him and didn't go after him, just like they told me. He was heading into the woods over there." She indicated a dense grove of oak forest that ran along the western wall of the park. "Come on, get in." She levered herself into the lo-float, which sagged visibly under her weight. Gabriel and Kipper leapt in behind her as she set it in motion. They covered the fifty meters to the edge of the wood in seconds, Gabriel jumping from the lo-float before it had even stopped.

"Where was it he went?"

"Just . . . there, between the trees . . . no, those."

Gabriel pushed his way gingerly through the low gorse that ringed the wood, searching the ground. He found what he was looking for in an area of sod: the fresh imprint of a foot.

Clear as daisies in coal seam. Gabriel smiled to himself, following the line his quarry had taken. The ground here was dank and ivy-covered, thickly overgrown with clustered daffodils and young tendrils of bracken. Dead branches spiked out of the tree trunks, all the way to the ground, impeding the passage of anyone who wanted to walk between them, like rust-frozen turnstiles.

That just made it easier. There, a disturbance in the pattern of ivy; there, a glint of exposed greenwood, where a fragment of bark had flaked off; there, the pale point of a snapped branchlet; Lazarus Wight's trail through the woods was painted in luminous colors.

"Gabriel?" Jael's voice was muffled by the greenery. There was a crash of breaking twigs and Kipper crowded in behind him. Gabriel put out an arm to hold him back.

"Stay behind me," he commanded.

"Why, what is it?"

"Here . . . there . . . he went that way."

Kipper's head twitched about like a chicken's. "Where? Where? Where? How d'you twenty that?"

Gabriel tapped the side of his nose. *Welcome to my element, Kipper.*

And he set off, moving through the woods like a phantom. Not that there was much point in moving like a phantom when your companion was making as much noise as a steamroller in a field of cornflakes.

"Shhh."

"I am, I'm not making a whisper!"

Stoically Gabriel blocked out Kipper's stumbling and concentrated on the trail, letting the ground tell him the story of Lazarus Wight's walk through the woods. Wight had set off confidently at first, with a clear sense of purpose. After a time, however, he had begun to have his doubts, stopping, scanning the area, adjusting his direction. He was becoming more and more uncertain, but that was hardly surprising. With all the dense growth, visibility was less than three meters. Here, next to this fallen branch, Lazarus had tripped and then stood around for a moment, probably swearing. Then he had set off again. Gabriel sensed that they were nearing the dome wall.

His phone pipped. He resisted the temptation to ignore it.

"Hello?"

"Gabriel, it's Jael. Listen, I just got a call down from Edom. Someone just opened the airlock."

Gabriel was taken aback. "Airlock? What airlock?"

"The park's airlock. We've got to be able to get outside the dome in an emergency."

Kipper and Gabriel exchanged a worried glance. "Okay, so where is this airlock?"

"Well, it's in the forest you're in now. Sorry." Jael sounded embarrassed. "I didn't think of it. I'm not used to the idea of someone walking around with override capacity . . ."

Gabriel cut off Jael's self-castigation. "Never mind; I think I'm almost there; I'll meet you there." *Pip!* "Strewth," he grumbled, "it doesn't seem to *end!*"

When Jael's lo-float arrived up the path that ran along the dome wall three minutes later, she found them waiting for her at the airlock door. "Edom is going out of his flocking lord up there," she puffed. "He's got TARCs and fairboys on-line, all telling him different things."

"Sounds like spookland business as it does," Kipper grunted, picking bracken out of his slaphappy slippers.

Gabriel demanded, "This door. Can you get it open?"

In answer Jael simply slapped the doorplate. The door opened into a small cubicle—the airlock itself was just beyond. Two evac-suits with their helmets were hanging against one wall. Jael pounced immediately. "There's a suit missing!"

The airlock chamber was empty as well.

"Shag it!" Gabriel swore. "What the flock is the point of that?"

"Ringside seat, dilly," Kipper said gravely. "He's a roofrunner, remember? That's where he's going to be." The little man jerked a thumb up at the dome.

"Oh, boy," Gabriel breathed. "I've got to get out there. Jael, can you help me into one of these . . . ?" He removed his coat, trying not to think about what he was about to do, and, with Jael and Kipper's assistance, started to climb into one of the sleek evac-suits. He had barely donned the leggings when both his and Jael's phones rang simultaneously. "Now, what?" He yanked the phone out of his collar. "Hello?"

"Kylie? It's Pelham Leel. If you don't have him already, you'd better get a move on. Klagham is . . ."

Gabriel missed whatever else he was going to say for

at that moment they were all nearly deafened by a magnified voice thundering through the park.

"This is a TARC order! Will all citizens in the park please proceed directly to the exit. This an official TARC order! Proceed to the exit. Do not run. Anyone still within the park perimeter in five minutes will be placed in custody. This is a TARC order . . ."

"Flockin' typical," Kipper snorted. "How's a dill supposed to be pattyfoot out of here in five minutes without running? Here, get your arm in this sleeve . . ."

Jael was speaking frantically into her phone. "Edom, you've got to keep this shagging door open! Stall them! Just . . . stall them!" She snapped it off. "Trouble, Gabriel, Edom's got Deputy Commissioner Klagham raising flames in central control. They've got toymen and half the TARCs in the city pouring into the park on their way here."

So the Bogy acts with its usual flamin' subtlety.

"Kylie?" Leel was still on-line. Gabriel changed hands as Kipper shoved his arm into the other sleeve and Jael busied herself with the survival harness on his back.

"Leel, I'm doing what I can . . ."

"Thanks, upside to hear that." Kipper snatched the phone out of his hand and tossed it aside as Jael placed the helmet over Gabriel's head. She was keeping up a running commentary, regardless of whether or not he was listening, "The faceplate'll compensate for Icarus Field distortion; you'll barely notice it . . . control panel's just above and below the faceplate; it'll track your eye movement and respond to it. Just stare at whatever it is you need . . . you've got the cooling system on the left there . . . communications, all the suits are on the same set frequency . . ."

Kipper was busy, meanwhile, forcing Gabriel's slaphappies over his gloved hands. Shouted orders and the crackling of undergrowth indicated that the velvet gauntlet of government authority was fast approaching. The woods were alive with the sparkle of toymen. As Kipper moved down to Gabriel's feet, Jael gave the top of Gabriel's helmet a pat. "You're ready." She glanced out of the cubicle doorway and immediately yanked her head back in as an iron voice boomed, "Halt, or bio-intrusive methods will be adopted!"

"Flock! And so are they!"

Kipper chattered, "Done here! Dilly . . . nearly!" Gabriel threw his arms out for balance as Kipper wrestled the second slaphappy slipper over his left foot. "Now . . . *yes*!"

Jael had slapped the cubicle door shut the moment she saw the TARCs approaching and, before Gabriel could even recover his balance, he found the third evac-suit and helmet being thrust into his arms.

"We've got to be fast, before they force Edom to override the door!" Jael bundled him into the airlock chamber. She paused before sealing it. "Luck, stike. Keep the hammer off us." Kipper said nothing, but as the airlock door separated them, he raised his hands and made a single clapping motion.

Jael had barely had time to set the airlock cycle in motion when the cubicle door started to open. The TARCs had overriden it. Kipper's hand hit the doorplate so fast that Jael barely saw him move. She heard the beginnings of an exclamation of dismay from outside which was cut off as the door shut again.

"Hey, what the fl . . . ?"

The airlock was halfway through its cycle.

Three seconds later the door began to open once more. Again Kipper slapped the doorplate—this time to no avail. A toyman arm shot through the opening to prevent it from closing, the hollow point in its index finger searching for targets.

Jael tried one last ploy to buy time, "Alright, wait a second, we'll open it . . ."

It was too late. She barely felt the spray of slumber-bullets that felled both her and Kipper.

The leading TARC agent pushed past the toyman, into the cubicle. She stepped over Jael and peered through the window in the inner airlock door with dismay.

"Sir?" she said into her phone. "We're too late, I think. The outer door to the airlock's open and there's no evac-suits left."

The reply was curt. "Then send out some A.I. modules!"

"Um . . . that may be difficult, too. I don't think we

can get the inside door open . . ." She had just noticed the empty evac-suit and helmet propping open the outer door.

Gabriel stood alone on the ledge outside the airlock door. A man's length from his feet the ledge ended in a drop-off of twenty meters onto the surface of Thor. It was also the beginning of the end of the Icarus Field. From the rim of the ledge to an armspan beyond, Thor's pull increased from one to thirty-seven gravs, a gravity gradient steep enough to rip a human being in half.

Below, Gabriel witnessed, for the first time, a sight which most Thor-bred natives had never and would never see: the surface of Thor, the Anvil, with nothing between him and it but three short steps and the dim flicker of the Icarus Field. So awestruck was he that, before he knew it, he had stepped forward to the edge of the drop-off and looked down.

Anvil-eyes. The term was apt, for the Anvil held you in a gaze so enticing, so powerful that you could lose yourself in its black surface and never truly come back. Close up, Gabriel saw that the Anvil was neither black, as he had first thought, nor gray, as he had thought later. It was like a tar slick, with glistening rainbows embedded in its surface and here and there a subtle gleam, beckoning.

Just a step.

And he could be standing there.

Touching it . . .

Gabriel drew back in sudden fear, feeling his center of balance being drawn forward.

Strewth, he thought, *that's a little . . . close to the knuckle.*

Anvil-eyes.

Dragging his attention away from the Anvil, he surveyed the dome above him. From where he was standing the curve prevented him from seeing very far. He thought for a moment that he had spotted Lazarus, up and to his right, but on closer inspection, it turned out to be a six-legged cleaning pod, such as the kind that he had seen clambering around the rooftops. There was nothing for it. He took a deep breath and began to climb.

Slap! Slap! His hands stuck fast. Except that now there was no sound, just a faint thud of impact running back up his arms, through his shoulders.

Up he went, ignoring all the aches, the agony in his shoulder, the chafing of his heel.

Slap! Slap! From outside the spun-diamond dome was semiopaque so Gabriel could not even look down into the park—there was just a milky iridescence filling his vision, against which his hands were hard-edged shadows.

Slap! Slap!

On and on he climbed. And on. Although the gradient gradually decreased the higher he ascended the curvature of the dome, by the time the slope had flattened out enough that he could crawl on his hands and knees rather than climb, Gabriel was half-delirious with exhaustion. He knew that there was no way that he could get back down again. If they wanted him inside, they'd have to come and flocking well get him.

Provided "they" were still around.

The dome surface was almost level when Gabriel finally thought to look up. And there she was. Kyara, in all her glory. Layer upon layer of spun-diamond domes, rising like a cumulus-cloud formation, burning with a rich, inner light and trailing a star-strewn sky. Beside this even the great dome of Rainer Park was dwarfed.

At the summit of the Rainer Park dome Gabriel spied a dark fleck. There, silhouetted against the bright glow of Kyara, Lazarus Wight stood, hands by his sides, gazing up in an attitude of reverence. He turned as Gabriel rose to his feet, almost as if he had heard him. His face was, of course, invisible behind the faceplate, but Gabriel would have recognized him by his manner of moving. There was a crackle in Gabriel's ears and his helmet was filled with the sound of someone else's breath.

"That's far enough."

"Lazarus?" Gabriel gasped.

Lazarus's helmeted head inclined slightly. His mirrored faceplate caught the sun and set him ablaze. "Gabriel Kylie. Welcome to freedom. No more cages or windowpanes to press your nose up against. This is it." He sounded almost glad, his voice trembling with a barely suppressed exultation. "They sent you, did they?"

"No . . . they didn't send me."

"So, you came to see the show!" Lazarus turned his gaze back on Kyara. He spoke absently. "Well, it won't be long now, it won't be long."

Gabriel climbed unsteadily to his feet. "Lazarus, you can't do it."

Lazarus's cut-glass laugh was mocking. "I can't do it? You came . . . all the way out here to tell me that I can't do it? In direct contravention of the facts? Watch me . . ."

"Wait!" Gabriel despaired at the shrillness in his own voice. "Wait."

"Oh, it's alright, I'm certainly in no hurry." Lazarus seemed to be smiling.

Gabriel searched for words, words that might mean something to this man, but all he heard coming from his own lips was, "Shit, Lazarus, why? You can't really mean to destroy the whole thing, everything, everything there is."

"Why not?" Lazarus said reasonably, and his voice grew distant. "It'll take the pain away . . . take . . . the pain away. No more voices . . . just silence."

Gabriel stumbled forward.

"I said, that's far enough," Lazarus said sharply.

"But there's four million people in there."

"Casualties," Lazarus said indifferently. "Casualties to the mendacities of moguls."

"What . . ." Gabriel stammered with incomprehension. "They're not casualties; they're people!"

"Aah," Lazarus sneered. "Is that today's aphorism from the well of your complacency?"

"Lazarus, they're people. They're men and nasty old ladies and children and . . . what's left of your own people and the dream you handed them and that they believed in. There's four million souls there! Why would you want revenge on them?"

Lazarus started. "Who said anything about revenge?" he demanded.

Gabriel held out his hands imploringly. "Lazarus, I know about what happened at Landing."

For a century of heartbeats Lazarus was silent. His voice, when he spoke, was fragile as a fall of Easter snow. "*He* . . . told you?"

"I'm from Landing. I knew him, the old man you killed. His name was Bulla, we used to call him Uncle Bull. He was family. He was why Elspeth came here."

"Looking . . . for me."

"No," Gabriel said firmly. "Looking for Saxon Rainer."

Another century went by.

Lazarus said, "I am—" Gabriel's heart froze—"the one," Lazarus finished, and Gabriel swallowed hard.

"I . . . he . . . he just came out of the trees. He was . . . he was drunk. I told Saxon we shouldn't . . . I told him we shouldn't be doing it, but he wanted his trophy. And then he came out and . . . I knew we'd had it if they caught us. We'd be spending the next five years in Retreat. It's when you became afraid and it lodges just below your neck like a steel balloon. You think if it just expands just a little bit, it'll choke you.

"And Saxon, he'd just gotten off his shot. There wasn't time to reload. And I'm there, and then he whispered, 'Shoot.' And it was as if, for a second, it all became so clear. Fate and providence and luck all rolled into one. Just a squeeze. Just a squeeze and he was lying there and it was over.

"Except . . . that it wasn't. All of a sudden that flash of clarity was gone and you're left with some old drunk lying dead with a laserburn between his eyes. And *he* didn't care. It was like . . . business, the challenge. Saxon even got angry when I didn't want to take the animal we'd shot with us. Just, 'Let's get going.' "

In that instant, Gabriel had an insight. He said urgently, "If you're waiting for another moment of clarity, it won't come. The first one was just a lie . . ."

"No!" Lazarus shrieked, and Gabriel cringed, his hands slapping instinctively at the sides of his helmet to try and cover his ears. "No! He promised. He comes every day, every night after I shut my eyes, he comes dancing out of those scrubby trees. Maybe if Saxon had said 'kill,' instead of 'shoot,' it might have been different. I might have thought. But it didn't feel like killing until . . . after. And Saxon knew it. *He* knew the difference. And still he turns up." Lazarus moaned. "With that open mouth and that . . . burn in his head. 'Kill.' "

"Lazarus." Gabriel kept his tone gentle. "You think this is going to be easier? He'll never leave you again."

"Is that a threat, Gabriel Kylie?"

"No, I've got nothing to threaten you with. I just think if you were going to do it, you would have done it already. But the truth is you can't. For all your threats, you've never killed anybody since that day. That's why you're still standing here."

Lazarus stood ever so still. His shallow breath rasped in Gabriel's ears and he moved his poor confused head to and fro.

"Lazarus," Gabriel pleaded, "Saxon Rainer has had it. He's buggered. He's in a TARC holding tank right now. The whole flocking thing is going to come down around his ears. He took away your life, he's carried it around, like a trophy on his wall. But nobody else did. There are four million Uncle Bulls in that city. What are you going to do when they all come dancing out of the shadow trees?"

Lazarus murmured something. Gabriel strained to catch the words and realized that Lazarus was reciting something: "And I shall rise victorious, and subdue my vanquisher, spoil'd of his vaunted spoil; death of his death's wound shall then receive, and stoop inglorious, of his mortal sting disarmed."

The words meant nothing to Gabriel, but his stomach knotted in dread. He gulped. "I'm sorry, I don't understand you."

Lazarus's shoulders tweaked upward. "Old English. An ancient bard and my delusions of grandeur." He spoke with a melancholy irony. "Sometimes all the leaves fall away. When I was young and I traveled and I stood in deciduous forests in winter. The leaves were gone and people would speak about it as if it was a curse. I never understood that. With the leaves gone, you could see so far. The hills behind, the sky. Sometimes the leaves fall away and I see what I've been doing. I see what I've done and I wonder, how the hell did I ever take it so far? How could I, knowing what I know, being who I am, feeling what I feel, how could I have done that?"

Gabriel opened his mouth and found it cottony with cheap aphorisms. *From the well of my complacency?* he wondered bitterly. Twenty meters separated him from Lazarus Wight and he could summon no wisdom to close that distance.

Lazarus mused. "I hate him. I see him and I know he is me, the one who committed those deeds. But I have to leave him out there, *as* someone else, or I know I'll just smother in the hate that I have for him. I hate him with my heart, with the bile in my belly, with the blood in my pores. And it doesn't do any good. As long as he's out there, he moves as he wishes and I can't stop him, I can't even see him, except for those few moments when the leaves fall away. I can't forgive him and he doesn't want the forgiveness. If I accept the forgiveness of those I've injured, I'll have to accept the pain of that injury. I'll have to hurt, too, I'll have to feel . . . really feel."

Gabriel whispered, "That's your terror, isn't it?"

Lazarus giggled softly. "Oh, he's been banging on my door for thirty years, that old drunk, trying to hand me some forgiving lie."

"It's no lie, Lazarus. It's why I'm here." And in that moment it was as if a great weight had lifted from Gabriel's shoulders. He repeated, more loudly, "That's why I'm here."

"To forgive me?"

"Yes," Gabriel said, with conviction. *Guess what, Old Man, the penny just dropped.*

"Ah." Lazarus turned and looked up at Kyara again. "I was born under the domes. Kyara raised me, nurtured me. As a young man . . . you know how it is, all raging hard-ons and contrariness . . . sometimes I'd look around and think, 'Shag-a-lackey, even if Thor doesn't drop the hammer, this town's going to collapse under the weight of its own bullyshag someday, anyway.' Then I'd shell out a few cues and catch the shuttle up to Orbit 1, just to catch a glimpse of her from the outside. And it would make me feel so proud! What a . . . stupid, pointless, anachronistic, *magnificent* dream! It would make me forget probabilities, which is what my fears would give me to hide behind. Instead, I'd remember that everything is possibilities, waiting to be born, and many of them more worthwhile than this glorious nonsense."

Lazarus sighed. "You were right, Gabriel Kylie. Am I supposed to add matricide to my other sins?"

As if in answer to his own question, Lazarus turned and started to walk, stumbling slightly as he did so, and Gabriel moved along a parallel path, keeping the distance between them the same.

"Just a little walk," Gabriel heard Lazarus muttering to himself. "Just a little walk."

A twinge of suspicion stirred in Gabriel. "Lazarus? Where are you going?"

The reeker's pace accelerated as the curve of the dome made the gradient steeper. By the time Gabriel actually accepted what Lazarus was doing it was almost too late.

"Wait! Lazarus!" Gabriel broke into a run to intercept him as Lazarus started to jog-trot down the slope of the dome.

"Give it up, Gabriel," Lazarus called back at him. "I'm going all the way."

"No!"

They ran faster and faster, the angle of descent increasing with every step.

They were both barely in control by the time Gabriel was close enough to fling himself at Lazarus, tackling him around the ankles. With a yell the roofrunner fell nosefirst, then they were sliding down the side of the dome.

"Leave me! Leave me!" Lazarus struggled madly in his grasp.

"No! I'm not flocking . . . ow!" Gabriel received a foot in his neck as he let go with one arm to try and stop their descent. The evac-suit protected him against the worst impact of the blow, but it was some seconds before he could draw breath properly. Meanwhile Lazarus's free foot pounded his helmet and shoulders, blinding and disorienting him. In desperation Gabriel slapped wildly at the surface of the dome.

Slap! His slaphappy stuck fast to the spun-diamond surface. The shock nearly tore Gabriel's arm from its socket and, ironically, it was only their speed which saved him. He gave a scream of agony, then the slaphappy fastenings gave way and the glove was ripped from his arm and they were falling again.

Down. They skated across the glowing dome like struggling rats on ice. There was no way to stop anymore—even if it had occurred to him, Gabriel would not have dared use his remaining slaphappy to break their fall. Even Lazarus had stopped fighting him.

There was regret in his voice as he said, "You're too late, Gabriel. This time you really are."

The Anvil spread its arms to receive them.

Then something seemed to rise over the approaching curve of the dome, something black and spider-legged and almost invisible against the dark surface. Gabriel barely had time to identify it as a cleaning pod before they struck.

It took Gabriel several seconds to realize that the impact must have knocked him unconscious. He could barely move from the pain in his ribs. Two of the cleaning pod's six legs had torn off and two more wriggled uselessly in the air. The pod was on its back, hanging from its two remaining legs, Gabriel and Lazarus jammed up against its body. Lazarus was trying feebly to get free, pawing at Gabriel's shoulders for leverage. His breath was dry bubbles and he was trying to speak.

"Please," he pleaded softly. "Please, let me choose . . . my moment . . . Let me . . ."

"Lazarus," Gabriel croaked, "you're forgiven. It's over."

"Not for me. Never for me."

And Gabriel knew that he had no option but to give in. In his mind's eye he saw the walls of the maximum security facility cocooning Lazarus—probably for the rest of his life, if he did not voluntarily submit to the Adjustment probes—and Gabriel knew that he could not force that on another human being.

There was, at least, dignity in choice.

So, in his pity, he made no move to stop Lazarus as the other pushed himself loose and tumbled free, becoming tinier and tinier before his speed flung him away from the surface of the dome. For a fraction of a second Lazarus seemed to hang weightless in space, still breathing loud in Gabriel's ears. Then it was as if a great, invisible hand reached up and jerked him downward and the breathing abruptly stopped. That was when Gabriel knew that the hammer of Thor had finally struck the demons from Lazarus Wight's soul.

rainer park

The Edelrice was bustling. Its patrons were shoulder to shoulder at the bar and more were piling in, looking for a late-evening snack and a late-evening-type drink to wash it down. This had been a good day for business, although one couldn't have told it from Mama Yamaguchi's countenance. She sat unmoving behind the bar and observed her customers with the equanimity of a trapdoor spider, whilst her wee service robots scuttled to and fro.

Gabriel himself had managed to secure a table by anticipating the departure of a school of Cornucopian diehards who refused to admit that the Meal-day Weekend party was long over and hungover. There was only room for four at Gabriel's table, so they had ensconced Aysha and Isaao at a neighboring table which had come free just as they were arriving.

Hitedoro Izeki was bellowing, "Right now, stike, there are nine High Court judges flockin' *inventing* things to throw at the bastards! Flockin' *inventing* things!" He guffawed loudly and Isadora and Gabriel chortled with him. Chuen just shook her head and looked prim.

If there was a taint of hysteria to Hitedoro Izeki's bonhomie, Gabriel was all too willing to forgive it. He would probably have been in far worse shape after three straight days in the slammer, which was how long it had taken to spring Hitedoro, even with Acting TARC Commissioner Raoul Klagham's reluctant cooperation. It was to celebrate Hitedoro Izeki's release that they had all gathered here.

The last forty-eight hours had seen them swept up in a whirlwind of activity. Meetings with lawyers, judges, law-enforcement officers—not all of them friendly—and all the while the media hovering at the periphery, like a plague of gnats; the eye of the public, ogling by proxy.

Kyara was finished, but she would be a long time dying. Any speculator who had been looking forward to the spectacle of twenty thousand independent businesses going bust simultaneously was going to be disappointed. On the contrary, the impending consumption of one's material assets by unknown, alien life-forms focuses the mind wonderfully. It would probably be four decades before the final evacuation of Kyara, and those entrepreneurs clear of mind, steady of nerves and swift of feet were out to make a bucket. Already talk was under way of converting the Orbit Stations into Orbital Colonies, industrialized cities in their own right.

Ah, well, there was no keeping a good dreamer down.

Or a TARC. Pelham Leel's future was not assured, but since he had never actually broken any laws—just put a few dents in them—the likelihood of his ever being prosecuted for anything seemed remote. Gabriel and he had not parted friends, but their last meeting had seen a grudging respect steal into the ferrety TARC captain's manner.

As for Gabriel himself, he had a couple of things to do tonight. *But not just yet,* he thought, *not just yet.*

Hitedoro had just told some blatantly offensive joke and Chuen was obviously trying to decide how to respond to it. Isadora had already decided and had her nose pressed against the tabletop, her shoulders shuddering with laughter.

Gabriel leaned back happily and let the conversation wash around him. These were fine friends to have. His glass was empty and he cast about for the nearest service robot.

Something moved in the corner of his vision and a withered hand set a new beer pouch down in front of him. Gabriel looked up in surprise to find himself at the business end of Mama Yamaguchi's most intimidating stare. The conversation at the table sputtered out and everybody gaped.

"On the house," she said coldly. "One time only. Don't get ideas."

"Why . . . thank you, Mama."

"You pay for your drinks, Mama 'Guchi keeps serving," she replied haughtily. She turned her back on him and Gabriel watched her crooked little form bobbing away through the tables.

"Hey, what about me? I was in the bastilla longer than he was," Hitedoro called at her over his shoulder. "Shit, I don't deserve a little appreciation?" he grumbled.

"Word gets around," Chuen remarked.

"What, that I don't deserve appreciation?"

There was a splutter from Gabriel's right and several drops of white wine struck his cheek. Isadora was giggling uncontrollably whilst at the same time choking on her drink, some of which was also running out of her nose.

"Your . . . face . . ." she gasped.

Chuen rolled her eyes in despair and emptied her glass. "I'm off. I promised Angela I'd be home before eleven. I'll leave you darlings to get on with whatever you're going to get on with the rest of the evening. I'll see you tomorrow."

"Hup, I'll head out with you." Hitedoro's hand descended onto the table's thumbplate, but Gabriel intercepted it with his own.

"Drinks are on me," he said.

"Flock me, it's contagious," the big man roared cheerfully, and staggered to his feet. Pausing at Isaao and Aysha's table to exchange a word with his brother, Hitedoro trailed Chuen out of the door.

"I wonder if maybe we should go with him," Gabriel wondered with concern.

Isadora waved dismissively. "Chuen'll stick him in a hangcab."

Gabriel raised his eyebrows. "Laying hands on a man?"

"She'll survive it . . . as long as she doesn't tell Angela." Isadora was watching him carefully.

"You all packed?" he asked.

"Well, we don't leave until next week."

"I'm always packed. It's a good habit. Second thoughts?"

"Lots."

"I wish it were simpler for you."

"You could make it simpler."

"You mean pack your bags for you?"

"No, I don't."

Gabriel grinned awkwardly. "Iz, I'm used to having friends. I'm not used to having a lover."

"What makes you think I'm used to it?"

"Er . . . you told me?"

"Did I? Oh . . . when?"

"I don't really remember, but you did."

"Oh. I don't remember."

"It doesn't matter." Gabriel leaned forward and took her hands. "Iz . . . I want to show you a place I know where there's an acacia tree growing, like a question mark coming out of the dirt, and you can breathe air so . . . sweet and so bitter and clear . . . and you can hear a whisper that goes on all day and all night. Just movement, things moving, living. When you smell the dust around Landing you'll *know*."

Isadora smiled a half smile and changed the subject. "Are you coming home with me?"

Gabriel shook his head. "No, I have something I have to do first. I'll follow on."

"I'll be waiting," Isadora said. Her gaze was warm.

Chuen and Hitedoro emerged from the Edelrice. They made their way to the first street corner together. There they halted. Chuen turned stiffly and extended her hand. "I suppose I'll see you around the place."

"Yeah. I guess." They shook hands awkwardly. Hitedoro did not release her hand immediately. "You don't call me by third person anymore. Not since . . . well, that night."

"You're not third person." She pulled uncomfortably away from his clasp, annoyed by his clumsiness.

"I am what I am."

"Well, that's nothing a few hormone shots and a little surgery wouldn't cure."

"Don't place any bets."

"No."

"You . . . er . . . I don't suppose you'd want to catch a jockeypuk match or something . . . sometime . . . I mean, I don't mean anything by it," he added hurriedly.

"I know you're Tanit and everything, but . . . well, you do have friends. Maybe I could be . . ."

"You wouldn't like my friends."

"No, I wouldn't. And they wouldn't like me much either."

"No."

"And you wouldn't like my friends."

"No."

"D'you need a lift somewhere . . . maybe . . . ?"

"No . . . no."

"Well, I don't have a hangcar anyway."

"I don't have a job."

"You quit? . . . Oh, yeah, foolish question. Well, I don't have one either."

"You didn't quit."

"I think I would have."

They stood in silence. The central weather authorities had ordained the evening warm and the population was out on the streets, enjoying the stars and the lights, rolling into restaurants, reeling out of bars. Chuen and Hitedoro stood and watched in silence and for a long time neither of them moved.

Gabriel's feet swished through the long, dry grass of Rainer Park. The park lamps were out and the Twist blazed through the spun-diamond sky, the trees and bushes a patchwork of still, black clouds, rising from the ground. Gabriel was following a scent, a scent to the last notes of a song that had traced a path fifty light-years through the stars. A scent of spinifex and gum tree.

The rustle grew sharper as the grass dried to brittle stalks under his soles. Then, suddenly, it ended, and Gabriel was standing on the edge of a clearing that he knew he would find. Flat stones covered the ground like the scales on a tortoise's back and in the center of the clearing a lone acacia leaned, entangled in the arms of a lazy gum. The two trees formed an arch over a rosette of tiny bushes, mere sprigs, worming their way out of the arid soil.

Through a blue, moonless night Elspeth's longing called to him and found its answer in this home a million million miles from home.

Gabriel moved over the ground like a desert spirit, his

feet disturbing neither twig nor pebble. As he walked, he shed his clothes, one by one, gathering them into his arms as they were peeled from his body, until at last he stood unclothed and shining in the desert night. A sweep of his arms laid his clothes in the shadow of a rock. Then, with the skill of his forefathers, who had walked the Green Desert in the days when its soil was dust red instead of beaded glass, he summoned the stillness from within himself and became just another dark shape, abstract, unmoving, invisible. And he waited.

Presently—and Gabriel did not know, or care, how long it had been—the grass whispered the presence of another. Something moved beyond the clearing, something that limped, coming, at length, to stand at the edge of the clearing. Edom Japaljarayi raised his face to the night sky as if waiting for a rain to wash him clean, a rain which would never come. Clumsily he removed his clothes, dropping them one by one on the ground beside him. At last he stood naked, but for the movement-assisting harness that gleamed silver against his dark skin, entwining his body like some skeletal lover.

Painfully he knelt on the ground and, with shaking hands, he unfastened it and let it rattle to the ground. To Gabriel, it was like watching someone remove their dignity as Edom lay, a stringless puppet, his arms and legs moving in uncontrollable twitches.

Whilst Gabriel looked on unobserved, Edom Japaljarayi began to drag his body across the stones toward the two trees, his painfully thin arms shuddering with the effort. At last he gained his goal at the center of the rosette. There he raised himself into a sitting position, painstakingly laying his useless legs one over the other, until he was sitting cross-legged. He spread his hands flat against the ground in front of him as if feeling for a heartbeat. Even though the air was cool, his body glistened with sweat.

When Gabriel stepped out of the shadows Edom went momentarily rigid with shock, then his face relaxed, not into fear, as Gabriel might have expected, but into relief, and Gabriel realized that there were no longer any secrets between them. With a single lithe movement, Gabriel lowered himself into a seated position opposite Edom.

For the eternity that lies between one breath and the next the two men regarded one another. Then Edom said softly, "How long have you known?"

Gabriel shrugged indifferently. "Since the second day, I suppose, or since the first. Maybe not till just now. The first words you said to me were a lie. You saw that I was Native Australian like you and you said to me—it was odd—you said, 'I might have known, with a name like Kylie.' But you must have at the very least seen a holograph of my sister's body, so how could you not know?"

Edom shook his head sadly. "Bad liars should know enough to live truth."

Gabriel continued quietly, "But it wasn't until I climbed what I thought was a sick tree to get away from a couple of TARCs that I knew how you did it. You could never have climbed up to the second scaffolding, much less have knocked Elspeth off. She could have backhanded you halfway across the park."

"She stole something from me," said Edom. Gabriel laid his hand flat against the patch of earth between them and Edom nodded. "Yes."

Gabriel explained, "An old eth-head called Ellis Quinn Macintire said he'd seen me once before, lying on my back in the park at night, with a stone in my hand. At first I thought he'd seen Elspeth. Then I realized what the stone was and that it had to be you."

Edom shivered and swayed backward and forward a few times, hugging himself. "I don't understand why she did it. Why would she do it?"

"Lazarus Wight blackmailed her, as she blackmailed you. She was being hunted by everybody. He offered her a way out of Kyara and off Thor if she got the plans for Rainer Park for him. Eslpeth found the lever to get them out of you." Gabriel paused. "You're a tribal man, Edom."

Edom bit his lip, his face masked by grief. "My parents were. They followed the voices of the Ancestors here. They sang them here. My mother died when I was . . . quite young. My father—" He broke off. "My father followed their singing out onto the surface of the Anvil. They found his remains right under where we're sitting now."

Gabriel nodded and gazed about the clearing for a few moments, feeling it better to let the little man recover before he went on. Then he said, "That's why your parents didn't have your spastic disorder fixed *intra utero*. That's why you didn't have your fear of heights Probe-treated. A block is one thing; altering an intrinsic part of a person's mental makeup . . . is quite another.

Gabriel sighed. "Maybe Elspeth found this place by accident . . . or maybe she felt it or smelled her birthplace from across the park like I did. But she found your father's tjuranga buried here, beneath the trees. And she stole it."

"She stole it," Edom repeated. "She . . . promised to give it back if I gave her the plans to the park."

"She found the lever to get past the block."

"No. Or I would have given them to her. But . . . I saw to it that she had access to the park after darkdown . . . after closing hours. I told her that the plans were up on the scaffolding. She was supposed to leave the stone down here . . . she did, but . . ."

"She'd broken the Law."

"She . . . the block stopped me from giving her what she wanted . . . the Law meant I couldn't go anywhere for help . . . What was I supposed to do?" Edom's breath was shallow, his face reflected his inner turmoil, so Gabriel took the story over from him.

"You talked her up to the platform by phone, that's why her phone was on when they found her. A couple of days ago I had Iz ask Jael to get me the records on debris from the park's cleaning pods. The information is only dumped once a year, so they still had it and you overlooked it. On the day that Elspeth was found dead here the pods collected three times as much debris as on any other day, mostly leaves, twigs and branches.

"The coroner's report said that Elspeth had fallen from a height of thirty meters, so she must have fallen from the second scaffolding. But I saw where they found her and she couldn't have ended up there if she'd fallen from the second scaffolding. So either somebody moved her, or she didn't fall from the second scaffolding. The spooks must have seen it, but they never asked.

"There was one other thing that showed me the way." He pointed across at where something gleamed, half a kilometer across the park. "Chandra's Clock. Chandra's Clock had gained three seconds.

"Elspeth didn't fall from the second scaffolding; she fell from the first. She must have been clinging to the ladder when you threw the switch on the Icarus Field." Gabriel smiled. "You know every strut, every join in this park. You'd know exactly how much this structure could safely take. I'd guess you threw it up to about two gravs. One minute Elspeth is sixth-five kilos, hanging on to a ladder, the next her weight had doubled in a split second. It must have been like a gorilla jumped on her back. Ellis Quinn Macintire thought that that was what had happened after they found him unconscious in the service tunnel. The next three days after it happened you insisted on sorting out the security systems yourself, so that no one could see that you'd shorted out all the Icarus Field alarms as well. Six seconds at two gravs sped up the pendulum on Chandra's Clock. Elspeth hit the ground at twice her normal body weight and twice the speed. No wonder everyone thought that she'd fallen from twice the height."

Edom was weeping now, jaw working, as if chewing on words that would not come forth. Gabriel looked away sadly. Edom's grief was his own and Gabriel had no right to intrude. Eventually Edom recovered himself and Gabriel spoke again.

"Nobody ever comes here, do they?" he said, gazing up at the branches overhead.

"Rarely." Edom managed to smile. "There's an ancient architectural term known as 'lines of desire.' It denotes the little natural paths made by people when they . . . cut a corner, for instance, or cut across a stretch of grass between two paths or through a hedge, anyplace where people choose a path other than that built into the design. A good architect can anticipate those lines of desire and incorporate them into the design. I saw to it that this place was at the furthest point from all the lines of desire in the park. The chances of anybody stumbling across it would be remote. The only ones who came here usually were children."

"And Elspeth."

"Yes."

"Something else you forgot."

"Something else?"

"That the first lines of desire were the paths taken by the Ancestors when they sang Creation into being. Their Songlines were the first lines of desire and precede all others. I think you heard one without realizing it and followed it and felt the djang at this place. I think your father did. And I think Elspeth did."

Edom sighed. "So what are you going to do?"

"To you?"

"To me. With me."

"Nothing. You didn't kill Elspeth. Anger killed Elspeth. Her anger and the anger of an old woman mourning a lover. I killed her by not hearing."

"But what about the law . . . ?"

Gabriel threw his head back and laughed. "What about the law, Edom? You want me to keep the circle going, is that it? Listen, twenty-two years ago an old man killed me to save my life. I spent nineteen years of my life running from world to world trying to keep out of his reach because I didn't understand. Shit, mate, you think you're so flaming important when you're seventeen, a kicker against the pricks. I hated him all my life. Layin' down the flockin' rules, layin' down the flockin' *Law*! I didn't understand the law because I didn't know the law, *his* law. The law's not just a set of rules, it's . . . an understanding. An understanding that comes up through the soles of your feet from the heart of all things. My grandmother tried to tell me just before she died, but I didn't understand. And Old Man tried to tell me himself, the last time he ever said a word to me, but I didn't . . . listen. I didn't even let him speak. And he died knowing I thought he'd tried to kill me."

Gabriel wiped his eyes and shook his head. "He knew. He knew where Elspeth had gone and he tried to save me so that I could save her. He did save me; without him I would have died last night in Saxon Rainer's office. But I didn't listen and I got here too late.

"I couldn't save Elspeth. I couldn't save Heloise Amiée. I couldn't save Lazarus Wight. Maybe not even Ellis Quinn Macintire.

"Every circle has an end, Edom." He smiled ruefully and shrugged. "It ends where you choose to stop. Right there.

"Uncle Bull, Old Man, Grandmother Lalumanji, Elspeth . . . they're all the same person. They're a part of me. Those we love are a part of us. We're born whole and as we go through life, parts of us fall away, stripping us, leaving us naked. The nakedness is what hurts, but it can also bring us closer to who we are." Gabriel gazed up and the Twist shone very brightly, the stars like footsteps. He bathed in a thousand landscapes, a thousand valleys and woods, deserts, oceans.

"Old Man. He sent me on a rare old trip," he said in wonder. "We can run . . . I've run. But toward it, or away from it, toward me or away from me. That's the choice, isn't it? Both paths hurt, you know? Every path leads us over thorns, and over islands of sunlight. I've just been tryin' to find my way. We're all just trying to find the way, Edom. Like following a track through the woods. And one day, I reckon, we all see that there's nothing waiting at the end of the path but ourselves. And that's okay. That's as it should be. The day you know that, that's the day you realize you were never really lost."

Edom did not look up. "You know that for sure? You even know what you're saying?"

"No." Gabriel grinned wryly. "No. It's just a picture. And a hope."

"There's always that."

"Yes."

Without really knowing why, Gabriel leaned forward and kissed the little man on the forehead. Then he stood and turned away. Gathering up his clothes, Gabriel walked to the edge of the clearing. There, in a good place, between two flat stones, he laid the parakeelya seed that he had found amongst Elspeth's belongings. He inhaled the fragrance of spinifex and gum, the bittersapped pine and the sweet grass that flowed up the hill to Chandra's Clock.

"So much life," he murmured. And with those words Gabriel strode out of Rainer Park for the last time.

But a small part of Nerita Elspeth Kylie would forever lie there, far from home, but joined by a thread of Song to a patient land, and waiting.

Waiting for the rains.

▓▓ BRINGS THE FUTURE TO YOU

ROC

EXPLOSIVE SCIENCE FICTION

☐ **DEATHSTALKER by Simon R. Green.** Owen Deathstalker, unwilling head of his clan, sought to avoid the perils of the Empire's warring factions but unexpectedly found a price on his head. He fled to Mistworld, where he began to build an unlikely force to topple the throne—a broken hero, an outlawed Hadenman, a thief, and a bounty hunter.

(454359—$5.99)

☐ **DEATHSTALKER REBELLION by Simon R. Green.** Owen Deathstalker—"outlawed" with a price on his head and the mighty warrior lineage in his veins—had no choice but to embrace the destiny that befell him. With nothing to lose, only he had the courage to take up sword and energy gun against Queen Lionstone XIV. (455525—$6.99)

☐ **FLIES FROM THE AMBER by Wil McCarthy.** An Unuan mining expedition has discovered an alien mineral they name centrokrist—a stone of incomparable beauty. Yet when the Earth scientists at last arrive to investigate, they find a phenomenon eclipsing the centrokrist crystals. For this double-sunned solar system is nestled right next to a black hole. (454065—$4.99)

*Prices slightly higher in Canada

FAR AWAY WORLDS

☐ **PETTY PEWTER GODS by Glen Cook.** P.I. Garrett knew he was in for it when two rival pantheons tried to hire him. A confirmed atheist, Garrett wanted nothing to do with the gods. But the gods wouldn't take no for an answer, and if Garrett didn't come up with something fast, TunFaire might be treated to a war that could rip the very fabric of the universe apart. (454782—$5.99)

☐ **BROTHERS OF THE DRAGON by Robin W. Bailey.** Caught in a war between dragon-riders and bloodthirsty unicorns, two brothers trained in martial arts lead the forces of Light toward victory. (452518—$4.99)

☐ **FLAMES OF THE DRAGON by Robin W. Bailey.** The domains of light had welcomed Robert and Eric, two brothers skilled in martial arts, when they were transported through a portal that linked the Catskill Mountains to a land where magic was real, where dragons soared the skies, and where angry ghosts roved among the living, seeking vengeance upon their slayers. (452895—$4.99)

☐ **TRIUMPH OF THE DRAGON by Robin W. Bailey.** Robert and Eric are revered by the people of Palenoc as their long-awaited champions. They are also desired by the Heart of Darkness, an evil sorceress whose ultimate goal is the complete domination of Palenoc. (454375—$4.99)

*Prices slightly higher in Canada

THRILLING SCI-FI NOVELS

☐ **EXILE by Al Sarrantonio.** It is the end of the 25th century. Human civilization has expanded into the Four Worlds of Earth, Mars, Titan, and Pluto. Recent progress in terraforming promises to turn Venus into the Fifth. But for Prime Cornelian, usurper of Martian rule, there will be no rest until all planets bow before him. "A very talented writer."—*Washington Post Book World*   (455215—$5.99)

☐ **FLIES FROM THE AMBER by Wil McCarthy.** An Unuan mining expedition has discovered an alien mineral they name centrokrist—a stone of incomparable beauty. Yet when the Earth scientists at last arrive to investigate, they find a phenomenon eclipsing the centrokrist crystals. For this double-sunned solar system is nestled right next to a black hole.   (454065—$4.99)

☐ **BEYOND THIS HORIZON by Robert A. Heinlein.** This classic tale portrays a utopian Earth of the future, in a time when humanity is free of illness and imperfection. Yet even in paradise there are some like the privileged Hamilton Felix who harbor deep doubts about the very point of human existence.   (166760—$5.99)

Prices slightly higher in Canada.